Also by Terry Spear

SEAL Wolf
A SEAL in Wolf's Clothing
A SEAL Wolf Christmas
SEAL Wolf Hunting
SEAL Wolf in Too Deep
SEAL Wolf Undercover
SEAL Wolf Surrender

Heart of the Shifter
You Had Me at Jaguar

Billionaire Wolf
Billionaire in Wolf's Clothing
A Billionaire Wolf for Christmas

Silver Town Wolf
Destiny of the Wolf
Wolf Fever
Dreaming of the Wolf
Silence of the Wolf
A Silver Wolf Christmas
Alpha Wolf Need Not Apply
Between a Wolf and a Hard Place
All's Fair in Love and Wolf
Silver Town Wolf: Home for the Holidays

Heart of the Jaguar
Savage Hunter
Jaguar Fever
Jaguar Hunt
Jaguar Pride
A Very Jaguar Christmas

Highland Wolf
Heart of the Highland Wolf
A Howl for a Highlander
A Highland Werewolf Wedding
Hero of a Highland Wolf
A Highland Wolf Christmas

White Wolf
Dreaming of a White Wolf Christmas
Flight of the White Wolf

Heart of the Wolf
Heart of the Wolf
To Tempt the Wolf
Legend of the White Wolf
Seduced by the Wolf

YOU HAD ME AT WOLF

TERRY SPEAR

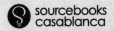
sourcebooks
casablanca

Published by Sourcebooks Casablanca, an imprint of Sourcebooks
P.O. Box 4410, Naperville, Illinois 60567-4410
(630) 961-3900
sourcebooks.com

Printed and bound in the United States of America.
OPM 10 9 8 7 6 5 4 3 2 1

To Angela Austin, thanks for being so dedicated to wanting a book, even when your own local store wouldn't get it in stock. I thank you from the bottom of my heart for loving my books and helping to share them whenever you can!

PROLOGUE

Fort Meade, Maryland

No one on Warrant Officer Nicole Grayson's special agent team had a clue what she was—a gray wolf shifter, or *lupus garou*—or that she had a decided advantage in locating criminals: her sense of smell. Not that she could use that in a court of law, since humans didn't know shifters existed. She loved that she could sniff out a perp but hated that she couldn't use that scent match as evidence. An eyewitness account could be inaccurate. Her sense of smell was extremely accurate.

She had just started working as a special agent in the U.S. Army Criminal Investigation Command, also known as the Criminal Investigation Division (CID), and was paired with a senior agent to learn the ropes in the field. Today, Nicole was on her own, interviewing a female second lieutenant who had alleged that a military police sergeant, wearing civilian clothes and a ski mask, had pulled a 9mm gun on her in an attempted armed robbery at her apartment off-post. Nicole was determined to learn if the case was legitimate.

When she arrived at the lieutenant's apartment, a dark-haired woman answered the door, identifying herself as Roxie Wolff. She stood about five four, her hair in a bob. Her large, dark eyes widened when she took a deep breath. Nicole knew the lieutenant had smelled her scent and realized Nicole was a gray wolf, too, surprising the hell out of her. Nicole had never met another wolf while serving at Fort Meade.

"I'd say the man was six foot one, about the same height as my brothers. And muscular." A finance officer, Roxie was pretty and petite, and she didn't look like someone who could overpower an MP with criminal intent, especially one who was so much taller, a muscular male, and trained in taking down suspects. Because Roxie was a wolf, the sergeant could have worn any disguise, and the lieutenant would still know him by scent if she ran into him again. That would definitely help. A suspect's appearance could change, but their scent wouldn't.

"I'm glad you're a wolf and can take care of this guy." Roxie narrowed her eyes. "I expect you will find the MP and charge him with attempted armed robbery."

"If I can prove he tried to rob you, yes." Nicole couldn't promise more than that. She knew that without any real proof, she couldn't do anything. "If you would, tell me everything that happened that you can recall."

"He was wearing a black ski mask and ski jacket, army boots, and camo pants. If I hadn't been able to smell his scent, I wouldn't have recognized him as the MP who had pulled me over on post for an expired safety-inspection sticker earlier in the day. He must have seen my coin books sitting on the seat beside me. I had just had them appraised and had a buyer for them. I had them for years, and I was tired of trying to safeguard them. Neither of my brothers nor my sister was interested in having them. Collecting coins was something my dad and I used to do when I was a kid."

Nicole understood how Roxie felt about that. Moving

with the service made it difficult to safeguard valuables and everything else a service member needed to "hand-carry" with them to each new assignment.

"Do you think the MP learned where you lived after seeing your driver's license?"

"That's what I assume. He could also have looked it up from my license tag. He was professional, very pleasant, and obviously clean-cut, being in the military. He gave me a warning to have the inspection done within the week and told me to have a nice day. I didn't have any negative feelings about him when we talked."

"Then he came to your apartment and...?"

"No longer in uniform and wearing a ski mask, he told me to hand over the coin collection. He had intense blue eyes that reminded me of the MP I'd met earlier in the day, but his scent was what really confirmed it. I was horrified to think one of our own military personnel, who is supposed to uphold the law, was breaking it. I couldn't recall his name. I never can remember names when I hear them, so that wasn't surprising. He might not have even given it to me. I was kind of rattled when I learned I had an expired safety-inspection sticker and thought I was going to be fined. Not to mention, any trouble with the military police could end with a call to the commander's office and a stern lecture from my commander."

"That's so true."

"He had dark-brown hair, military cut, and was clean shaven."

Nicole wrote everything down.

"He needs to be stopped. If he can get away with trying to rob me, what will he do next?"

"But he didn't get the coins from you?" That concerned Nicole, because the sergeant might try to break into Roxie's apartment or accost her at some other time.

"No. I slammed the door in his face and locked it."

Nicole's lips parted. The lieutenant had spunk, which Nicole admired.

"Don't tell me I should have just handed the coins over. They were in the apartment, and if I'd let him inside, it could have been far worse for me. When I slammed the door in his face, it automatically locked and he didn't have time to react. I think I really surprised him with my reaction. They were *my* damn coins, and I'd safeguarded them since I was a kid. He couldn't very well have kicked in the door or shot at it, or he would have caused a scene and left evidence behind. I think he had assumed it would be a quick grab-and-run scenario.

"Actually, I don't think he thought it out all that well. He didn't go to any of the cars parked where I could see them from my windows though. He must have parked out of sight of the apartment. I called the local civilian police, but they said they couldn't do anything about it because nothing had been stolen and there were no witnesses who had seen the alleged crime. They had nothing to go on. I knew he was the MP I'd seen, but I didn't want to tell the people at his workplace, or he'd learn I knew he'd been the one who tried to rob me. Without proof, it would be my word against an MP. I couldn't do anything. I called your office instead, hoping someone there could help."

"I see your dilemma but also the civilian police's problem with the case. Are the coins in a safe place?"

"I had a buyer for them, and he came and picked them

up right after the MP pulled his attempted burglary. The coins are gone, but the MP won't know that. What are you going to do about him?"

"You don't know his name?"

"No. Um, come inside. He had ahold of my driver's license when he was checking me out. You can smell his scent from that. I did capture a picture of him on my cell phone, but it's just a bit of a blur because he was moving so fast, and it only shows his profile."

"Okay, thanks." Unfortunately, learning the guy's scent wouldn't help Nicole bring him to justice. Roxie was right though. He needed to be held accountable for his actions.

What if this was just the beginning of his life of crime? Or what if it wasn't the first time he'd committed an offense? He knew military police procedures, which would give him an edge. Nicole looked at the photo, and other than the clothes he was wearing—the same as the description Roxie had given her—she couldn't tell anything about him except that he appeared to be tall like the lieutenant had said. He was still wearing the hoodie with the hood up so Nicole couldn't see his face.

"Did you notice if he took off the ski mask when he was headed away from your apartment?"

"I think he must have, or he would have looked suspicious. I thought his right pocket was bulging a bit when I didn't think it had been before. Since he still had his hoodie up, I couldn't see for sure." Roxie pointed to the hood. "But I didn't actually see him remove the ski mask. I ran for my phone to capture a shot of him, but when I returned to the window, he was nearly out of sight."

"Okay, I'll talk to your neighbors and check the security

cameras monitoring the apartment complex." Nicole took a whiff of the driver's license and had Roxie send her the photo she'd taken of the man. After that, Nicole left and talked to as many of Roxie's neighbors as she could. She also checked for video surveillance around the complex but found nothing that could corroborate Roxie's story. Nicole believed every word the lieutenant had told her, but without any hard evidence, she couldn't prove anything.

Nicole did go to the military police department to see if she could locate the police sergeant by scent. She was working on another case, an attempted rape, and she needed to see the officer who had been called to the scene first, which gave her a good excuse to drop by. That was when she got a good look at the blue-eyed cop, sitting back at his desk, drinking coffee and joking with another MP. She was careful not to be seen, and when he left the station, she noted the nameplate on the sergeant's desk. Oscar Kovac. Human and bad news, if Roxie's story was all true.

For an entire year, Nicole kept trying to prove Roxie's story was true, but she had no concrete evidence, and the MP didn't commit any other crime that she was aware of.

Roxie soon left the service, and Nicole was dismayed that her first case involving a wolf victim could never be put to rest.

CHAPTER 1

Silver Town, Colorado

NICOLE PAUSED TO WATCH A MAN DRESSED IN A GRAY ski jacket, hat, pants, and snow boots struggling to start a snowblower to clear a walkway to the parking lot from the Timberline Ski Lodge. She was conducting surveillance for her investigation into a fraudulent life insurance claim, but that was less interesting than the man before her.

What intrigued her was that he was the same hunky guy who'd been walking a Saint Bernard in the snow earlier this morning. The dog had taken chase after a rabbit and dragged the man off on a wild jaunt, with him hollering, "Rosco, heel!" Which hadn't had any effect whatsoever. Rosco had been hell-bent on catching the rabbit, and nothing would keep him from his mission. That was the last she'd seen of the dog and the man, who had disappeared from sight through the snow-laden trees. She wondered if the guy had ever reined the dog in or if the dog had finally given up on his own.

Now the *lupus garou* seemed to be having trouble with his snowblower. She could relate to both instances, having raised a yellow Labrador retriever who had a mind of her own when Nicole took her on walks or runs. The dog moved much faster than Nicole could manage. Unless, of course, she had been in her wolf form. But she hadn't taken the dog for runs while she was. No telling where Dusty would have ended up.

As to machines, Nicole had a bark mulcher that she'd always had to ask her neighbor to start for her. She knew all about uncooperative outdoor equipment.

She shouldn't watch the guy. But since he was also a hunky wolf, he really had her attention.

Nicole knew she should have continued on her way, but she was mesmerized by his antics. He poked at the push-button start with a gloved finger. Nothing happened. After three more pokes, he stared at the pull cord and finally pulled it out. Voilà, the snowblower started. He smiled.

She smiled. He must have been new on the job. Maybe a handyman at the lodge. She would have offered to help him, but she didn't know a thing about snowblowers.

The snow blades were throwing the snow up into his face, and he was frantically attempting to adjust the blades by pushing buttons and levers on both the right and left sides of the snowblower. Nicole stifled the urge to chuckle. She glanced around to see if anyone else was watching him, but everyone was hurrying to the ski slopes, eager to ski, and taking a different stomped-on path that also needed to be cleared of fresh snow .

Finally, the guy was blowing the snow off the path, creating an even higher snowbank than had been there. Once he finished, it would be like walking down a narrow path with castle walls of snow on either side. Nicole was about to continue on her way, the show over, when the wind switched and the snow blew straight into his face, covering him from his hat to his boots. This time, she couldn't help but chuckle. He was so busy fighting with the snowblower— and the equipment was so noisy—that he didn't notice her. Thankfully.

He unzipped his parka and shook out the snow. Not once did he curse, and he kept going, despite all the trouble he was having. She admired him for it. He zipped his parka back up and began to move the snowblower again. His boots must have hit a patch of ice and he slipped on it, landing on his backside.

Nicole laughed. Scolding herself for not being nicer, she headed in his direction to help him up. Before she could get close, he was back on his feet and clearing the path without any trouble. She chuckled again, imagining herself in his boots, and headed down the other path of trampled snow.

She entered the warm, toasty lodge, where a fire was crackling in the double-sided gas fireplace in the lobby. The mischievous Saint Bernard she'd seen running off earlier was sound asleep next to it on a big, soft dog bed covered in blue velvet-like material and little black dog paw prints, no doubt dreaming of chasing rabbits. Her thoughts again shifted to Larry Thornton, the human working as her partner on this case. Larry was suffering from high-altitude sickness, and Nicole thought he needed to go to the medical clinic in Silver Town to get checked out.

When she reached their room, she set his bag aside and pulled her ski boots out of the closet. She planned to wear them to make it look like she was skiing while she observed her suspects. Larry made his way out of the bathroom wearing gray pajamas. Nicole studied her sick partner. Even his skin looked gray as he stumbled back to bed. He insisted he was fine, though he had a major headache, was short of breath, and had thrown up in the bathroom twice already this morning. He said he would be up and out of bed in no time. According to him, he just needed to rest a little more while adjusting to the lower oxygen pressure at the higher altitude.

"Larry, you really need to go to the clinic." Nicole sat down on her made-up bed, the patchwork quilt featuring a block each of moose, bears, and wolves, surrounded by green and black plaid squares. She loved the lodge. It made her feel as though she was in a cabin in the woods. She pulled off her snow boots and slipped into her ski boots.

Photographic prints on the wall featured wolves running in a pack on the snowy slopes. She wondered if they were *lupus garous* or real wolves. The slopes looked like the ones the ski lodge was connected to. She noticed the signature of the photographer was Jake Silver and thought of the name of the town: Silver Town. Was he related to its founders? She'd initially thought it was called Silver Town because of the nearby silver mine that was now closed.

"Every time I go skiing at a higher elevation, I have this condition," Larry finally said. "This is all I do. Just rest. It's always worked for me before when I went skiing."

Nicole finished buckling her boots. "So you've said." But she wondered if he'd felt this bad before.

Larry worked for another private investigator firm, while Nicole had her own agency. They had been hired by the same insurance company to learn if a policyholder had faked his own death so that his beneficiary would receive the five-million-dollar payout. What she couldn't fathom was how people could get such high-dollar life insurance policies when they didn't earn that much normally on the job. And wouldn't you know, Oscar Kovac was the policyholder—the former army MP who had tried to steal from Lieutenant Roxie Wolff. Nicole had jumped on the case, wanting to prove he was alive and a fraud in the worst way since she hadn't been able to prove he'd tried to commit armed robbery against Roxie.

He had left the service two years after Roxie did. Through Nicole's sleuthing, she discovered he was now going by the name Rhys, a Welsh variant of the name Reese, pronounced the same way.

She tucked her ski goggles into her jacket pocket so she could wear them while she was outside watching for Rhys and his partner in crime, his cousin, William Kovac.

"What had you been working on before you were assigned to this case?" her partner asked.

"I'd been working on a case involving a burned-down steak restaurant that appeared highly suspicious. I found accelerant on the kitchen floor, the place was closed for business, and the wife had just received it in a divorce settlement. The whole situation screamed arson. I was eager to finish the case and prove the wife guilty. It appeared she had wanted some quick cash and didn't want the headache of running the business or trying to sell it in that small town, which could have been impossible." Nicole shrugged. "I had all the evidence that supported arson, but then the insurance company asked me to take this new case right away because of my military and investigative background. Somebody else took over my findings on the arson case."

"Bummer. I don't think I would have given up the other job."

"The insurance company did pay me for most of the work. This one pays even more because if Rhys and his cousin got away with this, it would mean even more of a payout to the cousin."

"Thankfully, I was between jobs. You be careful. They wouldn't have hired us to work together if the last PI the insurance company hired to search for Rhys hadn't vanished without a trace."

"That's what I was told." Nicole was glad that the company hadn't tried to hide the truth from them. Because the police couldn't find any sign of foul play in the private investigator's disappearance and he was known to go off the grid on cases, the police hadn't delved into his disappearance any further.

Even the guy's girlfriend was unconcerned about him disappearing, saying he did it all the time. Nicole would have worried the guy was seeing some other woman!

But this time, the company had hired Nicole and a male PI she didn't know so they could pretend to be a couple while keeping the suspects under surveillance. Safety in numbers. Except now her "marriage partner" wasn't going to be any help at all. Not in his condition. She felt bad for him and worried too. As much as she wanted to prove that Rhys was the policyholder and very much alive, she couldn't risk Larry's life if he insisted on doing the job but was too sick to do it.

"I can run you down to the clinic in Silver Town. It won't take any time at all, and they'll make sure you're fine." Nicole's wolf genetics meant she could heal faster, and she never had high-altitude sickness. Though she was from Denver, and Larry was from Kansas City, so the elevation, and the fact he was human, worked against him.

"I'll be okay. Really. Go look for Rhys and his cousin, and I'll join you after I get a bit of rest. Just…don't take any unnecessary risks."

Since the insurance company had been concerned about the missing insurance investigator, they had hired PIs who both had a military background: Larry, a former sniper in the army, and Nicole, who was trained in combat and police techniques. As an agent with the CID, she had supervised or conducted investigations into felony-level crimes against army personnel and property, drug sales and use, rape, robberies, and all kinds of other crime. She'd even had to look into a case of treason, the selling of classified documents to the highest bidder.

She hadn't ever had a case of terrorism, but it had always been a possibility. She'd had one case of a faked death, a soldier not wanting to be in the army any longer, which was another reason she had been asked to work on this case. She'd found him hanging out with his girlfriend in another state. And she'd solved three civilian cases where the dead person turned out to be very much alive but involved in life insurance payout schemes.

"All right. I'll check on you in a bit. Call me if you start feeling worse. I mean it."

He smiled a little at her. "I will."

She didn't trust that he would. She knew he didn't want her to have to go after Rhys and William on her own. And he really did want to work with her on the case. "Okay, I'll check on you after a while." Then she texted her mom. Her mom and dad had a stationery store and gift shop in Denver. She always let them know where she was on a mission so they wouldn't worry.

She texted: I'm at the ski lodge at the Silver Town Ski Resort. I'll let you know if anything interesting happens. Love you.

Mom: You're okay staying with a human male in
the same room?

Nicole: We tried to get a suite, but they didn't
have any available. And if we're pretending to be a couple and watching each
other's backs, we need to stay together.

Mom: All right. But if he gets fresh, you can
handle him?

Nicole smiled and texted: Yes, Mom. You know how
growly I can be. Talk later. Got to catch up with the suspects.

Mom: Be careful.

Nicole left the room and headed down to the lobby. She
was grateful she had this case so she had the chance to track
down Rhys and finally have him arrested, once she had
proof he was the man she knew he was.

But she had another concern. She needed to report to
the insurance agency that Larry was sick. She always went
by the rule book, so no getting paid for work when the work
wasn't being done. The insurance company might want to
hire another private investigator to work in Larry's place.
She didn't want to do that to Larry, but she couldn't let on
that she had a working partner when she didn't. Still, she'd
give him another day before she called it in, just to see if he'd
recover on his own like he thought he would.

She made her way to the lobby and then outside to see
if she could find Rhys or his cousin hanging around the
outdoor restaurant or in the snow, trekking toward the ski
lifts.

Co-owner of the Wolff Timberline Ski Lodge, Blake Wolff had to hurry to get Rosco ready for his canine avalanche training. He entered the lodge and saw his older quadruplet brother, Landon, feeding the dog.

"Hey," Landon said, grinning at Blake. "Hell, if I'd known all the trouble you would have with the snowblower, I would have come out and helped you."

"You watched."

"Of course. You were really entertaining this morning."

"I hadn't dreamed I'd have that much trouble with it."

Landon laughed. "You won't be so eager to volunteer when our hired help calls in sick again. I told you it wasn't a piece of cake."

"Next time, I'll be a pro." Luckily, no one else had seemed to notice, except for one pretty skier in pink and white, who'd made him smile when he'd heard her laughing when he fell on his ass.

He'd had a rough morning of it when the family Saint Bernard, Rosco, had shot off after a rabbit on a walk. Blake had barely been able to stay on his feet on the icy snow while trying to get the dog under control. He swore Rosco had pulled him for half a mile before finally giving up on the chase and doing his business. Rosco was usually well behaved and mild-mannered, until it came to rabbits and squirrels on a walk. The dog had never caught up with one, and Blake wondered what would happen if he ever did.

"Hey, Rosco, are you ready to train to locate avalanche victims?" Blake asked, petting the dog's head.

The Saint Bernard stood and wagged his tail.

"Okay then. When I return, we can take turns skiing?" Blake asked Landon.

"Yeah, you can go first."

"See you in a bit." Blake grabbed the equipment he'd need, then took Rosco out to where several volunteers were being buried in ice caves just out of sight so the avalanche rescue dogs could practice searching and finding them once they were given the signal.

The avalanche "victims" were wrapped in thermal blankets and had hooded, insulated cloaks. Thermal-insulated pads were used to line the snow inside the ice caves, which were dug large enough to give the volunteers plenty of air while the dogs searched for them.

Rosco had to take training every year, and this was a perfect situation where he could work with *lupus garous*. The Saint Bernard had saved two men's lives after an avalanche at the family's ski resort in Killington, Vermont, so the family was proud of their dog.

"Hey, Blake," Jake Silver said, coming over to shake his hand. He was one of the subleaders of the Silver Town wolf pack and glad they had another rescue dog in the pack. "Is Rosco ready?"

"Hopefully. This will be the first time he'll be looking for our kind buried alive."

"He'll do great."

"Thanks, Jake."

The dogs and their handlers were kept away from the victims' positions so they wouldn't see where the men were being buried. In only thirty minutes, a rescue dog could search two and a half acres of avalanche terrain, unlike humans who would take four hours to cover the same area. Of course, as *lupus garous*, the wolves also had the advantage of being able to smell the scent of humans up to fourteen feet underground.

Then the alert whistle called for the dogs' searches to begin.

And the hunt was on. Ten dogs ranging from German shepherds to Labradors and golden retrievers, plus one Saint Bernard, raced off to search for the buried victims. All their handlers ran after them with shovels, probes, and first aid kits.

———————————

Nicole was watching her suspects coming off the slope when they turned in the direction of the avalanche dog training. Her suspects and several other skiers had started to watch the trials so Nicole did too. Observing the rescue dogs in motion was fascinating. They ran one way, then another, noses to the ground, and were as excited to find their victims as she was watching them. Then she saw Rosco and his handler, and she smiled. Now she had a handler/dog team she really wanted to cheer on. Not that she didn't want the other dogs to find victims. That was the whole point, and everyone wanted them to work as quickly as they could. But she already had a soft spot for the wolf and his dog. After the business with him trying to get the dog under control on his walk, she really hoped they'd come out on top.

One of the German shepherds had already found a victim and was digging at the snow like crazy, his handler and rescuers ready with shovels to help dig out the volunteer. Rosco was still turning one way and then another, stopping, smelling, wagging his tail like crazy. And then Rosco barked and began digging at another location, snow flying.

Adrenaline was flowing through Nicole's blood, and she hoped Rosco had found his victim. Considering how many people were gathered around him as he started to dig, she figured he had succeeded.

The handler was encouraging Rosco, and then the dog was deep in the hole with only his backside hanging out, his tail wagging. The handler pulled the volunteer out of the ice cave, and the victim gave Rosco a treat as part of the game. It was a way of reinforcing the behavior of finding people or objects.

The wolf made sure the victim didn't have any ill effects from being in the ice cave, then slapped the victim on the back and turned his attention to the other handlers' dogs that also had found victims. The one that had found the first victim was already done. It had taken fifteen minutes for Rosco to find and dig out the victim.

He had done a good job. New dogs could be confused by the scents of all the different people who had passed through the area. When all the victims were rescued and checked over, the handlers and dogs took off for their vehicles, all except Rosco and his handler. He gave Rosco a treat and praised him generously. The dog adored him. Suddenly, as if the wolf knew somebody was observing him, he glanced in her direction and looked surprised to see her watching him. He smiled a cocky little smile and winked.

Nicole felt her whole body flush with heat, which never happened. Of course, she didn't often ogle guys, especially ones who were wolves, and get caught at it.

He led the dog on a leash to the lodge, and Nicole switched her focus to her suspects.

Then she saw Rhys and his cousin headed in her direction, returning to the ski lodge. They were smiling, talking to each other. Before they noticed her, she walked in ahead of them, thinking that this would be a really good time to have her partner to hug. She began looking for a male who appeared to have no female companion at the moment and that she could turn into her boyfriend for just a few minutes as her cover. Of course, it could all backfire if the man made a scene and the cousins witnessed it.

Then she saw the cute guy who had been trying to get the Saint Bernard and the snowblower under control. If anyone deserved a hug, it was him. As long as the wolf didn't have a mate or girlfriend and ruin her Good Samaritan deed. Besides, it was his fault he'd winked at her after the dog avalanche training.

———————————

"How'd Rosco do?" Landon asked Blake. "I wanted to come out and watch, but I got stuck on guest issues."

"Nothing bad, I hope." Blake unhooked Rosco's leash.

"No, typical stuff. Somebody had their TV playing loudly all night. I wish their neighbors had told us last night and we could have dealt with it. One person said he couldn't figure out the coffeemaker."

"We provide the easiest ones to operate to alleviate trouble," Blake said.

"Right. He still couldn't figure it out. Too simple, I guess. He had an aha moment when I showed him how it was done. Then a woman was having trouble with her alarm going off so she finally unplugged it—but she wanted to use it. I had to show her how to reset the times. We probably should have gotten a simpler model."

Blake smiled. "Kayla insisted we have the ones with the automatic change for daylight saving time so we wouldn't have to change all the clocks in the rooms twice a year. I'm glad you were here to take care of the issues. As to Rosco, he did great. He found an avalanche victim in record time."

"I'm glad to hear it. Saint Bernards suit the lodge, and I'm glad he's knuckled down to do his duty during avalanche rescues."

"I agree. He sure seemed like he'd be an avalanche rescue dog dropout when he was a puppy. Have you heard from either of our sisters about the closing?"

Roxie and Kayla planned to join them in Silver Town after closing the deal on the sale of the family's ski lodge in Vermont, but they still had to correct some issues with the lodge before the sale went through.

"I got a call from Kayla. She said she and Roxie accomplished everything needed to satisfy the buyers, so the closing took place and our sisters are on their way here. I should have told you earlier, but you were so busy, and I forgot."

"That's great." Knowing the Vermont lodge had sold was a real relief. Blake was glad his sisters had been able to manage that while he and Landon opened the ski lodge here. "Did they need one of us to pick them up at the airport?"

"No. Kayla said Lelandi was eager to pick them up and welcome them to the pack."

Blake was glad she would do that for them. "Since Lelandi's the coleader and psychologist for the pack, I wonder if she intends to warn them about all the bachelor males who are looking for mates and anxious to meet with them." That was all he and Landon had heard when they first arrived. Where were their sisters?

"Could be. And she wants to make sure they feel welcome. Which is one of the reasons we all wanted to be part of a pack." Landon glanced around at the hubbub in the lobby: skiers and other visitors were entering or coming out of the restaurant, others leaving the lodge to ski or coming in from skiing, some sitting around the double-sided fireplace. A couple of kids were sitting on the floor petting their sleepy Saint Bernard. "I'm glad our sisters are arriving soon. Kayla needs to help us with our marketing, and Roxie does wonders with the staff. We'll be a lot better organized when they're here. I bet they can't wait to try out the new slopes here too. Powder snow in Colorado instead of ice skiing in Vermont—they'll love it."

"Yeah, they're excited about it." There wasn't anything the family loved more than being part of the ski community. They were also looking forward to having visitors interested in hiking and other sports in the region. They loved being here with a wolf pack, which was why the family had solicited Darien and Lelandi Silver to allow them to open a ski lodge here, once they learned Silver Town was actually run by wolves. Not everyone in the pack had been happy about them opening the business at first. "I think most of the wolves in the pack accept us now," Blake said.

"Yeah. We knew we'd have to work at it a bit. I suspect when our sisters show up, some of the bachelor males will be even more agreeable to us being here."

Blake shook his head. "Roxie and Kayla won't be prepared for the onslaught of dating offers, I bet."

"They might not admit it, but I think they're looking forward to it. Little did we know there were so many males looking for she-wolf mates."

The brothers had worked super hard at trying not to take business from the bed-and-breakfast and the Silver Town Inn in town, doing everything they could to help advertise the other wolves' businesses too. It was good wolf-pack public relations. Most of the wolves were warming up to them being here. They'd finally opened the Howling Wolff Bar and Grill at the lodge, and that had also concerned some of the business owners in town.

The Silver Town Tavern, which boasted the best drinks and lunches and dinners around, was open exclusively to wolves, courtesy of a high-dollar membership that the wolves didn't really pay, so human visitors needed someplace else to go for dinner. Even so, the tavern's owner, Sam, and his mate, Silva, had worried the Wolff restaurant might take more of the wolf population's business. Silva ran the Victorian Tea Shop, which was open for lunches, but not everyone wanted to leave the slopes to eat lunch in town.

The ski lodge featured a large deck, offering dining for skiers who wanted to grab an appetizer, a drink, or a meal before they hit the slopes, and they had indoor dining too. A lot of folks came there on dates, not just to ski.

The Wolff brothers had downplayed their competitive nature, so this past Christmas, they hadn't participated in any of the competitions—snowmen or snow sculptures, gingerbread houses, even Christmas lighting. They'd decorated the whole lodge in lights, of course, but they hadn't entered their place in the competitions. Except for getting their business off the ground and making it a profitable venture, they hadn't had time for a whole lot of anything else.

"Looks like I've got some business to take care of." Landon frowned, his gaze focused on someone behind Blake who he could hear was fast approaching. From the sound of the ski boots on the tile floor, he thought the person was female. "You go ski, and when you're done, I'll take a few runs down the slope."

Blake glanced back and saw the pretty blond he'd noticed observing him and Rosco during the avalanche training. She was headed straight for them, her expression intense, brows furrowed, her gaze shifting from Landon to Blake. He smelled a whiff of her scent—fresh air and she-wolf. No wonder his brother was eager to assist her. At the same time, Blake was a little embarrassed that the woman approaching had witnessed him struggling with the snowblower. Good thing she hadn't seen him with an out-of-control Saint Bernard even earlier.

Blake smiled. "I can hang around for a moment and take care of whatever issues she's having."

"No, that's okay, Blake. The sooner you ski, the sooner I get to."

Blake knew that wasn't the only reason his brother wanted to take care of the woman's concerns. Landon had recognized she was a wolf too.

When she drew closer to them, she targeted Blake, and he was eager to be the one to handle whatever was upsetting her. *Happily.* Conflict didn't bother him or his brother. It was a chance to prove they could resolve any issues that arose at the lodge with the least amount of fuss. When he caught another whiff of her wolfish scent, that made him even more eager to help her. Though he reminded himself she could have a mate or a potential one.

She smiled brightly at Blake, her cheeks and the tip of her nose rosy from the cold. She was wearing a white parka, the furry hood down, a light-pink and white ski hat, dickey, and gloves, and formfitting light-pink ski pants and white ski boots, looking as if she'd just came off the slopes. She reminded him of cotton candy and snow bunnies, innocent and sweet.

When she reached him, she threw her arms around Blake in a hug, startling him. He smiled down at her, amused at where this was going. Since he was single, he didn't have to worry about a mate throwing a fit. If he had, all she'd have to do was smell this woman all over him, and he would have been in the doghouse. As long as the woman hugging him didn't have a mate either. Then again, wolves mated for life, so she probably wouldn't act this way if she were mated or courting another wolf. She could smell that he didn't have a she-wolf's scent on him either. Not until now.

He was surprised at her action. Did she think he was someone else? But she would recognize his scent, which quashed that theory. The only other thought that flashed through his mind was that she was trying to pretend she had a relationship with him because some guy was hassling her. Whatever the reason, he was all too willing to play along and take care of whoever was giving her trouble.

She kissed him, startling him even more, and his brother laughed. "It appears your day is looking up, and I think you have a handle on this." Still chuckling, Landon walked off.

Blake was enraptured with the woman. Her lips were soft and malleable as she pressed them gently against his, but she began building up the steam, licking his mouth and then nipping and melding hers with his.

Relishing the scent of the she-wolf and the crisp, cold out-of-doors that she carried with her, Blake wrapped his arms around her waist and pulled her tighter against his body, enjoying her soft curves and warmth, building a slow fire deep inside him. They were kissing like they needed a room, he realized, not family fare in the lobby of their lodge. He *very* reluctantly pulled his mouth from hers and smiled. "Do I know you?"

"Took you long enough to ask." She smiled up at him, and he wondered what he was getting himself into.

Hell, he was game.

"I'm Nicole Grayson, and you're my fiancé. For the moment. My life depends on it."

Blake frowned, worrying she was really in trouble, though she didn't seem overly anxious—not in her facial expression, and certainly not in the way she'd been so easily intimate with him. "Do we need to call the sheriff?" He should have already had his phone out, but he didn't want to let go of her if there wasn't any need. This was just too damn nice.

"No, I've got a handle on this."

He wanted to laugh at her choice of words since Landon had said the same thing about Blake. "All right, good show. By the way, I'm Blake Wolff."

"Wolf? I'll say."

He smiled. He liked her easy banter and didn't think she could be in any real danger. He would have smelled her anxiety for one thing, instead of her enticing arousal that was fueling his own. "I'd shake your hand, but I think we're beyond that."

"For this to be believable, yes." She smiled up at him as if she truly adored him. "I saw all the trouble you were having with the snowblower earlier."

"Uh, yeah." That kind of blew his macho image, he was afraid. He had hoped she wouldn't bring it up. "I've never used that kind before."

"I kind of figured that. I haven't either, or I would have tried to help."

He smiled. "You watched instead."

Her cheeks pinkened. "You were entertaining."

"You saw everything?"

"You mean the spill you took too? Yeah, you should have seen me hit a patch of ice on the slope this morning. I was sprawled every which way."

He chuckled, not feeling as bad now. He liked how she could make him feel better about it. "I was just going to ski. Did you want to come with me?" He thought that would be fun if it was in line with the ruse she was playing and because they would both be dressed for it once he put on some ski boots. Besides, he hadn't been this interested in a she-wolf since he and Susie Northrop ended things between them. She'd been so pissed off that he and his brother and sisters were moving to the "wilds" of Colorado, the Wild West, she said, that she broke it off with him a year before he left. Good thing for that.

"I just came in from out-of-doors. Take me to your room instead," Nicole said.

He raised a brow. He hadn't quite expected that. Then again, he hadn't expected any of this—the hug, the kiss, now this. He wasn't letting go of her though. "Because your life depends on it."

"It would seem more realistic. If we're lovers. And we can talk."

None of this seemed real to Blake. Well, the kiss sure did, but the rest? No.

He rubbed her arm, his other arm still keeping her locked against his body. His was hot and aroused, to be sure. He couldn't believe how much he didn't want to let her go. Then again, she was the one who had tackled him first.

He glanced around the lobby, looking to see if anyone was eyeing them with speculation. Their guests all seemed to be enjoying visiting with friends or were on their way somewhere—to the restaurant, restrooms, seating by the big center fireplace, out-of-doors to ski, or to their rooms. "Okay, we have a little problem with going to 'my' room."

"Don't tell me your roommate won't go along with it." She sighed.

"I'm not staying here."

"Okay, you can come to my room. But my partner has high-altitude sickness and might be sleeping."

"Partner. Male?" As in a *real* boyfriend? That could be awkward. Then again, he couldn't be, since Blake didn't smell a male's scent on her except his own. Blake hadn't met her before, but he was definitely showing any other eligible wolf bachelors here that he had a real interest in her. Was she part of the Silver Town pack, and he just hadn't met her yet? He didn't think so, or she wouldn't be staying at the lodge.

"Yes, he's a he. So you live in Silver Town? And are just up here for the day skiing?"

"I'm part owner of the ski lodge and restaurant, along with my brother and two sisters." He normally wouldn't have mentioned that to a she-wolf he'd just met who wasn't a member of the pack, feeling like it was bragging a little.

Her brows rose this time. "Oh, *Wolff* as in two *f*'s. Okay, this won't do. I need to find somebody else." She started to pull away from him.

He held on tight. "No. Wait."

She smiled up at him again. Then she frowned. "I shouldn't involve you. You seem like a nice guy."

"I'm already involved. And I can be a not-so-nice guy if you need me to. Ask my brother and sisters."

She chuckled, but then she grew serious again. "Okay, here the two men come. Make this look good. You can be my lover, and Larry is my brother."

"Larry, as in your partner?"

"Yes." She didn't give Blake a chance to ask any more questions as she kissed him again.

She didn't smell like she'd been around another male, so he didn't think the guy was really her partner as in mated. Instead, Nicole was wearing Blake's scent and he was cloaked in her sweet fragrance, making it seem, to other wolves, that *they* were together.

Blake had every intention of making it look real, but he wanted to see who she was worried about. He wanted to ask her who she was and who her "partner" was.

For now, he concentrated on the workout they were having, his mouth pressed hungrily against hers, and that was not faked in the least. She kissed him back just as greedily, her olive-green eyes feral as she gazed up at him, and then closed them again to concentrate on the kiss.

He could feel her pulling her mouth away finally, and he reluctantly went along with the plan. Her cheeks were flushed with heat, her gaze still on his mouth, as if she was thinking of kissing him again.

He smiled. She was hot and interesting, and he could have kissed her all day long.

She sighed. "Let's go."

Blake glanced back to see if his brother was busy working. Landon was standing near the fireplace, arms folded across his chest, watching them, smiling. Which was normal for a family member and a wolf who was curious how this would play out.

"Wow, we leave you guys alone for a couple of months, and what do we come home to?" Blake's sister Roxie asked. He turned to see her and their sister Kayla openmouthed and staring at him in surprise.

CHAPTER 2

BLAKE REALIZED ROXIE AND KAYLA HAD ENTERED THE
lobby, and instead of greeting him after their long trip, they
had been watching the situation between him and Nicole
unfold, just as Landon had.

"Ohmigod, you!" Roxie said to Nicole, finally really
looking at her.

"Roxie…um…*Wolff*? You're related to *Blake*?" Nicole
asked, sounding surprised.

Roxie folded her arms. "Yeah. I'm his *sister*. And this is
our sister, Kayla, and our brother Landon."

"You two know each other?" Blake suspected from his
sister's aggravated tone and posture that she did, and it
wasn't in a good way.

Roxie turned to Blake. "Unfortunately, yes. I know her.
Remember me telling you about that worthless CID investigation concerning the MP who threatened me with a gun,
ordering me to hand over my coin collection?"

Blake looked at Nicole, waiting for her to confirm.

"You can't be here!" Nicole said to Roxie, panic in her
voice.

"What?" Roxie wore a growly expression as she glow-
ered at Nicole.

"Can we talk about this in private? Please?" Nicole
asked, pleading with Roxie and Blake.

Blake knew from the change in Nicole's scent from
interested in him to highly anxious that something really

was wrong. "Yeah, we can go to the office," he said, worried Roxie might be in some kind of trouble.

"I just got here, and I fully intend to see everything and do my job. *You* can get lost." Roxie glanced at the restaurant, and her face brightened. "I love the decor. I know we helped plan it, and you sent us pictures, but it's even nicer than I had envisioned."

"If you haven't had lunch, you ought to check it out," Blake said.

"No!" Nicole said, even more anxious now.

Everyone looked at her like she was crazy.

"Can we *please* move this to someplace private? To your office, like you mentioned?" Nicole said.

"Sure. Come on." Blake led the way, and his sisters and Nicole followed him to the office.

As soon as they were all inside, he saw Landon give someone a quick word, then shake his hand and stalk across the floor to join them. Blake was glad they could all meet together to learn what Nicole thought was wrong. Landon hugged their sisters, and then Blake realized he should have too when he first saw them, but he'd been wrapped up in Nicole and the kiss and whatever the trouble seemed to be. He began to make introductions, explaining to his brother about Nicole having been with CID and investigating the unsolved crime against Roxie.

"Hey, I'm Kayla," his other sister said, stepping in to shake Nicole's hand. "So you're a member of the Silver Town pack?"

"Uh, no." Nicole smiled and shook Kayla's hand. "The town has a wolf pack then?"

"Yeah. Are you still with the CID?" Kayla asked.

"No. I left the army."

"Did you have too many unsolved cases?" Roxie arched a brow, her arms folded across her chest.

"That was my first case, and my first unsolved case, true. I had a few more, but I solved a lot more than I lost. That wasn't the reason I left the service. Okay, listen. Not all cases can be solved. I couldn't find any hard evidence to charge the MP with the crime, though I believed your story in its entirety. I even learned who the MP was."

Roxie's eyes widened. "And still you did nothing?"

"I smelled his scent, then found his desk and his name-plate sitting on his desk, so I knew he was the one who had held your driver's license. But you know we can't use our ability to recognize scents in a court of law. If I'd had a secu-rity video of him accosting you or one of him getting into his car and the license plate number, I could have nailed him. I even did surveillance on him until he left the service, whenever I had any free time, though I was often working seventy-hour weeks on cases. I was trying to pin him down on a different crime, to find a pattern of criminal behav-ior. At the time, I thought either he had never committed a crime before or he was lying low, afraid someone might realize what he'd done. But I never caught him doing any-thing illegal the rest of the time he was on active duty."

Her eyes narrowed, Roxie still looked miffed, but Blake understood Nicole's situation. With nothing to go on, she couldn't have done anything more. Wisely, he didn't com-ment and take Nicole's side though.

"What are you doing here if you're not part of the pack?" Roxie asked. "Besides kissing my brother like he's your long-lost mate. And why don't you want anyone to see me?"

"He's here, the MP, and I'm here to do surveillance on him with a partner who unfortunately has high-altitude sickness."

"Partner?" Roxie and Kayla both glanced at Blake, as if expecting him to look surprised, especially after all the kissing that had been going on between the two of them.

Roxie eyed Nicole again, then said to Blake, "I'd sure check out this 'partner' before I got much more involved with the former special agent. So the MP *is* here? And you're doing what? Looking to finally make this right? If you're no longer in the service, I don't see that you can. Unless you're FBI or something now and he's committed another crime, one you can do a better job solving."

Wanting to explain Roxie's animosity about the case to Nicole, Blake said, "Roxie was afraid she'd run into the MP at some other time while she was on active duty. She's not afraid of much, but that really spooked her. Especially since he had a badge and a gun. When she called us about it, Landon and I were there in a heartbeat and stayed with her for a couple of weeks at her apartment, just in case the bastard returned. We were running the ski lodge in Vermont at the time. We were glad when she got out of the service and joined us to help with the lodge. Had you seen him here, and that's why you kissed me?" He suspected she was a PI or undercover cop, FBI maybe.

"Larry and I are investigating a case of insurance fraud. We're independent private investigators working for an insurance company. I need to check on my partner and make sure he's all right. He's from Kansas and can't take this high altitude. He's human, not one of us. But the situation is this: we're looking for two men—Rhys Hanover and William

Kovac. They're cousins, and Rhys is dead. *Supposedly* dead. Rhys's real name is Oscar Kovac. He was the MP who tried to steal from you, Roxie."

"Hell. I'll kill the bastard. So what are they doing? Looking for a big insurance payoff and this is a case of pseudocide?" Blake asked.

"Yes, that's exactly what it is," Nicole said.

"I don't believe this," Roxie said.

"We're talking about a five-million-dollar life insurance policy. The problem is that he could see you here and realize you'd know who he is. He could worry you'd heard of his death but realize he is alive, and the gig is up. I know he'd run. Trying to track him down again could be impossible. Even though we couldn't get him for the earlier crime perpetrated against you, we want to get him for this one. Right now, he thinks no one knows him here and that he's perfectly safe."

"What about you? Wouldn't he recognize *you* if he sees you?" Roxie asked. "You said you'd seen him at the police department."

Blake was thinking the same thing. Nicole must have dealt with the police from time to time while handling her CID cases.

"I never had any dealings with him directly. He was never at the police department when I was there after the one time I saw him. He didn't see me. Thankfully, he's not a wolf or he might recognize me by scent."

Roxie's whole posture changed from highly irritated to excited. "I want to help catch him."

"No," both Blake and Landon said. Blake knew his sister would get involved if she could. Now he wished she had stayed in Vermont until this situation was resolved with Rhys, when before this, Blake had been hoping she and Kayla would hurry up and arrive in Colorado. Not only were they a great help to one another, but the family was close and enjoyed doing things together. Their new life was here.

"Nicole's right. If he sees you, even if he believes you don't know that he faked his death, he could still worry you might recognize him from the time he stopped you for your expired safety-inspection sticker," Blake said.

Roxie bit her lip. "Okay, but I want to do something." She eyed Nicole as if she thought she might be able to give Roxie a job that would help Nicole catch the bastard.

Blake knew his sister wouldn't be able to sit still when she wanted to help run the lodge, see the sights, visit with her new pack members, and adjust to her new home. He could see Kayla hiding away in the office, busy creating all kinds of plans for holiday specials, like a website that would feature all the fun folks could have at the lodge. They had to dig her out of the office just to get her out to socialize a bit. But Roxie? She was always out and about, greeting people, making everyone feel welcome, social to the max. If she was sick or needed to sleep, that was when she went home. Otherwise, she loved being with others. Confine her to house arrest? She'd go batty.

"I know it might seem boring, but if you could watch the security monitors and alert me where he is when you see him, that would help," Nicole said.

Roxie scoffed.

Blake knew Roxie wanted to be a whole lot more active than that.

"What are your email addresses? I'll send everyone a

picture of what Oscar looked like before he had some plastic surgery done, grew his hair and beard out, dyed his hair, and started calling himself Rhys. I also have some pictures of him and his cousin now and what they've been wearing for skiing while here."

Once Nicole had their emails, she sent them all the photos.

Blake was amazed at how different Rhys looked from Oscar's earlier photo. He didn't think he would have made the connection if he'd only met the man once before, when his hair was dark brown and cut short, military style, as a military police officer.

"Wow," Roxie said. "If you had a close-up photo of his eyes, I would have recognized him. But I wouldn't have known him if I'd seen him wearing the long, blond hair and the brown beard. I can't tell about the plastic surgery. I think his nose looks a little different. But the hair and the bushy beard really would have thrown me off."

"It appears he staged his death for the insurance money. Did he really have the accident and then hatch the idea? Or had he planned it all along? It really doesn't matter how it all came about. He didn't die, his cousin received the money from the life insurance payout, and that makes it a crime. Since they're together, I have to assume they both got part of the proceeds," Nicole said.

"And you think they're dangerous." Unless Nicole was being melodramatic... She had mentioned it could mean her life if Blake didn't pretend to be her lover. Rhys *had* threatened his sister with a gun when they were in the army, so he could understand Nicole's concern.

"Yes, if the men had anything to do with the last investigator's disappearance—which is why they sent two of us as a team this time. And knowing Oscar was armed the time he confronted Roxie, we have to assume Rhys is armed now."

"They killed the other investigator?" Roxie asked, sounding horrified.

"He vanished. We have no idea if he met with foul play. He told the insurance company that hired him that he had a lead on Oscar Kovac. He gave the insurance company Oscar's last known address, though he didn't have his new name. Rhys hadn't yet hooked up with William, the cousin, and that was the last anyone heard of the private investigator."

"So they hire a woman?" Blake couldn't help how that sounded after he spoke the words. If a man couldn't deal with these two men, how could a woman? In retrospect, he should have said it a little differently.

Nicole cast him an annoyed look.

Roxie and Landon were smiling as if they knew Blake had blown it. Kayla was frowning at him.

"I'm highly trained, have a double black belt in jujitsu, was weapons-trained in the military, and keep up my training. I'm trained in hand-to-hand combat and more. Usually when we're working an investigation, we have to do a lot of computer searches, following the trail the suspect left behind, looking for them on social media sites, and conducting surveillance. So it's not all about trying to take the men down but about proving they've committed a crime. As a private investigator, I've proven three prior cases of pseudocide and saved the insurance companies some hefty payouts. I'm good at what I do."

"Uh, yeah, sorry, I didn't mean that the way it sounded."

"Since there are two subjects involved in this, it's better for us to work as a couple, in case the men split up. Though

I've found that they're sticking together. Once Larry and I got the case, we were shadowing the cousin first, since he'd received the payout, knowing if he suddenly was chumming it up with a male who fit Oscar's description, it could be him. I really thought they wouldn't see each other for a good long while after getting so much money. For the first two months, they didn't have any contact. Then they must have thought they were out of the woods. Rhys and William seem to be really good friends, not just business partners. Maybe they assumed receiving the payout meant they were in the clear. Even after a payout, investigators will continue to search for the truth if no body is found. Or if foul play might have been involved."

"Wait, if they got rid of the other investigator, wouldn't these men be worried another investigator would come after them?" Blake asked.

"That's why the cousin left Florida and they ended up here. They were trying to hide their tracks."

"And you knew this how?" Blake asked.

"Facebook. I found the cousin's name, to begin with. Not Oscar's, because he had already changed his name. Rhys was a friend of William's on his Facebook account. William had over a thousand followers, so I created a fake Facebook persona and friended several of his friends until it looked like we had a lot of mutual friends."

"Sneaky. I've got to see this fake Facebook page of yours," Roxie said, sounding intrigued.

Nicole showed it to her. "Don't you go and do the same thing."

Blake smiled at his sister. Nicole seemed to have her pegged.

Roxie rolled her eyes. "Your picture looks like you are fun-loving. Single. But it doesn't look like you, exactly. Black hair? Bobbed?"

"Wig."

"I'm surprised you haven't been hit up a thousand times," Roxie said, while Blake, Landon, and Kayla took a look at Nicole's profile and Blake thought the same thing.

"I have. Anyway, once we had lots of the same friends, I friended William and he accepted my friend request. Then it was a matter of going through all the friends on his list and checking out their profiles. I narrowed it down to a guy who had just started his account a couple of months earlier. No earlier posts than that." Nicole showed them some of the comments Rhys and William had made.

"Which means he just suddenly came into existence," Blake said.

"Right. Luckily, no one seemed to think anything of the fact that I had started my Facebook account even more recently than that. Rhys mentioned kayaking with William. And that raised a red flag, since that's how Oscar supposedly died. The two of them made comments that appeared to be inside jokes about ways to die a dramatic death while kayaking or white-water rafting.

"Then I began researching what I could on Rhys. He had a new driver's license in Little Rock, Arkansas. It looked like he had moved there after the other PI disappeared in Fort Lauderdale, Florida. Then Rhys's posts were all about skiing and the places that he'd been. He didn't mention anything about being an MP in the army. He didn't share his birth date, but his driver's license says he was born a month and two years later than his original birth date. A lot of times, these guys will be so arrogant, thinking they've pulled one over on the system, that they'll post where they're living or vacationing."

"'Skiing at the ski resort in Silver Town, Colorado.'" Blake shook his head while reading more of the comments William and Rhys had made.

"Yep. Since it's winter, I figure that's why he's not kayaking, but come spring or summer?" Nicole said.

"Hopefully, he'll be in prison before that happens," Roxie said.

"I agree. *If* I get the evidence I need and have him arrested before he gets away again."

"His Facebook profile picture is of a guy skiing, ski goggles, ski mask, ski hat, so you can't tell who he really is," Blake said, looking at the masked figure wearing gray and black ski pants and jacket. "Some of William's friends might know Oscar, a.k.a. Rhys."

"Right. But they might not know that Rhys is Oscar. Just that he's a good friend of William. Some of the men listed as William's friends were ones who had been at a party the night Oscar's parents died in their home due to a fire. A lot of discussion about what had happened that night was posted on William's page. Nothing incriminating though. Just lots of discussion how awful it was that they had died and William and Oscar sharing a bunch of wonderful childhood memories."

"You think Oscar had something to do with their deaths?" Blake asked.

"Possibly."

"Do you think the discussion about how they were upset over his parents' deaths was contrived?" Blake skimmed backward to see earlier messages.

"Faked wonderful childhood memories? Could be to show anyone who might investigate William and his cousin's social networking sites that Oscar was the adoring son and his cousin was their loving nephew."

Nicole was looking over Blake's shoulder, and he loved the way her body was pressed against his. He was trying to concentrate solely on the business at hand, but she was definitely making that difficult. Not that he wanted to give that intimacy up.

Roxie was looking over his other shoulder at the comments.

Blake found the pictures of the kayaking trip where Oscar supposedly had drowned, the overturned red kayak wedged between rocks, the throw rope in the water, the men freeing the kayak, turning it over, and then realizing Oscar wasn't pinned beneath it. "Someone was taking pictures."

Blake looked at pictures of Oscar's funeral that a friend had taken. William was wiping away tears in a couple of them. "Man, these guys are con artists."

"Yeah, they are," Nicole agreed.

Blake looked much further back on William's page and found pictures of him and Oscar kayaking at the same location. "Okay, so this was two weeks earlier."

"The staging operation, I figured," Nicole said.

"Sure looks like it to me." Blake could really get into this sleuthing business.

"You wouldn't think they'd post all this stuff," Roxie said. "It's a dead giveaway."

"I think it's all a cover-up for when they actually did the deed. If you look further back, William posted about Oscar's younger brother Eli's drowning—which was real. There are pictures of Eli's funeral on William's page, but if you read the conversation between William and his cousin, when he was still Oscar and shortly after Eli's death, you'll see a lot of anger concerning the parents being mad at Oscar for allowing his brother to die."

"Wait, the younger brother died in a drowning too?" Blake asked.

"Yep."

Blake went back to see the comments on William's page, referring to the brother drowning earlier on.

> **Oscar:** If my mom hadn't forced me to take Eli to the damn lake, none of this would have happened.
>
> **William:** I agree, man. You shouldn't have had to be your brother's keeper. Hell, Tyson nearly broke my nose when he hit me with the ball. The ass. My eyes were swollen, and I could barely see! Let alone watch out for your brother. Besides, Eli was being a nuisance like usual and wanting to tag along. Then he sulked off when we wouldn't include him in the game of toss.
>
> **Oscar:** Yeah. It wasn't my fault.

That made Blake want to see how many times before that they had written about Eli tagging along with them. There were no pictures of Oscar and his brother, just of Oscar and William. There was no indication that Blake could see of Oscar complaining to William about taking care of his younger brother. Blake mentioned that to Nicole.

"Yeah, I had the same thought when I was looking at earlier comments on William's Facebook page, figuring if the parents were always forcing him to take Eli with them, he would have said something about it."

"What about Eli's Facebook account?"

"There is none that I could find."

Blake handed Nicole's phone back to her. "Great detective work."

"Thank you. You're not bad yourself."

"A PI in the making."

Nicole smiled at him.

"All right, so I've got video security monitoring duty." Roxie sounded resigned to her assignment, though Blake knew she would do a good job of it. "Give me your phone number so I can contact you."

Nicole exchanged her phone number with everyone. "Roxie, you'll need to wear a disguise whenever you're roaming the lodge when Rhys is around."

Roxie smiled a little evilly, Blake thought. "Okay, what else can I do?" she asked.

"I need his fingerprints or a sample of his DNA after he has eaten off a utensil or had something to drink. The military has been collecting DNA from soldiers since 1992, in addition to dental records and fingerprints, so if we can catch a break, we should be able to prove beyond a doubt that he is still very much alive. But he's been really careful about not leaving any evidence lying around. And I haven't wanted to go into his room and get caught."

"Housekeeping service? One of us could pose as a housekeeper," Blake offered.

"They've got a Do Not Disturb sign posted all the time on their doorknob. We don't want to have someone slip in there and get caught. That might tip Rhys off so that I wouldn't be able to find them again," Nicole said.

"It sounds to me like he is being somewhat cautious about anyone learning he's here." Blake couldn't imagine going through such a farce and getting a big payout and then being really careless about it. Mentioning on Facebook where Rhys was going to be skiing was plain dumb. Then again, he thought no one had discovered his alias.

"Right. People often go back to their old habits. Not only that, but again, there's the arrogance factor. That helps us as investigators to catch them."

Because Nicole was in their territory and her partner was out of commission, Blake thought they needed to contact Darien and Lelandi, their pack leaders, and get the whole pack involved in watching Nicole and her partner's backs. Even though the *lupus garous* usually didn't eliminate human criminals in their territory, instead turning them over to other authorities in the location where the crime had been committed, they protected their own kind. Well, humans, too, if they needed protection from the bad guys.

Kayla motioned to the office door. "Nice meeting you, Nicole. I've got to get to work on a marketing plan, and I hope you get this resolved soon. But I'll help in any way that I can. I'm going to the house to unpack first though."

"Thanks, Kayla."

Kayla left the office and shut the door.

Landon finally spoke up. "Okay, the problem is that Roxie could be in danger if Rhys eliminated the other investigator, since she's already thwarted him once. If he sees her, he could feel compelled to murder her to keep her from revealing that he'd been here."

"What do we do about it?" Roxie asked. "Believe me, I'd rather do anything than hide out here. Or at the house."

"I say eliminate him. He's already dead. The insurance money is paid out. Let him get his just deserts that way," Landon said.

Blake knew his brother was only half-serious. He wouldn't mind doing it himself, since the sergeant had threatened their sister with a gun, but he knew they couldn't. The guy was human, and the pack would have to be involved in any decisions of that magnitude.

"I'd go along with that," Roxie said, "but I'm sure we don't have that option, unless it's in self-defense."

"We could arrange that." Landon smiled.

"I'm going to help Nicole with this," Blake said.

"We'll all help," Landon said. "We need to end this guy's need to commit crimes."

"Since you are in charge of this, what do we do next?" Blake asked Nicole. He and his siblings were lodge operators, not criminal investigators. She would have to guide them in what they could do to help her.

"I need to go to my room to check on my partner's condition. I'm sorry about not being able to charge Oscar the first time," Nicole said to Roxie.

"I understand," Roxie said. "I don't like it, but at least he never got the coins and he never bothered me again before I left the service."

"Okay, and thanks for helping with the case. Just let us know if you see him." Nicole started to leave the office.

"I'm going with you," Blake said. "I'm her boyfriend," he reminded his sister.

Roxie scoffed. Landon just smiled. Smiling back at them, Blake hurried after Nicole.

"After the comment you made about a woman not being able to handle this job?" Nicole said, arching a brow at Blake as they entered the lobby.

"Uh, yeah, I apologize for that." He figured he might have to work a bit on mending fences if they were going to pull off being a couple, but he was certainly willing. They took the stairs to the second floor.

When they reached her room, she unlocked the door and Blake saw her partner in bed, a redhead, looking pale as he opened his blue eyes and stared at the two of them.

"Okay, that's it. You look awful, Larry. You're going to see a doctor," Nicole said to her partner.

Larry was frowning at Blake. "Who's *he*?"

Blake thought the guy sounded more like a real boyfriend than just Nicole's partner on a job. Not that he was surprised that the guy would be interested in more. If *Blake* had really been her partner, he definitely would have been intrigued enough to become a real boyfriend.

"He's my fiancé. You didn't last long enough in the relationship, though I told Blake you were my brother, in case anyone overheard what was going on. It's much more believable this way. He'll help look after me. Don't you worry about it. I'm truly sorry you're feeling so poorly."

"You just picked the guy up?" Larry sounded as if he couldn't believe how naive she could be.

Blake didn't blame her partner. Even though Blake was a wolf like her, that didn't mean he was automatically a trustworthy individual or that he was someone who could really protect her. Her partner wouldn't know Blake was a wolf either. If the guys Nicole was after had been wolves, that would have been a whole other story. The pack would have taken care of them themselves. Actually, he and his brother would have dealt with them with the pack leaders' blessing.

"Blake Wolff owns the lodge." She changed out of her ski boots into furry snow boots.

"Oh. Stepping up in the world." Larry tried to sit up in bed, and Nicole hurried to help him. "Does he have any combat training? Weapons training?"

Good questions. If Blake had been solely a business owner, maybe not. But being a wolf meant he'd dealt with lots over the years.

Nicole glanced at Blake, raising her brows.

"All of the above." Not that he'd been in the military or on the police force, except as deputy sheriff in the wolf pack, but over the years, he'd had his share of fighting with the bad guys, wolf and human. He even knew how to use a sword, but that was more for fun.

Nicole sighed. "I'm sorry, Larry. It would never have worked out between you and me." She smiled at Larry teasingly.

"Women are fickle." Larry finally got out of bed and began to dress. Slowly. The way he kept leaning to the side and losing his balance, he appeared to be dizzy.

Nicole helped him as much as she could. Blake would have offered, but she seemed to want to take care of him.

"You can drive him to the Silver Town Clinic. They'll take good care of him. If he needs longer-term care, they'll transport him to a hospital farther away." Blake thought maybe she could use his help getting Larry there. "Do you need me to drive you?"

"No thanks, we're good." She called the clinic. "I have a friend who needs to be seen for high-altitude sickness…right. I'll bring him in right away. Thanks." She pocketed her phone. "Dr. Weber can see him."

"Are you sure you don't need my help?" Blake realized he was reaching for any excuse to stay with her longer. It wasn't just the kiss they'd shared but the reason why they'd shared it. He wanted to make sure she stayed safe, if she really needed a partner on this mission. And he suspected she did.

"I can manage. We'll be fine."

"If you need my services any further, just come get me. I'll be down in the lobby. My brother will probably go skiing, but you and I can talk. And now that my sisters are here, they'll be helping us run the lodge so I can take off more time." Well, he guessed Roxie shouldn't until they turned Rhys over to the authorities.

"You can buy me lunch when I return if you're free."

"Room service?" Blake smiled a little.

Larry shook his head as they helped him out of the room.

"In the restaurant," she said, her chin tilted down, as if telling Blake that the kiss was purely for show.

But it had been the real deal to him—and to her, or she wouldn't have put that much effort into it. She sure had him worked up, and that hadn't happened when he was kissing other women he'd actually dated.

They were quiet as they helped Larry to the elevator and

took him through the lobby, outside, and to her car. Blake had decided to go with them out to the car, not wanting to learn Larry had collapsed in the parking lot. He noticed her license tag said she was from Colorado. That helped with the ploy of Blake being her fiancé. Unless she'd flown into the airport and the car was a rental. Her fake Facebook page said she was from Sacramento, California, but he suspected she had included that to throw Rhys and William off.

"You're from Colorado?" Was she with a pack or on her own? The only other Colorado wolf packs he knew of were Bella and Devlyn Greystoke's up north and Ryan and Carol McKinley's in Green Valley.

"Yeah, I'm from Denver."

Blake was glad to know that, in case he wanted to take some trips there to see more of her. He helped Larry into the front passenger seat and buckled him in.

"You take good care of her. The last investigator disappeared. Mysteriously," Larry said, giving him as stern a look as he could in his condition.

"I will. I promise. So will my brother, my sisters, and my friends. She'll be in good hands. Just you get better." Blake shut the car door for Larry.

Nicole climbed into the driver's seat. "I'll be seeing you."

"See you soon." Blake watched them drive off, then glanced around at the people coming and going in the parking lot, but he didn't see two males walking together who fit the cousins' descriptions. He headed inside to talk to his brother in the lobby and saw him speaking with a guest, but then Landon motioned to the restaurant and the man headed in that direction.

Smiling when he saw Blake approach, Landon shook his

head. "I always figured our sisters would pick mates first. We need to let the pack leaders know about this situation."

Blake agreed. "We do. Helping Nicole doesn't mean anything will come of this. Her partner didn't look well at all. She's taking him to the clinic to see Dr. Weber. I doubt the guy will be coming back to the lodge to help her anytime soon."

"Then we'll help her. Let's check the men out and see what we can learn." Landon and Blake returned to the office. Landon logged into a computer while Blake exchanged his ski boots for a pair of snow boots.

Roxie was watching the security monitors, but she came over to see what they were going to do. "What's the room number where the creeps are staying?"

"Twenty-three," Landon said. "Reserved to a Rhys Hanover."

"Is Nicole working the case alone?" Roxie asked Blake. He thought she sounded a little concerned.

He explained what had happened to Nicole's partner.

Roxie tsked. "You're taking her out to lunch? She sure has you wrapped around her little finger."

"What can I say? She's a great kisser and she's a wolf."

"Single?"

"I sure the hell hope so." Blake could just see some irate mate coming here to take him to task for getting fresh with his wife. It was one thing to have a partner, another to be kissing him as if she wanted to take this business with him a lot further.

"You don't know hardly anything about her."

"I know she's from Denver, a wolf, and goes after bad guys. That's good enough for me." For now.

"Okay, here's the news story on the men," Landon said, pulling up the page.

Blake summarized the news report. "Okay, Oscar is the dead guy. *Supposed* dead guy. From this account from his cousin, William, it looks like Oscar was kayaking with him, following him down the Gore Canyon, which is considered an intense if not extreme river challenge. That's where you and I went that one time we wanted to go kayaking in Colorado, Landon."

His brother agreed. "Yep, that's the same place all right. It can be hairy."

"According to this, William slammed into an abandoned throw rope strung across the chute underneath the water. He was jerked from his boat and forced to swim to the shore. He finally reached the rocks on the bank and climbed out. Oscar was following him in his kayak and hit the same rope and flipped out of his boat, only his kayak was pinned among the rocks. There was no sign of him when rescuers finally arrived and secured the boat and turned it over."

"It's plausible, as far as abandoned throw ropes go. Anyone who doesn't go back and retrieve their own rope ought to be hung with it. So did they hang the rope there themselves, or did they just happen to run into it? And then after Oscar was 'lost forever,' William mourned his cousin's loss and waited for the insurance settlement."

Blake agreed. "Not sure about the rope. It doesn't say anything about the payout here. From what Nicole said, the insurance company has already paid the money to William."

"Which is why they have all the money to spend up here. I take it you're not going to ski," Landon said.

"No, I'll be hanging around here, waiting for Nicole's return. You go ahead."

"I'd like to ski the white powder," Roxie said, "if anyone cared."

"Are you already tired of looking at the monitors?" Blake had known she wouldn't last long at it.

"Yes! Talk about a boring job."

"You know, if you wore a ski mask, your reflective ski goggles, and a ski hat, Rhys would never know it was you if he ran into you," Landon said. "Besides, he only met you twice."

"Just my thought," Roxie said. "I won't speak to them if we end up getting close to them."

"No giving him the evil eye," Blake said.

"He'd never know it if I did while I'm wearing reflective goggles."

Landon hesitated to leave. "Are you sure you don't want me to hang around, Blake?"

"No. We've got enough hired help to take care of the check-ins and checkouts and reservations. I'm really only needed if we have trouble. And everything seems to be running smoothly."

"Roxie, if you keep covered up at all times while we're out skiing, you can come with me. At the same time, we can see if we can locate them anywhere on the slopes." Landon asked Blake, "Are you going to check out Nicole's background while you're doing research on the internet?" Landon took off his boots and put on his ski boots.

Roxie was hurrying to do the same. They'd built a walk-in closet in their office for all their gear—emergency gear, skis, ski poles, boots, and snowshoes. They could take a break skiing or hiking, or they could help with emergencies while they were working at the hotel.

"Doing that right now." Blake did a search for Nicole on the internet and found her listed as living in Denver with a private investigator business there. He smiled. "'Mile High Investigations—no job too big or too small.'"

"Tell me what you learn when I get back. We'll be gone for a couple of hours." Landon slapped Blake on the back. "Just be careful."

Blake couldn't help thinking about the pretty blond and her mission. She should be working with a partner if these men had anything to do with the disappearance of the other investigator.

While he was searching on Facebook for her real profile, he had found five Nicole Graysons and one that had *his* Nicole pictured: blond hair, green eyes. But he couldn't see her posts without friending her. And then she'd know he was checking her out.

He smiled. They were supposed to be engaged. He friended her, and as soon as she accepted his friend request, he'd list her as being in a relationship with him. Her cover, right?

CHAPTER 3

NICOLE COULDN'T BELIEVE HOW BAD OFF HER PARTNER was, and she wished she'd made him go to the clinic earlier to have his condition checked out. He was going to be okay, but he needed oxygen and they were transporting him to another hospital at a lower elevation. Larry said he hadn't been skiing for a couple of years. He was in excellent physical shape, but sometimes that worked against someone visiting a location at a higher altitude than they were accustomed to.

Pulling off his oxygen mask, Larry reached his hand out to her.

She squeezed it.

"Be careful. And call Taggart if looks like you need real backup," he said.

"I will." She suspected Larry had thought he might get to know her better since she was running her own detective agency and was single like him, and she and he had gotten along from the beginning. But he had no idea that she was all wolf.

Speaking of wolves, she had been surprised to see Dr. Weber was a red wolf when they arrived at the clinic. So was the office manager. The nurses and the receptionist were gray wolves. Nicole had thought only the lodge was wolf-run. She wondered just how many wolves lived here. And she suspected if she really needed more help with her mission, she'd get it. She imagined the pack's members wouldn't tolerate anyone coming into their territory and causing trouble for other wolves, local or otherwise.

As an attendant wheeled Larry out to a waiting ambulance, Nicole got a notice from her Facebook account that she had a new friend request. She rarely got them, so she was surprised. She glanced at the friend request and saw it was from Blake. She chuckled and wished Larry well, then had to tell him what Blake had done. Larry just shook his head again. *Larry* hadn't friended her on Facebook. But then *he* wasn't a wolf.

She said goodbye to Larry and accepted Blake's friend request.

As soon as she climbed into her car, she saw that Blake had changed his status from being just a friend to being in a relationship with her. She laughed. He must have been waiting for her to accept his friend request. In a heartbeat, he had moved right into the role of being her boyfriend. But she was certain he'd be busy running the lodge and couldn't always watch her back. Still, it was good to know he was there and she could solicit his help if she needed to. She was certain Landon would help too. She just hoped Roxie kept a low profile so that Rhys didn't see her and make the connection.

Nicole called Blake on her Bluetooth as she drove back to the ski resort. "Hey, Blake, I'm on my way back. If you had qualifications to be a real PI, I could hire you at my agency and then ask the insurance company to hire you to help me with the investigation. Too bad we couldn't do that."

He didn't say anything for a moment.

"But you would already have to have all the credentials and a PI license."

"You want to hire me?"

"We're already dating and I could use a partner. For this job. But you'd need to pass a written exam and have a degree in an investigative field."

"Then you're going to throw me under the bus once this job is done?"

She chuckled.

"It wouldn't work out. I have a degree in hotel management. Since you're new here, you don't know the workings of the pack, but Sheriff Peter Jorgenson deputized us in case we were ever needed to help take down bad guys in the town, if anyone like that showed up. I have a permit to carry. Even though I couldn't get a PI license in time to do this job, I still am qualified to help."

"Excellent! I won't have to hire you and then have to let you go after the job is done."

He chuckled.

"I'm just pulling into the parking lot now. See you in a sec." Nicole had been watching Rhys this morning to see if he and William ate or drank anything so she could get Rhys's fingerprints off his trash or utensils, but they never seemed to eat or drink when she was around. She hoped she hadn't missed them coming in for lunch this time.

The first rule of staging one's own death—and getting away with it—was not being seen alive. They'd blown that already. She'd sent photos of the men to the insurance company, but that wasn't enough because Rhys didn't look like Oscar. Even though she knew it was him because she'd smelled his scent.

She parked in the ski lodge parking lot. Though her focus had to remain on the mission, she couldn't help but want to see the hot wolf again. By the time she'd driven to the clinic, the clinic staff had sent Larry on the road to the hospital, and she'd driven back to the lodge, it had been nearly an hour and a half. She hoped Blake would be ready to have lunch with her, and then she would plan her next course of action.

Nicole walked toward the lodge, loving the rustic appearance of the building with its log walls, steep roof, and big windows. The deck extended out to the slope, providing skiers the opportunity to ski to some of the rooms, or to the dining area and lobby, with ease. Even the hot tubs surrounded by snow appealed. Not to mention the inviting indoor-outdoor pool that would be fun to enjoy during all seasons.

She loved the laughter and smiles shared by skiers heading for the slopes, eager to enjoy their day.

Inside, the stone fireplace reached to the high ceiling and was double-sided so that guests could sit on either side and still enjoy the warmth. It made a beautiful gathering place for drinks, snacks, and conversation. A wall nearby had a fountain with water running down into a basin, making it sound as though she'd found a waterfall in the woods, and miniature potted alpine trees were sitting on either side of it, adding to the illusion.

Pillars featuring packs of wolves in different settings—sitting atop rocks, drinking at a stream, running in the woods—added to the wolfish feel of the lodge. She loved it. In a way, she wished she was here just enjoying a ski vacation, though she was certain she would never have dropped into Silver Town otherwise, since it was off the beaten path. But what an out-of-the-way treasure—and especially to find that so many wolves lived, worked, and played here.

Sleeping beside the fireplace was the full-grown Saint Bernard, curled up on his big, soft dog bed, and she walked over to pet him again. He lifted his head and she swore he smiled at her, his tail thumping against the tile floor when she reached down and ran her hand over his head. She noted that the little barrel fastened to his collar said Rosco. "You didn't mind your master this morning when he took you for a walk." She could imagine losing control of the dog completely if she had hold of his leash, or falling face-first in the snow when he'd yanked so hard to tear off after the rabbit.

Nicole observed Blake speaking to a man, so she took a seat by the fireplace while she waited for Blake to finish his conversation. Blake was rugged, his face chiseled, his hair light brown, and his eyes blue. He was wearing a sweater, ski pants, and snow boots, looking good enough to hug and kiss...again.

Then she saw Blake's brother heading straight for her, and she worried Rhys had seen Roxie. Landon looked so serious, she assumed it was bad news.

When he reached her, he asked, "How's your partner?"

She hadn't expected that at all, but she appreciated his concern. "He's on his way to the hospital at the lower elevation, but he's going to be all right."

"That's good news. Then he won't be returning to help you?"

"He might, if he gets used to the altitude. But for now, I'm on my own." She glanced around the lobby, and not seeing the men she was investigating, she relaxed a little. "Did you see any sign of them when you went skiing?"

"We did see them. They were skiing toward Dead Man's

Leap. We followed them, but they went down the run before we reached them. Which was what we wanted, for Roxie's sake. She was good. She didn't say a word, just pointed her ski pole in the direction she wanted to go. Other than that, we have nothing to report."

"Okay. I was going to ask Blake if he wanted to go skiing with me for a while after lunch."

"I'm sure he'll take you up on it. We've got things covered here. Roxie's back at work, watching the security monitors. I got her a meal to go. She can bundle up anytime she leaves the office so no one will recognize her."

"Your house is the big place next door to the ski lodge?"

"Yeah, we wanted to be close by so we could monitor things. Since you live in Denver, you must not be part of an organized pack there."

"No. A few of us work there and have wolf nights out though."

Landon smiled, then his expression turned serious again. "Blake said you needed him to pretend to be your fiancé because your partner is sick. Is that still your plan?"

"Right. Just for around here. Just to make it look like I'm not on a stakeout concerning these guys. I can't be made, or they'll know I'm investigating them. That's why two of us teamed up to investigate this. I mean, the missing investigator's disappearance could be unrelated to this case or even tied to another one he'd been working on. The insurance company did say he often disappears for a time while researching a case. We just don't know. Your brother doesn't have to be involved in this in any way if he doesn't want to."

"Are you kidding?" Landon glanced at his brother. "After

the way you kissed him? He's not letting go of you if he has a chance to keep you around longer."

She smiled. Blake *was* a great kisser.

Blake finally noticed them and ended his conversation with the other man. Blake looked a little growly at his brother, as if he was afraid Landon would attempt to steal her away or maybe deter her from using Blake as her cover.

He walked across the lobby to join them. "How's Larry doing?"

"My brother is feeling better." She was trying to keep up the charade they'd started in case anyone overheard them. "He really needed to go to the hospital, but even so, once they'd given him oxygen at the clinic, he was doing much better."

"Oh good, I'm glad to hear it," Blake said.

"I saw you talking with Darien," Landon said to his brother. "He and Lelandi Silver are our pack leaders, Nicole."

She wondered why Darien hadn't come over to speak with her since her business here could have an impact on the wolf pack.

"Yeah, I told him we might have a bit of a situation with these men. Our pack leaders always need to know what's going on," Blake said to Nicole. "In case it affects the pack."

"I completely understand."

"He would have talked to you, but he knew you are working undercover, so he didn't want to mess that up."

"Sure. Good thinking. What about Roxie?" Nicole was still concerned their sister would be seen and blow the whole case or put herself in unnecessary danger.

"That was the other thing I talked to Darien about. He and Lelandi offered to take her in so she doesn't run into these men up here, but she's glad to be home with our family. If she had to, she said she'd rather stay home and chill than make a nuisance of herself at someone else's home. In any event, the whole pack is here for you if you need any other help with this," Blake added.

Nicole hadn't considered that a bunch of wolves in a pack could help her out. She was used to having a small specialized team of special agents working with her in the army, and everyone knew what to do. No one here would. Except for their police force. "Thanks. That's great. Did you want to have lunch, or are you busy?"

They both looked at Landon. He shrugged. "Go have lunch. I already grabbed a bite. I can handle anything that comes up for the next few hours if you want to do some sleuthing. I told you Roxie and I had no problem skiing incognito. If the two of you want to go up on the slopes, you could do the same. It's cold enough for you to bundle up. Enjoy your meal."

"Thanks. We'll let you know before we go skiing." Blake looked inordinately pleased to be able to spend more time with Nicole. He took her hand and led her to the restaurant while Landon headed back to the office.

"I love the name, the Howling Wolff Bar and Grill. Who came up with it?" Nicole asked as Blake walked her inside. She noted that the glass dividers giving guests privacy while they ate lunch had wolves etched in the glass like with the wolf pillars. Some wolves were snuggling against each other, tending to pups, watching for danger, running, or playing, and the pack was depicted howling in unison with the full moon above, despite that wolves howled at any time, moon or no.

"Kayla. As our marketing director, she came up with the idea."

"She picked a winner."

This was a real treat. Not only did Nicole have Blake's wolf backup, but he was hot and part owner of this beautiful lodge and restaurant, which made her feel like she was on a real date with a celebrity.

Nicole and Blake took seats by one of the windows so they could see skiers up on the slope, and a server immediately came to wait on them. Nicole noticed the woman was a wolf by her scent. She suspected the Wolff brothers hired mostly wolves. It must be nice, not having to hide their true selves.

"This is Minx, born and raised here," Blake said of their server.

"Welcome to Silver Town," Minx said, smiling, then left menus and glasses of water and told them she'd give them time to look over their menus.

"Thanks." Nicole opened hers and decided on the Reuben: slow-roasted corned beef, melted Swiss cheese, and sauerkraut served on grilled marbled rye. Blake chose an Angus burger, topped with Swiss cheese and sautéed mushrooms. She might have to try that tomorrow for lunch.

"Why did you move from Vermont?" she asked Blake.

"Truthfully, *lupus garous* weren't very prevalent there. We were looking to establish a new ski lodge, but someplace where more of our kind congregated, so we could have more after-hour wolf fun. Though we haven't had a lot of time for it while getting this place up and running." Blake closed his menu.

"Oh, I agree. I didn't realize Silver Town had so many wolves."

"It's actually wolf-run, established by the Silver wolves in the beginning."

"Oh, wow, the whole town? I kind of wondered, then just thought a lot of our kind lived here and the lodge and clinic were wolf-run. That's even better. If you don't mind me asking, what does Rosco carry in the little barrel attached to his collar?"

"Doggy treats. It's said that in the old days, the kegs were filled with brandy to help revive an injured skier, which isn't medically sound. So we just filled his with treats."

"Poor dog. He has to carry them around all day, smelling them, wishing he could have them."

"Hey, it's like the rest of us who have to carry our snacks with us on long hikes and can't eat them right away."

"Okay, you're right about that."

Smiling broadly at them, their waitress came back and took their orders. Then with their menus in hand, she left to place their orders.

"I guess before I kissed the daylights out of you, I should have asked if you had a girlfriend. But you didn't have a she-wolf's scent on you, so I figured you would be fairly safe." Nicole took a sip of her water.

Blake smiled. "My brother was eager to take care of whatever issues you were having, if you hadn't noticed."

"I noticed. I just hope it doesn't cause you any grief if you are interested in dating someone locally."

Blake's mouth curved upward again, his eyes still smiling, and he shook his head. "We have a shortage of females in the pack."

"Oh, that's why those twin ski instructors kept wanting to give me ski lessons. Kemp and Radcliff Grey? They were too funny. Free lessons! I told them I knew how to ski. Even better, Kemp said. Radcliff said he was even better at teaching expert skiers."

Blake laughed. "Yeah, I can just see the two of them doing that. They're always taking breaks on the deck between ski lessons, just to see if they can meet some out-of-town she-wolves here for a ski vacation. And they were bugging my brother and me about when our sisters were arriving. I'm sure the word they're here will go out soon, and the twins will be back looking to offer them free ski lessons too."

"I guess they haven't had any luck finding their special mates."

"Not yet. They love what they do, and they're members of a rescue team when they're not busy teaching. They're good guys. Speak of the devil…" Blake waved at the brothers as they came in to have lunch.

The blond-haired twins smiled, and the one punched the other in the shoulder in a friendly I-told-you-so way. "We should have known the new guys would get the girls," Kemp said, joining them, sporting a light-blond beard.

"Yeah, if you didn't know, the Silver brothers and cousins and our sheriff all got their mates," Radcliff said.

Nicole chuckled. "I'm not staying here. I'm just here to have fun."

Kemp sighed. "That's what they all say. And the next thing we know, the lady's mated to one of our pack's wolves."

"Well, in truth, we are in a relationship," Blake said, pulling out his phone and showing his Facebook page to the guys.

Stifling a laugh, Nicole was amused that Blake seemed to really enjoy playing his part.

"So you knew each other back in Vermont?" Kemp asked, sounding surprised.

"Just met, but you know how it goes between wolves," Blake said.

It was a good thing she wasn't hanging around for long, because she suspected the news would travel quickly through the pack. If Blake was interested in meeting another she-wolf who was local, he'd have some explaining to do.

"That's why she didn't take us up on ski lessons," Radcliff said, sounding relieved.

"Sorry, Blake, we didn't know you two were an item. Well, we're off to have lunch," Kemp said good-naturedly and headed to another table across the restaurant.

"Yeah, nice meeting you, even if it is too late." Radcliff gave her a big smile and followed his brother.

"I hope I didn't mess up your plans if you wanted to keep this more secret." Blake smiled at her.

She didn't think he sounded sorry in the least. "I think you're having a great time playing your part."

"I am. The brothers will let everyone know you're off-limits, so no one else will try to hit on you. Our pack leaders will welcome you to the pack, and—"

Smiling, Nicole raised her brows.

"Just as a formality. They already know what you're doing here."

Her sandwich and Blake's burger arrived shortly after that, and they began to eat. "So what level skier are you?" Blake asked.

"Expert, though I like to get started on the intermediates

to warm up a bit…" She paused. "Speaking of the devil, here my potential frauds come."

"Do you need me to kiss you again?"

She laughed. "Not this time. We're eating lunch and looking perfectly harmless."

"Tell me what they're wearing, and I can keep an eye on them, too, when I have a chance."

"They're headed our way."

She glanced at their clothes surreptitiously, careful not to look at their faces, and spoke low, just for Blake's hearing. "R has a sky-blue parka and black ski pants, W's wearing a brown ski parka and black ski pants." She smiled at Blake, pretending to just be with him for lunch.

Blake glanced in the cousins' direction, being a wolf and protective of her. While she appreciated his concern, she hoped he wouldn't be too obvious about it. Then he motioned to the waitress, and Nicole smiled at him in relief. The men had passed their table and gone to one behind her—several tables away, from the sound of the chair legs moving against the wooden floor, courtesy of a wolf's exceptional hearing.

Blake raised his empty water glass to Minx to indicate he needed a refill, and she hurried over with a glass pitcher of ice water.

"I'm so sorry," she apologized.

"No problem. You're busy."

Minx poured more water in Nicole's glass too. "Is there anything else I can get you?"

"Not right now, thanks, Minx," Blake said.

When Minx left, Nicole drank more of her water. "Well, what do you think? Dead or alive?"

Blake chuckled and saluted her with his glass of water. "He looks very much alive to me."

"Yeah, just as I thought. We need to get Rhys's utensils or cups and check the DNA." She realized what she was saying as soon as she spoke the words, not meaning to involve him in that much of her investigative work.

"Sure, we can do that." Blake seemed pleased she'd include him. "I need to tell Minx not to clear their table once they've eaten."

"Okay, good idea."

Blake waved for Minx to come to the table again. She looked at his water glass, but it was mostly full. She hurried over. "Yes, sir?"

"The men you just waited on… When they've finished their meals, just leave their dishes for me to collect, will you?"

Minx's eyes widened and Blake quickly added, "Don't look at them. Act normal."

She nodded vigorously, wrung her hands, and looked ill at ease.

He took hold of her hand and squeezed it. "There's nothing to worry about. We just need to prove who the one man is, that's all."

"Okay, sure."

"Are you good? Or do you need to take the rest of the day off?" Blake asked.

"I'm good. I can do this."

"If they ask for anything else?"

"Oh, oh, they're getting meals to go. Triple cheeseburgers, fries, and apple pies."

"To go?" Nicole couldn't have been more disappointed.

"Yeah, and bottled water."

"Okay, well, if they leave anything behind, just don't touch it," Blake said.

"Okay. Yeah. All right. I can do this."

Nicole was sweating it out. She was afraid the young woman would give things away. But then Minx stiffened her shoulders and walked back to the kitchen, order pad in hand.

Fifteen minutes later, Blake said, "Minx just dropped off the sacks of food and bottled water. She was all smiley, as if she were acting in a school play. She seemed to overcome her nervousness."

"Good. I'm not entirely surprised that they got food to go. I haven't seen them eat here since I arrived last night. I came down early for breakfast and hung around most of the morning but never saw them."

"They might have gone into town to grab something from the grocery store or somewhere else. Maybe even brought some food with them." Blake straightened a little while they continued to eat but kept his gaze mostly on her. "They're leaving the restaurant with their sacks of food in hand."

"If we could follow them and find where they dump their trash, we might get something," she said, hopeful.

"We'll certainly watch for that. Are you done eating?"

"Yeah, thanks for lunch."

Blake left a tip on the table. "Meal's free. Courtesy of ownership, but we always leave good tips for the servers."

"That's good." She watched the guys leave the restaurant and sit at an outdoor table to eat their meals outside on the deck. "Okay, they're settling down again."

"What do you want to do now?" Blake asked.

"I can see them from here. We can just wait and watch. If they leave their trash in the bin, we can grab it."

"What else can you do to learn who these men are?" Blake asked.

"I'm continuing to monitor their Facebook and Twitter postings and reporting them to the insurance company."

"You would think they'd keep the secret."

"You'd think so. But you know what? Everyone is just a friend on their accounts. I believe they are showing off that they got away with it, thinking no one will ever look at the social media sites to see what they've done. Sometimes surveillance like this can make or break a case. In the case of a guy who claimed back injuries and said he couldn't even drive a vehicle after an auto accident, I took video recordings of him walking around with a rifle, getting ready to go on a hunt. He obviously had no trouble walking or driving. No limp or anything."

"And?"

Minx came back and asked them if they needed anything else.

"Coffee?" Nicole asked.

"Yeah, me too."

She left to get their coffees.

"The guy was charged with fraud, served a short term in jail, and is on probation. Plus, he had to return the money. In another situation, the guy was bragging on Facebook about the ski trip he took. He had taken workers' comp, claiming he was bedridden. Skiing?" She shook her head.

"A lot of dishonest folks out there."

"Yeah. A lot of honest ones too. Some feel that they've

paid premiums to an insurance company for years and never filed an insurance claim, and they're owed a little money back. But it's still wrong. The rest of us who are paying insurance premiums end up getting the increased rates for it. I know of a case where the family moved a lot of their nice things into their grown son's home, then torched their house. Claimed everything had been destroyed in the fire."

"I would think the insurance payout wouldn't be enough to cover everything."

"It was for them. He was the insurance agent who insured all that stuff. I look for a lot of things though. If a person dies and a beneficiary is getting a big payout, when did they get the insurance? Often, they take out the policy, and then it's not long before the person suddenly dies. Or the house or car is torched. Have they taken out other policies? In one case, the wife had died ten years earlier, then her widower married a woman whose first husband had died the year before. Then the current husband and his son took out three life insurance policies from different companies on the current wife, unbeknownst to her or the other insurance companies, and guess what?"

"She died."

Minx brought their coffee, and both Blake and Nicole added sugar and cream to their cups.

"Yep. Karma for her, since her former husband died falling off a bridge, and then she died in the same way. Oh, and she had spent all the proceeds from her husband's life insurance policy in a matter of months. Now, police are looking into the death of the guy's first wife to see if he received a payout for her death."

"You have an interesting line of work."

"Yeah, sometimes. Not that I always want to find people who are trying to defraud the insurance company. I'm happy when I see a case where the policyholder is legitimately owed the money and receives his insurance check to cover his expenses. Hey, the cousins are on the move." Nicole jumped off her chair and headed for the doors leading out of the lodge.

CHAPTER 4

Blake hurried after Nicole to catch up to her. Man, did she move fast when she was on a mission. When they got outside, he realized Rhys and William were returning to the lodge. Blake immediately took hold of Nicole's hand, pulled her into his arms, and kissed her. "Because they're headed back this way," he said, even though he knew she was well aware the men were returning to the lodge. He just was glad he could kiss her again. His mouth against her mouth, he pressed kisses on her lips and cheeks, then moved lower to her jaw and neck, not wanting the men to catch on that they had been observing them.

The men didn't dump off their trash in the can nearby as Blake and Nicole had hoped. They headed back inside the lodge through the lobby and walked in the direction of the elevators. He figured they were returning to their room. "Do you think they know someone could be trying to grab a sample of Rhys's DNA?"

Nicole let out her breath, forming a white puff of frosty air. "Could be. Or they are being careful, just in case."

"But not about their social media." He led her back inside, and they went to the office to talk.

"You're right," Nicole said as they entered the office. "I suspect these guys think they're protected on social media. Totally unseen."

Roxie was watching the security monitor and glanced at them. "You're back."

"Yeah, they took their lunch trash to the room," Blake said.

"That's not good," Roxie said.

"Or maybe they have leftovers to snack on and were taking them up to their room," Nicole said.

"That could be," Blake agreed.

"You've been investigating these guys for a while. What have you learned? Any dark secrets?" Roxie asked.

Nicole sat down on one of the office chairs while Blake sat nearby. "I'll say. When I investigated Oscar's background, I learned a lot that might indicate he's dangerous. He was in debt and had a string of girlfriends, but none of them lasted long. He has a short temper, and they called it quits when he got violent. His cousin William was at Oscar's funeral, playing up the grief-stricken close relative. Oscar's mother and dad had died a couple of years earlier. William's parents, Oscar's aunt and uncle, are still living. Oscar's brother, Eli, died in a drowning accident when the boy was twelve and Oscar was sixteen."

Roxie shook her head.

"That doesn't sound good. In Oscar's parents' case, did he receive an insurance payout?" Blake asked, even more concerned about this guy now.

Nicole smiled. "Now you're thinking like an insurance fraud investigator." She took a deep breath and let it out. "Not only did Oscar inherit everything, but he received money from their life, house, and car insurance policies since he was the only surviving son. He couldn't access it until he was eighteen, but he didn't have too long to wait before he could get to all that money."

"Did he have an alibi for the time they died?" Blake asked.

"That's what I was going to ask," Roxie said. "And to think this guy threatened me with a gun."

"I know. His brother's disappearance and his parents' deaths change everything. Even though he might not have had anything to do with any of it, it's possible he did. It just seems like too much of a coincidence that everyone in his immediate family died in accidents."

"I'll say. Would you like some water?" Blake asked Nicole and his sister.

"Yeah, thanks," both said.

Blake brought out bottled waters from the office fridge for each of them.

"Thanks." Nicole took hers and removed the top and sipped some of the water. "During the fire, Oscar was out partying with his friends and came home to a burned-out house. Everyone had seen him at the party—he made sure of it—but no one remembered the exact times. You know, drinking and drugs at one of those wild parties makes it hard for anyone to remember anything clearly. He could have been there the whole time, or he could have been there and gone and returned and nobody would have known the difference."

"Sounds to me like he has a history of making money off insurance policy payouts. Why the hell would he have gone after Roxie's coin collection when he had all that money?" Blake was still angry about that. Of course, he, Landon, and Kayla had scolded Roxie for not just handing over the coins when she'd risked her life by keeping them. Though she'd made the valid point that handing them over didn't neces- sarily mean he would have let her live.

"Maybe he thought it would be easy money? Thinking

YOU HAD ME AT WOLF

it was a win-win situation?" Nicole said. "Maybe it was the excitement of doing something illegal and getting away with it?"

"I agree with Nicole. He must have seen the coin books and coins in special plastic containers sitting on my passenger seat, and he thought it could be an easy heist," Roxie said.

"Exactly! Lots of red flags popped up when I learned all this stuff about his past. He went to live with his cousin and aunt and uncle."

"No one could prove the house fire was a case of arson?" Blake lifted his bottle of water to take a drink.

"They couldn't determine if it was arson. The house was older and had a couple of smoke detectors, but the batteries had been removed. Some people remove them because they don't want to have to change them when they stop working. There may have been nothing sinister in that, unless they told the insurance company they had working smoke detectors to receive a discount on their house insurance policy.

"The dad stored all kinds of gas tanks in the garage for his lawn-mowing business. That's where the fire started. But they couldn't determine whether it was an accident or someone had set it on purpose. Without being able to pin down Oscar's whereabouts during the time the fire occurred, and since no one had witnessed anything suspicious at the house, they really didn't have enough to go on. Except that Oscar received so much money from their deaths."

"Was there any question of his cousin's involvement?" As close as William and Oscar/Rhys seemed to be, Blake figured he could very well have had a hand in it too.

"William was at the party, and the party house was only a couple of blocks from Oscar's home. He could have easily walked there, set the fire, and returned to the party with no one the wiser. His cousin could very well have helped him. When I asked the police for details about the case, trying to learn more about Oscar, they said that the guests who had been at the party gave the same statements concerning William's whereabouts. Yeah, they saw him there, but no one could say when. Nobody actually saw them leave. All everyone else knew was that they stayed at the house party until they heard the fire trucks. It sounded so close by that several of the kids walked out to see what was going on."

Blake thought there were way too many coincidences. "What about the younger brother? Was there any question that Oscar was involved in *his* death?"

"The younger brother, Eli, was with Oscar and William and three other teens when they were out swimming in a nearby lake. He was twelve. Oscar and William were sixteen. One of the other boys was sixteen, and two had just turned seventeen. Oscar and Eli's parents had insisted Oscar take his brother with them. I'm sure Oscar resented being saddled with his kid brother when he wanted to be with his older friends. Anyway, again, all the boys told the same story. They were all swimming, the brother too. They were diving and coming up, but after some time, they realized Oscar's brother didn't surface. He'd just... vanished. Everyone but Eli was playing with a ball and roughhousing, so they really hadn't noticed what he was doing for a while."

"Convenient," Blake said.

Roxie shook her head. "I can't imagine doing that to a brother."

"Neither can I," Nicole said. "They never found his body

either. That made a lot of folks suspicious. But none of the kids had any defensive wounds, like you might expect if they had purposely tried to drown Eli. According to Oscar's friends, Oscar got nothing but grief from his parents over it. Until his parents died. With his parents and brother gone, he inherited everything."

"Since his parents held a grudge against him for the death of their younger son, that could have been another reason to eliminate them," Blake said.

"Right. The more I dug into Oscar's background, the more I felt he could have found the perfect way to make a living."

"Except that he was in the army for a time," Blake reminded her. "Why go through basic training and get a real job if he had all that money to live off?"

"He spent all that money, which amounted to $750,000, in three years on fast cars—wrecking two of them—trips, jewelry, and a house he lost due to not paying the taxes on it. Easy come, easy go. He joined the army to earn an income for the first time in his life. He had an eight-year service obligation, a minimum of two years on active duty. After that, he was required to be in the National Guard or the Army Reserves for at least two years. The rest could be spent in the Individual Ready Reserve.

"He took out a life insurance policy on himself, the beneficiary being his cousin. Then he left active duty. He'd taken the policy out about three months before his supposed accidental death. He served four years in the army, which was a surprise to me. Seemed like a long time to wait. Maybe he hadn't even had the notion at first, then he and his cousin hatched the idea. It's even possible that he tried to fake his death through an accident before this, experimenting to see how they could stage it to make it look realistic."

"Then he had no more military obligation either, once he was dead." Blake leaned back in his chair. "Oscar is just lucky his cousin didn't off him and keep all the money, since Oscar is supposedly already dead."

"Too bad he didn't," Roxie said.

"I agree with you there. What do you want to do now?" Nicole asked Blake.

"Do you want to sit in the lobby for a while and watch for them?" Blake finished his bottle of water.

"Nah. Let's grab our skis and hit the slopes."

Blake smiled. "All right."

"It will help us to keep some distance from the suspects for a while. If it appears we're always where they are, they might get suspicious."

"I agree with you there."

"Have fun," Roxie said, still monitoring the security videos. "They haven't left their room. I'll text you when they do."

"Thanks," Nicole said.

Blake got his skis and poles out of his office and put on his ski boots. Then they retrieved her equipment from her rental locker, and he crouched to buckle her boots. Afterward, they headed for the slope, their ski boots crunching in the snow as they made their way to one of the ski lifts. Everyone who worked at the ski resort was a wolf with the Silver Town pack. It was a way of keeping their own people gainfully employed. But it also meant everyone knew Blake was with a new she-wolf.

"Hey, Blake," one of the bachelors said, smiling at Nicole and waiting for an introduction.

Blake didn't give him one, smiling and moving Nicole toward the ski lift.

"Is he a friend of yours?" Nicole asked.

"He's one of the pack members. I don't know him that well. We just moved here ourselves, but everyone's been really friendly. All the people who work at the ski resort love our lodge and restaurant, now that they can get meals up here and take breaks while they work."

They put on their skis and skied the rest of the way to the lift. The two male-wolf lift operators smiled at them. "Hey, Blake." Both guys glanced at Nicole and smiled.

"Nicole," she said, since Blake wasn't volunteering her name.

"She's with me," Blake said. "We're in a relationship. Facebook, you know."

The guys smiled and shook their heads.

She laughed at Blake. He was glad she didn't seem perturbed by his wolfish need to stake a claim to his territory, even if she really wasn't his to claim.

Then she and Blake got on the ski lift and headed to the top, the wind whipping about them. In the snow, not as many other scents could be smelled, which was why snow made the air seem more...purified. He loved the winter weather.

"What are you going to do when I leave here after the job is done and you've got to explain to potential girlfriends in the pack how we weren't really in a relationship?" Nicole asked.

Blake wrapped his arm around her. "I've been on an undercover mission, providing you with backup. I'm sure everyone will be quite impressed."

She laughed. "So this is a way for you to earn some brownie points."

He just smiled at her. He only cared about earning brownie points with her.

Before long, they had reached the top and skied to an intermediate run Nicole said she wanted to go on. "I need to work up to the expert slope. I haven't skied this season at all. I hope that's okay with you."

"Hell, if you want to go down the bunny slope, I'll go with you. That's what being partners is all about."

She shook her head. "No bunny slopes. Unless you need them, and then I'll stick with you."

"Intermediate it is."

When they skied down the first blue slope, it was steep but no bumps, and Blake followed her, watching her beautiful ski form, the way she held her upper body facing downhill, with great edge control, while she rotated her feet back and forth all the way down the hill. On the next steeper slope, she was doing jump turns. She had good boot flex, dominating it, so she was headed down the slope and not falling backward like some skiers he had seen who attempted ski jumping. She was good, and he figured she'd be on the expert runs soon. Though he would have fun doing any of the runs as long as he was with her.

After a couple more runs, they headed up the lift for the expert slopes covered in moguls. After getting off the lift, they were skiing to the slope when Nicole's cell phone rang in her pocket. Blake waited while she fumbled to pull off her ski glove and unzipped her pocket to grab the phone.

His first thought was that her partner or medical staff had called to say Larry's health had worsened, or even that

Larry was feeling better and wanted to take up where he and Nicole had left off doing surveillance. Blake had been thinking about it and wondered when she'd get a call about Larry's status. He sure didn't want Larry taking his place to help her, even if the guy was more qualified to do investigations. Not to mention, Blake wanted to get to know her better.

"Hey," Nicole said, then told Blake, "It's Roxie. Yeah, go ahead."

Blake moved in closer, a good excuse to wrap his arm around her and listen in on the conversation, warming her up at the same time.

"Don't put this on speakerphone," Roxie said, and Blake knew the cousins were up on the slopes.

"I saw Rhys and William headed for the slopes. Or I should say, Landon did. I saw them on the security monitor heading outside and told Landon. He surreptitiously followed them outside. He called me to tell me they were going to ski lift Bravo."

"The one we took up. Okay, thanks," Nicole said.

Blake saw the cousins skiing toward the same run they were taking, and Blake whispered, "They're here."

"Got to go, thanks!" Nicole said.

Blake nodded at the men in greeting, like any civilized person would, though he'd rather tear into Rhys for having threatened his sister with a gun. Nicole didn't acknowledge the men, pretending to still be busy on the phone, though she had already ended the call with Roxie.

"No," William said to Rhys as they skied past Blake and Nicole to the slope they would ski down. "Are you crazy?"

Blake thought so. With their wolf hearing, he and Nicole

could hear the men's conversation. If they'd been strictly human, they wouldn't have been able to.

"Come on. No one's going to be able to recognize me," Rhys said.

"They might if we're together like we always are. We're not going kayaking there this spring."

Where Rhys supposedly died? Blake was thinking it was like the case of a criminal going back to the scene of his crime—in this case, a faked death—to relish the deed.

"Beat you down this time," William said and tore off down the hill with Rhys in hot pursuit.

"Too bad he doesn't just break his neck," Nicole said.

"That would be an end to his crimes," Blake agreed.

Clouds were beginning to cover the clear-blue sky and a cold wind was whipping up the powdery snow as Nicole skied down through the moguls. She was managing most of them, slicing through a couple of bumps before she lost her balance and nearly took a spill but recovered nicely and continued down the slope.

Blake headed down while she waited for him just past the moguls. He wanted to show off how good he was, but he could imagine getting cocky and taking a bad fall and breaking something. He'd never live it down. His brother and sisters would rib him mercilessly, and probably some of the pack members too. Maybe even Nicole would tease him.

He skied down to her in record time so she wouldn't have to wait too long for him. The snow began to fall, large flakes fluttering around them, whipped around by the wind.

"How are you feeling? Do you want to take a few more runs down?" He and Landon had been taking daily runs down the mountain, but since she hadn't skied this season, Blake thought she might be getting tired.

"I'm good. My 'subjects' are still out skiing, so I might as well be out here too. I saw them headed for the lift again."

"That works for me."

"But I want to stick to the intermediate slopes for the rest of the afternoon."

"You've got it."

They skied back to the lift and saw the cousins waiting in a long line to ride it. Blake never thought he'd be spying on subjects at the resort who were wanted in a criminal investigation. Or enjoying skiing with a she-wolf either. "What do you do for fun?" he asked as they steadily moved up in line.

"This."

He smiled. "Surveillance?"

She chuckled. "Skiing. I'm not a workaholic, though while I was working for CID, the hours were long, and it seemed that way. Most weeks, I worked seventy hours. My days can be long when I'm on a case now, but I usually can break away for a bit. Or like this. This is a terrific way to enjoy my hobby and watch my suspects. I've never had an assignment like this. That's the other reason why I really love the work I do. It's always something different."

"Do you ever regret leaving the service?" Blake asked as the lift line continued to move.

"I did love my work and the team I worked with. I didn't like how I couldn't have a family life. And I didn't meet any wolves I could be friends with, even if I'd had the time."

"You met Roxie."

Nicole laughed. "Yeah, and I felt bad I hadn't solved the case involving her, so friends? No. Time really worked against me though. It really made it rough on friendships. No wolf companionship and no time for friends were the reasons I left the service. I like my PI business. I can work really long hours on an active case, but when I'm done with the case, I can have some off time too."

"Why settle in Denver?"

"I was born and raised there."

Someone didn't get situated on the chairlift correctly, and the lift operators had to stop the lift and make sure the skiers were seated properly.

"What about your parents? Any siblings?" Blake asked her.

"My parents live in Denver and own a stationery store. I have a twin brother who's an Army Ranger. He's planning on going into the business with me. He's got a degree in criminology and has been interested in the cases I've been working. He's getting out of the service in a couple of weeks and we're going to talk about it further. I have more than enough business for the two of us, between my contacts with insurance agencies and just my own cases."

Blake was not really happy to hear it. He was already imagining dating Nicole, and if her brother wanted to live in Denver and help her with her business there, Blake was sure she wouldn't want to bail out on him. As to Blake leaving Silver Town, he couldn't imagine doing anything other than running the ski lodge with the wolf-owned town here, and he really wanted to stay with his own brother and sisters. "That sounds good. Your parents don't mind that they're not with a pack?"

"No. All the wolves living in Denver like their independence. They have discussed forming a pack, but everyone's

happy to be on their own. I've met maybe ten wolves there.
A couple are lawyers. One is a chef. We have ladies' night
once a week."

"No guys there?" He hoped he didn't sound too hopeful.

"Sure, there are guys. But nobody that I've been interested in."

"Good."

She raised a brow at him, smiling at the same time.

He shrugged. "You and I might not be in a relationship
now if there was someone else."

She chuckled.

Their subjects were a few people in front of them in line
and finally got on the chairlift. The snow was blowing hard,
and Blake suspected the ski resort would be shutting down
soon if the winds continued like this.

When he and Nicole sat on one of the chairs and rode
the lift up, the chairs were swaying in the wind. "I think this
is our last run down. The weather's getting too bad. I'm sure
the place will be closing down," he said.

"I agree. I think I'll be ready for hot cocoa and dinner.
Are you buying?"

He laughed. "Now I know why you kissed me. You
already knew I was a part owner and assumed we didn't pay
for our meals at the restaurant."

"Smart of me, wasn't it?"

"Very."

"The truth is I'd seen you taking Rosco for a walk this
morning—or I should say he was taking you for a run."

Blake groaned. "I had hoped no one had seen."

"Did you manage to stay on your feet? If it had been me,
I would have lost him for sure."

"Yeah, I slipped on icy snow a couple of times, but he did, too, which helped to slow him down a bit. He ran forever, then finally wore himself out. He probably lost the scent of the rabbit too."

"Well, between you and the dog and then your trouble with the snowblower…" She shrugged.

"Truthfully, once you kissed me, my whole day was looking up."

She laughed, then turned serious. "As long as nothing goes wrong with this situation."

"The good thing about the wolf community is we can always call for lots of backup, no questions asked. If we say we have trouble, you better believe we'll have a ton of wolves there in a heartbeat helping us out."

"Now, that's nice to hear."

They got off the chairlift and skied to an intermediate slope covered in moguls, but the bumps were spaced farther apart than on the expert run, the terrain was wider, and the run not as steep. Blake wanted to observe her, but he really had to watch what he was doing too. Visibility was getting worse as they headed down for their last run with near-whiteout conditions, and depth perception was almost nil. It was as if everything was flat and white and he couldn't tell if he was going downhill or flush with the ground.

As soon as he found Nicole at the bottom of the slope, they skied toward the lodge, which looked almost like a white castle, mystical in the blowing snow. The snow was coming down heavily, high gusts of wind whipping it about, and he was glad he was wearing ski goggles. People were heading out to their vehicles in the parking lot to leave while others were returning to the lodge. All the ski lifts had shut down because of the high winds. Everyone was covered in snow, but they were still laughing and enjoying themselves.

"Does it hurt your business when the ski lifts shut down?"

"Maybe for locals who would have stayed for drinks or something instead of heading home. But for those who are staying at the lodge, no."

He'd had a great time skiing with Nicole and hoped they could do this again tomorrow. It wasn't the same as skiing with his siblings, though he wished he and Nicole could just ski for fun and not because she was trying to keep these men under surveillance. Now it was time to warm up and figure out their next move.

"What are we going to do about the sleeping arrangements tonight?" Blake wondered if she needed him to stay with her like her partner had been. He was all for it, but he didn't want to presume anything. Except that if they were in a relationship on a ski trip, they would most likely be sharing a room.

Admittedly, he was hopeful she'd want him to spend the night with her.

CHAPTER 5

NICOLE WAS WATCHING SOME OF THE CARS DRIVING OUT of the parking lot when Blake asked her about sleeping arrangements for the night and she smiled at him. She knew he was only concerned for her welfare. Well, mostly.

She glanced again at the cars leaving the ski parking lot and hoped no one would have a wreck on the roads, as low as the visibility was.

Then she took hold of Blake's hand and entered the lodge.

"I should be fine by myself. You can go home." She didn't think she needed Blake to stay with her for the night. She understood why he thought he might need to, since she'd been bunking with Larry. But neither she nor Larry had a place to stay here, so they had shared the room and planned to talk over the case when they retired for the night. She could just call Blake if she needed to speak with him about anything. With Larry, nothing personal would have ever developed between the two of them. With Blake…he was too much of a wolf, and she was afraid she'd lose focus on her mission.

"My room isn't on the same floor as the men's. They always take the elevator. So I don't really need to continue the ruse overnight. I've walked by the cousins' room after they've gone up and they're in there watching TV, laughing about stuff, talking, so it appears they stay in for the night. Except for eating meals and skiing, there's not much else to do here in the evenings, unless they were wolves and then they might want to run. But just hiking out in the snow at night? No."

"Are you sure? I wouldn't want anything bad to happen to you while you're there by yourself," Blake said as they moved closer to the fireplace. "Unless you're afraid people will believe we're mated wolves."

"*Hardly.* I'm not part of the pack, and I don't intend to get to know everyone. You, on the other hand, need to keep up appearances. Staying with me won't help that."

"I'm more concerned about you not having anyone to watch your back like Larry was doing."

"I can call you if I feel I need help. You'll be close by."

"All right. Did you want to store your skis and boots in our office storage room? It would be easier anytime we need to ski if all our gear is in the same place. Otherwise, you have to continue to store your skis and boots at the ski rental shop, and it takes longer to grab them."

"Yeah sure. Since I'm seeing you."

"Except at night."

She smiled. "True. We won't be under observation. We can have breakfast together tomorrow. I'll be wearing something different, in case they've noticed me hanging around in my pink and white ski clothes. I figured they made me look perfectly harmless. Tomorrow, I'll be in pastel blue and white."

"Good." Blake led her into the office where they put up their ski equipment.

Roxie was sitting at the security monitor, concentrating on the influx of people. "Okay, they've gone into the restaurant for dinner."

"Great," Nicole said. "Hopefully, they won't get takeout this time."

"If they do, they might as well just get room service," Blake said.

"Then they'd have dishes, glassware, and silverware from the meal and would leave DNA evidence behind," Nicole said.

"That's true," Blake agreed. "Have you eaten yet, Roxie?"

"Landon was going to bring me dinner. Kayla is at the house fixing dinner for her and him there. But I was just thinking I should head to the house and eat there. Rhys and his cousin are probably not going anywhere for the rest of the night, except back to their room, don't you imagine?" Roxie asked.

"Sometimes they sit and drink by the fire, but we can take it from here," Nicole said, putting on her snow boots while Blake slipped on his.

"That'll be great. I need to unpack my bags, now that I'm finally here for good. Are you staying the night with Nicole?" Roxie asked Blake.

"Uh, no, I'll be home tonight."

"Aren't you supposed to be watching Nicole's back?" Roxie sounded worried.

"I'll be fine," Nicole said, appreciating Roxie's concern.

"Do you want me to stay with you?" Roxie asked, as if staying the night with another woman would make Nicole any safer. Unless, of course, Roxie turned into her growly wolf form.

Nicole smiled. "No, really, I'll be perfectly all right."

"Are you ready to go to dinner, Nicole?" Blake asked.

"I'm starving."

"See you later, Roxie," Blake said.

"Thanks for all your help." Nicole was grateful for their assistance with this.

"No problem."

She and Blake left the office and soon entered the restaurant. It was packed. Nicole thought that was good news for the Wolff family.

Blake glanced around at the tables and booths filled with guests. "Looks like the winds drove everyone inside to have dinner at the same time."

"I guess we'll have a wait to have dinner."

"Nah, we always have a couple of tables set aside for the family or our pack leaders and their families when they visit. There's Landon talking on his cell phone. Roxie probably told him not to get her dinner. And the suspects are getting takeout and leaving," Blake said.

"Well, one of these times, they're bound to slip up, or maybe we'll have to arrange a maid visit to their room after all and find what we can, despite their room having a Do Not Disturb sign on it," Nicole said.

"We can sure arrange that."

They saw the men leave the restaurant, but Nicole whispered to Blake, "They're eating their dinner by the fireplace."

"Okay, I see them."

"If they dump their trash and head for the elevators, I'm out of here to grab it," she said.

Blake and Nicole took their seats and soon ordered burgers and fries so it wouldn't take too long to get their meals.

"If they're still sitting around the fireplace when we're done, did you want to get a drink and we can take a seat by the fire? And visit with Rosco before he goes home with me tonight?" Blake asked.

"Sure, we can do that. Then we'll be closer if they dump their trash," Nicole said, though she really didn't believe they would. "Did you want to do a wolf run tomorrow night when the ski resort is closed down, if the weather isn't too bad?"

"I sure do. We might have company, if you don't mind my brother and sisters going with us. We haven't taken a run as family together in a few months."

She smiled. "That would be great."

The guy she'd seen speaking with Blake before, Darien Silver, the pack leader, came into the restaurant with a woman, and they both smiled and stopped at Nicole and Blake's table. The woman said, "I'm Lelandi Silver, and this is my mate, Darien."

Nicole realized Lelandi was the co-pack leader. She shook Lelandi's hand and Darien's. She thought they weren't going to acknowledge her, but maybe they assumed she was considering staying in Silver Town for good and they needed to semiwelcome her. No humans were sitting nearby, so the wolves didn't have to be careful about mentioning being mated wolves or pack leaders.

"Nicole Grayson, nice to meet you both."

"You're welcome anytime. We can always use good people in town."

"Thanks."

Then Darien and Lelandi went off to sit at another table.

"Do they come here often?" Nicole asked, because she wondered if they had made a special trip to see her or if they happened to be coming here and saw them.

"Usually they eat at the Silver Town Tavern, since only

wolves can eat there, and Sam's had the tavern there forever. I'm sure you had something to do with them coming here."

She smiled. "I'm not used to being with a pack. I guess everyone's really close-knit."

"We haven't been here long either. Before that, it had just been our family. So we're learning how it is to be with a pack too." Then Blake got a call from Roxie and leaned in closer to Nicole so she could hear what was going on in case it had something to do with her suspects.

"Hey, Landon was going home to help Kayla with dinner, but I was still monitoring the security videos and we've got trouble," Roxie said.

Blake glanced at the cousins still eating by the fire.

"There's been a four-car pileup in the parking lot."

"Great. All right. I'll go out there and see what I can do."

"I've called the sheriff, though he said they have had so many accidents in town due to the whiteout that they probably wouldn't get here anytime soon. Landon's out there already."

"It's a privately owned parking lot too," Blake said.

"Well, that didn't seem to matter. The sheriff said they would have been up here, but they're filling up the clinic and sending some of the injured people to the hospital in Green Valley, so apparently it's really a mess due to the snowstorm."

"Okay, thanks. I'll check it out."

"Landon might not need your help, but he wanted me to make you aware of the accident. He's texting me the license plate numbers because two of the vehicles that were hit were parked. Two were trying to leave the lot," Roxie said.

"Um, since Darien and Lelandi are eating at the restaurant, you might want to give them a heads-up."

"All right."

"Will Nicole be okay at the lodge while you're gone?" Roxie said.

"Yeah, her suspects aren't going to pull anything in front of anyone inside the lodge. Talk to you in a bit." Blake ended the call. "Did you hear everything?"

"Yeah. A four-car pileup occurred in the parking lot. What a mess. I *was* worried the snow might cause some accidents," Nicole said.

"I'm going out to check on it. Will you be okay by yourself?"

"Yeah, sure. I promise I won't eat the rest of your hamburger."

Smiling, Blake leaned down and kissed Nicole's forehead. "Okay, I'll be right back."

She smiled back at him, her expression saying he was probably pushing his luck. But hey, he was playing his role to the max as long as he could. He went over to Darien and Lelandi's table to tell them about the accident, and Darien said he'd join them in a moment.

Blake nodded, then pulled on his ski jacket, hat, and gloves and left the lodge. They'd had fender benders before when cars slipped on ice or bumped into each other because of low visibility during snowstorms, so Blake knew how to handle it.

Outside, the wind was bitterly cold and tempers were flaring.

"If you hadn't been in such a damn hurry, you wouldn't have plowed into me, making me hit the two other cars." The one speaking was the owner of the bank. Mason didn't ski so he must have had dinner up here. He looked as growly as any wolf Blake had ever seen.

The guy driving the pickup truck said, "Hey, dude, you pulled in front of me."

"You were driving too fast for conditions."

Landon was taking down everyone's license plate numbers, including the plates of the two vehicles that had been smashed while just parked in the lot. *Hell.* Blake recognized the one car as Nicole's.

He got on his phone and said, "Hey, it's me, honey. Your car was wrecked. From the extent of the damage, I'd say it was totaled."

"You're kidding. I'm on my way," Nicole said.

"Okay, we'll get it straightened out."

"Roxie just made an announcement about the other license plate. No one staying at the lodge has registered that license number. The owner must be eating here and not staying at the lodge. I'll be out in a minute. I'm going to leave our hamburgers in the kitchen so they can be kept warm for us. Don't worry about paying for the meal," Nicole said.

Blake chuckled. "Don't tell me you're getting the bill."

"The tip, anyway."

Then they ended the call. Landon was acting as deputy sheriff and taking witnesses' statements. Several of the people who saw the accident had luckily stayed to give their eyewitness accounts. When Nicole joined them, so did a man and woman Blake didn't recognize—the owners of the second parked car. Humans.

"I can't believe this," the man said, frowning at his car. It was the perfect way to ruin a good outing.

"He's the one at fault. If he hadn't hit my truck, slamming it into your cars, none of this would have occurred," Mason said.

"We've got enough witness statements proving it was as Mason said it happened. We even have a couple of videos to corroborate it," Landon said.

Blake was glad the wolf had been exonerated on video.

Nicole and the other couple shared insurance company information with the other drivers.

"I'm so sorry, Nicole," Blake said, putting his arm around her shoulders.

"You couldn't help it. Had the guys who caused the accident by hitting Mason's truck been drinking?" Nicole asked.

"Yeah. And they were trying to get out ahead of everyone else. In these conditions, visibility is just too low. Drivers have to slow down. It's just a good thing no one was injured," Blake said.

Two tow trucks finally pulled up. Blake helped Nicole get everything from her car. Then he asked the other couple if they were driving through town or had planned to stay the night.

"We were driving through, but we heard the restaurant was really good up here, so we came here to have dinner. But the weather became so bad, we planned to get a room tonight if we could," the man said. "Not to mention that we don't have a vehicle to leave in now anyway."

"I'm Brandon Wolff, and that's my brother, Landon. We own the lodge and we'll make sure you have a room, free of charge." Brandon shook his hand.

The man smiled. "You're the owners. Thanks. We'll sure spread the word about your place."

"We appreciate it. A garage in Silver Town can loan you a car."

Some of the witnesses came over to help the couple move things out of their car so they could have it towed. Mason's truck and the other guys' truck were drivable, so once Landon had everyone's statements, he released them.

Then Blake and Landon helped Nicole carry her belongings from her car into the lodge.

"What if you don't have a spare room for the stranded couple?" she whispered to Blake.

"I may have found a Good Samaritan who will give up her room and stay with me at the house, since the cousins just lock themselves in their room and don't go anywhere at night, so you said."

She frowned at him. "Assuming stuff like that could get you into trouble, you know."

He chuckled. "I'm sure we have a couple of rooms left, unless more people decided to stay because of the storm."

Landon smiled at his brother. "You better hope so."

———————————————

No way was Nicole giving up her room for the night and moving to Blake's house when she was on a job that required her to stay at the lodge. She intended to check on the men at intervals throughout the night like she'd done last night, though her partner was supposed to have assisted her. Yet she couldn't help feel sorry for the couple who needed a room.

She was going to go up to her room to drop off all her stuff, but instead, she followed the couple to the registration desk to see if they had a room for the night or not. "Yes, we have a room for you," Landon said, checking on the monitor. He took their information down and handed them a card. "Free night on us."

"Thanks so much," both the man and woman said. They looked relieved and thrilled to hear the news.

Nicole thought the world of the Wolff family for helping people out.

Four of the people who had carried the couple's bags and other items in from their smashed car hauled them up to their room.

"Let's drop off my belongings in the room, and we can finish our meal," Nicole said, relieved she still had a room. She had thought of just camping out in the lodge office if she'd had to.

She and Blake and Landon dropped off her things, and then they returned to the lobby.

"You can borrow my truck if you need it," Landon told her.

"Or my Jeep," Blake said.

"Thanks. I'll call my insurance company tonight to get a loaner car. Do you want to finish our hamburgers?"

"Yeah, but knowing our staff, they'll have made fresh ones for us," Blake said.

"But I told them to warm them." She noticed the cousins were still sitting by the fire and no longer eating, so she wondered what they'd done with their trash. They were drinking beers now.

"Did you want me to take Rosco home?" Landon asked. "Roxie and I are headed that way."

"No, that's okay. He'll keep me company when I head home, and he loves being around the guests."

"Okay, good show," Landon said.

"See you soon," Roxie said.

When Nicole and Blake returned to the restaurant, fresh hamburgers had been prepared for them, courtesy of Roxie calling ahead.

"Wow, I could really get used to the royal treatment," Nicole said.

"We have to have some perks for owning the place. Are you sure you're okay about your car?"

"No. I'll cry into my pillow tonight."

Looking concerned, Blake frowned.

She sighed. "All that matters is no one was injured, but yeah, I'm perturbed about it. That one driver wrecked four vehicles just because he was being an idiot."

"I agree with you there."

Nicole pulled out her phone and called Roxie. "Did you see what the cousins did with their trash?"

"Left with it. I think they took it up to their room. Then they came back for beers."

"Okay. I think we need to have some maid service, but we should probably wait until the cousins are out on the ski slopes tomorrow."

"Sounds good to me. Though I guess I can't volunteer to do it. Kayla could," Roxie said.

"No. It's my assignment. I have the training for investigative work. I'll do it."

"All right, but we wish you'd take Blake with you."

"Thanks, Roxie, but I'll be okay. Are you headed home?"

"Already there. We'll see you in the morning."

"Okay, see you then." Nicole just hoped she didn't get caught breaking into the cousins' room. She really wanted to do it now, but the cousins had been downstairs so long that they might go up to their rooms at any time. Still…

Once they finished their hamburgers, she asked Blake, "Are you done?"

"Yeah. Do you want to grab a drink and sit by the fire and make out?"

She chuckled. "I want a key to their room."

"Okay, and you're going to try to search it in the morning?"

"Tonight. While they're down here. You watch them, and I'll run up there and see if I can find any trash. I'll just do it quickly. I was planning on doing it tomorrow when they went skiing, but at this rate, I'm never going to get anywhere with this."

"All right. We'll try it."

"Just text me if they head toward the elevators. I need to get a key really quick though. You can watch them from the restaurant without being obvious."

"Just go to the registration desk and ask for the key to the room. I'll text the girl working the desk that you're going to come for it. I gave Kayla my master key, so we need to get another made."

"Thanks." She leaned over and kissed him briefly on the cheek, then hurried out of the restaurant. Heart hammering, she sure hoped she could get away with this.

She passed by the fireplace, and Rosco smelled her scent and raised his head. She had to pat his bony head, no matter that she was on a mission. Then she got the key at the front desk and took the back stairs up to their room.

When she reached it, she texted Blake: Still good?

Blake: They're still sitting there drinking their
beers.
Nicole: Okay, going in.

She opened the door and heard someone using the bathroom. Her heart nearly beating out of her chest, she quickly closed the door and hurried back down the hall to the stairs, worried the person in the room might have heard her and run to peek outside the room to see who it was.

Nicole: Someone was in the room using the
bathroom.
Blake: They only have Rhys's name on the
room. We've only seen the cousins
together.
Nicole: Okay, well, it appears there are three
of them. The scent indicated he was
another male. But we haven't seen any
sign of anyone else. Any time that I've
observed them, no other guy has been
with them either.
Blake: It sounds like we're going to have to do
room service tomorrow and learn what's
going on.
Nicole: All right. Is there any way for me to
have the other room across the hall from
theirs? I thought about doing that initially,
but I was afraid I'd run into them all the
time. But if there's another guy staying

> with them, we need eyes on the room to
> see if he leaves and what he looks like.
>
> **Blake:** The security camera should tell us the
> story if we look back to the day they
> arrived and then watch it from there. The
> camera is in the hallway, not really close
> to the room, but it should show when
> anyone else went into the room.

She finally reached the restaurant and decided to stay there with Blake and have a drink. They could still see the men, but they weren't as visible to the cousins this way. "Okay, that sounds like a good idea to me."

They observed the cousins having a couple more beers, and then they purchased two more and headed for the elevators.

"Okay, maybe that's why they're taking food and drinks back to the room," Nicole said. "Maybe it's not so much that they're destroying DNA evidence, but they're feeding someone up there. Someone who is on the lam, too, maybe. And that's why they don't want housecleaning."

"Did anyone else who was posting on the Facebook page mention going skiing with these men?"

"I'll have to look at the comments again. I don't recall that there was."

"The person in the room couldn't be a hostage. Not if he was using the bathroom and could have left the room or called out to you," Blake said.

"I agree. I sure hope I didn't spook them. Hopefully, he didn't know I'd been in the room. I tried to be really quiet."

"That would be the best-case scenario. Are you ready to look at the security monitors?" Blake asked.

"Yeah, let's do it."

They returned to the office and began to review the security videos. "Here's the video for when they checked in. Rhys was the only one there to check in. But here's the one for the hallway where their hotel room is located. Two men carried bags in, and then Rhys came in after that with more bags," Blake said. "So three of them are staying in the room. The one is William, but the other?"

"Another friend?" she asked. "I looked again, but I didn't see any mention of any of their Facebook friends coming here to stay with them—unless the other person doesn't have an account or doesn't actively post. Can we find a video of the parking lot for the time when they must have arrived before they checked in?"

"Yeah, let me pull that one up." Blake found the video and began examining it. "Here."

"But we can't see the car license plate."

"It's a blue Jeep Cherokee though. We should be able to get their license plate number and run it through the Division of Motor Vehicles to learn who it's registered to," Blake said. "Rhys should have listed his license plate number when he registered at the lodge, but he said he didn't have a car."

"Do you want to get bundled up and go out in the blizzard to check?"

"Yeah. Let me grab Rosco and take him out." Blake put on Rosco's leash, and they took him outside to relieve himself in the snow.

A lot of cars were still sitting in the parking lot, but they were buried under snow. "I don't know that we'll be able to tell which is their car," Nicole said. "We can't even see the colors with all the snow."

"You're right. We'll have to try this as soon as the snow quits and the sun melts the snow off the cars, or people go out and unbury them."

"Okay, well, I'm going to bed."

"Are you sure you'll be fine?"

"Yeah. I'll see you in the morning for breakfast."

They walked back inside, and she was certain Blake wanted to walk her up to her room, but she didn't need him to. "Night, Blake."

He looked like he was hoping for a good-night kiss. But really, she didn't want him to get the idea this was for real, except it sure felt like that. She smiled. What the hell. She pulled him in for a hug and kiss, and he kissed her back, but she quickly ended the kiss before she gave him the idea that she wanted him staying with her tonight.

"Tomorrow," he said as she said good night again.

She hoped she didn't run into any trouble after rejecting his offer to stay the night.

CHAPTER 6

WHEN BLAKE ARRIVED HOME WITH ROSCO, ROXIE MET him at the door, arms folded across her chest. "I can't believe you've got a chance at having a worthwhile girlfriend, and you've left her alone to watch the wolves, so to speak."

"She said she'd be fine." Blake removed Rosco's leash. "She didn't want me to stay with her. Forcing the issue could make it seem like I don't trust her instincts when she's highly trained in this kind of work. She'll call me if she needs me." He hung up his ski jacket in the coat closet.

Landon was turning off the gas fireplace before they all went to bed for the night. "He's right, Roxie. I thought you didn't even like the former CID agent."

"I changed my mind. I can't believe that on top of her mission here, her car was totaled," Roxie said. "I feel for her."

Wearing her snowman pj's, Kayla joined them. "What's the deal with the third man in the room? Someone in hiding? That doesn't sound good. What if Nicole has to deal with three bad guys, not just two? Heck, two is bad enough."

Blake agreed with his sister, but what could he do? He couldn't force Nicole to allow him to stay with her. He was fascinated with the kind of work she did though. It was sure a lot different from running the lodge.

"If you hadn't found a room for that couple with the totaled car, I could have convinced her to stay here with us," Blake said to his brother.

"Maybe. Maybe not. She looked determined to stay at the lodge tonight. It seems like once she's got a mission, she's resolved to complete it," Landon said.

"Yeah, but she went with us to the registration counter to see if the couple had a room. I'm sure she was thinking of giving up her room if they didn't have one. She might be hard-charging, but she also seems to have a soft spot for people down on their luck." Blake removed his snow boots and set them by the door.

"True," Landon said.

"In other news," Kayla said, "I've redone the lodge's website again, the restaurant page is refurbished, and now the menus can be accessed online. I added some pictures of the winter activities we had going on today. I'll have to do more when we have the spring thaw. I can actually play around with updating pictures on a daily basis to give interest to the site for people who want to see the ski conditions each day."

"That sounds great." Blake pulled up the ski lodge website. Landon and Roxie were looking over his shoulders. He found the pictures Kayla had uploaded showing people eating in the restaurant and sitting by the fire, drinking cocoa and petting Rosco. Everyone looked so happy, and that was just what they needed to help promote the place. "These pictures are perfect." Then Blake saw a photo of himself kissing Nicole in the lobby and he laughed.

"That's my favorite picture on the website," Roxie said.

Landon chuckled. "Now you'll really have to do something about this business between the two of you. Any she-wolves in the pack won't let you live it down."

Blake was hoping he could do something about how he felt about Nicole.

"Well, are you going to call Nicole before you go to bed to make sure she's all right?" Roxie asked.

Blake smiled. "I just left her and she was fine. She said she'd call me if anything was amiss, and I don't want to be bugging her about her job."

"All right. It's your call, but if I were you, I'd give her a ring. I'm off to bed." Roxie headed up the stairs.

"Night all." Kayla followed her up.

Rosco had settled on his bed by the fireplace for the night.

"How are you going to keep her here?" Landon asked. "The way she selected you to be her knight in shining armor and the way she kissed you made me believe she's got a real thing for you."

Blake chuckled. "You know why she picked me instead of you? She saw me fall on my ass when I was trying to operate the snowblower."

Landon laughed. "She's got a good sense of humor and felt sorry for you."

"I had it in mind that we could involve her in family activities so she gets to know all of us. She already talked about running as wolves tomorrow if the brunt of the storm has passed. I told her we hadn't run as a family for a couple of months, so if she didn't mind running with all of us, we could do that. She was agreeable."

"Okay, though you could have run with her on your own. Still, that will work." Landon slapped him on the back. "See you in the morning."

"I'm having breakfast with Nicole too."

"Then I'll see you at the lodge sometime or another."

Landon headed up the stairs and Blake turned out the lights in the living room, then followed him up.

As soon as Blake was in his room, he stripped out of his clothes and climbed into bed, then called Nicole anyway. "Hey, we didn't set a time for breakfast." He didn't want her to think he was checking up on her, but he did want to talk to her.

"Would seven be all right? These guys don't get out of bed until around ten, so I figure if we eat early, I can begin to watch for them," Nicole said.

"That sounds good to me."

"If you have any chocolate-covered almonds lying around, I'd love to have some to snack on. I meant to get some more. I should have run to the grocery store in Silver Town when I was down there checking on Larry's health, but…"

"You were in a hurry to see me for lunch."

She chuckled. "I had to get back to doing my surveillance. Now I don't have a vehicle. The auto body shop is sending one tomorrow afternoon, depending on the weather."

"Okay, sure, I think we have some chocolate almonds. I'll be sure to bring some tomorrow when we have breakfast. Can you hold out until then?"

Nicole laughed. "Yes, and if you don't have any, don't worry about it. I'm not desperate or anything. See you tomorrow."

"Night, Nicole." But Blake was desperate to locate some of her favorite candy and was already jamming his feet into a pair of boxer briefs and heading down the stairs to the kitchen, hoping someone had packages of chocolate almonds so he could take one to Nicole tomorrow morning. He looked in their candy and cookie stash in the pantry. No chocolate-covered almonds.

Roxie headed down the stairs to the kitchen. "Got the

munchies?" She opened the fridge and grabbed the container of milk, then poured herself a glass.

"I was looking for chocolate-covered almonds."

Roxie glanced in the pantry. "Hmm, Kayla and Landon like them, but it looks like we're all out. I didn't think you cared all that much for almonds."

"I do, but I just don't eat them that often."

"Then…why are you looking for them?" Roxie's face brightened with a smile. "Ohmigod, Nicole likes them."

"She was having a craving for them, and she doesn't have a car to go get them."

"Too late now. The grocery store isn't open until six in the morning." Roxie drank some of her milk.

"I'll pick up some before I have breakfast with her."

"Here?" Roxie asked.

"No. At the lodge. I think she wants to stay there in case the guys leave some evidence around that she can grab."

"This gets better and better." Roxie finished her milk and put the glass in the dishwasher.

She and Blake headed back up the stairs.

"Here I was worried she might be having real trouble." Roxie smiled at Blake.

"Yeah, well, believe me, when you or Kayla run out of your favorite foods, you feel the same way."

Roxie laughed and headed into her bedroom.

Blake returned to bed and thought about the candy. He would walk Rosco first, since that was his morning duty, and then run to the grocery store to pick up some chocolate almonds for Nicole and a few more packs to have on hand for Kayla and Landon. Then he would meet Nicole at the restaurant. Unless she had an emergency in the middle of the night, and then he was at her beck and call.

_____

Before she left her room to check on the cousins, Nicole sent another text to her parents to let them know she was fine and gave them the name of the lodge and a little about what she was doing. She always kept in touch, not wanting them to fret when she was working on a case.

Nicole put on her black cargo pants, black sweater, and sneakers that didn't make a sound. She made her way down the stairs to the cousins' room, thinking she needed to be in the room right next door to theirs. Now that she knew the owners and was friends with them, surely they could arrange it. Then she could listen to what was going on by pressing her ear to the wall. She had one of those highly sensitive, wall listening devices, but with her wolf hearing, she could hear well enough unless they had a TV blaring.

Now that the Wolff family knew her purpose here, she would not have to worry about being caught on the security cameras doing things that seemed a bit odd. But the person in the room across the hall might see her listening at the door and call security.

Still, she wanted to chance it, to see if she could learn anything about the men's plans and who the other man was. She pressed her ear against their door and listened for any sign that anyone might leave their rooms. It was ten that night, and hopefully everyone was settled down. The restaurant was already closed.

"You can't go out. Get that through your thick head," Rhys said.

The third man in the room? That's who Rhys had to be talking to.

"You're dead too. You shouldn't be able to go out either," the unknown man said.

Nicole's jaw dropped. Another pretend dead man? Another life insurance payout?

"Hey, that's the way it's gotta be," William said. "Your brother helped save your ass, so deal with it. Hell, you didn't have to come with us."

"Yeah, he did." Rhys sounded irritated.

Rhys saved his brother? The brother who supposedly drowned? Nicole didn't think there was another brother. She heard the elevator coming and took off for the stairs. When she returned to her room, she called Blake. "Can you get me into a room next to the cousins' room? Even if both of the rooms are booked right now, maybe you can say you have plumbing problems and need access to the room. You could give them my room instead. It's got a view of the mountains instead of the parking lot."

Blake chuckled. "Here I thought you were calling about an emergency, and I was ready to jump out of bed and come to your rescue, clothes or no."

She chuckled. "My wolf without his shining armor."

"You bet."

She put her phone on speaker and set it on the bedside table so she could undress and get ready for bed. She pulled out the jammies her brother had gotten her for Christmas, featuring spy glasses and 007 printed on the pink fabric. She would have to reciprocate after Nate joined her agency as a PI.

That was another thing she loved about being a PI on her own. She could work in her jammies while she did research if she wanted to.

"He's got a brother." She pulled her sweater over her head.

"What? Rhys? I thought his younger brother had died. That he'd drowned."

"I know. I did too. Maybe it's another brother. Or maybe it is the same one. I need to do more research." She sat down on the bed and pulled off her boots and then her socks.

"Do you want me to come over and help you do some research? I can be there in just a few minutes."

He sounded so eager that she smiled. She loved that he wanted to be with her longer and to help with the case. "You need to get me into a room that's next to these guys' room so I can listen through the wall to learn what's going on."

He paused. "Don't tell me you were listening at their door in the hallway."

"I was. But it's too easy to get caught at it."

He let out his breath. "Hell, Nicole. What if someone had seen you and called the sheriff?"

"You know him, right?"

"Yeah, but you don't want other guests to catch you doing anything that appears illegal. Not to mention you certainly don't want your suspects catching you at it. As to moving guests, I'd hate to have to say one of our rooms has a problem when our lodge is so new, but since your room does have a better view of the mountains and the outdoor part of the indoor-outdoor swimming pool, that could be a selling feature, and we'll try to swing it. It would be good if we could get this case of yours resolved. I worry that you have three men now to deal with."

"I have you and your brother and sisters to help me. So not to worry."

"And glad to. While you're chasing after the cousins, I bet Roxie wouldn't mind staying in your new room to listen in on what she can hear. She can take a computer with her and still monitor the security cameras. That way, you can be free to do your investigation outside your room."

"That would be great, if she wouldn't mind." Nicole pulled off her pants and panties, then slipped on her jammie bottoms.

"Okay, I'll let her know in the morning. Anything else?"

Nicole unfastened her bra and removed it. "No. Thanks, Blake. It's great knowing the owners of the lodge. I would never have thought I'd be able to do anything like this. And it's really going to help."

"You're so welcome."

She pulled on her jammie top. "You all have been the greatest help. Not to mention I've really enjoyed our time together. I'll see you in the morning."

"Same thing here. Night, Nicole."

They ended the call and she thought about trying to do more research but decided to get some sleep instead and start early in the morning. She turned onto her stomach, slipped her arms under the pillow, and smiled. She couldn't believe how well things were working out with all the help she was getting on her surveillance. Not to mention she'd had a wonderful time skiing with Blake and enjoying his company.

She hadn't yet fallen asleep when she got a call from Taggart at the insurance company.

"I apologize for it being a little late, but Larry called

to tell me he isn't helping you with your job. He says you picked up some other guy to help watch your back."

"Blake Wolff. He's co-owner of the Wolff Timberline Ski Lodge. I didn't realize he and his siblings were running the ski lodge. We go way back." As in she and Roxie, but Nicole wasn't about to mention that or how they knew each other.

"But he's not a trained private investigator."

"No, even better. They're moving me to a room next door to these guys so I can listen in. And the Wolff family is watching my back." The insurance company wouldn't pay for laymen to help with her investigation, but she suspected the Wolff family was going to be much more help than any other PI Taggart could hire. She hadn't told Taggart that she knew of Rhys before this investigation, afraid he might pull her off the case. Which meant she couldn't let it slip about Roxie knowing him either.

"I'll be moving to the new room tomorrow." She thought of telling him about the conversation Rhys had concerning the brother, but she needed to confirm Rhys didn't have another brother, or half brother, or stepbrother or something. She couldn't assume beyond a doubt that the one who was in the room was the dead brother.

"Any new news?"

"There's a third guy in the room. He's staying there, not ever leaving the room, so that sounds like someone else on the run. Or involved in some kind of illegal business. I'll try to nail down who he is tomorrow. The Wolff family let me look at the security videos, but he was wearing a hoodie and it was impossible to see anything about him."

"Sounds like you've got some good aid with this Wolff family. But what about muscle?"

"Blake is a volunteer deputy sheriff. And his brother is too."

"Okay, as long as no one makes a slip and sends these guys packing."

"They won't." She decided she would tell Taggart about Roxie's help so he would be convinced not to send someone else. "One of Blake's sisters has been watching the security monitors to let me know when they're on the move, so it's working out great. If Larry doesn't have to come back, it would really work out best in the long run."

"I'll tell him. He'll be disappointed. He called to tell me he wasn't working with you and couldn't for another couple of days, doctor's orders, and he worried about you in case things go wrong."

"I'm good. I would have called you about him, but he kept saying he'd get better on his own."

"I understand. Keep up the good work and keep me informed."

"I will." She sighed, figuring she needed to give Larry a call next to let him know he wasn't working with her any longer. She assumed if he had just called Taggart, he was probably still awake. When she got ahold of Larry, she said, "Hey, Taggart called. I told him I've got help on this one."

"I was hoping for that. I called him because I was worried about you," Larry said.

"I appreciate it. Maybe we can work on another case sometime in the future. Except we'll have to make it one at a lower altitude."

Larry laughed. "All right. It's a deal."

"Good luck on your next mission." Nicole didn't figure she'd ever work with him on another case, but who knew?

"Thanks. Good luck on this one. And stay safe."

"I will." Then she ended the call and hoped it was the last one she'd have to make tonight. She wondered if Blake always walked the dog in the morning or if taking the dog out this morning was because it had just been his turn. She would try to catch up to him first thing.

CHAPTER 7

EARLY THE NEXT MORNING, BLAKE WAS OUT WALKING the dog when he saw Nicole hurrying to catch up to him, wearing the blue and white ski clothes she had told him she would be wearing. He smiled, glad she wanted to join him. She was a breath of fresh air. "Did you think Rosco would get away from me again?"

"Possibly, if any more rabbits were around. You both provided great entertainment for me yesterday morning. I didn't know if you regularly walked him in the morning, but I could use some exercise before we eat breakfast. If Rosco gets away from you again, I'll enjoy the run with you this time."

Blake chuckled but hoped Rosco minded him this time and the rabbits were smart enough to stay away. "Did you learn anything more about the brother who drowned?"

"No. I was too busy trying to catch up to you this morning."

Blake smiled, a little surprised that she'd placed seeing him ahead of her mission, but he was grateful. "I'm glad you came out to join me."

"I'm glad I didn't miss you. Last night, I talked to Taggart, the insurance guy who hired Larry and me. It's official. Larry isn't working with me any longer. I told Taggart I have you and your family's help, so he isn't sending anyone else to replace Larry. Thankfully."

"Good. That could complicate things between us." Blake was really glad Larry was out of the picture.

Nicole smiled at Blake. "Did you arrange for me to move to one of the rooms next door to the cousins' room?"

"Landon's checking who the guests with the two rooms are first thing this morning. He'll let us know. Roxie is thrilled. She wants to know if you have a listening device she can set against a wall while she's listening in."

"I do. I also have a recorder she can use if anything important is revealed. With her wolf hearing, she'll be able to hear a lot. She'll be able to make out different conversations better with the listening device, like if someone's on the phone in the background and someone else is talking in the foreground."

"Okay, that sounds good. By the way, we didn't have any chocolate-covered almonds in the house, but Kayla and Landon love them, so I was going to take a run down to the grocery store and grab some for everyone before we have breakfast."

"Are you sure? You really don't have to make a special trip. I just thought if you had some lying around your house, I'd be forever grateful."

He chuckled. "Yeah, I'm sure. When we get back, we can check to see what Landon learned about the guests in the rooms on either side of the cousins' room. He can't really ask them to move until it's a decent hour though."

Nicole sighed. "True. I'm just grateful that you're willing to try to do this for me."

"Hey, we're all for helping to catch bad guys, and we certainly don't want them staying at our lodge if they're dangerous criminals."

"That's true."

Blake glanced down at the dog. Rosco didn't look like he

was planning to stop and do his business anytime soon, the way he was sniffing around and moving on, checking out a new spot—no doubt rabbit or squirrel scents left behind—and continuing his walk. "Okay, Rosco, do something already."

Nicole smiled. "They have to find just the right spot."

"Yeah, fresh snow means it's harder to find where he went last time."

Then Rosco did his business and Blake picked up after him. It didn't matter that this was all wilderness out here beyond their home and the ski lodge. They still picked up after Rosco as if they lived in a neighborhood. It was just the right thing to do.

"Did you want to go with me to the grocery store? Since you don't have a vehicle, in case you want anything else?" he asked.

"Sure. Are they open this early?"

"At six. By the time we return to the lodge, drop Rosco off, and drive to town, it will nearly be seven. Is that okay? I had planned on getting your candy and being at the restaurant at seven, but Rosco wasn't cooperating."

She chuckled. "No problem. You're going above and beyond the call of duty to help me get my fix. And really, the cousins waste half the morning sleeping in, so I normally have the time for myself."

"Good." Blake was glad he wasn't messing up her surveillance, but at the same time, he got more time to spend with her.

After they reached the lodge, Blake dumped the trash in the outside dumpster, then released Rosco inside the lodge. The dog headed straight for his spot next to the fireplace. Then Blake and Nicole went to see Landon in the office.

"We have a couple of guys in one room, and a family in the other. Both are staying through the week. I plan to approach the two guys first. Not sure if they care about more of a view, but they probably don't have as much gear to move as the family of five does," Landon said.

"That sounds like a good plan," Blake said.

"If that doesn't work, I'll ask the family. We'll help either of them move, and I can throw in a complimentary dinner."

"Thanks so much." Nicole sounded relieved.

"Hey, anything to help you in your mission. Blake says you want to go running with us tonight. The weather is supposed to be good for it. The winds have settled down, and we've got great powder for skiing today. A wolf run would be fun for all of us," Landon said.

Nicole smiled. "I'd love it. I don't get to go on wolf runs much in Denver, and when I get out to a place like this where I can really run, it's something I love to do. Especially when I can run with other wolves. That's even more enjoyable."

"Okay, well, we can discuss the time later," Landon said.

"I appreciate that."

"We're running into town to pick up a few things," Blake said. "Do we need anything else?"

"Yeah, we need another bag of dog food for Rosco. I swear he's eating us out of house and home. Next time, we get a smaller dog," Landon said.

"He'd get lost in the snow," Blake said.

They all laughed.

Then Blake and Nicole headed outside to his Jeep. The vehicles parked there were still buried in snow, so they must have belonged to their lodge guests. He brought out a snow brush and scraper to remove the snow and ice from his Jeep.

A plow had cleared the parking lot, and their regular handyman was out clearing the walkways to the lodge from the parking lot.

"Now *he* looks like he knows what he's doing," Nicole said as she watched the guy blowing the snow off the walkways.

"He does. But his absence helped me catch your attention."

Nicole laughed. "You and the dog first though."

They got into the Jeep, and Blake drove them out of the parking lot.

He smiled. "So you think maybe that's all you needed to choose me over my brother to help you out?"

"If I had any doubt, the snowblower tipped the scales in your favor."

He laughed.

When they reached the grocery store, he grabbed the largest sack of dog food he could find for Rosco. Nicole was going to buy bottled water, but Blake said, "No, we've got it for you."

"Oh, thanks. I figured you just get one complimentary bottle of water at the hotel room."

"You're our guest. Is the insurance company paying for your room?" Blake asked.

"Yes."

"Okay, we'd get it for you otherwise."

"I hit the jackpot when I met you."

Blake only smiled. "Did you need anything else? I know you want to eat at the restaurant to stay in close proximity with the cousins, but I was thinking you could come over to the house in the morning before they get up or have a late dinner with us after they've gone to bed. I could pick up something special for you."

"You're a real sweetheart, you know that? I'd like that."

Okay, so far, he was making the right moves. "Tonight? Dinner?"

She laughed. "Okay, yeah, dinner would be great. Thanks for the offer."

"You're welcome. I can make waffles for breakfast if that appeals."

"Yeah, sure, and we can talk about the case too."

"That works for me." Blake had to let his family know he was having a special dinner for Nicole so they could have some privacy. Some things he thought would be fun to do with the family, but some things he and Nicole needed to do alone. He'd play it by ear on the breakfast.

Still, as fast as things were moving along with him and Nicole, he knew he had to talk to her about the issues his family still had with shifting during the new moon and full moon. They couldn't shift during the new moon. They mostly had their shifting under control during the full moon, except on its fullest night. If Nicole and her family were royals, meaning their family had been turned generations ago, she might not want to dilute her line with a wolf whose lineage had a way to go. *Lupus garous* always had to think about their offspring, as important as wolf pups were to them. And a diluted wolf line would affect the kids. If she wasn't a royal, and her family had even fewer wolf roots, he would be fine with that, and he hoped they could continue to bond.

She was heading down the candy aisle, and he was amused. She truly had a sweet tooth and a one-track mind.

"If we have your room changed, one of my family will monitor the conversations while you and I have dinner." He grabbed a couple of packages of chocolate-covered almonds for Landon and Kayla. "What about salmon for tonight?"

"That would be perfect. And thanks for your family helping out. I'd hate to miss anything if I can get into a new room that will help with surveillance."

"Roxie is eager to assist you on this, especially since she has to keep a low profile."

They picked up some spinach to go with the salmon, and then they returned to his house first and dropped off the dog food and other items, all except for Nicole's chocolate-covered almonds. She had wanted to pay for them, but he wouldn't let her. Then they had breakfast at the lodge's restaurant.

Roxie came to see them, sounding excited.

Nicole was frowning, looking worried that their suspects might see her. Blake worried about it too.

"We've got your room. I told Landon we needed the family's room because it has an adjoining door to the suspects' room. That way, if the suspects leave for a while, you can slip into the room and gather your forensic evidence. The family was delighted with the better view and the promise of a free dinner for all of them. Anyway, we need to clean out your room, get it ready for them, and then do the same with theirs for you. Oh, and don't worry about me. Kayla's watching the hall to make sure your suspects aren't leaving the room while I talk to you."

Blake was glad to hear it.

"Okay. I can move right after breakfast?" Nicole asked.

"Yes. The family is coming down to breakfast with

their bags, and we'll hold them until we can clean up your room."

"All right, perfect."

"And I get to start doing wall-listening duty after that?" Roxie asked, sounding eager to be of help.

Nicole laughed. "Absolutely."

"Okay, I'll leave whenever you need me to, but when you need me to cover for you, I'll be there," Roxie said. "And while they're gone, I can watch the security videos on my laptop from there too. That way, I'll know if they're returning to the room."

"Sounds good to me."

And to Blake. He was glad they could help Nicole out in this way. Once Roxie left the restaurant, Blake and Nicole ate their pancakes and watched for any sign of the cousins, but as Nicole had said, they seemed to be late risers.

After breakfast, Blake, Landon, Roxie, and Nicole went up to her room. She packed her things, and they moved her to the room next to the cousins' room. They hadn't all needed to go, but they wanted to so they could see the setup.

Inside the room, Nicole looked at the three pictures on the walls, all photos of various wolves walking or sitting among Colorado wildflowers of purples and pinks and yellows. "Jake Silver," she said, noting the photographer on the prints.

"He's the pack leader's brother, subleader of the pack, and a professional photographer," Blake said. "We were eager to showcase his prints in all the rooms. He was happy to oblige. It helps to support each other in a pack and it suits the Wolff's wolf theme."

"I love them."

Nicole showed Roxie how to use the recorder and the listening device. "They're still asleep," she said quietly to Roxie as she listened at the wall.

Blake and Landon were observing what Nicole was showing them in case either of them needed to do it.

"What's next on the agenda?" Blake asked.

"I have to do some research on who the other man is. I need to look into the drowned brother's situation. As soon as these guys go down for breakfast, I'll head on downstairs," Nicole said.

"Should I stay with you until then?" Roxie asked. "I can listen at the wall while you're working on your computer and let you know when they say they're going down to breakfast."

"Sure, that will work," Nicole said.

"Do you need my help with anything?" Blake asked.

"I can meet you when the guys go down to breakfast. I'll just tell you when they're going down there."

"Okay, sounds good," Blake said.

Landon said to Roxie, "If you need a break, just let me know."

"I'll do that."

Blake and Landon left the ladies to do their work. He was glad Roxie wanted to help Nicole with this. It kept her occupied and feeling necessary too. Though she would have to be careful with coming and going from the room to make sure that Rhys didn't see her. Watching the security monitors should help with that. The guys seemed to always use the elevator, so at least Roxie would be able to use the stairs when she needed to leave the room. The staff elevator wasn't as convenient to this location as the stairs were, but if they needed to use it, they could.

Blake wished that he could have stayed too. Landon smiled at him as they headed for the stairs as if Blake's thoughts were transparent.

———————————

While Nicole was doing her research, the police reports she'd read made it appear that the guys who had been with Rhys when his brother had drowned had rehearsed what they'd done—playing, diving, swimming, then noticing Eli was gone and diving for him before they called the police. It was too practiced, to her way of thinking. Often, with the passage of time, stories would change if the witnesses or people responsible for a crime had lied. Sometimes witnesses were less afraid of telling the truth years later, and sometimes they just wanted to get it off their chests.

If these men bolted on her, she would return to their original family home and try to locate the witnesses and learn what she could. Even though it wasn't part of her investigation for this job, what if it led to learning more about where they'd flown the coop to? So it was something she made a mental note of for later.

"Discovering anything from your sources about the supposed brother in the room?" Roxie whispered.

Not that the men would hear her if she was speaking normally, but with their enhanced wolf hearing, it was easy to think everyone had it too. "I'm checking to see if either of Rhys's parents had prior marriages, in case this person is a stepbrother or half brother," Nicole said. "Or, as incredulous as it seems, the brother who supposedly drowned."

"Was there a life insurance policy on the one who drowned?"

"On Eli Kovac? Yes, payable to the mother."

"Mother. Not both parents?"

"Yeah, I thought it was odd at the time, but I was looking more into the situation with *Oscar*. I'd suspected Oscar killed his younger brother, and that would show Oscar had a propensity for committing crimes with monetary gain."

"What if the younger brother didn't die and the mom got the insurance payoff for the pretend death?"

"Then where has the boy been living all this time?" Nicole figured that was also something she'd have to look into. "Would friends have taken him in? Other relatives? But the news would have gone out that he had died. They'd all be part of the conspiracy to defraud the insurance company. He'd have to change his name. So what is it now?"

"It sounds like even more of a mystery. Your work is fascinating," Roxie said.

"It's like putting together a puzzle. Sometimes I get some really unique cases. Sometimes I can't believe how people thought they could pull off the crime. But some, like this one, keeps unraveling into more threads that make it curiouser and curiouser." Nicole could get lost in her research when she had a lead on something new concerning a case, which was why she'd wanted to see Blake first thing this morning and take a brisk walk in the snow with him while he was walking the dog. That was so not like her. Usually, when she was working on a case, she would be so wrapped up in it that she'd skip meals and not get enough sleep. Blake made her want to enjoy life around her work, which made this trip extra special.

She was enjoying having Roxie to bounce her findings off, too, when she normally only did that with someone trained in investigations. She'd found that the siblings could provide some great input.

"Okay, it appears neither of Oscar's parents had other spouses or kids," Nicole told Roxie as she searched through her investigative resources. "The mother's name was her maiden name when she married her current husband. I couldn't find any other marriage certificates for the dad. So it appears they had no stepchildren or half siblings."

"What about an illegitimate son?" Roxie asked, not taking her ear off the listening device next to the wall. She was really getting into this spy business.

"Ohmigod, yes. What if there was another son who was illegitimate? Or Eli was an illegitimate son? The mother is the true mother, and she had a lover or—"

"The father had an illegitimate son, and his wife was raising the boy instead of the birth mother for some reason."

"Okay, I'm checking for birth records on the younger brother, Eli."

"Or maybe it was an adoption. Maybe he wasn't even a birth son," Roxie said.

"True. No, wait. Okay, according to his birth certificate, he's the son of Rhys's mother, but the dad is listed as unknown."

"Aha. Another fly in the ointment. If her husband knew that the boy wasn't his, he could have been angry about it. He might have taken it out on the son. Why would they pay for a life insurance policy on her son and make it payable only to her?" Roxie asked.

"Because Oscar's father wasn't the boy's father. Due to

the insurance payout, I'd say she'd have a motive for getting rid of the boy, but her older son was with him at the lake, not her."

"Unless she gave him part of the proceeds if the boy should die," Roxie said. "And the parents did make Oscar take Eli with him and his friends."

"Hmm." This could get more and more complicated. "The father would also have a motive because Eli would be a constant reminder that his wife had had an affair with another man. If Eli knew Arthur wasn't his father, he might have even thrown that in his face. You know how rebellious teens can be. 'You're not my father. You can't tell me what to do.'"

"Yet Arthur stayed with his wife. He might not have known Eli wasn't his own son. Eli might not have either. Though if Arthur was clueless, you'd think she would have named him as Eli's father on the birth certificate. Unless there's another son. Do you see a pattern there?" Roxie asked.

"Yep," Nicole said. "I'm checking with the insurance company. They show that the mother was the one who signed the policy. The father, or I should say her husband, didn't. He might not have known about it. And the policy was taken out only six weeks before her son's supposed drowning. The mother received the money for her son's death. Then her living son inherited everything else upon his parents' death."

"And then for his own faked death," Roxie said.

"Right. So Oscar learned about getting life insurance payouts from his mother."

"Exactly. What about Oscar? Was he legitimate?" Roxie asked, her voice still hushed.

"Checking. Yes. Louise and Arthur Kovac were his birth parents."

"I hear movement in the bathroom. No one's talking. Just someone's getting out of bed and the bathroom door shut. The shower's running now. A light was turned on in the bedroom. I heard the click of the lamp going on. I love this hearing device. Box springs are squeaking. No one seems to be very talkative first thing this morning." Roxie sounded disappointed she couldn't help break the case wide open with some damning recorded conversations that would give Nicole more to go on.

"It can take months to learn the truth, even years sometimes, unfortunately." Nicole was hoping she'd learn the truth about the men at the ski resort though. With as many people hanging around the place as there were, she could blend in more than usual while doing her surveillance. And the Wolff family were incredibly helpful. Not to mention she really, really liked Blake.

Then Nicole had another idea and began looking for police reports that showed Eli might have been suffering from abuse. If his father knew Eli wasn't his son, he might have abused him. Then again, once the boy was gone, wouldn't the dad be glad? Supposedly, Oscar's parents had given him a rough time when his brother had died—unless that had all been for show.

"Did the mom have a life insurance policy out on the other son too? Or her husband?"

"Not on Oscar, which I thought was odd. But yes, both the husband and wife had them."

"What if Eli didn't drown and just went to live with his real father?" Roxie asked.

"Huh, that's a possibility. Though he would have to keep the secret about being dead, unless he lived in a different country." Nicole went to the wall to listen in. Drawers were opening and closing. The shower was running in the background.

"I'm going out today. I'm going skiing too. I don't have to go with you. Nobody's going to be looking for me. I'm dead." The voice sounded like the younger man Nicole had heard before. "You're the one who should worry about being seen."

Nicole couldn't believe it. She truly hadn't believed the brother was alive.

"Nobody knows me here. I told you that already," Rhys said. Then there was a rustling sound. "Fine. I'll give you some money for the lift ticket, skis, boots, and a rental locker for the rest of the week. If you get injured and give yourself away, I'll end you. Here's some money for food. Don't buy anything alcoholic. You're bound to blab your mouth off. If you're in the room, fine, as long as you stay quiet."

Roxie's mouth was agape as she stared wide-eyed at Nicole. "Wow," Roxie mouthed.

Nicole nodded. Some of Nicole's cases were really straightforward, like the arson case she'd been working on before she got this assignment. Some of them seemed straightforward until she delved further into the case and found herself caught up in multiple webs of deceit.

Nicole whispered to Roxie, "See what he's wearing when he goes by our room."

Roxie hurried to the door and watched out the peephole.

Nicole texted Blake: Check man on elevator in a couple

of minutes or so. It's the younger dead brother. Roxie is watching to see what he looks like.

> **Blake:** Living dead brothers seem to run in the family. Scoping out the elevator. A family with two small kids got off.

Ski-boot buckles were clamping in place in the cousins' room.

> **Nicole:** Should be soon. If you can pretend to be taking a selfie of yourself, get a picture of the guy, okay?
> **Blake:** You got it.

The shower shut off. "Hey, where's your brother going?" William asked.

"Skiing," the man they thought was Eli said.

The door to the room opened, then clunked shut.

"He's leaving his room now," Nicole whispered to Roxie.

"I hope you're right about letting him loose," William said to Rhys.

"Hey, how do you think we'd feel if we were cooped up like that? He'll be okay. He knows what's at stake."

At the same time, Roxie was giving Nicole Eli's description, and Nicole was texting Blake: Eli's headed to the elevator.

"Shaggy blond hair, black ski hat, dark-gray ski jacket with pale-gray and red stripes, gray ski pants, and white snow boots. Lanky male, older teen," Roxie reported.

Nicole texted Blake the guy's description.

Blake: He's coming out now and headed to the ski rental shop. I got a couple of pictures of him. Do you want me to follow him?

Nicole: Carefully. See if he grabs a bite to eat after he leaves the rental shop.

Blake: Will do. I'm sending you the pictures now.

In Rhys's room, drawers opened and closed.

"He's staying away from us," Rhys said to William.

"All right. Let's go get some breakfast."

Their door opened and shut.

"I'm off to follow them. As long as they're gone, you could watch them on the security monitors," Nicole said to Roxie. She didn't know what she would have done without having the Wolff family backing her on this, especially with three men to watch. At least Rhys and William seemed to stick together most of the time.

"Okay, I'll monitor the security feeds until I see that someone has... Wait, they're all gone. What if we can get some DNA evidence on Rhys in their room?" Roxie asked.

"We would have to replace whatever trash we would take or water glasses if they had used those," Nicole said.

Roxie pointed to the disposable cups and water glasses in Nicole's room. "You can use those to replace anything they've used. I've got a master key. Here. Use it to unlock the adjoining door to their room. I'll call Landon to tell him to watch the cousins, but I'll keep watching the security monitors too."

"Let me know pronto if someone is returning to the room."

"I will."

"I'll return here to grab what I need once I learn what they've used."

"Landon said they're going into the restaurant," Roxie said. "There they are." Roxie pointed to them on the security video.

Nicole watched the cousins walk into the restaurant. "Okay, good. They'll be there for a while. Wish me luck." Nicole slipped forensics gloves on, stuffed a bag to gather evidence in her pocket, unlocked their adjoining door to the other room, and moved to their adjoining door. Her heart was pounding as she unlocked the suspects' door to their room.

Without having any maid service since they arrived and being three young males, she expected the room to be a mess—unmade beds, clothes everywhere, rank wet towels, trash on the counters and filling the wastepaper baskets. They were empty, the water glasses unused, and the towels hadn't even been used! The beds *were* unmade. But no clothes were lying about. They had to be removing all their trash. Then she saw a package of paper towels. So that was how they were drying off. Which made her think about Rhys being a former MP. She wondered if he had learned a thing or two about leaving DNA evidence behind and how to cover his tracks.

They hadn't even left hair or beard hairs anywhere.

Well, damn it. She couldn't even find their toothbrushes. She opened drawers, and underneath several pairs of boxer shorts, she found a 9mm gun. *Crap!* She'd hoped they wouldn't be armed, though she had considered they might have a gun in the glove compartment of their vehicle. She'd never suspected they'd leave one in a drawer.

She pulled out the magazine—full of rounds. Was it the same gun Rhys had pulled on Roxie in the attempted coin heist? She rushed back into her room with the gun.

Roxie's eyes grew huge.

"Is it the same one Rhys pulled on you?" Nicole started to dust it with the powder used to obtain fingerprints.

"Yeah, could be. Looks just like it. Is it loaded?"

"It sure is." Nicole finished lifting fingerprints and cleaned off the weapon. She took a few pictures of it. "The serial number is filed off. Which means whoever did it has committed a federal felony."

"Great."

Nicole started to head back to the cousins' room. She didn't want to return it. She wanted to remove the rounds. She wanted to turn them into dummy rounds or blanks. But if done improperly, they could be lethal too, like in *The Crow* when someone attached a tip accidentally to a blank and it killed Brandon Lee. The bottom line was she didn't want to tip the three men off that she'd been in their room, so she left the gun the way it had been.

"You're not going to return it to them, are you?" Roxie sounded astonished.

"I can't disturb anything. If these guys notice anything's changed, they could make a run for it."

"Eli's returning to the elevator," Roxie suddenly warned.

"All right. I'm putting the gun back." Nicole was sweating it out, even though she knew she had a few minutes before Eli showed up at the room. She tucked the gun under the boxer shorts, shut the drawer, and ran to the adjoining doors.

She left the room and locked their adjoining door just as she heard the outer door open. She took a breath and hurried out of the space between the rooms and shut and locked her adjoining door.

Roxie's mouth was agape. "He didn't catch you."

"No, we're good. Why did he return to the room?" Nicole asked. "I thought he was going skiing."

Roxie listened to the wall. "He's in the bathroom."

Nicole returned the master key to Roxie. "You would not believe how clean they leave that place." She explained in detail what she'd found.

"Because the bastard was an MP," Roxie said before Nicole could mention that.

"Yep. Rhys could very well have a permit to carry a gun, since he's never had a felony conviction, but the business with the filed-off serial number? That changes things. I just couldn't take it from his room and charge him with it, unfortunately. Okay, I'm going down to watch the cousins. Are you going to be all right?"

"Yeah. I'll let you know where they are. Well, right now, they're waiting on food in the restaurant." Roxie pointed to them on the monitor. "Maybe you ought to wait. The younger brother is still in the bathroom. Flushing the toilet. Did *not* wash hands. Door just opened and shut. He's headed down the hallway to the elevator."

"I hope you clean the elevator buttons frequently."

Roxie smiled at her.

"Okay, see you later." Nicole hurried out of the room and went down the stairs to sit by the fireplace.

Landon saw her and came to join her. "Hey, the cousins are getting takeout. Roxie texted me to let me know you were delayed while you checked out their room for DNA evidence."

"Naturally, on the takeout. They cleaned their room. I couldn't find any evidence I could use, until I found a 9mm in a drawer."

Landon frowned at her. "The one Rhys used on Roxie?"

"Could be and it's loaded."

"I didn't expect them to have a gun in the room."

"It has a filed-off serial number."

"Isn't that illegal?"

"It sure is. I took fingerprints anyway. Maybe we can learn whose it is that way."

"I'll let Peter, our sheriff, know about the gun."

"Thanks." She handed the fingerprint evidence from the gun to Landon. "If you can give this to Peter, that will be great."

"I sure will."

"Where's Blake?"

"When Eli went back up to the room, Blake made a pit stop," Landon said.

"Okay, he's allowed."

Landon laughed. "But Eli just got takeout, so Blake grabbed another cup of coffee and he's headed out to the deck."

"Thanks, off to catch up with my boyfriend." Though she was thinking about skiing because the cousins were on the slopes.

Landon winked at her. "Blake will be delighted to hear it."

CHAPTER 8

BLAKE WAS SITTING OUT ON THE DECK, DRINKING A cup of coffee and watching Eli eat eggs, bacon, and toast with a cup of cocoa. The sun was rising in the morning sky, casting a golden light through the tree branches laden with snow, the breeze crisp, the clouds gone. He wished Nicole could be out here with him, drinking a cup of coffee or cocoa too. After the blizzard last night, it was a beautiful day to ski.

Eli rose from the table and started unzipping his back-pack. Blake assumed he was being as careful as his brother and cousin about getting rid of his trash. As Blake expected, Eli tucked his trash in his backpack, then went off to the chairlift. Roxie had sent Blake a text saying Nicole was in the room looking for evidence, but she wasn't able to find anything but a gun. That was bad news. He was glad Nicole had made it out of the room before Eli had caught her, but now they knew these guys were armed and dangerous.

Blake was torn between wanting to help her prove these guys had defrauded the insurance company and wanting to date her, knowing that once she was done with Rhys, she would be moving on to another assignment and out of his life. Which he didn't want! But this business with the gun really worried him.

He got a call from Nicole and wondered if she needed him now. He loved hearing her voice, so cheerful and sweet-sounding. She didn't sound like a hotshot investigator searching for clues.

"Hey, Blake, the cousins are skiing, so there's nothing else for me to do. Do you want to go skiing? Maybe we can overhear their conversation on the slopes if they pause at the top of the runs to talk." Nicole asked.

"Yeah, I sure do. I'll meet you at the office to get our skis. The other one is already out skiing too."

"Okay, I'm headed to the office now."

Blake saw the cousins heading outside, and he dumped his empty coffee cup in the trash, then walked inside the warm lodge. As soon as he met up with Nicole at the office, she gave him a big smile and an even bigger hug. She was wearing a soft, pale-blue sweater and ski pants, and she felt warm and cuddly, while he had to feel wintry cold, his ski jacket carrying the scent of the outdoors with him.

Not wanting to chill her, he wrapped his arms around her, pulled her even tighter, and gave her a hot-blooded kiss. Mouths melding, her warm lips heated up his cold ones.

"You're cold," she said, smiling up at him.

"But getting a whole lot warmer." He didn't let her go, wanting to revel in the feel of her against his body. He noticed her ski jacket was sitting on one of the chairs, and he liked how she'd made herself at home at their lodge.

"This business can be so slow. But this time, I'm glad it's allowed for some entertainment." Nicole didn't let go of him either, and he knew there was more to their interest in each other than just her using him as her pretend partner.

She didn't seem to be in any rush to release him. He knew the cousins would have made it to the top and probably skied down before Blake and Nicole could reach the chairlifts. The guys weren't going anywhere, and listening in on their conversations would be tricky unless Blake and Nicole got lucky.

"I don't like this business with the gun," Blake said.

"I don't either." She ran her hands over his shoulders. "In the worst way, I wanted to get rid of it."

"And they'd panic when they learned it was missing."

"Exactly."

"Not to ignore this situation with the cousins, but I was thinking, after dinner, we could watch a movie," Blake said, hoping he could keep her company for a little while longer tonight.

"We won't even be eating until around eight if the guys head up to their room by then. We could watch a movie while we're eating," she suggested.

"Okay, that would work." A nice, long movie would allow him to have more time to spend with her.

Nicole smiled. "Listen, if I were able to get the evidence that I need from these guys tomorrow, I wouldn't be leaving. Okay? I need a vacation. And this is the perfect place to take one with a bunch of fun-loving wolves, doing what I love to do. Running as a wolf and skiing."

Blake wasn't convinced. "What if they leave before you're able to prove who they are, and you have to follow them to their next destination?" She wouldn't have backup, and with three guys she was investigating, she'd need assistance. She couldn't do this on her own. He could just imagine her vanishing like the other private investigator had.

"I still need a partner. I don't care if he's an investigator or not. You're the perfect one for the job. All wolf, you've proven you and your family can be a real help. I need you for my protection in case things get hairy. As long as your family can do without you for a few days, I'd want you with me."

Hot damn. "They can do without me. They won't even miss me."

She chuckled and kissed him again, and their tongues tangled.

He loved the taste of her, sweet and chocolaty, the way she smelled of lavender and spice, she-wolf and woman.

But then she pulled away from him. "They would miss you and all the excitement we're getting ourselves into. I wouldn't be surprised if Roxie tried to come along." Nicole grabbed her ski boots from the closet and sat down on one of the office chairs to remove her snow boots.

"I couldn't be gladder to be there for you. As for Roxie, I think she believes there's more to me helping you than just doing a job, and she might be interfering if she came along. Not to mention Rhys might still recognize her. About our dinner tonight... I talked to my family, and they're all going to eat here while we have dinner at the house."

"Aww, they didn't have to do that. They could eat earlier than us if they want to be at the house to have their meal."

"They love eating at the restaurant, and they don't have to clean up anything afterward. I told them we'd have break-fast with them, and they were glad about that."

"They really don't have to stay away while we're having dinner," Nicole said, putting on her ski boots. "Especially if we watch a movie on top of that."

"They're happy to. Believe me. Any excuse to eat out. Landon and I have been doing it a lot while our sisters were away—so we didn't have to cook meals and clean up after ourselves—but our sisters are enjoying having some meals there too now. Or at least Roxie's enjoying the takeout until we can put these guys away for good."

He finished slipping his ski boots on and buckling them, and then they grabbed their skis and poles and left the office. They saw Landon taking Rosco out for a walk. They waved at him and went outside and finally skied toward the chairlift where they saw Eli going up the lift.

"We'll follow him," Nicole said as they moved into the line for the chairlift the cousins seemed to be using the most. "If we could get him to talk, it would be great, but I'm afraid that he might not, and then he'd tell the others we'd interrogated him, and they'd flee."

"I'd certainly love to try it, but I'd be afraid of the same thing. The younger brother isn't to be trusted. He's in the same boat as the older one, it sounds like to me. Except he didn't receive the life insurance proceeds resulting from his death. His mother did."

Nicole glanced at Blake. "Wait, what if he *did* get the proceeds? What if his mother was involved in this to protect him and gave him the money to live off, maybe to help pay for his upkeep while he lived with someone else?"

"I wonder how that would work. The boy would know his mother had gotten the money to give to him for his death. So he would be a witness to the crime. Actually, an accessory."

"Maybe he didn't. Maybe the mother didn't want to tell him for fear he might talk and give them away. She could have said the money was from her savings or work money or something. In truth, she wouldn't even need to say where she got the money."

Blake leaned over and kissed Nicole's cheek. "That

would make sense. Kids talk. And since she's dead, she's beyond worrying about being prosecuted for this. Then again, he went along with the charade to fake his death."

"True."

They rode the ski lift up, and when they reached the top, they headed past the easy run and in the direction of the intermediate slope where they saw Eli skiing to the run.

Then they saw Rhys and William waiting to talk to Eli. That was a surprise, since they thought Rhys didn't want to be seen with his younger brother.

"Now what?" Blake asked, sure Nicole wouldn't want to get on top of the three of them when they were talking.

"We'll slowly slip on past to the expert slope, and we'll hopefully hear something important."

"Hell, you're going down the blue slope?" Rhys said to his brother.

"I haven't been skiing in a couple of years." Eli turned and dashed down the run, pretty much in control, wobbling a little, like he was trying too hard to prove to his brother that he was good at this.

Rhys laughed and raced after him. William followed.

"I didn't get much from that except that his younger brother has been skiing when he was supposed to be dead, albeit not recently," Nicole said as she and Blake stopped at the top of the expert run.

"I thought they didn't want anyone to see them together," Blake said.

"From the looks of it, the two brothers have been close, don't you think? Just like William and Rhys are?" Nicole asked. "I bet you anything that Rhys was involved in this with the mother from the very beginning."

"Yeah, I'm starting to think that. What about the friends who were with them when the brother supposedly died?" Blake and Nicole were standing at the top of the expert slope, watching a couple of skiers making their way down to the bottom.

"They may not have known about it. William and Rhys could have been keeping their attention while Eli slipped out of the water and vanished into the woods. It sure turns everything upside down to know Rhys and William lied about Eli's drowning."

"Still, what if they hadn't known at first? Maybe they thought he had. But Eli sneaked off while his brother and his friends were goofing off. They might not have known he hadn't drowned. Not until later. It would make it easier for the brother and his friends to tell the story like they knew it."

"Hmm, I hadn't thought of that. So the person who would have been in on it was the mom. She was the one who sent him with his brother and Rhys's friends to the lake in the first place. She got the money, and she made him stay with someone else," Nicole said. "Maybe they went there before to plan how he would slip away and she'd pick him up, or someone else would and take him somewhere safe."

"Too bad we can't corroborate that with witnesses who saw the mother and Eli going to the lake earlier. I had another thought too. What if the fire in the Kovac home wasn't started by Rhys or William?" Blake asked. "What if Eli came back and started it?"

Nicole adjusted her ski glasses. "Wow, that could be. We didn't even know he could still be part of the equation, but where was he at the time of the party? Where had he been living at the time? If Eli did set the fire, he wouldn't have gotten anything out of it financially if Rhys hadn't been involved and given him some of the money."

"So that goes to a new motive. His mother forced Eli to die, live elsewhere, get money for his death, and he came back for revenge. Possibly."

"True. I didn't believe I'd have this many people who were dead come back to life. Come on. Let's make some runs down the slope and then go have lunch."

After making several trips down the slopes, they finally headed in to have lunch at the restaurant and found the cousins together at a table inside, talking about the powder snow. Nicole went for a table out of their sight but near enough that they could hear the conversation with their wolf's hearing, as long as the chatter in the restaurant didn't get too loud.

"I thought we weren't going to be seen with him," William said.

"Yeah, but you know how I worry about him. I wish he'd just stay in the room."

"We should have left him behind." William pulled a bottle of water out of his backpack. "He's eighteen now. He needs to make his own way in the world."

Blake smiled at Nicole. She was eyeing the water bottle, but that wasn't the one they needed to get. They needed to get Rhys's. Since he'd been in the military, they had his DNA on file.

"Like I did? He hasn't done anything wrong," Rhys said.

Nicole raised her brows at Blake.

"We both know that's not true," William said.

Blake wanted to force the truth out of them in front of their sheriff, Peter Jorgenson. Especially since Nicole said she'd stay a while longer, even after the job was done.

Then the men grabbed their food to go and left the restaurant. Blake and Nicole ordered grilled cheese sandwiches and cheesy broccoli soup.

"Eli could have done anything," Nicole said.

"Like being involved in the fire that killed his mother and his stepfather?" Blake asked.

"Yeah, like that too. Or it could have been something entirely different. I haven't heard either of the guys call him by any name that would help me to search records to see what he's been up to if he has an alias, and I'm sure he must," Nicole said.

"And no one that sounded like it could be him on their Facebook friends' lists?" Blake figured that might be easy to catch him up on there.

"I'll look again, but there wasn't anyone else who said he was joining them at the ski resort. I've been monitoring the posts that William and Rhys have where they've been uploading photos of all their skiing fun. Eli hasn't posted any. Other friends say how cool it is that they're having so much fun and wish they were there. Here's the picture of Eli at the age of twelve, before he supposedly drowned." She showed it to Blake.

"That doesn't look a whole lot like him now that he's an adult. You can imagine Eli has been disgruntled about being hidden away while his cousin and brother are off having a ball."

"Yeah. I'd say he's been really sucking it up for them. Maybe they said they'd take him with them only if he stayed

YOU HAD ME AT WOLF   147

in the room, and he was agreeable, but then enough was enough." Nicole took a sip of her water.

"I can imagine so."

Their grilled cheese sandwiches and bowls of soup were served, and they moved to a window seat so they could watch the guys eating outside.

"It's easy to keep track of them. They don't seem to vary their routine," Blake said.

Nicole agreed. "I hope they continue to keep on schedule. If they suddenly change things up, it would worry me." She began eating her soup.

"There's Eli. He's walking past them to take a seat at another table and ordering from a menu outside. He does favor his older brother."

"Yeah, if I had seen them together, I would have realized they were related."

After Rhys and William finished eating, they went inside to the restrooms, then went to the lockers in the rental shop and picked up their skis.

Eli watched them, then headed inside to do the same thing, used the restroom, then went to grab his skis from a rental locker.

"What now?" Blake asked.

"Let's go skiing."

"Seems like we have a routine too."

She smiled. "Except tonight I'm having fine dining at your place and we're taking in a movie. And then a wolf run with your family."

That would be the highlight of his day.

After the cousins and Blake and Nicole skied for the afternoon, they all ended up back at the lodge. The brothers and their cousin went to the restaurant to get dinner, Eli taking a separate seat. Landon and Kayla went in to take a booth near where Rhys and William were sitting to see if they could overhear anything while they ate.

Blake and Nicole took seats near the fireplace and had hot cocoa.

"Looks like Rhys and William are just playing games or checking emails or something on their phones," Nicole said, checking Facebook on her cell. "They're not posting new pictures of their skiing."

"Eli looks like he could be playing games too," Blake said.

William and Rhys finally grabbed bottles of beer and their meals and headed for the fireplace.

"Here they come," Nicole said under her breath. "At least with all of you running the lodge, it makes it seem safe."

"That's true. And you're with me." Blake wrapped his arm around Nicole's shoulders.

She smiled.

They cuddled next to the fire, petting Rosco's head. When the brothers and their cousin headed to the elevator after eating, Roxie came to speak with Nicole. "Do you want me to go to your room and listen in on the cousins while you're with Blake at dinner and the movie? I saw them going up the elevator to their room."

"Yeah, thanks, and then we'll all go running as wolves together," Nicole said.

"I can stay in the room, just to make sure they don't spill the beans and we miss it. I can run with you all later," Roxie said.

Nicole frowned. "Are you sure?"

"Yeah, I don't want us to miss anything if it could mean a break in the case for you."

"Okay, thanks." Nicole stood and gave her a hug. "Really, thanks."

"You're welcome. I can see how hard it is to prove these guys are guilty, and I want to help if I can. You know I have a personal stake in it. That will teach Rhys he can't get away with committing crimes." Roxie headed for the stairs, pulling her sweatshirt hood around her face in case Rhys came out of the room to get ice from the dispenser or something.

"Come on. Let's take Rosco for a walk and then get our dinner." Blake was looking forward to spending some alone time with Nicole where they weren't having to conduct surveillance on the bad guys the rest of the night.

They walked Rosco to the house, and then he fed the dog. After that, he and Nicole took the dog for another walk, brought him home, and removed their outer gear. Rosco immediately went to his bed by the fireplace.

Blake started the gas fire. "In the spring, we're going to put up a fence around the back so we can let Rosco explore for rabbits and squirrels to his heart's content. We don't mind taking him on walks, but he needs to be able to have time to just explore the yard without us having to keep him on leash all the time."

"I agree. When I had my Lab, she had a nice big yard to run in and explore."

Blake and Nicole started cooking the salmon, spinach, and a baked potato for dinner. After dinner was ready, they sat in the living room, having white wine and eating their dinner on table trays. He would have extended the time they had to enjoy their dinner and movie out a bit by having their meal on the dining room table and then moving to the living room to start the movie afterward, but she wanted to combine the two so they could run and then she could return to the lodge and free Roxie from her duty.

They watched a romantic comedy about a man who was an assassin. A woman's father was his target, but then he began dating the daughter, having missed the opportunity to take out the father. Blake and Nicole laughed and cuddled while they watched the movie together. He loved doing this with her, and he thought about how nice it would be to do it on a regular basis. The movie had a cute ending, and Nicole and Blake began kissing each other, his hand slipping up her sweater to run over her lacy bra.

"I want you to solve this mission, but I don't want you to go," Blake said, kissing her cheek and nibbling on her ear, being perfectly honest with her.

She sighed and began kissing him. "You're making it hard for me to want to return to my empty apartment in Denver."

"Don't then. We don't have any PIs in Silver Town. We desperately need one."

She smiled and kissed him again. "Just keep thinking those thoughts."

He would. But he would do more than that. He would let Darien and Lelandi know they could have a valuable pack member if they could encourage her to stay in the area. He would do everything to convince her of it too.

Blake was afraid she'd return to Denver and forget all about him. He knew he'd miss her. He could visit her there if she was agreeable, but keeping up a relationship could be difficult. And what about her parents? He hadn't considered having to win over a prospective mate's parents, but that was the next step. If he wasn't getting way ahead of himself.

"I want you to know how much I'm enjoying your company. I mean, *really* enjoying it," he started out. "I just have to be honest and tell you we're not royals."

"So how far back do you go?" Nicole sounded worried, and that bothered him. She must be a royal.

But it was better to get this out in the open rather than wait and cause hard feelings. If she were a royal and she couldn't live with what he was, it was better to end this deep-seated infatuation he had with the she-wolf.

Blake cleared his throat. "We're all wolf lineage back to my grandfather. My great-grandfather was the one who had been bitten. He was a sheep farmer and trying to protect his livestock from a wolf."

"A *lupus garou* was attacking his sheep?" Nicole sounded horrified that one of their kind would do that and jeopardize all the wolf shifters.

"In defense of her, a hunter had killed her mate and she was on her own, trying to teach her three wolf pups how to hunt. But one of them found sheep were easier to tackle. He didn't believe she was teaching her wolf pups to go after sheep. Of course, he didn't know that she was a *lupus garou*. Werewolves were the stuff of legends, not real."

"He didn't kill her pup, did he?"

"No. He loved animals. He knew enough about wolves to realize she could abandon them if he tried to seize the pups first. He planned to relocate them far away from his sheep farm, but he needed to capture her initially. They came at night, and he shot her with a tranquilizer gun, then hurried to place her in a cage. He assumed the pups would go to their mother, but not when he was putting their sleeping mother *in* the cage. He was certain they'd be wary of him. He was going to leave food for them in other cages so they'd be tempted to come for a free meal, except one of the six-month-old pups bit his hand."

"And broke the skin," Nicole said.

"Yep. My great-grandfather wasn't angry, just surprised. Then again, the pup had to be more alpha than the others and he was defending his mom. My great-grandfather understood that. He kept thinking the pups would go into the cages for the free meals, but they wouldn't go near them. He didn't know what else to do. He was afraid the pups would starve. Mom finally came to and was pacing in the cage and whimpering for her pups, so he thought. But later he believed she was telling them to stay away. He couldn't move her and not gather up the pups first. He had a real dilemma."

"Until he turned, I bet. Did he have a family?"

"No. He was young, a bachelor, his parents had died of typhus, and he continued to run the sheep farm. So he was all alone."

"That was a good thing for his family."

"True. That night, he thought he was hallucinating. He knew it had to do with being so concerned about the wolf and her pups that he thought he'd turned into a wolf and was on a mission to rescue her."

"Did he release her?"

"Or one of the kids did. She could have shifted during the night while he was sleeping, and the alpha son opened the cage and released her. In any event, they ate the meat he'd left for them and took off. He thought he was back to square one.

The mother was out with her pups hunting in the nearby woods, and he assumed they'd go after his sheep again."

"He didn't intend to kill her this time, did he?"

Blake smiled at Nicole and rubbed her arm. "No. He loved animals, and none of us in the family give up easily when we're challenged with what seems to be an insurmountable task. But everything was changing for him too. He could see them in the dark, lurking in the woods near the pasture, observing him. He could smell their scent on the breeze when they were close. He was certain that the bite that had healed so miraculously had made him connect somehow with the wolves and he was seeing their plight more clearly now.

"Despite knowing it was a bad idea to feed the wolves, he put out meat again so they wouldn't go after his sheep. He didn't want them getting used to him and then being unafraid of other humans who would kill them. But he was trying to come up with a plan to capture them again to safely relocate them much farther from any sign of civilization. Yet the third night after he'd been bitten, he had the greatest urge to run with the she-wolf, to court her. He thought he'd been alone on the farm for way too long and was losing his mind."

Nicole smiled. "The wolf love bug had bitten."

"You could say that." Blake was feeling the same way about Nicole. "Instead of following the crazy inclination he had to chase after the she-wolf, he decided to make his monthly trip into town a few days early and see if he could get up the courage to talk to a young woman who worked in the mercantile. Her father owned the shop and also worked there. Other than going in to buy supplies, he'd never been able to actually speak to her about anything other than the weather."

Nicole laughed.

"He wasn't shy about anything else. Just about her."

"But it wasn't to be." Nicole seemed interested in the story and seemed to approve of the fact that at least his great-grandfather hadn't wanted to harm the wolves.

"Nope. The she-wolf made sure of that. When he was gone, she entered his unlocked home. The kids joined her, and they found some clothes to wear. My great-grandfather never got rid of anything. So she wore one of his mother's dresses, and she found some of his kid-size clothes and dressed her kids in them. She cleaned the place and baked an apple pie and made beef stew for him, a way of thanking him and letting him know she was moving in."

Nicole laughed. "He didn't know what was in store for him."

Blake smiled. "He didn't know it, but he really needed her and the kids in his life. When he arrived home, she and the kids were sitting on the front porch, waiting for him. They were wary, none of them smiling, and he was just as wary. Until he smelled her scent and that of the two boys and one little girl. The same as he'd smelled on the she-wolf and her pups. He smelled the stew and the apple pie too. He didn't know what to think."

Nicole snuggled up next to Blake. "No way was he going back to the girl in the mercantile shop."

"Yeah. The she-wolf teased him about that for years. My great-grandfather didn't do much talking. He just went inside and found the meal set out, and he sat down at the table to eat."

She laughed. "Too funny. He didn't ask her where she'd come from?"

"Nope. Eventually, once he learned her son had turned him into a wolf shifter, she told him she'd lost her pack in a flood. She'd hooked up with a lone wolf and lost him when a hunter shot him. She had been barely surviving with her three little ones, who had been born after her mate died. My great-grandfather's whole world changed from the moment he tangled with the wolf. His kindness to her and the kids meant the world to her. He had been her hero when she'd so needed one.

"Still, changing a human hadn't been in the plans. That night, they all ran as wolves together, and she and the kids showed him the ropes. She was a royal and didn't have any issues with changing during the full moon. Her kids couldn't change unless she did until they were about six or so. He suddenly had a family, wolf and human all in one. And he never regretted it for a minute."

"I love that story," Nicole said, kissing his jaw. "We're royals. But so was your great-grandmother and that helped to add more wolves to the mix. Still, it must have been hard for them to become mated wolves when we have to find a mate who is our forever companion. How did she feel about it? Since she didn't make the choice to turn him?"

"My great-grandmother knew he was the one for her and the kids. She'd been watching him ever since her pups were born. There were no other wolves in the area, and she couldn't travel very far with her young charges. She saw the way he helped his ewes with difficult births, how he took care of the moms and the lambs, and he'd even saved a bird that had fallen out of a nest during a storm, taking care of it until the bird could fly away.

"My great-grandmother never once killed one of his beloved sheep either. She'd actually been chasing a rabbit for her little ones when it had taken off toward the sheep farm. She had been so focused, she hadn't realized how close she'd come to his sheep in the pasture. That was when he saw her the first time. After that, she was trying to formulate a plan. The problem was that he was human. He had no family, sure, but it didn't mean he could accept wolves or being one of them. Turning someone is a tricky business, and she didn't have the heart to do that to him."

"So her son did."

Blake laughed. "Exactly. He said he was rescuing his mom from the cage, and he was angry the sheepherder had shot his mother."

"They must have had more kids, or you would be the offspring of the she-wolf's pups."

"They did. They had three more kids, two boys and a girl. They all got along as kids do—fighting, playing, being a family of *lupus garous*. My great-grandfather had thought he would be all alone in the world if he didn't convince the girl in the mercantile to marry him. Instead, he brought his mate and a passel of kids in to the mercantile once a month, surprising everyone in town. He even took my great-grandmother to dances, but only when a new moon was out."

"What a lovely story."

"I won't lie to you and say everything worked out. There were times when my grandfather was ashamed of not being a royal wolf like the older half siblings. It had a big impact on them. They vowed to find royals to mate. It was easiest for their sister since there was a shortage of female wolves.

She found a mate right away. But my grandfather and great-uncle were turned down a number of times after they'd fallen in love with the she-wolves they'd wanted to mate."

"And?"

"My great-uncle found the she-wolf he couldn't live without who was similar in wolf roots' lineage to his own. He didn't care. He loved her. My grandfather lucked out and also found a mate whom he truly loved, and she loved him back. Her parents didn't want her to mate him because she was a royal and he wasn't, but she broke from convention and mated him anyway, though they moved out of state. That's how we ended up in Vermont."

"Wow. I have to admit my parents want my brother and me to mate wolves we love, but no turning anyone, and if we have a choice, mate a royal. Of course as kids, we're agreeable. But when you're in the real world, you realize that what makes your heartbeat quicken has nothing to do with whether the wolf you're dating is a royal or not."

"So there's hope for me yet?"

She chuckled. "Are you kidding? There's a lot more to any of this than that. Chemistry, which apparently your great-grandfather and the she-wolf had. It just goes so much deeper than the need to provide royal offspring. I can see where your grandfather was coming from, observing his half siblings who were able to run as wolves during the new moon. Maybe wanting to go somewhere around humans on a full moon night but unable to. Feeling different from humans when they were trying to sort out their differences with their wolf half siblings. I imagine when they were younger, it would have been difficult to understand the differences."

"It was. They were fortunate the half siblings didn't tease them about it. It was something their mother and my great-grandfather were strict about. They'd have enough ridicule from other royal wolves when they grew older, not to have to suffer it from their own stepsiblings."

"That's good parenting. So where does that leave us?" she asked, pulling him in for a kiss.

In heaven. He began kissing her again, her lips tenderly pressing against his, and then the pressure intensifying, growing more passionate, more like a courtship than just a sweet friendship between wolves. He nuzzled her cheek, her skin soft and warm. He moved his lips against her mouth again. He hoped she was being perfectly honest with him because he really, really wanted to take this a whole lot further with her.

She dragged her mouth away from Blake's and ran her hands through his hair. "I need to check with Roxie and see that everything is okay, and you need to tell Kayla and Landon they can come home to run as wolves with us. Then I need to return to my room so poor Roxie can come home."

"Yeah, you're right." He knew his siblings would do anything to allow them as much time as they needed, but Nicole was right.

"Hey, how are you doing, Roxie?" Nicole asked on her cell phone.

"Everything's quiet."

"Okay, we're going for a run and then I'll call and you can return home."

"Okay, no rush," Roxie said. "Talk later."

Blake got up to clean the dishes and texted Kayla and Landon to tell them to come home.

Landon texted: We're on our way back.

It wasn't long before Landon and Kayla arrived at the house. Nicole was helping Blake with cleanup, and then they stripped and shifted. As wolves, they ran out the wolf door and chased each other across the fields of snow, through the woods, woofing and having a blast, the waning moon shining on the night. The chilly air made their wolf breaths turn into frozen mists.

Blake wished Roxie had been able to join them and hoped that they would be able to take her on a run with them soon. He thought Nicole was having lots of fun, and she proved she was when she stopped and howled at the moon. They heard a howl off in the distance—Jake Silver, a wolf's greeting and connection—and that set off the Wolff siblings, each of them howling to let the others know that they were with Nicole and she was one of them. Though with the ski resort being open, they had a lot of out-of-area wolf visitors, so the pack didn't necessarily think a wolf howling meant trouble.

Suddenly, Nicole nipped at Blake's ear. He pinned her to the snow. Maybe he should have gone easier on her, but his brother tackled him and so did Kayla. They were play-protecting Nicole, bringing her full force into the family.

Blake loved them for it. And the way Nicole was aiding them and cheerfully barking, he suspected she did too. They played in the snow for about an hour, running, chasing, biting, and then they finally headed home. He and the others had so much fun playing with the new she-wolf that he hoped they could do this nightly before they all turned in.

They ran inside the house where Rosco greeted each of them in turn, as if making sure his whole wolf pack had come home, though Roxie was missing. Then they shifted and dressed.

"We've got to do this every night," Landon said.

Kayla agreed. "Except we need Roxie to join us."

"I agree," Nicole said.

Blake smiled. "Let me take you home and Roxie can come home."

"Would you like to have breakfast with us in the morning?" Kayla asked.

"That sounds good." Nicole bundled up. "Night, Kayla, Landon."

They both said good night to her and headed upstairs to bed.

Blake and Nicole pulled on their jackets and gloves. Then he escorted Nicole back to the lodge. Nicole was texting Roxie to let her know they were almost to the room.

Roxie texted her back, and Nicole showed the text to Blake.

"They're still watching TV," Blake said. "It's midnight."

"Yeah."

They reached the door and unlocked it. As soon as they walked inside, Roxie smiled at them. "Hmm, you guys smell like the fresh outdoors. I'll give you a moment. I'll be downstairs, Blake."

Blake nodded. "See you in a minute."

Roxie left, and Blake pulled Nicole into his arms. "You let me know if I need to stay with you at any time."

She kissed him, and he loved this with her. "I will," she said.

"I'll see you in the morning. You let me know anytime if you are having trouble before then."

"I will. Thanks, Blake. I loved having dinner with you, the movie was so much fun, and the wolf run... That was great. I think everyone really enjoyed themselves."

"We did. Roxie will enjoy it with us tomorrow night too." Though he could envision Roxie aiding Nicole and Landon while tackling him to protect Nicole. He didn't mind as long as it was all in good fun. "Good night, Nicole." He kissed her again, not wanting to let go, but it was late and Roxie had to be tired too. Then he left Nicole, even though he wanted to stay the night with her in the worst way. He told himself it was just to protect her, but he knew it was a lot more than that.

Nicole started stripping off her clothes, but she didn't want to shower tonight, wanting to keep Blake's scent wrapped around her all night long. She knew she was falling for the wolf when she had no intention of doing so. She had a mission, and he was helping her with it. That was all.

So why didn't she just wash him right out of her hair?

CHAPTER 9

THE NEXT MORNING, NICOLE LISTENED TO WHAT WAS going on in the cousins' room but didn't hear anyone stirring yet. It was seven, and she'd overslept herself. Her suspects must have watched TV until two in the morning, which they'd done the night before, and then slept in late.

She hurried to take a shower, then dressed warmly, wanting to catch up to Blake while he was walking Rosco. When she reached the first floor of the lodge, she saw Blake smiling at her and Rosco on his leash. Rosco was wagging his whole body and trying to greet her. That was the nicest morning greeting she'd ever had.

"I wasn't about to run off until I learned if you wanted to go with us. I would have texted you, but I was afraid you might be sleeping. Rosco is getting used to you coming with me on our walk."

She smiled and gave Rosco a hug. "I was hoping I wouldn't miss you, but I didn't expect a welcoming committee."

"A good-morning kiss." Blake pulled her into his arms and gave her a hug and a kiss.

She hugged him back and kissed him. "You sure do a great job on your role as my boyfriend."

"Yeah, but I'm doing something wrong. You hugged Rosco first."

She chuckled. "True. He was wagging his tail so hard, I couldn't ignore him. But I didn't kiss *him*."

Blake smiled and kissed her forehead. "I have to admit

Rosco was a bit confused when I walked him to the lodge instead of out into the woods or field first thing. He thought he was going to miss his morning walk."

"No rabbits to chase at the lodge. He did so well at the avalanche victim training that I wondered why he chases after rabbits. I mean, he seems well-trained."

"About everything except for squirrels and rabbits. One of these days, he'll figure it out."

"Does he belong to the whole family?"

"Yeah. We've always had one in the family. We have our own jobs to do with him—feeding, so we're not forgetting or feeding him twice or more, grooming, his regular potty walks, and any scheduled training he needs to do."

"So who washes him?"

"Landon and I do that together. Rosco loves the water, not so much baths. He's so big that it's easier for us guys to take care of it."

"And brushing out all that fur?"

"We take turns. Roxie does all the vacuuming to pick up both our fur and Rosco's. No sense in getting a nonshedding breed when we all shed."

Nicole laughed. "I agree with you there."

Rosco was eager to take his usual walk, as though he'd been afraid he was going to be shortchanged this morning. But after a nice, long walk in the cold, crisp snow, they went to the house for breakfast with the family.

"I bet Rosco was confused when you took him to the lodge to pick up Nicole, thinking he was just going to sleep by the fireplace and not go for his regular walk." Roxie served up the pancakes while Landon dished out the sausages and Kayla made coffee for everyone.

Blake set out the butter and maple syrup. "Yeah, he was really confused when I made him head for the lodge first thing. Dogs have just as much of a routine as the rest of us. Tomorrow morning if we do the same thing, he'll begin to expect it."

"No trouble with rabbits this morning?" Landon asked.

"No, thankfully."

"Breakfast is great," Nicole said.

"We're glad you could join us," Roxie said.

Then they all finished their breakfast, helped to clean everything up, and walked to the lodge as a family. Blake thought Nicole fit right in. His family seemed to accept her as one of their own.

"Do you want me to listen to what's going on next door from your room and let you know when they wake?" Roxie asked when they reached the lodge, looking eager to do so.

Nicole had the greatest urge to take Blake up to her room instead and ravish him. What was wrong with her? "Uh, yeah. Let's go."

Blake kissed Nicole before she left with Roxie. "I've got to take care of some lodge business. Let me know when you need me."

"Thanks, Blake, and thanks for the lovely breakfast." She kissed him back, and then she and Roxie headed to Nicole's room. They set up the same way as they had the day before with Nicole on her laptop, sitting on the bed, searching for information, and Roxie listening at the wall.

Nicole figured she'd start with trying to learn more about Eli. "Okay, when Eli was ten, he broke his arm. There were conflicting reports at the time about how it had happened, which made the situation suspect. He said his father

YOU HAD ME AT WOLF 165

knocked him down, then changed his story and said he slipped on a toy. He refused to say his father abused him after that."

"It sounds like Arthur silenced him. I wonder if he learned Eli wasn't his son about that time and took it out on him," Roxie said. "He must not have been present when she gave birth to Eli."

"Could be. The next year, a teacher reported Eli had bruises on his arm. Eli said he bruised easily, but the handprints were that of an adult and severe enough to be noticeable. There were several more reports of unconfirmed abuse. A broken leg, bruises, cuts. Reasons given: falls, clumsy, fighting with schoolkids, but he wouldn't give names."

Roxie frowned. "Did it happen at school?"

"Nope. It happened after his dad was home from work. But Eli said it was after-school fights, not on school property."

"And the mother wouldn't protect him?" Roxie asked.

"She wasn't home. Either she was at work or out shopping or running errands."

"Feeling guilty she had the affair, maybe," Roxie said.

"Maybe. And maybe she was just glad her husband took it out on the boy instead of her," Nicole said.

"I was thinking the same thing. It was easier just to make the boy disappear than to deal with her husband's anger," Roxie said.

"Yeah. But Arthur was also the older boy's birth father, and I don't find any indication he ever had broken bones or bruises, at least none that were reported. Maybe Eli was exceedingly clumsy. When I saw him on the slopes, he did look a little out of control and like he was hotdogging it for his brother and cousin, but still, I think he was trying to show them he wasn't a kid anymore. That had to be an awful environment for Eli to live in. His mother wasn't protecting him, and it wasn't his fault Arthur wasn't his dad."

"And Oscar wasn't protecting him either," Roxie said.

"He was just a kid too. Think about it. If your dad was leaving you alone and beating up on your brother, what would you have done? If the dad's paying for most everything, Mom would hate you if you turned him in for abuse. Your brother would deny it. And Arthur was your biological dad. Would you turn on him?"

"I would have tried to stop him."

"Okay. This isn't really a fair assumption since we're wolves. I would have protected a sibling from a threat. And we don't know. Maybe Oscar tried to protect his younger brother."

"I hear them getting up."

Nicole came over to the wall to listen.

"Hey, I'm sleeping in," William said, his voice sounding muffled under a pillow.

"I told you that you were drinking too much," Rhys said. "Okay, we'll see you later. Did you want to ski with me, Eli?"

Confirmation! Eli was the drowned brother!

"Yeah, sure." Eli sounded enthusiastic that his brother had asked him.

The shower ran for a while, and then it quit. Drawers opened and shut. Then the shower started to run again.

After another hour, the door to the room opened and closed, and Roxie ran to Nicole's door to see Eli and Rhys walk by. "They're wearing the same clothes as before. Do you want me to stay here and listen to learn when William gets up?"

"Yeah, sure." Nicole called Blake on her cell phone. "The brothers are going to the elevator. They're probably headed for the restaurant. Rhys finally called his brother Eli by name. William's in bed with a hangover. I'll meet you for a cup of hot chocolate if you're available."

"I sure am. And that's great news on the confirmation concerning Eli. See you soon."

"They're wearing the same ski clothes," Roxie told her.

Nicole pulled on a new ski jacket.

"You sure have a lot of different outfits," Roxie said.

"When I'm home, I ski a lot at Breckenridge on my time off, so I have some changes of clothes. On this mission, I hoped I would look different while I'm on the slope. All bundled up in different colors that hopefully would make me blend in and not stand out as someone who would always seem to be in the same place day after day."

"You do look different, and that's a great idea. Oh, and about tonight, I'm not missing the wolf run this time like I did last night."

"Good. We all missed you on the run. Thanks so much for all your help with this. I'll see you later." Nicole left the room and found Blake downstairs, holding on to two cups of hot cocoa, waiting eagerly for her to arrive.

Blake gave her a big smile and handed her one of the hot cups. "They're just getting breakfast in the restaurant. I wish we could catch up to them when they get rid of their trash."

"I'm thinking they must do it in the middle of the night when I'm asleep. I can't imagine not catching them otherwise," Nicole said. "I'm a light sleeper, but I still don't hear them opening and shutting the door to their room in the middle of the night. We need to see if we can catch them on the videos leaving the room in the middle of the night."

"Yeah, that sounds like a good plan," Blake said.

Then they took seats by the fire. Rosco curled up at their feet.

"This is the hard part of the job. All the waiting and observing and not getting very far with anything."

"I'm certainly not complaining. You have added some real spice to our lives."

"Thanks. I've been having fun with you and your family too."

They were enjoying their cocoa and watching the brothers getting their lunch takeout when Nicole got a call from Landon. "It's your brother," she told Blake and answered her phone. "Yes, Landon?"

"We've got a problem."

"What's wrong?" She knew from the darkness of Landon's voice, it had to be trouble.

"Do you know a Clay Strand?"

"Yeah. He's the private investigator who went missing. What's happened?" She envisioned the worst-case scenario: Clay's body had been discovered somewhere at the lodge. Why else would Landon know about the man?

"He's here, and he's been asking for you," Landon said.

"What?" Nicole was so surprised. She supposed she should have been grateful that he was alive and well.

"I told him I couldn't give out guest names. He said the insurance company said you were here, and he had to stay here. I told him the lodge was booked. We don't have any available rooms. He repeated that he'd stay with you."

"Like hell he will." Though Nicole thought about how she and Larry had been rooming together. "What's his excuse for vanishing?" She thought if he'd been injured by Rhys or his partners in crime, she'd view the situation differently. Though she really didn't want to work with the guy now. She loved working with the Wolff siblings.

"I didn't ask. I didn't let on we knew you. I was waiting to see how you wanted to handle this. Have you met him before?"

"No."

"He's a gray wolf."

"What? Oh, that's just great." No way would she room with the wolf. Not that he would come on to her, but she still didn't like staying with a male wolf—other than Blake.

"Yeah, and he's alpha."

"He sounds like an ass."

Landon chuckled. "I had the same thought. He's in the restaurant getting something to eat."

Blake was waiting for her to tell him what was wrong.

"I'm calling the insurance rep that hired me for the job. Hopefully, I can get this straightened out with them."

"Okay, good. I can tell you right now, the guy grates on people."

"Thanks. I know what he looks like, but I doubt the insurance company would have sent him a picture of me." Then she let out her breath in exasperation. "He knows my name. He's a PI. He can find out everything about me that he wants."

"Except that you're a wolf."

"Right. Thanks, Landon. I'll let you know what I learn."

"We all back you on this, and I don't mean just our family but the whole pack of Silver Town."

She kept forgetting about that part. She smiled. "Thanks."

When she and Landon ended the call, Nicole took Blake's hand. "Come on up to my room."

"I would take that as a good thing, but I understand we have trouble."

She sighed. "Yeah. The PI who vanished is a wolf, and he just arrived at the lodge, stating he's staying with me in my room."

"No way in hell."

She smiled at Blake as they took the stairs. "He's a wolf."

"Really, no way in hell." Blake smiled back at her. He looked like he was trying to make it sound like he was joking, not trying to tell her what to do, but she was sure he wasn't.

"I agree. I need to know why he vanished. I had agreed with the insurance company to work with Larry and stay with him in the same room because we thought Rhys and William were dangerous. Now that I know they have a gun, they still could be. And now there are three of them."

"You have all four of us to watch your back, and a whole pack besides."

"Right, and I don't need Clay, but if he's anything like me, he will want to finish the job since he was hired to do it first."

"Which is why he's here."

Nicole reached for her room key, but Roxie opened the door before she could, and Nicole and Blake entered the room and shut the door.

"Landon called and told me the missing PI just turned up and is a total-pain-in-the-ass gray wolf. And the guy says he's staying in your room, but it's not happening," Roxie said.

Nicole smiled. Roxie was being as territorial as Blake.

"You're right about Clay. He's not staying with me. I need to talk to the guy who hired him though. He should have let me know Clay was coming here." Nicole got on her phone while Blake sat at the table in the room and Roxie continued to listen at the wall. "Hey, Taggart, it's Nicole. Clay is here making a nuisance of himself." She put the call on speakerphone.

"I hired him first, and you need a PI partner on this job. I know you said you didn't, but Clay's still contracted to do the job, now that we know he's alive."

"How come he disappeared and didn't let us know he was fine?"

"He was working on this case."

Bull! She wondered if Clay had another, more lucrative case he was working on. "Okay, listen, I've got a team of people on this, and you don't have to pay for their services. He's going to cause trouble for me and not help me with the case. He's extremely abrasive, and from everything I've learned about him, he doesn't work with partners."

"He will on this one. He's got a proven track record. I want him staying with you at the lodge, just like we'd arranged for Larry to stay there with you for safety sake."

"*I* have a proven track record."

"You do. Which is why I also hired you when we couldn't get in touch with Clay any longer. Either do it, or you can give up the assignment. I'll pay you for your time on the job. He can take your room."

Man, did she wish Blake had a PI license so she could have had Taggart hire him! Then Clay could just waltz out of here and get some other assignment.

Blake wrote on a complimentary lodge notepad on the table and handed it to Nicole.

The room is yours. You're vacationing here then. It's free for you to stay at.

Nicole smiled at him. "Okay, look, Taggart, I'm not working with Clay. I suspect he had another case he was working on that paid more than this one, and that's why he did his disappearing act. He was being totally unprofessional not to let anyone know what was going on with him. In any case, I'll stay here on my own penny, so you can't force me to share a room with Clay. The lodge is booked, so he can camp out in his car for all I care."

Taggart chuckled, sounding darkly amused. "If I pay you for the work you've done up until this point, you will turn over all you've learned about the cousins."

Nicole was disappointed she couldn't continue working on the case for the insurance company, but she wasn't giving up her job. "Of course." Anything that pertained to actually proving Rhys was Oscar Kovac. But everything else she learned, like about Eli? Not happening. She might not be paid for the job, but she planned to still prove Rhys was Oscar and put his butt in jail once and for all.

"Have you even talked to Clay?" Taggart asked.

"Not yet. I will. And I'll ask him where the hell he was when he was supposed to be working on this case for you."

"Talk to him first before you give up the case. Maybe you'll change your mind."

Not happening. Unless the guy turned out to be way less aggressive than he sounded right now. "I'll let you know."

Taggart gave her Clay's phone number. Then they ended the call.

"Taggart sounds like a real jerk too," Roxie said, "but you're not really giving up the case, are you?" She sounded worried.

"No way. We have the perfect setup here. If Clay learns the truth before I do, more power to him, but I'm still going to try to nail Rhys's butt." Nicole wouldn't give up on the case, knowing how much it meant to Roxie too.

Roxie gave her a hug. "We'll get Rhys this time. I know we will."

"We will. They'll slip up eventually. These people always do," Nicole reassured her.

"Do you want to talk to Clay on the phone or in person?" Blake asked.

"In person. I don't want him to think I can't speak with him face-to-face." Nicole looked at the video feed for the restaurant. "That's him. The bearded redhead eating a steak. Let's try to meet up with him down there."

Blake looked pleased she wanted him to go with her. Roxie was smiling. She motioned to the wall. "Do you want me to continue to monitor William? He's showering now in his room."

"Yes, and thanks."

"I'm glad you're still doing the job. You've worked too long on it not to finish it," Blake said as they left the room.

Nicole told him about Eli and how she suspected Arthur abused him, maybe because he learned Eli wasn't his son.

"That's really rotten. But I'm glad the boy didn't drown."

"I am, too, though if he's been in on all this, he may serve some prison time."

"I hope the kid gets a break."

"I do too," Nicole said.

Blake slipped his arm around her waist, and they headed for the restaurant.

Roxie called her and said, "I see you on the security monitor. William is leaving his room, probably to get something to eat. Unless he's too hungover. Clay is still eating at the table."

"Thanks, Roxie. We'll let you know how it goes."

"Sure thing."

Nicole slipped her phone in her pocket, and she and Blake went straight to the table where Clay was sitting. He looked up from his meal and smiled at her but frowned at Blake. "You must be related to the guy at the registration desk who said he couldn't tell me where Nicole was. You look just like him." He turned his attention to Nicole. "Well, so you're a wolf too. That's a surprise."

"Yeah, and we've got this covered. You can tell Taggart you're leaving the job to me." Nicole raised a brow at him. "After all the work I've done on it because you were too busy with other obligations."

CHAPTER 10

His expression amused, Clay motioned for Nicole and Blake to take seats at his table. They did, and Blake asked the server to get them a couple of coffees. "So who's 'we'? Larry isn't on the job any longer, Taggart told me," Clay said.

"No. I've got friends here who are watching my back."

Clay sat back in his chair and turned his attention to Blake. "You? Do you have any investigative training?"

"Enough."

"He's deputized, in case anyone needs to be taken into custody," Nicole said. "So is Landon, his brother, the man you talked to at the registration desk. They own the lodge. *And* the restaurant."

Clay's green eyes widened. Maybe he was finally getting the gist of the matter. Whether Clay got a room or not was up to them. And being wolves like Clay, they made the rules.

He folded his arms as the server brought Nicole and Blake's mugs of coffee. Both of them added cream and sugar to their drinks.

"Did you talk to Taggart about this? Our working together as investigators?" Clay asked.

Nicole saw William enter the restaurant, and she lowered her voice, "That's William, Rhys's cousin. They come in here to get takeout but don't dump their trash. I haven't figured out when they're getting rid of it or where." She figured she'd let Clay know that much. She didn't want him giving them away by talking about being PIs and having the cousin overhear them, though as noisy as the restaurant was and as far away as he was sitting, she figured they were good.

Clay eyed William for a moment, then said, "Okay, so I'll learn where they're taking it. Do you have security videos we can look at?"

"I do."

Clay frowned. "I get the impression you mean that you can look at them but I won't have any access to them. What's this all about?"

"Look, I'm working with the Wolff family. You…vanished, and I was assigned to do this job."

"With Larry. I know. He went home after being sick, and you've got me now."

"I don't have you." As if Clay would really work *with* her. "I've got the Wolff family watching my back. Thank you very much. You know, everyone thought the cousins did you in. You could have let someone know you were fine."

"That's how I work. You don't have to like it."

She smiled evilly. "You got a higher-paying job after you received this work. I get it. I've had that come up, but you know what, unless I can't get any leads on a case I'm currently working on, I decline the job and let someone else handle the new case. Even if the pay is more lucrative."

"I can work on more than one case at a time."

"Sometimes I can too. But this case is special. Besides, it wasn't so much that you were working on another case but that you didn't let anyone know what had happened to you. Taggart thought the cousins had gotten rid of you and that they were dangerous. That's why *two* of us were hired to learn the truth about these guys. Since I know you're alive and well, I don't need you."

"It was my case *first*. I'm not giving it up."

Nicole shrugged. "Fine. It's your case. Good luck."

"You haven't told me everything you've learned on the case since you started working it. Forget it. I'll figure it out and be way ahead of you." Clay sounded as conceited as Nicole thought he would be.

"You do that." Nicole rose from the table.

Blake joined her.

"Wait." Clay took a deep breath and let it out. "Listen, I need a room."

"Landon told you we are all booked," Blake said.

"Right. I still need a room."

"Check with the bed-and-breakfast in town or the Silver Town Inn," Blake said.

Nicole hoped they didn't have any vacancies either.

"Who owns the house next door? Maybe I could rent out a room there. I need to be close by," Clay said.

Blake smiled. "The Wolff family."

Clay frowned. "I'm not giving up this job."

"You shouldn't have disappeared, and they wouldn't have called me to work on the case instead," Nicole said.

"Taggart won't go along with this. Either we work together, or you're off the case," Clay said.

Nicole smiled. "That's just what I told him." She turned to Blake. "Do you want to go skiing?"

"Yeah, let's get some fresh air. Oh, and by the way, don't do anything illegal in our lodge, Clay. Nicole's right when she said my brother and I are sworn in as deputy sheriffs. If you didn't know it, the town is wolf-run, and we belong to the pack. So don't give Nicole or us any trouble."

Clay's jaw dropped.

Nicole smiled again, then took Blake's hand and led him out of the restaurant and into the lobby. William had already left the restaurant and was eating his takeout outside.

Blake and Nicole went to the office to pick up their skis. Landon joined them. "So what's the deal with this wolf?"

"I'm not working with him. I told Taggart that already. Though I guess I need to update him to tell him for sure that I'm not going to. If Clay nails Rhys first, that's fine. As long as Rhys gets caught for defrauding the insurance company, that's all that really matters." She got on her phone while Blake got on his.

Blake explained to Darien about the situation with Clay and Nicole. "Can you ensure he doesn't get a room at the bed-and-breakfast or Silver Town Inn?" Blake smiled at Nicole. "Thanks, we sure appreciate it. That's all we need, but if we see him breaking into the suspects' room or doing anything illegal, we're arresting him and letting you deal with him." Blake nodded. "Good show. Thanks, talk later."

Nicole loved Blake for being on her side. "Thanks."

"That's what wolf boyfriends are for." Blake put on his ski boots while she was still trying to get ahold of Taggart. Then Blake put her ski boots on.

Landon was looking over the security monitors. "Clay is on his phone, looking frustrated, running his free hand through his hair, frowning."

"Good." Nicole finally reached Taggart on the phone. "Okay, so I talked to Clay in person, and he's as bigheaded as I figured he'd be. I'm not working with him. He's all yours."

Taggart didn't say anything right away.

She really did want the money for resolving the case. She felt real satisfaction settling a case one way or another, and she'd given up her arson mission just to take this one on. So she really didn't want to give up this one. Not when she already had a personal connection to Rhys. And she felt she owed it to Roxie. Especially since most of the family had been involved in helping her with the case all this time.

"All right. There's nothing in our policies concerning investigations that says the two of you have to work together. If you want to share notes, fine. If you don't, it's up to you. I checked with Clay's PI agency, and his secretary told me he had been on another case. I had to threaten to remove him from this case if I didn't learn the truth. Since you've been diligently working on the case all this time, it's yours. If he wants to try to get the evidence we need and he gets it before you, more power to him. But you're both working on your own."

"Thank you."

"Don't thank me. If you worked together, you might get somewhere with this faster. I don't want to hear that either of you impeded the other in learning what you can about this."

Like not allowing Clay to spend the night here on the mountain at the lodge or in Silver Town?

"So get cracking on it and get some results."

"I'm working on it, Taggart. Believe me, I want to get the evidence soonest so I can get on to other business."

"Good. Let me know if you have any other developments."

"Rhys's dead younger brother is alive," Nicole said.

"What?"

"He's staying with Rhys and their cousin. I learned there was a third man in the room, and Rhys called him his brother. So I began researching to see if the brother was another or just something he called him, as in friend."

"Okay, keep up the good work. Let me know if you need anything else."

"Will do. And thanks." Smiling, she ended the call.

Landon and Blake were waiting for her to give them the news.

"It's still my case. Clay can work on it too, but we can work separately."

"And he's not staying in your room." Blake sounded adamant.

"That's a given. We're going to look for these guys on the slopes," Nicole told Landon.

"I'm checking the security monitors for the middle of the night when the cousins might have taken out the trash," Landon said.

"Oh, good, thanks," Nicole said.

She and Blake headed outside to ski and were soon riding a chairlift. They saw the brothers skiing down the intermediate slope together and William waiting at the bottom. Nicole figured he'd want Rhys to ski with him instead, not with his younger brother. She felt sorry for the younger brother for all that he'd been through.

"Do you want me to stay the night in your room?" Blake asked.

"Clay doesn't know what my room number is."

"How long do you think it will take him to learn where the brothers and their cousin are staying? And how much longer will it take him to learn where you're staying?"

Nicole smiled. "You know you could just say you want to stay with me."

"I want to stay with you in the worst way, but this sounded like a really great excuse—a gray wolf who could give you grief."

"I wanted you to stay with me in the room this morning, but Roxie was there."

Blake chuckled.

"She's having so much fun listening in on these guys, I couldn't tell her I needed some private time with you. And don't you go telling her that either."

"I won't." Blake put his arm around Nicole and warmed her up.

"You better not."

"Not if I can stay the night. Did you want to have dinner with the family tonight, go for a wolf run, and then we'll return to the lodge?"

"Yeah, that sounds like a good plan. What about taking Rosco for a walk?" They reached the top of the lift, skied off, then headed for the expert slope.

"Someone else will walk him or bring him to the lodge early and we can walk him."

"Okay, that sounds good. I'd miss our chilly morning walk otherwise."

Blake stopped at the top edge of the expert run. "I'm glad Clay arrived."

She laughed. "So you could be with me for the night."

"Works for me."

"The truth is, it works for me too. Are you ready?"

They looked down the slope and witnessed someone crash and burn.

"From the angle of his leg and the way he's not getting up right away, that does not look good," Nicole said.

"No, I'm alerting the guys in case he needs to be brought down on a sled."

Nicole skied off down the mogul-strewn slope, noticing

the guy was all alone. No one seemed to be waiting for him at the bottom of the run, and since he hadn't been in front of them earlier, she suspected he'd cut across the path through the trees that allowed travel from the intermediate run to the expert, or vice versa if someone thought the expert was too difficult.

She could hear Blake behind her, keeping enough distance from her in case she took a spill so he wouldn't collide with her. And then she finally reached the skier. He was groaning, holding his leg, and she was afraid he'd broken it.

Blake reached the skier right after her.

"We're getting medical assistance," Blake told him, getting on his phone again and calling the injury in.

The guy looked young, and Nicole asked him how old he was.

"Fifteen."

"Isn't there someone skiing with you?" Nicole asked.

"My dad, but he got tired."

Nicole held his hand. "Okay, we need to let your dad know you're injured. What's your name?"

"Tommy Jacobs. My dad is Wendell."

"Okay, Tommy, just hang in there. Help's coming. Were you staying at the lodge?" Nicole asked.

"Yeah."

Nicole got on the phone to Landon. "We're with an injured skier who he says his dad is Wendell Jacobs. Can you see if you can locate him? He returned to the lodge."

Tommy patted his ski jacket pocket. "Phone."

Blake reached into his pocket and pulled out the teen's phone.

"His number is listed under contacts as Dad," Tommy said.

Emergency personnel were already riding up on snowmobiles, bringing a sled.

Blake called the dad. "Sir, this is Blake Wolff, part owner of the Timberline Ski Lodge. I was skiing when I witnessed your son take a bad spill on the expert slope. Uh, yeah. Looks like a broken leg. Emergency personnel are on their way. They'll have him down to the infirmary to evacuate him to the hospital in a few minutes. Here's your son."

"Sorry, Dad. I thought I could cut across and just get the tail end of the expert run, but you were right. It's too much." The boy chuckled. "Yeah, see you."

Blake took his phone from him and tucked it in his pocket.

Medics arrived and began to splint the teen's leg.

"What did Dad say to you?" Tommy asked Blake.

"He's taking a video of you for your mom and sister and girlfriend." Blake smiled at him.

Nicole appreciated Blake's humor, setting the teen at ease while the emergency staff worked on him.

The boy groaned. "My sister will show it off to everyone at school."

"You've got a camera that took a video of the spill. That will be a winner on YouTube, I bet," Blake said.

The kid laughed and groaned again. "Yeah. Now *that* will be worth showing off."

The rescue team members were smiling. "We're taking you down now, all right, bud?" one of the men asked.

"Yeah, sure. Thanks."

Then the rescue team took the boy down the slope, and Nicole asked Blake, "How did the dad sound?"

"He laughed. I suspect the boy got his recklessness from the dad."

Nicole smiled, and they headed the rest of the way down the slope.

"You might have a room cancellation at the lodge," Nicole said to Blake as they watched the boy being taken to the first-aid hut, thinking that maybe they should just let Clay have a room. She normally thought of herself as a nice person, and she was feeling mean about not allowing him a room to stay there to do his investigation, even if the guy was being a jerk.

"True. The boy's dad will probably pack up and drive his son home once they take care of his leg at the bigger hospital in Green Valley. Is this about having the room available for Clay?"

"Yeah. I was thinking about it and figured he can do his own research, and maybe he will find the evidence we need to solve the case. What would it hurt? If Larry had, I would have been happy. What difference does it make if Clay solves the case instead? I just want to make sure Rhys doesn't get away with the fraud, and we need to expose him for what he is."

"It's up to you whether you want to allow the wolf to stay at the lodge and work on his own."

"I still think he's an ass for worrying all of us when he went missing to do another job, but we need to get these guys, so if he gets the evidence before we do, mission accomplished, and we'll just have some fun."

"All right. If you're sure—"

"Yeah, I am."

Blake got on his phone and made a call. "Hey, Landon, the call I made to you a few minutes ago? It looks like the boy broke a leg on the slope. I'm sure his dad will be taking him home, and we could have a vacancy soon. If so, Nicole said Clay could have the room." Blake glanced at Nicole and rubbed her back. "Yeah, she's sure. Okay, I'll tell her." He ended the call. "He's got a room for him already. The couple who were here during the snowstorm got a rental car and are leaving, but Landon was waiting for us to give him the okay."

"All right, that works."

"Clay asked what room the cousins were staying in. He's got to realize we're not here to help him with the investigation. Landon told him he couldn't give out guests' room numbers. Standard privacy policy. Even if he is a wolf and investigating these guys."

"Good thing that you were all right with giving me the room number and the room next to their place."

"You bet. You're my girlfriend. Clay asked my brother if *you* knew the cousins' room number."

Nicole raised a brow.

Blake smiled. "He told him you were a top-notch investigator, and you probably knew just about everything there was to know about the cousins."

"I sure lucked out when I met you all."

"The kiss you gave me to seal the bargain didn't hurt at all. He better not bug you."

"I'm sure he'll think he's too good at the job to ask me anything." At least that was what Nicole believed.

CHAPTER 11

BLAKE SUSPECTED CLAY WAS GOING TO BE TROUBLE NO matter what they did. Give him a room. Don't give him a room. But Blake liked that Nicole was willing to allow the guy the opportunity to remain there and do his investigation. Hopefully, Clay would stay out of Nicole's way. Blake knew Nicole would love to complete the task, and he and his brother and sisters would do anything they could to aid her in finishing it. He thought the world of her for being good-natured enough to be okay with Clay solving the case so she could spend more time with Blake.

Besides, staying with her while the guy was here was definitely a good thing. At least he hoped so. He remembered going on a trip with his siblings to Grand Cayman Island once, and Roxie talking to a middle-age couple about why they were there. Was it a honeymoon? Anniversary?

She learned the couple had dumped their spouses and were doing a trial vacation in paradise. They were each paying their own way, but this was like a honeymoon before the marriage, if it went that far. Blake wasn't surprised Roxie would talk to the woman. She was always so interested in what was going on around her, and she thought the couple looked so happy. Blake and his brother and sisters were out on the beach walking one afternoon as a family when Roxie saw the woman by herself, not with the dream guy, and asked her how it was going.

"He hogs the bathroom, stinks it all up, won't put the

toilet seat down after he uses the toilet, leaves toothpaste all over the sink. He's a total grouch until he's had his fourth cup of coffee. and sometimes even after he's had that. I can see why his wife wasn't really happy with him. There are two sides to the story. I'm seeing the wife's side now."

Blake and his siblings had laughed about it later. From the sound of it, even a trip to paradise wouldn't fix the troubles those two were bound to have.

But he hoped sharing close quarters with Nicole wouldn't prove to be a disaster. Then again, if things didn't work out between them, it was better to know sooner than later.

"You look like you could use a hot cocoa," Blake said to Nicole.

"I could, thanks." They took seats on the deck and ordered hot cocoa and saw Clay coming. "Oh, brother."

Blake smiled at her.

"Hey, thanks, Nicole, Blake. I know you gave Landon the go-ahead to allow me to have a room. Believe me, I really appreciate it, and I'll share anything I find on these guys with Nicole."

"Thanks," Nicole said, but Blake swore she didn't trust him.

Probably because of the issue with Clay doing his disappearing act. He seemed like an opportunistic wolf. Blake didn't blame her.

Then Blake saw Jake Silver's wife, Alicia, coming to see them, holding her five-year-old daughter's hand. Both were dressed in blue jeans and matching blue sweaters featuring a snowman family: momma, daddy, and baby. Alicia's long hair was dark-chocolate brown and curly. Her daughter's hair was the same color, but little blue bows tied up her hair in long pigtails. She reminded Blake of his sisters at that age.

"That's Jake Silver's wife, a former bounty hunter, and more newly turned. Jake's our subleader, Darien's next older brother," Blake told Nicole. When Alicia and her daughter joined them, he said, "Alicia, Carly, this is Nicole Grayson, our guest at the lodge for a week. Hopefully for more." He smiled down at her.

Nicole was smiling back. That sure gave him hope that she might consider sticking around longer.

"Hi, Nicole." Alicia shook her hand. "I'm Alicia Silver, and this is my daughter, Carly. I know you are busy with important work of your own, and we would love for you to stick around longer too. Carly has something to ask of you."

"Daddy said the sheriff is too busy taking care of car accidents 'cuz of the snow. My cat went missing, and he can't come up here to look for her. Uncle CJ can't either. He's a deputy sheriff. But Daddy said you look for missing things and you'd find her." Carly's eyes were brimming with tears.

Nicole crouched down in front of Carly, took her hands in hers, and looked her in the eye. "I do, Carly, and I sure will help you find her. What's your cat's name?"

Blake thought the world of how Nicole was handling this.

"Mittens, 'cuz she has all white paws, but she's black, caramel, and white." Carly showed Nicole a picture of the cat wearing a blue doll's dress.

Nicole smiled. "She's cute."

Carly frowned. "But she's missing."

Alicia said to her daughter, "Show her Mittens's dress."

Carly pulled the little blue dress the cat had been wearing

in the photo out of her small purse and handed it to Nicole so she could pick up her scent.

"When was the last time you saw her?" Nicole smelled the dress, then handed it back to Carly, and she tucked it in her purse.

"I'll see you around," Clay said with a smirk. Then he left them alone. He went out to the parking lot to a dark-blue pickup truck.

Looking cross, Carly folded her arms, her dark-brown eyes narrowed. "Mittens was sleeping with Rosco. They are best friends. But a little kid ran at Mittens and Rosco, and then Mittens got scared and ran away. We looked all over for her."

Through the windows, they could see Clay pull out a couple of bags, and then he walked through the parking lot to the lodge.

Blake gave the wolf a caustic look.

"She went missing a couple of hours ago, and we've looked everywhere," Alicia confirmed, rubbing her daughter's back in a comforting way. "We've usually just let Rosco and Mittens sleep together at the Wolffs' house when we've been over to have dinner. And Rosco does the same thing with Mittens at our house when we've had the brothers over for a meal. The sisters weren't here yet. This was the first time we tried letting Rosco and Mittens be together at the lodge. Jake is up here taking photos for the collection he showcases at art galleries. He thought it might help to promote the lodge after all the Wolff family has done in showcasing his photography. We couldn't have been more thrilled."

"But Mittens is missing," Carly said as if the adults forgot that part. She handed Nicole a five-dollar bill. "That's my birthday money to pay for finding Mittens. Daddy said you have to get paid to do a search job."

"Okay," Nicole said, returning the five-dollar bill. "I don't charge for locating a cat that's friends with Rosco. I'm friends with Rosco, too, so friends help friends. Do you want to take my hand, and we'll see if we can find her together?"

"We looked all over," Carly said plaintively.

"Right. But this is the kind of work I do all the time."

"Okay." Carly didn't sound as though she trusted Nicole to help find Mittens if Carly couldn't while she looked for the cat with her mom.

Blake sure hoped she could locate the cat. He knew Carly and her two brothers would be heartbroken if she didn't.

Nicole took Carly's hand, and Blake dumped their empty cocoa cups and followed behind Nicole and Alicia's daughter, Alicia walking beside him.

"Cats like to hide when they get scared. Where does Mittens like to hide when she gets scared at home?" Nicole asked.

"Under the bed," Carly said. "Or sometimes in the closet. But she hides under the couch too. When she's not hiding, she likes to get inside a laundry basket filled with clothes. Momma said she can't when the clothes are clean 'cuz she sheds. She loves boxes too. And once I found her in a Christmas bag. She loves to bat Christmas ornaments off the tree, and she curls up in it to sleep."

"She sounds like a fun cat. Take me to where she was when she ran off."

Carly led her to where Rosco was, and he wagged his tail at them.

"Would Rosco be able to find Mittens?" Nicole asked Blake.

Carly leaned over and gave Rosco a big hug.

"Uh, I'm not sure. He can find his dog toys, and we used to have him find us when he was younger, playing hide-and-seek with him. He does rescues of avalanche victims, but I'm not sure if he would know how to search for the cat," Blake said.

"Come on, Rosco, you're going to help us look for Mittens," Nicole said, looking down at him. "This will be your first cat rescue mission. Where did Mittens go?" Rosco wagged his tail even harder. She chuckled.

Smiling, Blake shook his head, but he thought that wasn't a good sign that Rosco would be of any help.

"Can you let him smell Mittens's dress?" she asked Carly.

Carly pulled out the doll's dress and showed it to Rosco. He smelled it.

"Find Mittens," Nicole said.

But Rosco just continued to stand there, wagging his tail as if they were going to take him on a walk.

Nicole and the others followed the cat's scent, knowing that it wouldn't have left one at any other time here, so it should be easy to follow. Which made Blake wonder why Alicia and her daughter hadn't located Mittens already. He worried the cat had gone outside, with so many people coming and going from the lodge. The doors were opening and closing all the time.

He saw Clay coming in with his bags and heading for the elevator. He looked just as amused as before to see Nicole offering to search for a missing cat. The guy didn't have an ounce of decency in him.

Landon smiled at Blake, and he assumed his brother had

told Alicia and her daughter where Nicole and Blake were so they could request their assistance.

The more they searched for Mittens, the more Blake realized the cat had gone everywhere! One way, then another, probably attempting to avoid guests.

"Where's Mittens?" Carly asked Rosco. He wagged his tail and brushed her hand with his nose. She petted his head. "I don't think he knows."

The door to the stairs was closed, unless the cat had slipped up them when guests opened the door. They went in that direction, but they didn't smell Mittens's scent near the stairs. Luckily, their sense of smell really helped in cases like this.

"She went in the direction of the elevator," Nicole said. "It doesn't mean she went up in it, just that she went to it." But when she pushed the button for the elevator and it returned to the first floor, she smelled that the cat had been inside it. "Okay, she took the elevator somewhere." The lodge had three floors, so they took it up to the second floor but found no scent of the cat there. They took the elevator to the third floor and that was where she'd gone.

"She hadn't gone to the elevator when we came looking for you to help us," Alicia said.

"No," Carly said, shaking her head.

"She must have come out of her hiding place and hurried into the elevator afterward," Nicole said.

They all got out on the third floor where Nicole's room had been. Then they turned left and began to follow the scent. That was when they saw a maid's cleaning cart at a room, the door propped open, and Blake wondered if the cat had slipped into the room and was hiding under a bed.

"She better not be under the bed in there," Carly said.

But the cat's scent disappeared before they reached the cart. Maybe she had slipped into the room before that. The cat's scent just stopped at the room.

"I've got a master key," Blake said and knocked on the door first. "Housekeeping," he called out.

No one answered, and he opened the door. "Housekeeping!" he said, just so no one would be alarmed to see him in their room if they hadn't heard him at the door. The room was all straightened up already, but the cat hadn't been in the room.

Nicole eyed the cart, and Rosco headed for it. "Is Mittens in the cart, Rosco?"

He ambled toward the cart and poked his nose at the dirty towels and wagged his tail vigorously and woofed.

"Mittens?" Carly said.

Nicole and Carly, standing on her tippy-toes, peered into the bag with the dirty linens.

"Well, hello, Mittens," Nicole said. "You've worried everyone. What did you find?" She slipped her arms into the dirty linens and pulled out the pretty calico cat. She had her claws dug into a paper cup and teeth marks on the rim. "Uh, Blake," Nicole said, sounding excited and worried at the same time, "can you reach in my jacket pocket and get the plastic evidence bag from there?"

"You're not going to put Mittens in the bag, are you?" Carly asked, frowning.

"No, just the cup."

Blake found the bag and carefully slipped it around the coffee cup. Alicia gently pulled Mittens's claws from the cup. But he smelled that Eli had been using the cup. Where in the world had the cat picked it up?

Nicole handed Mittens to Carly, who hugged her to pieces. Rosco was standing next to her, his tail wagging like crazy.

"Thank you," Alicia said with heartfelt gratitude.

"You're so welcome. I know how difficult it is to lose a beloved pet." Nicole gave Carly and Mittens a hug. "Now you stay with Carly and don't go wandering off again, Mittens."

"She's staying home from now on," Alicia said.

"Unless we go to Rosco's house." Carly sounded worried that the cat would be forever locked up at home.

"Yes, where no other little kids will scare her off. The lodge is way too big. It's too easy to lose her." Alicia eyed the cup. "That's something important, I gather?"

"Possibly. I just wish I knew where Mittens picked it up. She might have helped solved part of our case for us."

"Does that mean she gets paid for it?" Carly asked.

Blake and the women laughed.

Alicia ran her hand over her daughter's hair. "No. It means that's payment for Nicole for being so kind to look for our cat for us. Let's go. Your daddy will be up here forever taking pictures, but we need to get home to your brothers. The lady who's watching them didn't expect us to lose our cat and be up here for so long."

"Okay, thank you." Carly gave Nicole a hug.

"She's a good cat, but with all the strange people around, it's easy for her to get scared. She's so pretty. Take good care of her," Nicole said.

"I will."

"Thank you," Alicia said again, and then they all took the elevator to the first floor.

"I need to get this to the lab to see if we can get any DNA off it other than Mittens's," Nicole said to Blake.

Alicia chuckled and said goodbye, then took her daughter outside to their vehicle.

"I can ask our sheriff to handle it. Peter and our deputies—including CJ Silver, who is Jake's cousin—are eager to help in any way they can."

"Thanks."

After leaving Rosco off at the fireplace, Blake and Nicole went to the privacy of their office. Blake got ahold of Peter and told him about the cup. "There will be domestic cat saliva and hairs on the cup, but we're looking for the DNA of the man who was drinking from it. He's one of the three people Nicole is investigating."

"Three? I thought there were only two. The cousins."

"We believe we also have the younger brother who supposedly drowned."

"Whoa, two dead brothers, both alive? That's a record. Okay, I'll send CJ to pick it up, and we'll get it processed for you as soon as we can. Landon said you also had fingerprints from the gun. He can get those too."

"Thanks, Peter."

Nicole was smiling, taking a seat on one of the chairs.

"We don't know if we can get any evidence off it yet or not." Blake didn't want her feeling bad if this didn't pan out.

"I know." But Nicole's smile didn't falter.

"What?"

She laughed. "Well, if it does, it's a good one on Clay. He was smirking about me helping Carly."

Blake smiled. "I like your way of thinking."

"I can inform the insurance company that paid out on

Eli's life insurance policy that he appears to be very much alive, even though the policyholder is dead. I'll also let Taggart know about it, as it can show evidence that Oscar/Rhys followed in his mother's footsteps of obtaining life insurance proceeds for a pretend drowning victim."

"Sounds good to me. It's about lunchtime. Did you want to grab a bite as soon as CJ picks up the evidence?"

"I do. I sure wish I knew where the cat picked up the coffee cup."

"I was wishing the same thing. Though it might have been a fluke. Just a lapse of good judgment on Eli's part. He dumped it or dropped it, and the cat got hold of it."

Landon came into the office. "Your loaner car is here, Nicole, from the Silver Town Auto Body Shop. You made a great impression on Carly, Alicia, and Jake. They're beholden to you for finding their cat. Especially Jake, because he said you would be able to, and he didn't want to explain to his daughter that it could be hard finding lost pets."

"We got lucky." Nicole smiled, holding up the bagged coffee cup.

"That's not Rhys's, is it?" Landon sounded hopeful.

"Eli's. But if our luck holds up, we'll have some DNA and more will be on file with a database, and we can confirm he's one and the same. Even though Rhys called him Eli, I'd still love to have some physical proof."

Landon eyed the cup in the bag. "It looks a bit chewed up."

"Mittens was using it as a chew toy. She probably liked the cream and sugar Eli had in his coffee."

CJ Silver knocked on the door.

Blake hurried to introduce CJ to Nicole. "She hopes we

can get some DNA off this pretty quick before these guys take off."

"I was already on my way up here for the gun fingerprints when Peter called and said you had a cup too." CJ took the bag and eyed the cup. "Mittens's claw and tooth marks, Peter said."

Nicole smiled. "Hopefully, the cat didn't mess up the DNA if Eli left any on the cup."

"We'll sure do our darnedest to learn the truth as soon as we can. Nice to meet you. I met my cousin Jake on the way in here, and he said you located Mittens for them. They're one happy family, believe me."

"I was just glad she hadn't gotten out of the lodge and we found her quickly."

"Well, they're grateful. We'll contact you as soon as we know anything, good or bad, about the evidence." CJ left the office with the cup and gun fingerprints tucked away in a bag.

Nicole went up front with Landon to fill out the paperwork on her loaner car and thanked the body-shop owner.

"Are you ready for lunch?"

"Yeah. Are you all right here without me?" Blake asked Landon.

"Yeah, I already ate. I think Kayla went home to eat lunch. I left a hamburger and chips with Roxie in your room," Landon told Nicole. "I hope you don't mind. She says Eli just went up to his room with his lunch takeout from the restaurant."

"Maybe he'll leave more evidence behind and I can snag it," Nicole said. "It's possible his brother has been making sure the trash is taken out, but once Eli was on his own, he got careless or figured there really wasn't any threat."

Blake agreed. "Which there might not have been if it hadn't been for Mittens." Then he escorted Nicole to lunch and saw the cousins sitting together waiting at a table for their lunch, drinking bottled water.

"How much do you want to bet they're getting take-out," Nicole said, sounding resigned. Then she saw Clay at another table watching the cousins. He smiled at Nicole as if he thought he'd found them first. "Wait until they get take-out and deflate his balloon." She sat with Blake at a booth that had a view of the deck so that when the men moved to that, they could watch them.

Clay would have to move to another spot to see them.

Blake and Nicole ordered mushroom-topped burgers and water. "I don't think I've ever been this obsessed with trash on a mission before. Though I often find myself digging through it to help solve a case, but usually, it's an easy deal. Not like this where I have to keep following the suspects around, waiting for them to ditch their trash. I was thinking the snow might have melted off the cars still sitting in the parking lot, and we could see if we can find DNA evidence in Rhys's car. Hair, trash, fingerprints, et cetera. But it would be tricky not getting caught. I'm not sure we could break into it without alerting them. Anyone from one of the rooms could see us down there trying to get into the vehicle, including Rhys and his companions."

"Yeah, it's too bad we couldn't tow it away. We could wait until there's an open spot between their vehicle and the hotel and park a tall truck there to block the view. We can just take a casual walk out there at night and see if there's anything in the car that we could use to obtain DNA evidence from."

"They could still see us peering into the windows if they're looking out and suspect the worst."

"Then we try to get a tall vehicle in there to block the view first." Blake texted his brother about it.

> **Landon:** A lot of the cars are still snow-covered. But the windows should be clear and the license plates should be visible. We need to locate the car. Wait, Kayla said she's on it. She's taking Rosco for a walk.
>
> **Blake:** Okay, thanks.

Blake told Nicole what Landon had said.

"Oh, good. By the way, I never would resort to getting into his car to obtain DNA samples if it wasn't for my concern that he's going to leave and get away with this."

"I understand." And Blake knew Kayla had wanted to help somehow, but she'd been busy creating marketing materials for the lodge. Though he'd seen her watching the security monitors a few times and pointing out where the men had gone. He loved his family.

They watched the cousins move to the deck with their takeout meals.

Nicole took another bite of her burger. "Clay didn't look happy that the cousins went outside to eat their lunches."

Blake smiled. "I knew he would be surprised. But even more so when he sees they're going to stuff their trash in their backpacks."

She chuckled. "I can't wait to see the look on his face. What does he think? I don't know what I'm doing?"

Blake shook his head. "He'd be an idiot to believe that.

I'm sure the insurance company wouldn't have hired you if they didn't know your track record."

They finished their hamburgers and saw the cousins stuff their trash in their backpacks, then head inside to use the restroom. Same old routine. They would go skiing after that.

"Bathroom break?" Blake asked.

"Yeah, sure." They used the one for the staff so they didn't have to run into the cousins.

Afterward, they left the lodge to go skiing and saw Clay watching the cousins head for the ski lift.

"You're not going skiing?" Nicole asked Clay.

"I have a job to do."

"Good luck." Nicole smiled at him.

Blake and she skied off to the lift. But then she got a text message and stopped to check it. Blake waited to see what it was.

"Kayla says she didn't see anything in the car. No trash. But we can still find hair and fingerprints probably," Nicole said.

"Okay, Landon's going to try to get a vehicle in the spot next to their car, once the car that's already there moves."

Blake and Nicole continued to the chairlift and stood in line. He wrapped his arm around her. He knew he shouldn't be thinking of being with her tonight, and he wasn't planning to sleep in the bed with her, though he'd love to, but still, the idea of having her in his arms tonight certainly appealed.

CHAPTER 12

Nicole was having so much fun skiing with Blake, deciding different runs they would take, as if they were really on vacation here and just enjoying themselves.

When they headed back to the lodge, Landon called them with good news. "The car sitting next to Rhys's car finally moved, and we borrowed one of the wolf member's vans to place in the empty parking space. We've looked from one of the second-floor rooms and third-floor rooms to see if the car is visible on the other side of the van, and it isn't."

"Terrific! So that means we'll be able to try to collect evidence from the car when they go to sleep tonight," Nicole said.

"Yeah, but just don't get caught. We have the tools for getting into the car without breaking the lock or window, since we've had to help a few people who have locked their keys in their cars while getting all their ski gear out. We'll have to have someone watching the security monitors so you can be alerted if anyone goes out into the parking lot. Most of the time, it's quiet all night long," Landon said. "There's no real nightlife except for the Silver Town Tavern, and that's for wolves only. If you go out to search the car after the Silver Town Tavern is closed and any guests have returned to the lodge and their beds, you shouldn't run into anyone in the parking lot."

"Okay. I'll have to come up with a plan. We can talk about it over dinner," Nicole said, thrilled.

"Sounds like a good idea. We're all ready to help you however you need us."

"Thanks, Landon."

Later that evening, after the cousins had retired to their room for the night, Blake and Nicole headed over to his house. The rest of the family was there already, cooking dinner. Roxie was glad to eat with them tonight. Kayla had fixed fried chicken. Roxie had made mashed potatoes and salads, and even Nicole got involved, making the gravy while the guys set the table and brought out glasses of water.

"White wine?" Blake asked.

"Yeah, sure." Nicole noticed everyone was waiting for her okay first, since she was still on a mission no matter the time of day or night. But a glass of wine wasn't going to affect her ability to do her job.

"I was watching that Clay guy on the security videos as much as I was observing the suspects." Roxie served up the salads. "Clay must not ski. He never once went out in the snow. He just went up to their room and stared at the door, then sat by the fire, watching for them."

"I wonder if he tried to take fingerprints off the door." Nicole brought over the bowl of mashed potatoes, and Landon set the gravy server on the table.

"It wouldn't matter." Kayla placed the platter of fried chicken on the table. "I watched them enter the room a number of times, but every time, they were wearing glove liners, so I doubt he'd find anything on the outside of the door. But I was making sure Clay didn't try to sneak into the room. I don't know if he realized there are three of them, not just two."

They all took their seats, Nicole sitting next to Blake as if they truly were courting, and everyone began serving up their food.

"Well, Clay is an expert investigator. He's supposed to be smart enough to figure that out on his own." Nicole ate a bite of her chicken drumstick.

"But he could blow it if he tries to get into the room and the younger brother is in there." Roxie spooned up some of her mashed potatoes and gravy.

Nicole blew out her breath. "I figured Clay would know right away. But if Eli isn't hanging out with his brother while Clay's watching, he might not realize they're all together. Then again, I've got a great team of superspies."

Blake and his sisters and brother laughed, raising their wineglasses to her. "To supersleuths," Blake said.

Nicole drank to the toast. "You all are the best." Then she got on her phone and called Clay. "Hey, it's Nicole. I just wanted to let you know there are three men rooming together. Not just Rhys and William." She put the call on speakerphone.

"I've only seen the two men together."

"The other man had been staying in the room. He might have had high-altitude sickness to begin with. In any event, just be careful. If he comes down and you're watching the cousins, he might see you and get the idea that you're on to them. And then they'll run."

"Hell, how long have you known that?"

"Not right away because he never left the room until yesterday." She wasn't about to tell Clay she'd gone inside the room and realized the guy was in the bathroom. "But I figured you would already know. Still, better to be safe than sorry."

"Thanks for the heads-up." Clay didn't sound grateful in the least, more sarcastic than anything.

"You're welcome. Good night."

"Night."

Nicole set her phone on the dining room table, glad she'd told Clay there were three men staying in the room. But if Clay wanted to figure out who the third man was, he'd have to do it on his own.

"This is sure the best fried chicken." Nicole picked up a wing off her plate.

"That's one of my favorite meals to make," Kayla said. "Everyone loves it no matter what time of year we have it."

"We'd have it a lot more often if she'd agree to it." Landon winked at his sister.

Kayla laughed. "You'd have it every day if you could."

"Okay, so how are we going to work the surveillance situation while you're trying to break into Rhys's car and gather evidence?" Landon asked.

"I thought Blake could watch from my lodge room and give me warning if he sees anyone leaving the building," Nicole said.

"You'll get more done if two of us are there, trying to gather evidence," Blake said.

She got the impression Blake wanted to be with her for more than just the evidence gathering. He wanted to protect her if things went haywire. She was glad he did.

"We can monitor the security videos at the house. Blake can go with you in case you need some assistance," Roxie said. "I can't even imagine how unnerving that could be—trying to break into someone's vehicle and gather the evidence without anyone catching you. I was a nervous wreck when you went into their room, looking for anything we could test for DNA. And then when you brought the gun back in to fingerprint."

Nicole smiled at her. Roxie had seemed okay about it at the time, and Nicole hadn't realized she'd been stressed out about it. "Okay, Blake can come with me. If we get lucky, maybe we'll find some trash tucked under the seats or something."

"Can you use it as evidence?" Kayla asked. "I mean, if you didn't get it through a search warrant or some other legal means, like he threw it out in the trash."

"We'll make sure it appears as though he left it somewhere that I could easily pick it up. But really, all we need is proof he's alive. It's not evidence to use in a trial. They can take swabs of his mouth to learn if he's the person who's perpetrated the insurance fraud once I have proof he is who we know him to be—because of his scent. Once we have the DNA, it's just a matter of turning the information over to the police and the insurance company and having the men arrested. William is an accomplice. We don't know about Eli yet. He might have been involved in all of it. And the fire that was set in the family home? That's something else that needs to be looked into further."

"Will the insurance company hire you for that?" Blake asked.

"The company that insured the house and cars was a different insurance company. They have their own team of investigators."

"Sounds like they didn't do a good job of investigating," Kayla said.

"Maybe, or maybe it really was just an accident. But it's not something I would look into unless someone hired me to learn the truth. And then, I might find the same thing the insurance investigators found. Inconclusive evidence that anyone set the fire that claimed Rhys's parents' lives."

"If you were to give an educated guess, what would you say about the circumstances?" Landon asked.

"That it was set on purpose, and the one who got all the proceeds from it was the one responsible. But that's the problem with this work. Without evidence to support my theory or a confession from the culprit, it won't matter. And I might be howling up the wrong tree in any event."

Roxie shook her head. "Sounds like a confession is what we need."

Nicole laughed. "As if that would be forthcoming."

After they finished eating and putting away leftovers and cleaned up the kitchen, they agreed it was time to run in the snow as wolves.

"If Clay had been a nicer guy, he could have come with us," Kayla said.

Everyone agreed as they stripped off their clothes, then shifted.

Landon went out the wolf door first, Kayla following, then Roxie, and Nicole ran out next. Blake followed her, and they all ran through the woods, exploring, marking territory, and telling other wolves in the pack they'd been there.

Nicole wondered why Rosco didn't join them on the runs. Not that they'd want to worry about him. He was a dog, after all, and that didn't mean he'd stick with them. A rabbit could send him racing off to the moon. Maybe they had trained him to not use the wolf door.

Before long, they saw a few other wolves out for a run. They barked at each other in greeting, and she knew they were *lupus garous* and figured they were part of the pack. Maybe not though. Some of the wolf guests at the lodge could be taking a run, just as she was. It must be nice being part of the pack and knowing most of the wolves by sight though.

She was so focused on the other wolves that she didn't see Blake come up beside her and lick her cheek, as if letting her know the wolves were safe. She nipped his ear in fun.

He tackled her, which she hadn't expected, but she delighted in it. She had never had a "boyfriend" wolf to play with, so this was a new and welcome experience for her. Even though she fully intended to get him back, his sisters ganged up on him, and she woofed at him in pure enjoyment.

Landon was letting his brother get "whipped" by the three females this time, and Blake was so endearing, taking all of the play nips and bites in good measure. Nicole would really miss this time with Blake and his siblings when she finished up her assignment here.

When they let Blake up from the snowbank, she noticed other wolves of the pack watching, probably getting a kick out of the goings-on.

Nicole and Blake and his family ran for a good stretch, then returned to their home. While she was getting dressed, Nicole said, "Rosco never leaves through the wolf door?"

"He can't. He wears an ultrasonic collar that opens the door only when it's turned on." Blake finished dressing.

"Okay, I wondered. I thought he was one of the world's best-trained dogs."

Everyone laughed.

"Not Rosco. He's great at the lodge and won't leave when everyone's coming and going," Kayla said, "and when he's on a search mission. But to run with us when we're wolves…we're afraid he'd get sidetracked."

"I kind of wondered."

Blake took ahold of Nicole's hand and squeezed. "I'm going upstairs to pack a bag. Be right back." He went up to his room.

"Do you really think Clay will cause problems for you at your room at the lodge?" Kayla asked.

"Maybe. If he figures out I'm staying in the room adjoining the cousins' room. He might want to have access to my room to get access to theirs. I wouldn't let him into my room, but it will be nice to have Blake there to impress upon Clay that I'm not alone."

Roxie laughed. "You are so getting yourself in trouble with Blake."

Blake called down from the second story, "I heard that."

Everyone laughed.

"We'll be planning a move on Rhys's car once they're fast asleep." Nicole hoped they didn't get caught at it and the mission didn't turn out to be a disaster.

CHAPTER 13

BLAKE WASN'T SURE HOW MUCH HELP HE WAS GOING TO be to Nicole once he broke into Rhys's car later tonight. He'd had enough practice helping out folks who had accidentally locked their keys in the car. So that would be his job.

But right now? He set his bags on the floor in Nicole's room, pulled off his gloves, and set them on the desk while Nicole shut and bolted the door, then pulled off her gloves and set them next to his. Right now, they had some time to kill.

She turned on the TV.

That wasn't really what he had in mind. But then she turned it to a channel that had music. Okay, so no movie time. Just background music to mask what they were up to. Hopefully.

They were still wearing their ski jackets and hats and scarves, and she came over to him and put her hands on his shoulders and tilted her head back for a kiss.

A knock sounded on the door.

"Hell." Blake went to the door and peeked out the peephole. "Clay," he said under his breath.

"You're kidding," Nicole said.

"Nope." Blake opened the door. "What do you want?"

Clay looked surprised to see Blake was in Nicole's room.

"So that's why you wouldn't share a room with me," Clay said, glancing beyond Blake to see Nicole.

"You got a room," she said, all growly.

"And your room is right next door—"

"What do you want to do? Talk out in the hall and sabotage things?" she said, her voice hushed and dark.

"He's not letting me in to talk," Clay said with a shrug, referring to Blake.

"That's right. This is my room. Go to yours. You don't have any business being here," Nicole said. "If you want to talk, we can do it in the morning. If Blake will allow it, we can talk in their office."

"Yeah, that would be fine," Blake said.

"Tomorrow, after we have breakfast and before these guys get up," Nicole said.

"All right. You've got my number." Clay sounded disgruntled that Nicole seemed to have the advantage on this mission, but he was the arrogant ass who acted like he knew everything.

Blake shut and bolted the door. They heard Clay walking toward the stairs.

Nicole shook her head. "I can't believe he actually came here."

"I can. He was just waiting for the right time, figuring you'd be alone, I bet. But he wasn't getting in. You don't trust him, do you?" Blake asked Nicole.

"Nope. I believe he'd use everything I learned and then solve the case, but he wouldn't help me back. I would like to think otherwise, since he's a wolf, but his going missing to work another case put him in the untrustworthy category for me."

Blake wrapped his arms around her in a bear hug and kissed her lips. This was what he'd wanted to do since he'd first met her—kiss her in the privacy of a room. Her mouth, and his, were still cold, but the movement of their lips against each other's soon warmed them up.

Then she yanked off his ski hat and tossed it on one of the beds. He pulled hers off and threw it on top of his. He unfastened her scarf and she was unwrapping his, and their scarves joined their ski hats on the bed.

She ran her hands up his ski jacket and kissed him again, as if enjoying the slow seduction. At least he hoped that was where this was going.

While their mouths were still pressed against each other's, kissing, nuzzling, sharing pure joy, Nicole and Blake were fumbling for each other's ski jacket zippers. They unzipped them as if in slow motion, then helped each other out of them, not wanting to pull their mouths from each other. Then they were wrapped in each other's embrace again.

"You are so…" Nicole said, pausing. "Incredible."

"You're a delight." He pulled her sweater over her head, and as soon as he tossed it, she pulled his sweater over his head.

He sat her on the bed and crouched down to unfasten her boots. She ran her fingers through his hair, her touch thrilling his senses as he breathed in her magical scent. She was so sexy and tempting. He pulled off one boot and then the other. Then he was sliding her socks off.

He was thinking they were going to have to get dressed and go out in the cold again, but that would be in about three hours. The guys next door had started a movie, which would help disguise what was going on in this room, though they were being quiet.

Nicole had him sit down on the bed and began to remove his boots, then his socks.

She kissed his knees, then leaned in between his legs to start unbuttoning his shirt. His hands went around her head, and he kissed her forehead. But as soon as she unbuttoned his shirt and pulled the shirttail from his jeans, he yanked it off. He rose to his feet to pull her to hers and remove her shirt. Ski pants came off next.

Then he was stripping off her bra and panties. She slid his boxer briefs down, and then they were together on the bed, naked, hot skin to hot skin, bodies writhing, lips kissing. Her hands were on his chest, rubbing his nipples, her fingers firing him up, stirring his cock to life. She felt divine beneath him, and he was in heaven with the she-wolf.

He kissed her neck, her throat, licking, nuzzling, loving her soft skin and she-wolf scent, her arousal, and sweet fragrances of lavender and mint. She was taking deep breaths of him, and he smiled, then cupped a milk-white breast and massaged.

"Hmm," she said, "keep going."

He intended to as long as she was agreeable. He suckled her nipple, and she ran her hands through his hair. He wanted to convince her to stay here and not return to Denver. To set up her PI shop here. She could work in town or up at the house. Their house. The one he would share with her. They could ski together and take Rosco for walks in the snow in the winter and on hikes in the summer. And run with the family as wolves. Their own little family pack within the pack. He couldn't think of anything nicer than that. Not that she was thinking about anything beyond this mission.

She moved her face closer to his chest, and then she began to kiss his pecs, and he flexed them a little under her lips.

She smiled. "You're such a wolf." Then she nibbled and licked his nipples, and the heated sensation was like a jolt of electricity that shot straight to his groin.

He moved his mouth to her breasts, kissing, licking, nibbling, and she groaned, her hands tightening in his hair, encouraging him. He could already smell her rampant arousal, his too, their pheromones aiding in the seduction process.

He'd never been around a she-wolf like this, and he'd never wanted to take things this far in a relationship. She was special.

She slid her hand down to take hold of his ironhard erection, and his cock convulsed in her grip. He sucked in his breath and slid his hand down her smooth skin until he reached her short, blond curly hairs and found her erect nubbin. Her eyes were darkened and filled with lust. Her head dropped back to the pillow, and her lips parted on a sigh as he began to stroke her.

But she didn't give up on stroking his cock either. He was finding it hard to concentrate, trying to keep touching her to bring her to fruition. Likewise, her hand would still on his arousal, as if his touches were stealing her attention and carrying her away. Which he was happy to do. Anything that would prove he could be her wolf lover for now and forever.

He couldn't even believe he was thinking along those terms this early in the relationship, but after she'd kissed him in the lobby, knowing he was a wolf, she had claimed him.

He was all too willing to be hers, even if this was really a rash decision for him.

Still, he groaned when she began stroking him again. He leaned in to kiss her parted lips, tonguing her, his finger dipping between her legs to stir things up there, to moisten his finger and work on her nub again, but she cried out, to his surprise.

He smiled and kissed her again.

She pushed him onto his back and straddled him, stroking him again while he watched her smiling eyes and lips, her blond hair hanging over her shoulders, her breasts jiggling with the movement. In the worst way, he wanted to flip her onto her back and consummate the relationship. They would be mates for life then. What if there was another she-wolf out there who was more perfect for him?

He didn't think so, and when she stroked him to the point of no return, he couldn't believe how good it felt to be with her, only he still couldn't help wanting more. He exploded, feeling satiated and complete with the world.

She left him to turn on the shower, and he wondered if he should let her have some time to herself. He didn't want to crowd her.

But what if she wanted him to join her?

He wasn't second-guessing this. He entered the bathroom. "Do you mind me joining you, or do you want me to wait?"

She pulled the shower curtain aside and smiled at him. "I made a mess of you. Join me."

In a heartbeat. "Gladly."

Then they washed up, using her bodywash because it was the only soap in the bathroom.

It didn't matter if he smelled like peaches, not when they were rubbing the bodywash all over each other's bodies in silky caresses. Every bit of her was a tactile delight, just like her fingers tracing across his heated skin sent his adrenaline soaring. She began washing her hair with coconut shampoo, and he took over. Then she did the same with his. They smelled like they were sunbathing in the tropics. He wouldn't have ever worn the sweet-smelling fragrances, but he had to admit it was like wrapping her scents around him, and all the next day, that was all he'd think of.

Afterward, they dried off and he blow-dried her hair, combing his fingers through the wet strands while he swore she was purring, her eyes half-lidded. When her hair was soft and dry, she ran the dryer over his hair, though it was mostly dry. Her fingers combing through his hair felt damn good, and he could see why him drying her hair had such an effect on her.

Then they climbed under the covers of the bed they'd already messed up and cuddled together, listening to the music in their room and the TV playing in the other room.

"Should we set an alarm?" Blake asked.

"No. One of us will notice the TV is off after a while."

They turned out the lights, and she pressed her head against his chest, her arm dropped lazily over his stomach saying he was hers, and he was all for it. He used the remote to turn off their TV.

They had slept maybe for three hours when he finally stirred awake, realizing the TV had been turned off in Rhys's room.

"Hey," Blake said to Nicole, his voice whispered against her hair, "are you ready to see if we can find some evidence?"

"Yeah, I sure am." But she didn't make a move to unwrap her body from his.

"I'll call Roxie to make sure she's awake and watching the security videos."

"Okay, I'm getting dressed. I don't feel like it though." She still didn't move a muscle to leave the bed.

Blake smiled and kissed her lips. "I feel the same way." He pulled her into his arms. "I'd love to keep going with more of this."

She smiled up at him. "Man, is it tempting. But look at all everyone did to set this up for us."

He chuckled. "I think they'd understand. Then again, Roxie might give me hell for thwarting you in your mission."

Nicole laughed. "I can see her doing that." She got out of bed and started dressing.

Blake called Roxie. "Hey, did I wake you?"

"Yeah, but I've been waiting for your call. Are you guys ready? I checked the video, and they're still in the room," Roxie said.

"TV's turned off. They're probably asleep."

"Okay, good. I'll let you know if anything happens."

"All right. We're just getting the equipment together to go on our mission."

Nicole was smiling at Blake while she was dressing.

"Hey, talk to you in a bit," he said to his sister.

"Out here."

Blake started getting dressed. "I couldn't tell her what we were really doing."

"I bet she guessed."

He chuckled. "No doubt." He finished dressing, and then they left the room, carefully shutting the door, and headed for the stairs. His adrenaline was pumping, and he could hear Nicole's heart beating hard too.

He ran his hand over her back. "You've got this."

"We've got this. If we find any evidence." She smiled up at him. "I hope we do."

They left the lodge on the snow-covered path, strode through the parking lot, and finally reached the driver's side of the van.

Blake used a wedge and rod to open Rhys's car door. They both smelled the scents in the car—Eli's, Rhys's, and William's. Nicole first looked for trash in the car and found an empty soda can. She gave it to Blake, who put it in an evidence bag. "Eli's." Then she dusted powder on the steering wheel and began trying to lift prints with standard lifting tape. She placed it in an evidence bag. Then she brushed hair from around the seat into another evidence bag.

She searched more through the back seat but mostly concentrated on the front seat, since it was Rhys's car and he would probably be sitting in the driver's seat most of the time. It smelled like it too.

Blake kept hoping she would be done quickly, but she was taking her time like a good investigator would. He wished he could do more, but she was the one who was trained in this, and all he could do was watch her and help carry any of the evidence she gathered.

Nicole was finally finished and was now carefully cleaning up the powder. He was planning to help her with that when he got a text from Roxie and read it: Hurry! Eli just left the room.

Aw, hell. Blake told Nicole the news.

"I can't leave any powder on the interior of the car, or they could see it and suspect something."

"Let me help." He was helping her remove the powder

when he got another text. He paused to check it, but Nicole
kept cleaning, dedicated to getting this done properly.

Roxie: Eli's going outside.

"Come on, Nicole. We've got to go. Eli's on his way outside the lodge."
"Okay, that should be good enough."

Roxie: He's headed into the parking lot, walking toward the car.

Blake locked the car door after Nicole, but they couldn't
leave now without Eli seeing them. Even if Blake had a key
to the van, just opening the door would spill light all over
the place. So they couldn't sneak inside it without Eli knowing they'd been next to his car.

They couldn't chance it.

He texted Roxie: Going silent.

Blake motioned to Nicole to slide under the van. She
nodded, looking resigned to the fact, and hurried to slide
under there on top of a thin layer of snow. He quickly
joined her. The footfalls grew closer. Blake slid his arm
under Nicole's head so she didn't have to have her head on
the snow.

Their hearts were pounding. He was glad Eli and the
other suspects weren't wolves, or they could smell Blake
and Nicole had been in their car. They remained still, their
breaths frosty underneath the van.

The car door opened, the light came on, and they heard
him rummaging around in it. Blake was glad he had told

Roxie not to text him any longer. He could just imagine Eli hearing the text ping and coming to look for the "lost" phone underneath the van—and finding a man and a woman hiding there.

They heard Eli continuing to rummage around in the car. He unwrapped the seal around a package of cigarettes, then tapped one out, and lit it. Cigarette smoke wafted in the air while he smoked next to the car. He finally shut the car door and walked slowly back to the lodge. Since he couldn't smoke inside the lodge, Blake figured Eli was taking his time returning so he could finish his smoke. They waited until they heard the door to the lodge open, then close. Then Blake slid out from under the van, and he helped Nicole up when she reached him. They brushed snow off each other.

"Hiding under a vehicle to avoid detection is a first for me. What about you?" Blake asked.

"Me too, believe it or not." They were heading back to the lodge when Nicole saw the discarded burning cigarette in the snow. "Yes! The one time I'm glad someone's a litterbug. Otherwise I want the person charged with a federal crime."

He chuckled. He knew how she felt though. A trash bin could be only a couple of feet away from where some inconsiderate person dumped their trash on the ground. As if that was all the people who worked at the lodge had time for, cleaning up other people's trash.

They put out the cigarette and stuck it in a fresh evidence bag.

"That was so worth it. Though I wish it had been Rhys smoking the cigarette," Nicole said.

"Me too."

Blake called Roxie before they reached the lodge. "Hey, we're done. We'll have to call Peter to come pick up the evidence."

"Eli returned to his room. I'm so glad you didn't get caught. I was hoping Eli was planning to take their trash out to the dumpster or the car, and we'd catch them at it, but then I saw him moving around the van and lighting up the cigarette. I thought we finally had them. I was worried about the two of you. Where did you go?"

"We had to hide under the van. At least we weren't caught, but man, that was a surprise," Blake said.

Roxie laughed. "Did you find anything in the car that might be useful?"

"Possibly. And he dumped the cigarette in the snow, so we have that. We'll have to have the stuff sent to the lab to have all of it analyzed, but hopefully we got what we needed." Blake put his arm around Nicole's shoulders.

"I saw Clay went up to Nicole's room earlier tonight. Looks like you chased him off," Roxie said.

"I did. I really couldn't believe he'd come up there. I think he was aggravated that she had the room next to the cousins' room. Nicole's going to use the office in the morning to talk with him."

"Okay. I hope you're going with her to set him straight. I'm off to bed if you all are done and don't need my help further."

"I'm just going to call the sheriff's office to let them know we have evidence to send to the lab."

"Okay, night, Blake. Give Nicole a hug for me."

"I will. Night, Roxie." Blake opened the door into the lobby, and then they made their way to the office. Inside the lodge, he called Peter. "Hey, it's Blake. We've got some more evidence."

Peter groaned. "Don't you ever sleep? It's three in the morning."

"Nicole and I were on a mission. We had to do it in the middle of the night."

"Hell, Blake, you're really getting into this."

Blake smiled. "Yeah, you know it."

"Good show. I knew there was a sound reason why I deputized you. I'll be up there in a few minutes to pick up the evidence. Where will you be?"

"If you don't mind, meet us in the lobby. It's empty right now." Blake figured they shouldn't be talking in Nicole's room and possibly wake the suspects.

"Yeah, sure. Be there soon."

"Let's get some cocoa from the kitchen, and then we can wait for Peter to show up. After that, we can retire to bed for the rest of the night," Blake said to Nicole.

Nicole took hold of his hand. "Now that sounds like a winner. And we might end up staying in bed nearly as late as the cousins tomorrow."

Blake smiled down at her as they went into the kitchen of the restaurant. "That sounds all right to me."

"Better be more than just all right."

"It is." He made them some cocoa topped with whipped cream, and then they went out to the fireplace and waited for Peter.

The sheriff didn't take long to arrive, and he gathered the evidence. "I sure hope this works," Nicole said.

"I do too." Peter shook Nicole's hand. "Always love to meet one of our kind who does investigations into criminal behavior."

"Thanks. If I was going to be here longer, I'd help you with your investigations."

"About that…"

Raising a brow, Nicole smiled.

"Silva owns the Victorian Tea Shop in Silver Town, and she's missing one of her antique tea sets. Her favorite one. I thought, if it wasn't too much trouble, you could help us find out how it went missing."

"You're serious."

"We heard you found Mittens for Alicia, Jake, and the kids."

Nicole smiled. "That was easy. Finding tea sets isn't your thing, huh?"

Peter smiled at her. "CJ, my deputy, asked around, but he couldn't figure out what had happened."

"Sure, I'll take the case. I'll need a picture of the tea set, and I'll have to ask everyone about it and see the video surveillance."

"She's good," Blake said, pulling her into a hug.

"Wait and see if I can find the tea set first," she said.

Peter asked for her email and then sent her a picture of the tea set.

"Okay, when I can, I'll run into town and see Silva," Nicole said.

They said good night to Peter, and he left. After throwing away their empty hot cocoa cups, they returned to Nicole's room.

As soon as they were inside, door shut and locked, they began removing each other's clothes. They didn't have to, and she didn't plan to ravish Blake again tonight, but it was just more fun this way and a nice ending to a long day spent with him. They were soon naked in bed, snuggling together, and this time sleeping for the rest of the night, and that was really nice too.

———————————

The next morning, Nicole's phone woke her, and she saw it was Clay. "Sorry, I'm getting a late start this morning. I'll call you when we can talk."

"Don't make it too much later."

Now that irked her. Clay didn't tell her what to do. He didn't need her help. Though she smiled about that. If he had half her resources...but that was partly due to being a nice wolf and kissing Blake in greeting first thing. If she hadn't been here and Clay had talked to Landon, nicely, he might have been where she was. Wolves usually helped other wolves.

She nuzzled Blake's chest with her cheek. He kissed the top of her head. Well, Clay wouldn't be exactly where she was, unless he'd made some courting progress with one of Blake's sisters. But they weren't happy with him either. She suspected, because of his arrogance, he wouldn't have made inroads with either sister if he'd shown up before Nicole had.

"I have a runaway tea set to find. I'm sure you can solve this other case on your own if I don't first. I'll call you when we can get together." She had no sooner ended the call than Roxie called her.

"Hey, um, Landon walked Rosco so Blake and you wouldn't have to do it, since we were all up so late last night. Did you want me to come up to listen to the cousins' room a little later?"

Nicole sighed.

Blake smiled at her and got out of bed, motioning to the bathroom. He soon started the shower.

"Yeah, I'll let you know when to come up. Blake's just taking his shower now. We'll run down and have breakfast at the restaurant before the guys get up." She hoped.

"Okay. See you soon."

For the first time on an investigative mission, Nicole just wanted to sleep in. With Blake.

"I heard you telling Roxie we were going down to breakfast at the restaurant." Blake turned off the shower.

"Yeah, Landon walked Rosco for us."

"Oh, good. I guess Roxie told him we were up late."

"I'm sure he figured that out because of what we had planned." She joined him in the bathroom, his towel wrapped around his waist. She gave him a hug. "Good thing we did it instead of skipping it like we wanted to."

He chuckled. "Yeah, we would have had some explaining to do. Though I still say that they would have understood and given me a hard time for it in a good-natured sibling way."

"We might need to take a nap sometime today."

"With you? I'm ready!"

"To nap."

He chuckled. "That's what you say now."

She agreed with him there. No telling where it would go when they got naked together again.

As soon as they were both dressed, she called Roxie. "We're heading down to breakfast. Come up anytime you'd like."

"Thanks, I'm on my way."

CHAPTER 14

WHILE NICOLE AND BLAKE WERE WAITING ON BREAKFAST in the lodge restaurant, she called Silva to learn more about her missing tea set. "Hi, I'm Nicole Grayson. Peter asked me to check into your missing tea set?"

"Yes, thanks. He told me he'd asked you. I'm sure you have better things to do, but if you have any free time to look into it, I'd pay you. I've asked everyone, and no one knows a thing. I purchased most of the tea sets from antique shops over the years, but this one was my great-grandmother's."

Nicole didn't blame her for being upset about it. Her parents' stationery and gift store had been broken into a couple of years back, and they'd felt violated, afraid it would happen again. She'd finally tracked down the thieves, proved they'd done the crime, and they'd gone to prison for that and a string of other break-ins and thefts, but her parents were still afraid they'd open their store some morning and find they'd been robbed again. "I'll need to talk to everyone who works at your shop concerning the theft. When was the last time you saw the tea set?"

"A couple of days ago. It might have been gone for longer than that. I don't know. I had it in a glass display case, but someone has moved a similar-looking tea set into its place. We've been so busy lately, I only just noticed the switch a couple of days ago."

"Did it have any special value? I mean, besides that it

was your great-grandmother's? Did it have a high antique value?"

"I never had it valued. Why? I never planned to sell it."

"Okay. Do you have security cameras monitoring your shop?"

"Outside, not inside. I never thought I'd have any need to watch patrons. I've never had any trouble, and you know we're a wolf-run town, right?"

"Yes." Which Nicole would think would keep wolves from stealing from others, but humans wouldn't know that the wolves would be looking out for one another. "I'll need a list of any potential suspects you can think of."

"No one, really. Peter said you had a serious case you're investigating, so I don't want you to feel you have to be tied up with investigating this when you have this other business to take care of."

"Oh, don't worry. I'll see what I can do about your case. I have downtime where I can't do a whole lot on a case, and the Wolff family is helping me with it. If I could contact your employees first, I'll talk to them by phone so I won't have to leave the lodge. If you could send me the outside security video for the couple of days prior to the disappearance and the day it went missing, I can look over that. I'll drop in to the tea shop when I can."

"Free lunch on me if you can get away."

"Uh, yeah, sure, I'll try to do it this afternoon if I don't get tied up here with this other case. I'll let you know one way or the other."

"The whole pack is talking about you finding Mittens for the Silvers."

Nicole smiled. She knew finding the missing cat had

been important to the family. She just hadn't realized how much the pack would share and that everyone would think she had done something so heroic.

"I'm glad I could find her so quickly to give them peace of mind. She's adorable."

"She is. I'll let you go, but I'm sending you the information you wanted."

"Thanks, Silva. I'll let you know what I come up with."

When they ended the call, their server brought Nicole and Blake's waffles and sausages, and they began eating. She got a text and checked her phone to see that Silva had sent the security video and a list of contact numbers for employees. Nicole set her phone aside. Even though she was dying to see the video and get started on this, she was having breakfast with Blake and not about to ignore him.

"Silva sent me the video surveillance and a list of employees to talk to. But she only has a security camera on the outside of her tea shop."

"That's a shame."

"Yeah, she'll probably have to install one inside. I would think the town was pretty safe," Nicole said.

"It is. We really do have the advantage of having a great pack, and everyone will keep their eyes and ears open in case they can learn something about it. In the meantime, though, I sure hope you can find it for her."

"It's her great-grandmother's. It has a real sentimental value."

"It's not valuable for resale?" Blake asked.

Nicole ate another bite of her maple-syrup-covered waffles. "She didn't have it appraised. But I'll try to find one online that has been valued or submit the photo Peter gave me to an online appraisal site and see if I can get a price that way. Oh, and I want to meet with her and see her shop. She said I could have a free lunch, so unless I'm tied up here, I'll probably run down to town, eat there for lunch, check out where she had the tea set, and sniff around for clues."

"If you need my help, just let me know."

"Maybe you can be my ears and eyes on these guys while I'm down there."

Blake smiled. "You know it."

A guy who looked similar to Deputy Sheriff CJ Silver came into the restaurant and headed for their table. Nicole suspected he and CJ were related.

Blake introduced them. "This is Eric Silver. He runs another pack with his mate. He's a forest ranger."

"Wow, that must be interesting."

"It can be. Chasing off bears. Saving folks from eating poisonous mushrooms growing in the woods, served up with a nice grilled steak at a campout. Missing persons getting lost on hikes. Rescuing people caught in bad storms. We even had a Bigfoot sighting. You never know whether it will be just a so-so day or a day filled with danger. It's nice to meet you. I heard all about Mittens. Jake is my cousin."

She laughed.

Eric smiled. "I just dropped in to grab something quick to eat, so I'll let you get back to your breakfast. I hear you're on an assignment here."

"Thanks, yes." She got a call from Roxie. "Excuse me for a second. Yeah, Roxie?"

"They're headed down to breakfast."

"Okay, thanks."

"Good luck with your case," Eric told Nicole.

"I've got the best of help, between the Wolff family and CJ and Peter."

"If you need mine, just let me know." Eric glanced at Rhys and William as they entered the restaurant, and Nicole was certain Eric knew just who they were.

Had Peter told the whole pack that she was investigating these men? She smiled. Unless Clay got really lucky, she did have a whole pack behind her.

Eric took a seat in a booth across the restaurant and ordered his breakfast.

"Has he eaten here before?" Nicole asked Blake.

"Never. To be fair, the restaurant has only been open for a little over a month. And Eric doesn't even live in Silver Town, so between his work and pack commitments, I'm sure he doesn't get into Silver Town much, except to check on his brothers."

Nicole chuckled.

Blake finished his waffles. "I told you. You're good for business. Your help with Mittens endeared you to the whole Silver family and the rest of the wolf pack."

She smiled. "I wonder if Clay would have done it if he knew the goodwill it provided."

"Are you kidding? That guy is in it for the money. Searching for a missing cat when there's only five dollars in it for him? I doubt it."

"From the way that Eric was sizing up the cousins, I suspect Peter has sent out word to the whole pack."

"I imagine so. For your safety and for that of the rest of the pack."

"I bet your sisters are also drawing more of a bachelor crowd."

"Not yet. I think Lelandi has told the males to watch their p's and q's so my sisters can have time to acclimate, meet with the pack members, and do their jobs here. Lelandi is a psychologist, so she's good at assessing people's needs."

"That's good then."

"Yeah, the pack leadership is great. They seem to really know how to lead in a good way."

"Had you expected that when you first came here to open the lodge?"

"We were hopeful, and we're doing everything we can to ease tensions resulting from the concerns of some of the business owners in Silver Town that we would steal all their business away. We're finding lots of acceptance now. And with our sisters' arrival, I'm sure even more."

Nicole laughed. "Did you realize that would help influence your acceptance here?"

"Well, not at first. But when we mentioned we had a couple of sisters who would be joining us once the lodge in Vermont sold? Landon and I learned the Silver Town wolf pack had a shortage of females. Good news for our sisters, not so good for us. But we're happy for them if they find good mates."

"That's what my brother always tells me. I need to be somewhere I have some dating possibilities. Denver doesn't have any."

"Me? Here?"

She smiled. "Here is a long way from there."

The cousins left with their takeout meals, and Nicole saw Clay headed her way. She was surprised he wasn't following the cousins, but maybe he was worried about the other man rooming with them catching on that Clay was after them.

Not asking permission first, Clay took a seat at Nicole and Blake's table.

A server came and gave them refills on their coffee and asked if Clay needed to see a menu.

"No, I've eaten," Clay said. When the server left, he said to Nicole, "Who's the other man?"

"I don't know for sure right now." Which was the truth. Until they got the results back from the lab and only if it was conclusive would she know for certain.

"Have you found the tea set?"

"I'm working on it." Or she would be, if Clay would get lost.

"They're hiding their trash," Clay said.

"Correct. So even though they spilled the beans about where they were going to be, they're being careful about leaving DNA evidence behind," Nicole said.

"I know. So how are we going to nail them?"

"Keep watching them until they make a mistake. I've skied after them to learn what I could. But that's pretty iffy. People don't usually have long conversations on the slope, and we've never been close enough to them in the lift line to hear what they're saying. Mostly, they talk about the next run, when they're going to stop for lunch, great powder, their great moves, stuff like that."

"I've tried to listen in on them for lunch, same thing."

"There's the third guy now. I need to do some work on the missing tea-set case." Nicole finished her coffee.

Blake had already finished his. "Do you want to go to the office, and you can look at the video of the tea shop there?"

"Yeah, I sure do. And I can call the employees. Good luck," Nicole said to Clay. Then she and Blake left the restaurant.

When Nicole and Blake entered the office, Kayla was on a computer doing some promo work.

"Clay didn't look happy that you couldn't enlighten him further," Blake said to Nicole.

"What can I say? We don't know if the third man truly is Eli until we get the DNA report."

"I saw Clay sat down with you while you were having breakfast," Kayla said.

"Yep, he was trying to learn if I knew anything further," Nicole said.

"I had an idea," Kayla said.

"What?" Nicole asked, all ears.

"What if I got friendly with Eli? I'd tell him my name and he'd have to tell me his, even if it's a fake. Then you'd have something else to go on."

Nicole liked the idea but was afraid it might spook the others. Maybe even Eli. And he might just give another alias.

"I don't like the idea," Blake said, more from the perspective of a protective older brother.

"I could let him know I do some billing for the lodge or something, so I work here. I could just be superfriendly, clumsy maybe, bump into him or something. Maybe I could greet some other guests and then turn to greet him so it doesn't look like I'm singling him out."

Blake raised both brows.

"Or Roxie could do it."

"No," both Blake and Nicole said.

"She's undercover. We don't want Rhys to see her. What

if she was in the lobby, and Eli pointed her out to Rhys? That could blow the case to smithereens," Nicole said.

"That's true. Okay, so it would have to be me."

"I still say no," Blake said.

"I would do it for Roxie and for Nicole," Kayla insisted. "Fine. Whatever."

"Thanks, Kayla. It's a good idea, but we'll hopefully get the DNA evidence soon." Nicole sat down on one of the office chairs and began watching the security video outside the tea shop.

Blake was looking over her shoulder at it. "Silva has lots of customers."

"Almost all women, except for a woman bringing a man in to eat lunch there."

Nicole began looking up the value of tea sets. She found one that was valued at over $38,000!

"Incredible," Blake said.

"It's not like her set, but it just gave me pause. If hers was valued that high, I could see why someone might want to steal it for the resale value. Okay, here's one that looks just like hers. It's valued at ninety dollars. Since it was in a glass display case, someone might have believed it was worth more."

"What are you doing now?" Kayla asked, joining them.

"A tea set in Silva's tea shop has gone missing," Nicole said.

"Don't they know you've got an important job here to do?"

"It's her great-grandmother's set and important to her. I figured I'd look into it whenever I have a moment. I'm going there this afternoon to check out the place. Have you

234   TERRY SPEAR

been?" Nicole was thinking that if Kayla was kind of shy about meeting others in the pack, maybe she'd go with her.

"No, I haven't, but it looked like a fun place for soups and sandwiches."

"Teas, pies, and cakes too. Did you want to join me when I go?"

Kayla glanced at Blake as if worried he wouldn't want Kayla's company too.

"Girls only," Nicole said. "Roxie could come too if she wanted. Or she could continue to monitor these guys for me. That's what Blake is doing."

"Okay, yeah, sure, I'd love to."

Nicole smiled.

"I'll ask Roxie." Kayla started texting her sister.

Nicole said to Blake, "I'm going to call the women who work for Silva. It'll take me a while if you want to do something else."

"Yeah, I'll go see what Landon wants me to do."

Before Blake left the office, Kayla said, "It's just you and me, Nicole. Roxie's going to continue to monitor the security videos. She said Clay's sitting outside on the deck having coffee, watching Eli eat his breakfast. Rhys and his cousin are out skiing."

"Okay, good."

Blake left and Nicole began calling tea-shop employees. One woman said she hadn't noticed because they'd had so much business lately. Another said the same. One said she thought Silva had changed out the set to make a different display because she did that periodically, changing the scheme of the tea shop so frequent visitors would enjoy the new scenery. Nicole thought Lila, one of the women she'd talked to, might know something, her voice hesitant and unsure as she answered, but Nicole needed to see her in person, question her, and smell her scent to see if she was anxious about the missing tea set. Since Lila was working at the shop today, Nicole would talk to her there but not let on she was going to be there.

"Any leads?" Kayla asked as she continued to work on a brochure for the lodge.

"One of the women appeared to know something."

"Oh, good." Kayla sounded like she was thrilled to be part of the new sleuthing business. "Did you see anything on the video that would make it look like someone was taking off with a tea set? Wouldn't the person have to take it at night when the shop was closed?"

"According to Silva's website, it's closed for business at four and then she works at her husband Sam's tavern. He's also open for lunch, but she manages her tea shop during that time. The video camera in back of the shop was blanked out for a bit, it appears."

"Whoever took it must have gone in the back way. Did he or she have lockpicks?"

"Or it's an employee with access to the shop. There's nothing more for me to do here until lunchtime, so I'm going to grab Blake for some runs on the slope."

"You're spoiling him." Kayla frowned. "Do you think it might work with me trying to get Eli's current alias?"

"I do. But Blake's also right. It could go totally sideways. Let's wait. If the evidence comes back inconclusive on the cup, the cigarette, and the stuff I took from their car, we can talk again about you meeting up with the guy somehow."

Kayla brightened. "Okay."

Nicole wondered if Kayla was just looking for an excuse to meet a guy. "I'm off. See you in a bit."

"Unless you are getting somewhere with your case. And I'll completely understand."

"True." Nicole thought Kayla sounded a little disappointed. "But if so, we'll run by there another time."

Kayla smiled.

Nicole left the office and found Blake talking to a guest. Once the man left, she took ahold of Blake's arm. "Ready to ski?"

"Yes! I thought you'd never ask. Did you get anywhere on the tea set?"

"I might have a lead." They returned to the office to get booted up for skiing.

"Good show. I hope you do."

Then with skis and poles in hand, they left the office, moved through the people milling about with hot cups of cocoa in the lobby, and went outside. The blast of cold air hit them, and Nicole pulled down her ski goggles and lifted up her dickey.

"We might miss out on our nap," Blake said.

"We might. We'll just have to see how things go."

"Roxie said she's taking a nap in your room at lunchtime in the spare bed, if that's okay with you. Landon's going to deliver a meal for her for lunch."

"Sure, as long as she's not there when we slip up to the room to take our nap."

"We could go to my room at the house."

Nicole glanced up at him.

He smiled. "No one's home until dinnertime."

"Okay, we could do that."

They skied for the rest of the morning, him following her down the expert slopes, and then later they skied a couple of intermediate slopes. The sky had clouded over again, and Nicole smelled snow in the air. "More snow."

"Yeah, coming in tonight."

She looked back at the lodge. "The cousins are headed in for lunch."

"I'll go watch them if you want to take Kayla to the tea shop. And thanks. You asking her to join you meant the world to her."

"I think she has caught a little bit of the sleuthing bug."

Blake chuckled. "You've had that effect on all of us. And we're delighted. But this is great for her to meet some of the other ladies without feeling too uncomfortable. And that means everything to us. Getting her out of her shell can be a task."

Nicole was glad she could help Kayla out.

CHAPTER 15

NICOLE AND KAYLA ARRIVED AT SILVA'S VICTORIAN TEA Shop that afternoon, the large windows sporting ivory lace valances as well as miniature white lights surrounding the window frames and reflecting on the glass, pretty and sparkly on a cold, wintry day. A covered patio with café tables outside for when the weather was warmer was covered in fresh snow.

When Nicole and Kayla walked inside, a little bell jingled on the door, and the fragrance of tea, roses, chocolate, and savory meals permeated the air. Tables were covered in lace, and chairs had high ladder backs and cushions for the back and seat in blue, silver, and white plaid. Antique teapots, tea sets, and floral, antique hot chocolate pots were on display all over the tea shop that boasted a main eating area and tucked-away seating for small groups or couples. Victorian figurines of girls and boys ice skating sat on shelves for a wintry, festive look.

Nicole imagined how cute the tea shop could be for Valentine's.

Pillars were adorned with white lights, white flower garlands, large white bows, miniature ice skates, and skis. Pictures of winter scenes were hanging on the wall, and when Nicole looked closer, she saw the photography had also been done by Jake Silver, but he had antiqued them to make them look more Victorian for Silva's shop.

Nicole loved the decor, and she was glad Kayla had

come with her. Kayla seemed glad too, as she was smiling and admiring all the different tea sets.

Her beautiful dark-brown hair swept up in a bun, a woman hurried to greet them. She wore high-heeled boots, formfitting, pale-blue leggings, and a soft white sweater that showed off the rest of her curves. Nicole had expected a sweet, older lady wearing a floral dress.

"I'm Silva, owner of the Victorian Tea Shop. And you must be Nicole and…?"

"Kayla Wolff," Kayla said.

"Oh, I'm so glad to meet you. As soon as I have a chance, I'm going to eat at your restaurant. It's kind of hard when I'm working either here or at Sam's tavern, but one of these days, I'm going to make it up there. Everyone's talking about how good your food is, and the lodge is beautiful."

"Thanks. I only arrived a few days ago myself. I love your tea shop," Kayla said.

"Thanks and, Nicole, thanks so much for helping me out." Silva led them to a table.

"You're welcome," Nicole said, taking a seat. "I needed to ask you about the video blacking out at a certain point that must have been the day the tea set went missing."

"I need to get a new system. It periodically stops working. If you look at earlier days, it was doing the same thing. I normally don't ever have to look at it, but when this happened, I saw that had happened, and I viewed other days and found it doing the same thing. I have a new security camera on order."

"Oh, okay." So that didn't help. Nicole eyed the menu, then ordered a grilled cheese sandwich.

"That sounds good. I'll have the same," Kayla said.

"And tea?" Silva asked, notepad in hand.

"Of course. Peppermint?" Nicole asked.

"Got it."

"Lavender for me, please," Kayla said.

"All right. I'll bring it out in just a few minutes."

"Is there a Lila working here today?" Nicole asked.

"Yeah, sure. She's at the register. Do you want me to send her over to speak to you?"

"Yeah, that would be great. Thanks."

Lila appeared to be around nineteen, and she looked and smelled nervous when she came over to speak with Nicole. "Hi," Nicole said. "We spoke on the phone."

"Yes."

"Can you take a seat?" Nicole wanted to speak softly to her so Lila would feel comfortable enough to tell her what she knew.

"I, uh, have to work."

"Silva said you could talk with me."

Her eyes cast downward, Lila sat on one of the chairs, looking unhappy, as if she were getting ready to have her head on the chopping block.

"Okay, just between you and me—" Nicole said.

Lila looked at Kayla.

"She won't say anything," Nicole assured them.

Kayla nodded. "I'm just here for lunch."

"I was driving home after being at the tavern late, and I saw...I saw..."

Nicole frowned. "What? If you know something, I'm sure we can work this out somehow."

"It was Laurel. She came out of the tea shop through the back door," Lila blurted out under her breath, as if she had to do it that way or she wouldn't have the nerve to 'fess up.

"Laurel?"

"Silver. She's mated to our deputy sheriff, CJ. Cousin to our pack leader." Lila looked like she wanted to cry.

"Okay," Nicole said. "No problem." She patted Lila's hand. "Go back to work. Don't worry. I'll be careful, and I won't say anything to anyone about this until I learn what's going on. No one will know you told me, okay?"

Lila nodded and got up from the table. Then she went back to managing the cash register, and Silva brought out their grilled cheese sandwiches.

Kayla didn't say anything, just ate her sandwich, but Nicole was sure she was thinking plenty. Just as she was.

Silva was busy serving her customers. Nicole ordered a chocolate cream pie after she finished her grilled cheese sandwich. Kayla had a blueberry scone.

"Free lunch on me, ladies," Silva said, "and thanks again for trying to find my tea set, Nicole."

"You're so welcome. And thanks. Everything was delicious. We've got more work to do, and it's so nice meeting you," Nicole said, but before she left, she looked over the glass display case where the tea set had been sitting before it went missing.

"You can have a meal on us any time," Kayla said. "So good to meet you."

"Breakfast! That works for us," Silva said, snapping her fingers. "Sam and I could run up there for an early-morning breakfast before we open up our places."

"That would be great," Kayla said.

Then the ladies left, and Nicole said, "Okay, we need to talk to Laurel."

Kayla let out her breath. "She's the deputy sheriff's wife, Lila said."

"Right. We still need to talk to her. Or I do. You can wait in the car while I speak with her. She runs the Silver Town Inn with her sisters."

"I'll…I'll go with you."

"Really, you don't have to."

"I'd like to see their hotel."

"Okay." The hotel was just down the road from the tea shop, and they soon parked there. As they went inside, Nicole was trying not to be nervous, especially in front of Kayla. She'd made a lot of goodwill with the pack already, and though it didn't mean she was going to join the pack or anything, she still liked making friends among wolves who were good people. She didn't know what to think about the tea set, but she thought Lila might have been mistaken about what she'd seen.

Nicole saw what she thought could be one of the three sisters at the registration desk, but she didn't know for sure.

Kayla looked at the lobby decorations while Nicole went to speak to the lady behind the registration desk. "Hi, I'm Nicole Grayson, and I'm looking for Laurel Silver."

"She's in the office. I'm her sister Ellie. Did you want me to tell her what you're here for?" Ellie had a pretty Irish accent that Nicole would love listening to all day long.

"I'm working on a case at the lodge. I'm a private investigator."

"Oh, you're the she-wolf who found Mittens." Ellie smiled, her blue eyes alight with happiness. "Thanks for doing that. The family is so happy you found her."

Now Nicole felt worse about questioning Ellie's sister, but she had to. She was sure it could all be explained and Lila had made a mistake, but still, she had to ask. Nicole smiled, then Ellie pointed to where their office was, and Nicole went to the door and knocked.

"Yes?" a woman asked inside the room.

Nicole said, "I'm Nicole Grayson, and I need to talk to you about something."

The door opened, and a pretty woman smiled at her and offered her hand. "I'm Laurel Silver." She had the same lovely Irish accent.

Nicole shook her hand.

"You're the PI."

"Yes, I'm staying at the lodge and working on a case."

"And you're here at our hotel because?"

Nicole let out her breath and went inside and took a seat. "I'm searching for Silva's missing tea set. It was her great-grandmother's."

Laurel took a deep breath, let it out, and smiled.

About that time, Ellie poked her head in the door, and so did another woman who looked similar. Meghan? The other sister? They were all pretty redheads of varying degrees of blond or purer red. Two had green eyes, the other blue.

"She's a private investigator, looking into Silva's missing tea set," Laurel said, sitting down at her desk.

"Oh no," Ellie said. "She's good at her job."

Meghan smiled. "We've been caught."

Nicole suspected it wasn't something bad when all the ladies acted so happy about it. That was a first for Nicole on a case when something went missing.

"I guess we could have Silva's birthday party just a little early," Laurel said.

"You took it to throw her a birthday party?" Nicole asked, astonished.

"No. We had a professional antique restoration service restore her set completely. We wanted it to be a surprise. A birthday gift she'd love. We hoped she wouldn't notice her set was missing. I swapped it for one that looked similar in color, but I guess she still noticed."

"Oh." Nicole smiled. "I'm so glad and I'm sorry I troubled you."

"No, you're great at your job. We could use someone like you living here," Laurel said.

"Thanks. When is the party?"

"Tomorrow afternoon. We have to sneak the tea set back into her shop tonight while she is working at the tavern. Brett and Ellie are going to make sure she doesn't go anywhere while Meghan and I are sneaking the set in. The guys don't know anything about it, or CJ, my mate, would have told Peter what was going on. We just wanted it to be a surprise for all that she's done in welcoming us to Silver Town."

Nicole loved how everyone did so much for everyone else in the pack. She'd worried when she'd thought someone in the pack had stolen from another pack member or that humans broke in and stole it. She was glad to know that it wasn't anything of the sort.

"Your secret is safe with me. Silva knows I'm looking for it, which will hopefully give her some peace of mind until the birthday celebration."

"Yeah, but we want you to come to the party tomorrow afternoon if you can."

"All right, if I can. I've got a case I'm working on, and the Wolff family has been helping out. But I don't want them to be the only ones watching who I have under surveillance."

"I understand. Tell Roxie and Kayla to join us if they can too."

"I sure will. Nice meeting you all." Nicole said goodbye and walked out of the office.

Kayla looked worried. Nicole smiled. "Come on. The mystery is solved, and you, Roxie, and I are invited to a birthday party. We just need to figure out what to give her."

Kayla began looking at her phone and showed it to Nicole. "This antique, Bavarian hot chocolate set?" Aqua with gold trim, it was beautiful.

"That works for me," Nicole said.

"Good. It's at an antique shop in Green Valley, just a short way from here. I'll pick it up tomorrow," Kayla said.

———

Blake couldn't believe how much he missed not having lunch with Nicole. He hoped she and Kayla had a nice lunch at the tea shop and had learned something useful about the missing tea set. Nothing was going on here. Like Nicole had said, the cousin and the two brothers had the same old routine as usual. Clay was either on his laptop or trying to watch the men as surreptitiously as possible.

Then Blake got a call from Nicole, and he was glad to hear her voice.

"Hey, did anything good come of your investigation?"

"You would not believe it. Laurel Silver and her sisters took the tea set to have it restored for Silva's birthday. She invited your sisters and me to the birthday party they're having tomorrow."

Blake laughed. It sounded like the longer Nicole stayed

here, the more she was beginning to become part of the community. He hoped she wouldn't want to leave after all was said and done. Here he'd thought he would have to solicit others to convince her that her work was needed here.

"We're almost home, but I'm still on for taking a nap," Nicole said.

"Sounds good to me."

"We're here."

They parked the car, and Blake joined them outside. He couldn't wait to see Nicole.

She gave him a big hug and kiss, telling him she had missed him too.

Kayla was grinning. "Have a nice nap." Then she went inside the lodge.

Blake kissed Nicole back. "I need you in my life. No matter what. I want you to know that."

Nicole smiled up at him. "I think I've been missing a lot in mine."

"You know it."

She chuckled. "Come on. Let's head to your place for a much-deserved nap."

He was ready for it. He was just hoping it meant they'd do a little loving before or after the nap. In the two months they'd had the lodge and house up and running, he'd never believed he'd be having his potential mate in his bedroom, enjoying a nap and whatever else he could get away with.

Once they were inside the house, he chased her up the stairs, and she squealed in surprise and fun. In the hallway above, he caught her up in his arms, feeling like he was truly claiming her, and she laughed.

"I should have let you catch me earlier and you could have carried me all the way to your room."

He chuckled. "Next time." He carried her into his room and set her on the carpeted floor next to his bed, the blue covers matching the blue curtains. He pulled the bedcovers aside, and with urgency, he began stripping off her clothes.

"Not just a nap, eh?" She was tugging at his clothes to remove them just as fast: gloves, hat, scarf, ski jacket. Then she shoved him to a sitting position on the bed and tackled his snow boots and socks.

"Not on your life. You know where this is headed." At least he damn well hoped so.

"So you think," she teased.

He leaped to his feet and then sat her on the bed. He removed her boots and socks, then slid her ski pants down her legs. "I know so." Even if he didn't.

At one time, he'd thought his old girlfriend, Susie, and he were going to be mated wolves, but once he'd talked about moving, that was the end of that. She had been a lone wolf, and the family needed to be with a pack. It was perfect here for them in Silver Town, and family meant everything to him. Staying in Vermont with Susie hadn't been an option. Which meant she hadn't really been the right wolf for him.

He realized that even though Nicole wasn't from here either and she hadn't said she'd move here to be with him, he felt so much differently about her. So connected, not wanting to lose her. If he had to give up his family to move to Denver, it would be hard, but losing her would be unbearable. Unless she *really* didn't want to be with him in the long run, like he wanted to be with her.

Already he was fully aroused, and when he yanked off

his sweater, Nicole's eyes were centered on his bare chest, raking it with her hot gaze before she smiled at him and then sighed. She pulled off her sweater. "How did I get so lucky to find such a beautiful specimen of a wolf?"

He pulled off his ski pants. "I was thinking the same thing about you."

It was amazing how invigorated he felt, even though they'd been up so much last night. But being with her, alone and eager for some loving, he felt the adrenaline rush, his pheromones ratcheting up a few notches to sing with hers.

He leaned over to unfasten her bra, and she licked his nipple. He groaned. He was ready to burst. He removed her bra and panties, and she climbed into bed and stretched out on her back like a wolf waiting for a belly rub.

He ditched his boxer briefs and joined her. Her darkened gaze met and held his, her lips turning up fractionally. "I told you that you wouldn't want to just sleep." Her voice was sexy and tantalizing.

"You either," he said, his voice already heavy with lust. Then he moved in to kiss her, to touch her soft skin all over.

His erection ached for her touch, but he knew if she began to stroke him, he wouldn't last. He licked her nipples, kissing her breasts with fervent desire, and slid his hand down her belly, ready to move forward with the foreplay, conscious of her need to return to the lodge to do her job after they napped.

He was glad she wasn't such a workaholic that she couldn't spare the time to be alone with him. It made him all the more determined to help her with her mission and get on with the courting business.

His fingers swept through her curly hairs, and he found

her nub, engorged, ready for his strokes. He started to stroke her clit, his mouth tackling hers with a passionate kiss. She ran her fingers through his hair, her nails lightly raking his scalp, her touch sending a spark of need straight to his groin.

Her body was tense with need, and her mouth kissed him ravenously back. That heightened his rampant craving for her all over again.

He inserted a finger between her feminine folds before stroking her even harder when she cried out his name. He smiled at her, surprised she had come so soon. But then she was pushing him onto his back, climbing on top of him, her legs spread across his thighs, and seizing the moment. She began stroking him, her smile bright, her gaze shuttered. Her pink feminine lips were spread to his view, a beautiful sight.

It didn't take long before he exploded, his world splintering into a million pieces of ecstasy. "Holy hell, Nicole. I'm keeping you."

She chuckled and rolled off him so he could get cleaned up. "I'll be right back," he said, but he meant what he'd said.

When he returned to bed, she had pulled the covers over her, but she was still awake, waiting for him. He loved her for it. He joined her under the covers, and this time, he spooned her, his hand lazily caressing her breast. He would never get enough of touching her.

After pressing kisses on the top of her head, they both finally truly had a nap.

By the time Nicole and Blake had napped, kissed, and dressed, then left the house, it was snowing and the wind was blowing hard. "Will they be closing down the ski lifts again?" Nicole asked.

"Yeah. If the winds are gusting this high down here, it'll be worse up on top of the mountain."

"Avalanches could be a threat too."

"Yeah, with high westerly winds and significant snowfall and with it being midwinter, avalanches can break deeper, enough to bury people. It can happen due to natural causes, or they can be triggered. We've got ski patrols out checking the conditions before they open the lifts in the morning. The patrols trigger avalanches with explosions to alleviate the trouble. But if the snow comes down too fast while the lifts are running, that's when we can have real trouble. Even in December, we had an avalanche caused by snowboarders. Luckily, no one was killed, but we had search and rescue out looking for buried skiers. It also helps that we are all gifted with a heightened ability to smell, just like avalanche rescue dogs. A lot of the Silver Town wolf pack members were out doing search and rescue."

"I hadn't thought of that."

"Yeah, and because of the incredible snowfall, we were just packed with skiers the day after it happened."

"You'd think people would be afraid to come up here after that had just happened."

"No, they were eager to get out in all that powdery snow."

By the time Nicole and Blake reached the lodge, they were wearing a layer of snow and shook it off before they went inside.

Rosco came running over to greet them, licking Nicole first. Blake smiled. "He's found a friend in you."

"He's so sweet." She rubbed his head.

Frowning, Landon waved for them to come to the registration desk.

Blake was afraid it was some kind of trouble.

"There's a guy called Nate here, looking for his sister, Nicole. He's a wolf, but since you didn't tell us he was coming, I was suspicious."

"Nate's here?" Nicole sounded horrified.

Blake and Landon exchanged looks. Blake recalled that she had said he was an Army Ranger. He hoped he wouldn't be angry that Blake and his sister were spending a lot of time together.

"He's in the restaurant. Your parents told him you were here. I told him you were keeping her safe, Blake. I think he's worried about her and wanting to check you out."

Nicole shook her head and took Blake's hand. "Come on. I need to straighten my brother out. I love you, you know, and I'm not giving you up for anything."

Blake was in heaven. "I knew it!" He lifted her off her feet, hugging her tight to his breast, and swung her around, so elated, he could barely think straight. "You are the only one for me. I love you right back."

CHAPTER 16

NICOLE COULDN'T BELIEVE HER BROTHER WOULD TRACK her down at the ski lodge. Once Nate left the army, she had planned to get together with him. She hadn't thought he had that much terminal leave left.

She sure didn't want him to know she was sleeping with one of the owners of the lodge and cause all kinds of trouble for Blake or the rest of his family.

Her brother was as tall as Blake, six feet, just as muscled, just as much of a wolf. He was wearing a blue ski jacket and ski pants, and she swore he looked like he'd come here just to ski. He loved it as much as she did. Maybe *that was* why he'd come here. Not to check up on her but to take a mini-vacation while she was working and maybe even back her up on her job.

She and Blake walked toward the table where Nate was chowing down on a hefty rib-eye steak, potatoes, gravy, and green beans. That was his kind of meal.

"Hey, Nate," she said. "I thought you had another week or two before you left the service."

Nate gave her a big smile. "I had extra terminal leave." He rose to his full height and gave her a big hug. "Mom says you're working on a dangerous case and I needed to provide you with backup. I got my PI license. I can join your agency." He glanced at Blake.

"This is Blake Wolff. He is part owner of the lodge and restaurant. He and his family, his two sisters and brother, have been helping me with my work."

"Much obliged," Nate said, offering his hand to Blake.

Blake shook it. "The missing PI is now working on the case, so if you were concerned he'd vanished, don't be."

"Larry?" Nick asked, frowning.

"Uh, no, he went home sick with high-altitude issues. Clay was the one first assigned to the case, and the insurance company thought he had run afoul of the suspects. But he was just working a higher-paying case," Nicole said.

"He sounds like an ass."

Nicole smiled. She and her brother often saw things the same way. "Sit and eat your meal before it gets cold."

Nate sat back down. "I figured I'd stay with you and get some skiing in and help you with your case."

"Stay with me in my room?" Normally, Nicole would have been fine with it. But not now. Not when she wanted to stay with Blake and work with his sister.

"Uh, yeah. Like we normally would?" Nate put his silverware down and eyed Blake. "Is there something I should know? I thought we would be going into business together, Nicole."

"Yes, we will. I'm excited about it. But I've got a room-mate already."

Nate glanced at Blake again.

"Blake's sister Roxie is in my room whenever the men are settling down at night or getting up in the morning, and she's monitoring the security videos. The Wolff family set me up in the room adjoining the suspects. But at night? Blake's got my back."

Nate's gaze shifted again to Blake.

Blake shoved his hands in his pockets and shrugged.

"What can I say? She kissed me in the lobby before I even knew her name."

Nate's jaw dropped.

"I knew I was in love." Blake smiled at Nicole and wrapped his arm around her waist and pulled her close.

Nate was on his feet in an instant, and Nicole shoved her hand at her brother's chest. "Cool it."

Nate laughed. And pulled her in for a hug. "I hope you feel the same way about him," he said with a growly voice. "I'd hate to hear you were leading him on. My own sister."

She laughed. "Well, I hadn't exactly planned it this way, but yeah, we're good for each other, and"—she looked up at Blake, knowing he was the one wolf for her—"I love him."

Nate shook Blake's hand. "Well, you did something right. My sister is particular about the guys she dates. Real particular, so if she's kissing you when you don't even know her name, she must have seen something in you." Nate sat back down to eat his lunch.

Nicole knew Nate was all show, that he had realized at once she saw something special in Blake.

Nicole and Blake sat down with him this time.

"Okay," Nate said, cutting off a piece of steak, "am I still joining you in the business?"

"Absolutely. I guess the choice we have is we can work here, set up shop in Silver Town if the Silver wolf pack is fine with it, or we can split our forces and you work out of Denver and I'll work here. I have to tell you Silver Town is run by our kind."

Nate raised his brows. "You're kidding."

"Nope. The whole town."

"What do we have to do to get accepted around here?" Nate asked.

"Nicole found a family's missing cat." Blake reached over to rub her back. "Jake's one of the subleaders. Nicole's definitely got an in. Not to mention she's becoming one of our family, and we're members of the Silver Town wolf pack. They don't have any private investigators in town. And Nicole's already solved another mystery, a missing tea set at a tea shop in town. If the pack accepts Nicole, I'm sure they would accept you too."

Nate cut up some of his steak. "I need to talk to Mom and Dad first. They might want me to stay around Denver."

"We can always work out something where we have two offices." Nicole was excited about the prospect of really mating Blake and staying here with the Silver pack and the Wolff family. "Yours in Denver, and mine here."

"You really don't need me to help you here on your case?" Nate asked.

"No. You can go skiing and have some fun. I'm sure you need a break after leaving the service."

"And I'll help you if I can."

"Yeah, sure, Nate. That'll work." Nicole loved her brother, and she knew no amount of encouraging him to just have fun would work. She wondered if he was also eager to show off in front of Blake, just a little.

Kayla came into the restaurant and walked straight to their table. "You have another case, Nicole." Then she smiled at Nate in an interested she-wolf way. Boy, would the bachelor wolves of Silver Town be upset if one of the Wolff sisters suddenly took up with an out-of-town wolf.

"Uh, Kayla, this is my brother, Nate Grayson, who's started working in the business with me."

Kayla blushed.

"Nate, this is Kayla Wolff, Blake's youngest quadruplet sister. Roxie is the other."

"How do you do?" Nate hurried to rise from his seat to shake Kayla's hand. He was usually a fast eater, but he wasn't getting very far with his meal. But he also looked eager to meet the blushing Kayla.

"What's the job?" Nicole asked her.

"Our restaurant manager said four cases of beer went missing from the restaurant last night. She said two cases of packaged chips and other snacks were also stolen," Kayla said. "It sounds like someone had a room party."

"Did you want to go with Kayla to talk to the restaurant manager, Nate? He also has a PI license," Nicole said to Kayla.

"Yeah. Sure." He was about to join Kayla, but Nicole stopped him.

"You need to eat your food." Nicole was amused with her brother. Now it appeared he wanted to make some points with Kayla.

Kayla sat down at his table. "I can fill you in on the details while you finish eating."

Nate sat back down to eat, and Kayla said, "We've smelled their scent—three human males had been down in the wine cellar where we also store other food supplies. We don't have any humans working for us, so no one should have been down there but us wolves."

"And the security video?" Nate asked.

"I've got it on my phone." Kayla showed it to him.

"We're going skiing," Nicole said, taking Blake's hand.

"Catch up with you later. Oh, and I need to get a room of my own, I guess." Nate winked at Nicole.

YOU HAD ME AT WOLF

"I can get you a room." Kayla got back on her cell phone to get a room reserved in his name.

Blake and Nicole went to the office, though she changed her mind about getting their ski boots. Once she'd declared her love for Blake, it was time to mate.

"That was a smooth move," Blake said.

"What? Giving my brother a job? I wanted him to bring Kayla out of her shell. He's good with people like that. He's more into the shy violet type than the splashy, bold type."

"Like Roxie?"

Nicole smiled.

"You want him here working with you, don't you?"

"Yeah. My twin brother and I have always been close. We had always talked about going into business together, which is why we wanted to join forces once he left the service."

"Staying here kind of messed up your plans though."

"Doesn't look like it." As soon as they were in the office, she shut the door and pulled Blake into her arms for a hug and kiss. "You really want to be mated wolves?"

"You bet. You only said you wanted to go skiing in front of your brother, right? I was thinking we would do something else. Let me give my brother and Roxie a heads-up to call us if anything happens with the case because we need to return to the house."

"Speaking of which, how are we going to work that?"

"Build a separate house? The forty acres beyond the house is ours—woods, rabbits, squirrels, and all. We planned to have our own places when we mated. And Darien and Lelandi wanted to ensure developers wouldn't hassle them any longer about building more lodges, restaurants, or shops near the ski resort."

She laughed. "So the Wolff family has to field all the offers."

"Yep." Blake smiled. "The Silvers knew how to work that. They knew we could handle it too. The last one of my siblings who finds a mate will keep the main house, and we'll continue to use it for our family gatherings."

Nicole smiled at him. "I love you."

"Oh, man, I so *hadn't* wanted you to see me make a mess of that snow-blowing operation, but now I know it was the right thing to do."

"And lose control of Rosco that morning. Remember, those were the two things that made me fall in love with you, just a little. You were too cute, and I felt sorry for you."

"Man, am I lucky for that." Blake touched base with Landon and Roxie, putting it on conference call and speakerphone. "Nicole and I are heading over to the house for a little while."

"Is this what we are hoping it is?" Roxie asked, sounding enthusiastic.

Blake smiled. "A mating? Yeah, it is."

"Hot damn, brother," Landon said. "And here I thought I would be the lucky wolf first."

"I got damn lucky."

"We'll have a celebration tonight," Roxie said. "I'll get with Kayla and Nate."

"Okay. Sounds good. See you later." Then Blake took Nicole's hand. "Let's go to my place."

"That works for me." She couldn't be happier. Finding people and things was part of her job, but finding a loving wolf mate while on a case? It certainly hadn't been in the plans, but she hit the jackpot.

Instead of trudging through the snow from the lodge to the house, she felt like she was practically walking on air. Blake wasn't taking a leisurely stroll to the house either. He was moving like a wolf on a mission, his gloved hand clutching hers, pulling her along, keeping her on her feet, their warm breaths making a frosty mist in the air.

When they finally reached the house, he hurried to open the door, closed and locked it behind them, and swept her up in his arms. "You are mine."

If he didn't sound like some dire wolf from caveman times. She loved it.

She loved the gesture, but she really didn't want him to carry her all the way up the stairs to his bedroom. But he did. He was being super romantic, and she loved him for it.

There was going to be no slow seduction this time, not as he set her on her feet in his light and airy bedroom and began removing her outer ski clothes and boots with urgency. And then she was frantically removing his, their clothes tossed this way and that as if the blizzard had stripped them away and blown them asunder. His need for her was only met by her need for him.

It was if they were afraid one or the other might change their mind. But there was no going back.

He crushed her against his body in a ravenous hug, and she wrapped her arms around him in a heated embrace. A wolf could survive on its own, but two wolves made a family, a small pack within a pack.

His eyes were hungry and dark, aroused and focused solely on her. But then his large, warm hands cupped her face and he kissed her, slowly, thoroughly, deeply. She had to hold on to his waist, feeling the sexual need to make him hers building, the passion in his kiss heating her blood, and she felt unsteady on her feet. She needed him to be her rock.

She was just as eagerly kissing him back, his hands shifting to her shoulders, rubbing her soft sweater against her skin, kicking up the heat.

"You don't know how glad I am you came into my life." Blake said, his voice low and resonant, mesmerizing. "I love you."

"You're irresistible to me," she said against his lips, then pressured him for another deep kiss. She slipped her tongue into his mouth, toying with his, claiming him. "I love you right back, you old wolf."

He smiled but then was right back to kissing her.

She'd known from the moment she kissed him in the lobby that he was someone really special. A hot kisser, a sexy wolf, someone who would jump at the chance to protect her, and more. Even when she'd suggested getting someone else for the job of being her pretend boyfriend, he was all for persuading her that he was the only one who need apply for the job.

And he was right. He was the only one for her. There was so much more she wanted to do with him—dance nights, movie nights, hiking trips where they could be wolves or humans to their hearts' content. Game nights, though she suspected his family and hers would be part of that too. Trips, near and far. So much to do.

She couldn't be happier.

The wind howled outside the window, the snow swirled around, and they began stripping off the rest of their clothes, alone together, apart from the hustle and bustle of the ski resort. No one in the rooms next door or wandering down the hall. They needed this moment to themselves.

He slid her sweater over her head and tossed it, and she pulled his sweater over his and did the same. And then he wrapped his arms around her and unhooked her bra. Once he'd ditched it, he ran his hands over her breasts in a loving caress. She moved her hands over his chiseled abs to his hard pecs, smiling. He was perfection. She had him smiling, too, and leaning down to kiss her again, but his hands remained on her breasts, massaging and weighing them. His wondrous touch made her feel uplifted and loved.

She shifted her hands from his broad shoulders to his ski pants and felt the bulge in his crotch. This time, he would join her all the way, and she couldn't wait to have the thick length of him sliding inside her, consummating the mating for life. She pulled off his ski pants and slid her hands down his boxer briefs, sliding her fingers over his warm ass. He matched her action and slipped his hand down her pants and cupped her buttocks, his hands warm against her skin.

She gave his ass a squeeze, his mouth on hers again, kissing and tonguing her. Then she tugged his boxer briefs off him, his cock springing free, stretching out to her, poking her. An inspiring, impressive sight, and, she realized with satisfaction, all hers.

He quickly slid off her ski pants and her panties. They were still wearing socks when he scooped her up, laid her on the bed, and joined her. His socks were gray like the wolf, while hers had cute little fox faces and ears. Who would have thought she'd be wearing them to make mated love in?

He took in a deep breath of her, smelling her pheromones kicking his into high gear, just as she was smelling his and basking in his arousal mixing with her own. He licked and kissed her sensitive and taut nipples, and she arched against the mattress and pillow in response, his actions stealing her breath. He suckled a nipple, and a charge of electricity shot straight to her groin. She moaned with need.

He laved the other nipple with his warm, wet tongue, suckling it before he skimmed his hand down her belly and found the juncture between her thighs.

As soon as he began to stroke her clit, the desire for him to join her made her ache in ways she didn't think she'd ever feel with a man—giving herself to him, allowing him to claim her, to accept him into her most intimate chamber.

Yet now, waiting with rampant expectation, she wanted to tell him to hurry it up, to finish this before she died in glorious anticipation.

But he was taking his time, stroking her, wanting her to climax first, considerate of her needs. She was dripping wet, ready for him already, and she went to say so when she felt the climax hit, shattering her into a million bits of astonishing pleasure. Then she was pulling at his strong arms, wanting him to join her. He moved his muscular leg between hers, preparing the way. She quickly spread her legs, willing him in, telling him she was his.

He inserted the broad head of his penis between her legs and surged forward like a wolf with a mission. She was his mission. Mating her. Loving her. For life. He was hers. Forever more.

Blake couldn't believe Nicole had chosen him over any other male wolf she'd encountered over the years, and he knew he was incredibly blessed. He thrust into her, wrapped up in the sweet and spicy scent that was all Nicole, from wolf to human. She branded him, and he would never be the same. Once they'd met, he hadn't wanted to do anything but prove he was the right wolf for her.

She seemed to believe that with all her heart, just as he knew she was the one for him.

Even now in sex, she moved with him, anticipating his moves, matching them, enhancing them. He was afraid she was going to tell him to quit trying to make her climax and just mate her already, the expression of impatience on her face dissolving with the sexual peak she'd experienced, right before she spoke. He loved that he could do that for her. He loved that he could make love all the way to her.

"You are my beautiful wolf," he said, kissing her mouth again.

"You are mine," she barely breathed out as he continued to thrust.

He felt the end coming and held himself rigid for a moment, then surged into her again and again until the climax hit and he spilled his seed deep inside her with a groan of great satisfaction, a stellar finish to a great mating. She truly was his.

There was no going back, and he didn't want to leave the bed again today. Instead, he wanted to cuddle with his mate the rest of the day and night and forget about the celebration his brother and sisters wanted to put on. Forget about the case she was working. Nothing else mattered but this. Mated bliss and being with the wolf he loved.

Yet he knew that wasn't possible, so instead he pulled the covers over them. They would have a nice wolf's nap, make love again, and return to the world to resolve this case of Nicole's one way or another.

CHAPTER 17

AFTER NICOLE AND BLAKE SLEPT FOR AN HOUR AT THE house and made love again, they'd jumped in the shower, cleaned up, dressed, and returned to the lodge. And done a lot of smiling. She couldn't believe they were mated wolves, and she felt on top of the world. But she had to get back to business and get the evidence against Rhys. She and Blake had returned to the office and were reviewing security videos taken of the dumpsters at night when Peter called her.

"Our pack leaders said you and Blake are mated, and you're staying in town and joining the Silver pack, right? That your brother also wanted to join. Landon called to let Darien know."

"I'm sorry, I guess we should have run this all past the pack leaders."

"No problem. Darien and Lelandi want me to deputize the two of you since you're helping us with criminal and other investigations. Even without being deputized, you can make citizen arrests, but we'd rather you had the backing of the sheriff's department behind you. We know both of you were in the army and are weapon trained, and we've done background checks."

"Already?"

Peter chuckled. "Why do you think everyone was asking you to help them with their cases? Well, they needed them solved, sure, but they wanted to show you that they believed you were a valuable resource to the pack."

YOU HAD ME AT WOLF

"Thanks, Peter. Here I thought I might just get some skiing in while I was doing surveillance on my suspects. I never thought I'd find a mate, a family, and a pack all at the same time."

Peter said, "Silver Town can have that effect on wolves. Oh, and tell your brother there are going to be some growly bachelor wolves if he mates one of the Wolff sisters. We have a lot of males who have been anxiously awaiting their arrival."

"They'll have to take that up with my brother." If Nate found a she-wolf he couldn't live without, no one was changing his mind.

"I'll be up there in a few minutes. I'm driving there now."

"Okay, we'll see you soon. I'll let my brother know." After they ended the call, she told Blake what Peter was going to do.

Blake smiled. "Good show."

"I need to find Nate and let him know."

"Unless you need me for something else, I'm going to keep looking at these nighttime videos."

"No, go ahead. We need to resolve this case." She left the office and found her brother looking intense as he moved around the lobby, brows furrowed.

"I'm smelling the scent of the men who stole the beer and snacks," he said, his voice low for her ears only.

"Well, Peter Jorgenson, the sheriff, has good news for us. He's deputizing us, so we can arrest suspects who are involved in criminal pursuits."

Nate smiled. "Hey, this is the perfect place to be."

"Yes, but he also warned me you'd better not 'steal' any of the single she-wolves that the bachelor males have been dying to court."

Nate laughed.

"I told him they'll have to take it up with you. Peter will be here soon to deputize us, so don't wander off too far. We'll need to do it in the office, in case my suspects, or yours, are about when he arrives. How are you doing with that case, by the way?"

"I have an inventory of everything that was stolen—four cases of beer and two cases of individual bags of snacks. Three males wearing black ski masks picked the lock on the back door to the restaurant. They were wearing all black, except for their jeans, like a bunch of thieves in the night. I've made casts of their boot prints in the snow. I want to catch them taking out the empty trash or find some of the stolen items in their room."

"You were following their scent?"

"They've walked all over the place. Kayla's working on some promo stuff for the restaurant, but she's going to help me sniff around a little later."

Nicole was thrilled Kayla was offering to help her brother. Then she saw Peter. He stalked across the lobby to join them. "I thought we could do this in the privacy of the office," she said. She was glad the sheriff wore jeans and a jacket and didn't look like he was a law enforcement official in case anyone saw him and worried the police were on to them.

When they entered the office, Blake and Landon were there to witness the deputizing. And then Peter wished them good luck on their current cases.

"Oh, and I have to warn you, we always do background checks on anyone who wants to set up a business in Silver Town or join the pack. Lelandi wanted me to ask you if you can do that for us. The pack pays for the investigations, and we could really use your help," Peter said.

Nicole smiled. "Nate and I will be happy to."

"You might check out a new couple that want to join our pack. A Nelda and Gary Grayson. I hear they're looking to move their stationery and gift store down here." Peter smiled.

"Mom and Dad? Ohmigod, yes!" Nicole looked at her brother, surprised to hear the news, and she wondered if he had anything to do with it. Neither of her parents had indicated to her that they wanted to leave Denver.

Nate smiled at her. "Hell, Sis, when you and old Blake here start having little wolf pups, you know Mom and Dad would want to be nearby. They told me after lunch they had talked to Darien and Lelandi, and it was a go."

Nicole brushed away tears. "That was my only regret about leaving Denver, but Mom and Dad have always said we needed to do what we wanted in life, and if that meant following a career and finding mates somewhere else, they supported it."

"They said that because we were both going into the army and they knew we'd be on the move."

"And they knew we wouldn't find mates in Denver either."

Kayla came into the office. "Nate, are you ready to start checking the floors for these guys' scents?"

"I sure am." Nate left the office with Kayla.

Smiling, Peter shook his head. "We'll talk soon, I'm sure."

"No word back on the DNA evidence?" Blake asked.

"Not yet. We're trying to get it rushed through, but it could take a week or longer."

"Thanks for everything you're doing, Peter," Nicole said.

"You're welcome. And thanks for becoming my newest deputies." Peter said goodbye and left.

Later, Nate and Kayla returned to the office and gave Nicole and Blake an update on their progress. She was glad he was keeping her in the loop. He'd brought Landon with him too.

"I was thinking you, Blake, Landon, and I can help arrest these guys for the theft. We found the three rooms where they're staying," Nate said. "Since we're all deputized, I figured we could arrest them. I called Peter for backup because there are three rooms of three people each. He's bringing his two deputies, CJ and Trevor."

"We've had alerts within the last hour that three stolen credit cards were used in reserving the rooms, meals, ski lift tickets, and ski rentals," Landon said.

"I can't believe these guys were involved in so much more criminal activity. With the number of deputies we have, that gives us two deputies per room, plus the sheriff," Nicole said.

"As sheriff, Peter's coordinating the searches and arrests. I needed to see if you all were fine with this," Nate said. "We'll arrest them at the same time so none of them get away."

"One of the rooms is near your suspects though," Kayla warned.

"Then someone other than Blake and me has to go there," Nicole said as they all looked over the rooms' schematic. "We can take this room on the other side of the lodge." She pointed out the room farthest away from her suspects' room. "Nate, you can take this one."

"That's the one where all the partying went down. They have the Do Not Disturb sign on the door," Roxie said.

"That sign is going missing." Nicole smiled at her.

"Maybe Peter and his deputies can take the room near your suspects' room since they're not staying at the lodge," Blake said. "Roxie can be monitoring our pseudocide suspects to ensure they're on the slopes, eating, or otherwise occupied. It would be best if they don't see any law enforcement activity around the lodge."

"I can do that," Roxie said.

"I can run interference somehow if one or more of them suddenly comes in about that time and looks like they're going to their room," Kayla said.

Peter showed up with his deputies and took charge. "Here are the search warrants for each of the rooms." He passed them out. "All right, what do we have, intel-wise?"

Blake liked that Peter didn't just start giving orders but was making sure he knew all the facts before they did this.

Peter looked over the rooms' schematics and considered all the evidence they had on the young men, and Kayla showed him the video of the guys carrying the boxes of beer and snacks into one of the rooms. Since their suspects had used either stolen IDs or fake IDs, no one knew their real names. They'd get it all sorted out at the jailhouse later.

"We thought you or your deputies could take the guys into custody who are in the room nearest our pseudocide suspects," Blake said.

"Yeah, good idea," Peter said. "Since this is a felony, they should get jail time."

"I've been keeping track of the men. They all went out to the ski slopes. Their rooms are clear, if you want to see if you can find any evidence," Roxie said. "And the other guys? Rhys and his brother and cousin? They're out on the slopes too."

"Roxie and I are monitoring the security videos, and we have all your contact information, so we can text you if anyone is headed back to the rooms," Kayla said.

"Is everyone armed?" Peter asked, "Just in case we have trouble with any of these guys."

"Yeah, Nate and I carry concealed weapons. We have permits for them," Nicole said.

Blake agreed. "Same with Landon and me."

"We do too," Roxie said, motioning to Kayla. "But that's just for our personal protection."

Peter looked over the bills that the guys had racked up for food and services. "This constitutes a class 6 felony, between $2,000 and $5,000 worth of merchandise stolen. Okay, if everyone's ready, let's do this."

Blake smiled at Nicole as they left the office and went to the stairs that led up to her room. "You gave your brother the room where they had the party."

"Yes, I gave him the job. I figured he needed to take credit for finding what remains of the stolen merchandise, if anything."

"He was glad, but he was waiting for you to say which room you wanted."

"We've always been close. But I've solved over seventy cases. This will be my brother's first."

They made their way to the third floor on the other side of the lodge. Blake was thinking how they'd have three more rooms available, since they already had proof the cards used to reserve the rooms had been stolen and the lodge would be out the money.

Nicole reached over and took Blake's hand and squeezed, smiling at him. "Are you ready for this?"

"I sure am. Working with you is a pleasure." He smelled her nervousness. He could understand how she felt. He'd had to check out rooms before, even called the police a couple of times in Vermont when he found guests involved in illegal activities after the maid had gone in to clean the room. Actually, investigating a crime scene and arresting someone was new for him. He sure didn't want to screw this up, not when it was his first deputy-sheriff assignment and Nicole could witness it.

"Hey," she said, "you'll do fine."

He guessed she could smell his anxiousness too.

With the master key card against the security panel, Blake knocked, called out, "Housekeeping!" unlocked the door, then opened it.

Nicole smiled at him.

He smiled back and shrugged. "If someone was in there, I figure they're less likely going for a weapon if they think it's just maid service."

No one had answered, and it appeared the room was empty.

He set a copy of the search warrant on the desktop, then began looking for evidence relating to the crimes they already knew the men had committed.

As soon as they began searching through drawers, Nicole found a couple of passports hidden under some socks. "Looks like more stolen IDs, unless these are their real IDs. The names are different from the credit cards."

"Betcha they're not theirs either." In the fridge, Blake found some of the stolen beer. The guy who had put it in the fridge had been one of the men who had broken into the wine cellar. "Here's some of the beer."

"I found one of the boxes with packages of chips and one of the cases the beer was in. You'd think these guys would have gotten rid of the boxes at least," Nicole said.

"How much do you want to bet they didn't think we'd be onto them." Blake checked through the rest of the drawers while Nicole went through their clothes.

"I'm sure of it."

Blake got a text from Roxie, and he hurried to check it.

"Don't tell me… Trouble is headed our way," Nicole said.

> **Roxie:** Two of the suspects have returned to the lodge. I'm watching to see where they're headed.

"Yeah, two of them are in the lobby."

Nicole was taking pictures of where they'd found the evidence: closet, drawer, fridge.

Peter texted Blake: We've got receipts for everything they've charged, including the rooms, ski equipment rentals, locker rentals, lift tickets, and meals. We have a number of empty beer bottles and packages of chips that the lodge sells in the restaurant in the room.

Blake texted him what they'd found but warned him two of the men were in the lobby: We need to confiscate the evidence, but we might be making an arrest first.

Roxie: They're headed up the elevator. Kayla
ran to check it out and said they're
headed for the room on your floor.

Blake texted Peter: We have two headed our way.

Nicole had gloves on and was placing all the evidence in the box in the closet. Blake hurried to help her, wanting to make the room look like it did when they first arrived so the suspects wouldn't turn tail and run. "We've got two coming to the room."

Peter: Arrest them first. I'll send CJ to intercept
the third guy rooming with those two so
he's not alerted and warns the rest of
them.
Blake: Okay.

"We're arresting them, Nicole," Blake said, his voice low. Now he felt the heat was on.

The way the lodge rooms were laid out, the door opened to where the closet was on one side of the entryway and the bathroom on the opposite side, both along the hallway walls. The bathroom wall provided privacy for the first queen-size bed, and that was where he and Nicole would have to hide until the men were fully inside.

"Over there," he said.

Once they were in place, he and Nicole were hidden from the mirrors on the sliding closet doors and the one over the chest of drawers—luckily. When they had gone over the designs for the rooms, he never thought he'd be hiding with his mate in a guests' room, waiting to arrest the guests.

"Are you ready?" Blake whispered, both of them leaning against the outer bathroom wall so the men could come far enough inside without seeing them. He was glad there would be only two of them, or the third one might have run off before they could grab him and then warn the others.

"I sure am."

Roxie texted: The other guy staying in the room just entered the lobby.

Blake texted Roxie: Okay. Tell CJ. We're going silent.

The men's footfalls headed for the room, and Blake and Nicole tensed, but then they clomped on past in ski boots. Blake and Nicole glanced at each other. Then they heard two more pairs of ski boots headed their way. This had to be them.

The key card activated the green light, and the door opened. "I wish we could stay for a few more days," the one man said.

"We can't chance it. The owners of the credit cards are going to realize they're missing, and once our purchases are declined, we're going to be in trouble."

Nicole was recording the conversation, and Blake smiled at her. He wouldn't have thought to do that. The one guy clomped farther into the room and the other guy joined him, shutting the door behind him.

"We still have the lift tickets for tomorrow. We could have at least skied in the morning first thing."

"Janus stole the cards, and he's calling the shots."

Blake came around the wall and said, "Deputy Sheriff Wolff. You're under—"

The one guy tried to make a break for the door, but Blake ran and tackled him, slamming him against the door.

Nicole got the other guy and forced him down face-first on the bed. "Deputy Sheriff Grayson," she said.

Blake read them their rights as he tied the man's hands behind his back with a plastic tie and forced him to sit on the bed while Nicole finished tying the other guy's hands behind his back.

"What are you charging us with?" the attempted escape artist asked.

"If you hadn't interrupted me and tried to flee, I would have told you. For stolen merchandise and IDs to begin with," Blake said.

Blake got a call and checked it. CJ. "I've got the other roommate for the room you're in," CJ said, "just down the hall."

"We can take them down the service elevator and out the back way if you can bring a cruiser around to pick them up," Blake said.

"We have a van waiting for them," CJ said, "and some other deputized men to watch them."

"We're headed out then," Blake said. "Come on, you two. Your friend's waiting for you."

"I don't know what you think we've done wrong, but you have the wrong guys," the attempted escape artist said.

Blake called Roxie, ignoring the guy. "Hey, can you secure the door?"

"Doing now."

That meant the rest of the guys couldn't get into the room in case any of the others had a key and tried to drop by.

"We have rights. We get to make a phone call," the escape artist said.

They joined CJ down the hall, and he said, "After you're processed at the jailhouse."

"We didn't steal anything," the guy insisted.

"Beer, snacks, passports, and using stolen credit cards for goods and services," Nicole said. "You're looking at felony charges."

"That's just for what we know about. No telling what else you've done wrong," CJ said.

The men looked miserable. Good. Blake hoped they knew they weren't going to easily be able to talk themselves out of this.

CJ loaded them in the van. Three other men were there, all deputized in the pack: the Silver brothers, Jake and Tom, and their cousin Brett.

"I'm going to return to the lodge to help Peter and Trevor out," CJ said.

"We'll head up to the room where Nate and Landon are," Blake said, "since we don't want to be seen around the other room."

Roxie called Blake. "It looks like all the rest of them are coming in. Maybe to have dinner."

"I think they were planning on skipping out of here." Blake had also mentioned it to CJ before they parted company. He just hoped Rhys and his party didn't learn of the arrests so close to their room.

CHAPTER 18

BLAKE AND NICOLE FINALLY MADE THEIR WAY TO THE other room and decided to wait in the hallway so they could catch the men outside their room while Landon and Nate planned to remain inside the suspects' room. He hoped this went as smoothly as the other operation.

The elevator doors opened down the hall around the bend.

"Showtime," Landon said. "We get to hide behind the outer bathroom wall inside the room."

"Nicole and I are going to have a special moment nearby in the hallway."

Smiling, Landon shook his head. "Come on, Nate. One of these days, that will be us."

Nate and Landon moved back inside, and Blake and Nicole leaned against the wall, having their moment, talking to each other softly, running their hands over each other's arms, nuzzling and being sweet. And listening to the sounds of footfalls headed their way.

The three men were laughing, the one saying, "I couldn't believe you took that spill, Janus."

"Hopper got in my way."

"Hopper is disgruntled about leaving."

"I know, but we can't stay." Janus used his key card on the door. "We shoulda left yesterday."

"We've had fun."

Janus opened the door and walked inside, the other two men following him. Nicole and Blake hurried after them before they shut the door.

"What the hell?" Janus said to Blake as he stopped the closing door with his boot. "Did somebody give you our damn room key?"

"You're under arrest," Nate said. "For felonious theft." They began tying the men's wrists.

"I don't know what you think we've done wrong—" Janus said.

"Enough," Landon said.

Janus stared at Landon and then Blake. "I thought you worked behind the desk. Since when do hotel clerks arrest innocent citizens?"

"Since they're sworn-in deputy sheriffs with search warrants and evidence of crimes committed at the lodge," Blake said. "We might not have caught up to you if you hadn't stolen the beer and snacks from the restaurant. Whose dumb idea was that?"

None of the men admitted to it.

"We took the others down the service elevator to a van out back," Blake said, then called Roxie on his phone. "Roxie, can you secure the door?"

"On it."

Then they escorted the men to the service elevator.

They soon had the men downstairs and packed in the van. Before they could call Peter to see what was going on with the men in the other guest room, he and his deputies were bringing the last of the suspects down.

Blake was glad to get that resolved before their pseudo-cide suspects learned of it.

They gathered the evidence and put it in Peter's vehicle so that he could take it to the sheriff's office.

Afterward, Blake and Nicole had gone to the office to look over last night's security videos of the dumpsters when Peter called. Blake put it on speaker and motioned for Landon to join him. Kayla was in the office working on promotional videos so she paused to hear what was up.

"The guys we arrested have done this before. They're all on probation and are all returning to jail in Missouri," Peter said. "Everyone did really well."

"That's good to hear," Blake said, though he suspected the thieves would be right back at it once they were out if they hadn't learned the last time.

"I hope they get some real time in the joint this time," Landon said.

"Me too," Kayla said. "We spend a lot of money on this place, and we need to keep rooms rented to pay for all our costs."

"I hope you get some restitution," Nicole said. "It's a good thing the insurance company I'm working for is still paying for my room."

"We can afford your room," Blake said, smiling at her.

"And meals?"

"Those too. Hell, now you're family." Blake kissed her.

"I just wanted to let you know we did good," Peter said.

"Thanks," Landon said, "for all your help."

"Just doing my job."

Then they signed off.

"Well, that's great news," Blake said.

"I'll say," Nicole agreed.

Blake and Nicole started reviewing security videos while

Kayla went back to work on her promo videos, and Landon left to do whatever he needed to at the lodge.

"Nothing." Then Nicole looked up from the monitor. "We don't have security cameras in the bathrooms."

"No, by law, we can't have any in there." Blake was looking at her now, realizing just what she was saying. "They go there after they've eaten and before they hit the slopes. We just figured they were making a pit stop before they went skiing. Hell, they could have stuffed their trash in there, and the janitorial service just got rid of it."

"Even if they drop their meal trash off now in the men's restroom, and you go retrieve it, the guys will leave Silver Town before we can get the analysis back," Nicole said.

"But I still have to do it."

"Unless you want me to," Nicole said.

Blake chuckled. "Actually, we can have the janitorial staff grab the bags after they've used the men's room, and we'll take it to the office to sort out."

"Okay, that works for me. I wonder what they do after dinner. We know they use the men's room after breakfast and lunch, but after dinner, they head up to their room."

"We didn't watch the security video in the lobby that would catch who might go to the restroom late at night," Blake said.

"Right. We were thinking they were using the big dumpsters outside."

They pulled up the security video for last night, and sure enough, Rhys was headed into the men's room in the middle of the night with a full backpack, and it had lost most of its contents by the time he left the restroom.

"And the janitorial staff cleans it out when?" Nicole asked.

"Early, before the restaurant opens. They clean the restrooms then and check on them periodically throughout the day. So they would be emptying out the trash if it was full enough."

"And Rhys and his coconspirators would see that the next time they had a meal and left off their trash."

"Correct. Which means tonight we need to come down after whoever attempts to dump their trash and seize the contents."

Nicole looked at the security videos for the other nights. "You know how I said these guys had such a routine? Every night at three in the morning, Rhys heads down to the restroom."

"There's nobody in the lobby, just the night staff, so no one's really paying attention to a guest who uses the restroom down there."

"Tonight, we will be."

———

Before they had dinner that night, Nate joined the whole family for drinks at their house while Roxie and Kayla cooked T-bone steaks and baked potatoes, and Blake and Nicole made a salad. The family had made Nate feel at home, too, as they encouraged him to tell some of his Army Ranger stories.

Roxie and Kayla had put up purple balloons with black paw prints and purple and white streamers. Blake wondered when they'd done all that, but Nicole was smiling broadly and looked happy to be celebrating their mating.

"Congratulations," Landon said, serving everyone

champagne. "Welcome to the family, Nicole, and you too, Nate. Now, you're stuck with us."

Nate smiled and raised his glass of champagne to Landon, telling him he was good with it.

Everyone cheered Blake and Nicole, and he was glad they all loved her as much as he did.

When they finally sat down to dinner, Landon began cutting up his steak. "We have a proposition to make to you and Nicole, Blake. Once Nicole's case is resolved and you are ready to leave the lodge, you and Blake can have the guest room downstairs until your house is built and you're ready to move in."

Blake smiled. Nicole blushed.

"Do you think we'll be making a little too much noise up there for you to get any sleep?" Blake asked.

"Hell, yeah. We'd expect nothing less," Landon said, toasting him with his wineglass.

"Yeah," Roxie said. "We agreed on it. Since Landon has the master suite, that means only Kayla and I will have to share the upstairs bathroom now. We thought we might find mates locally who already had a place of their own, so this wasn't exactly planned. But it should work out perfectly for the two of you. The guest room has its own bathroom too."

"I was the one who suggested it," Kayla said. "I'm a really light sleeper." She winked at Blake.

He laughed. He figured he and Nicole could slip away from his and her work whenever they had a chance, once this situation with Nicole's suspects was resolved, and return to the house when the rest of the family was at the lodge working. Sometimes, Kayla liked to work out of the house, but maybe he and Nicole and she could work out more of a schedule until their own house was built.

That was something else they had to look into—house plans. Of course, building a house together could create a lot of conflict in their lives. He hoped they could agree on what they wanted.

"That works for me," Nicole said, squeezing Blake's hand.

Blake was glad his brother and sisters had suggested it. He'd been so wrapped up in being with Nicole that he hadn't thought about what they'd do once she was done with the case.

"Nate, if you like, you can continue to have a room at the lodge free of charge until you get settled, since you're family, too, or you can stay in Blake's room, if he's agreeable. That'll give you some time to get moved here and figure out where you want to live," Landon said.

"Thanks. That's really generous of you." Nate didn't say one way or another what he wanted to do.

Blake didn't blame him. The guy probably needed his space to get to know the pack and Nicole's new family before he decided what else he wanted to do.

Once they finished dinner, Nicole, Blake, and Nate said good night to the others, then walked back to the lodge.

"Do you want me to look for the trash in the middle of the morning?" Nate asked. "I'd be happy to take care of it for you."

Blake was all for it, but that was because he wanted to keep her for himself in the room all night long.

Nicole gave her brother a big hug and smiled up at him. "Yes, thanks. You are the best PI partner ever."

Nate hugged her back. "I'm enjoying this new job and working with you on it."

"Good." Nicole wrapped her arm around Blake's waist. "You're an extremely valuable member of the team."

Nate laughed. "Yeah, because I'm doing trash detail so you can stay with your mate all night. But I'm happy to do it."

Smiling, Blake slipped his arm over Nicole's shoulders, and when they made it back to the lodge, they said good night to her brother, then headed up to their room. All he could think of was making love to his mate, and he was pretty certain the look of hunger in her eyes and the smile on her lips said she was thinking along the same lines.

———————————

Nicole couldn't believe Blake was her mate as they entered her room. Not a PI partner or a hunky wolf who co-owned the lodge but her mate. She couldn't have been more thrilled, and she was finally settling into her new life. Though they needed to build a place of their own and she needed to move her household goods here from Denver. She supposed she could put it all in storage in Silver Town until they could build their home.

As soon as she locked the door to the room, thinking only of ravishing Blake, she got a call from Laurel Silver and she put it on speakerphone.

"You're the PI on this case, and you are the one who solved how Silva's tea set went missing. We don't want to mess up your track record. Instead of sneaking the tea set back into her shop tonight and chancing getting caught, my sisters and I would love for you to pick up the antique tea set at our hotel and take it to her at her tea shop. We'll come in right behind you to wish her a happy birthday," Laurel said.

Blake smiled at Nicole.

"Sure, I'd be happy to."

"Thanks. We'll see you tomorrow."

Even though Nicole had thought she might stay behind to work on the pseudocide suspects' case, after Laurel called her, Nicole knew she had to go and play this out. Especially since the missing tea set had been her case, and she liked happy endings. They ended the call.

Blake began helping her out of her hat and gloves and scarf.

She unzipped her ski jacket and slid her arms out of it. "Now that Nate is here—not to mention Clay is still looking into the case—they can both watch over the men. Roxie said she was driving the three of us women to the party."

Blake ditched his hat and gloves, then pulled off his ski jacket. "I'll help your brother with the case in the meantime."

"Okay, thanks. I feel bad making you all work while I'm off to a birthday party."

"It's part of your missing-tea-set case that you're finishing up. Besides, if me assisting you with your case helped in any way to convince you to be my mate, it's all good."

She smiled. "I love you. All I thought was that I'd be working with a human PI and doing my job. I never expected to move into a new place to join a mate. But the more time I spent with you, the more time I wanted to spend with you. Because of all the time I spend away from home on cases, I kind of feel that my apartment is no more than a way station.

With you and your family and mine living here, it will be a real home. I haven't really had that in years."

"I feel the same way about you and your family joining us. As much as we enjoy being with the wolf pack, we're still new to the pack. The Silver Town pack promotes family, so now we're not just a bunch of single wolves but family. And we have our own autonomous family too."

"And," Nicole said, pulling his sweater over his head, "if we don't start using some protection, we're going to be expanding that family."

"Any problem with that?" Blake raised a brow, his mouth curved up a bit as if he liked the idea of seeing her carry their babies.

"Not for me." She smiled at him.

He scooped her up and set her on the bed, then removed her snow boots and socks. "Good." Then he lifted her sweater over her head and kissed her belly as if kissing the babies that might already be there.

Which made her wonder just how many she'd have, since he had three siblings and she had one. She wrapped her legs around him. "Hurry up, slowpoke. We have a busy day ahead of us tomorrow."

"And a busy time ahead of us tonight." He smiled.

She chuckled. "We can't keep taking naps to make up for it."

"Sure we can."

She smiled and ran her hand over his crotch, his erection straining for release, jumping to her touch. He groaned, but that prompted him to hurry and remove her ski pants. He shucked off his pants and his boxer briefs, then removed her panties and bra.

Then they were in bed together, kissing, panting, rubbing against each other in a frantic way. She thought about their next-door neighbors and how she and Blake would have to keep the noise down. Which was one good thing about making love in his bedroom in the house when his siblings weren't around. She couldn't wait to have a place of their own for that reason alone. She didn't know who was staying in the room on the other side of them. She hoped it wasn't a family.

Then she heard groaning and the bed hitting the wall rhythmically next to them. Not a family.

Blake smiled at her, and then they were back to kissing, touching, and rubbing their bodies together in a frenzied, passionate way, his hard body pressed against hers. He felt so good against her. Protective, sexy, heating her blood to fiery lava. Raw need surged through her as he began to kiss her jaw, then her throat, his warm lips giving her passionate, lingering kisses down to her breasts. She loved him and loved the way he made love to her.

She was feeling all his gorgeous muscle groups, loving how strong and able he was. And all hers.

He moved from her breasts to kiss her mouth again. She began kissing his, their kisses growing bolder, more insistent, their tongues dancing, stroking, twirling, tips touching. He smelled like a bit of heaven. Being with him like this felt so right, so good. His hand swept down her belly, and before she knew it, he was tackling her clit, making her body sing to his touch.

"Ohmigod," she moaned out as he circled her nubbin, then stroked it again. She was climbing toward the peak, and she dug her fingers into his biceps.

288   TERRY SPEAR

His dark gaze caught hers, and he smiled a little before
he brought her to the top. She tried to stifle a cry of pleasure
while he surged forward to drown out her cry with a deep,
stroking kiss.

She pulled at him to join her, spreading her legs for him,
and when he centered on her, she wrapped her legs around
him, and he pushed deep.

He felt so perfect, his erection thick, hard, and long,
thrusting into her, their kisses hot and eager.

He angled himself and dove in, making her reach for
the top of the world again. The pleasure stoked her all the
way to the top, and she climaxed again, shattering. He came
apart, too, groaning with completion, filling her with his
hot seed.

"God, I love you," he ground out, still pushing his cock
into her until the very end, then collapsing on top of her in
a loving, satisfied way. He gave her a smirk.

"You are the only one for me. I love you, my sexy wolf,"
she said.

And then he pressed soft kisses against her cheek, not
done showing her just how much she meant to him.

Early the next morning, Blake and Nicole had showered
and were getting ready to head down to breakfast once
Roxie arrived to monitor the cousins in the next room. In
the meantime, Nicole was listening to the suspects snoring.
She would be glad to finish up this case. She had a lot of
time invested in it and had uncovered a lot of interesting
information about the case, which had only piqued her

curiosity more. But she loved getting resolution in a case too.

"Did you know that testosterone and estrogen are released during sex, and that helps keep the body looking younger and more vigorous?" Blake said.

She glanced at Blake and smiled. "I thought you were looking up house designs."

"I am. I was just sharing what Kayla told us."

Nicole laughed. "Okay, so what else did your quiet sister say?"

"You get a good workout—toning your abs, back, butt, and thighs while thrusting."

Smiling, Nicole shook her head. "I could see Roxie saying that."

"Kayla often surprises us."

"Is that a recommendation for another romp between the sheets?"

"Always."

"Roxie's on her way soon. So we'll have to hold that thought." She called Nate, hoping she didn't wake him too early. But she had to learn if he had found anything. "Hey, are you awake?"

"Are you kidding? You're talking to an Army Ranger."

She chuckled. She should have known he'd say that.

"I found their trash from dinner and have already turned it over to the sheriff. Peter said Blake called him in the middle of the night and I called him at an ungodly hour in the morning—that we were conspiring against him."

Nicole laughed.

"He sent CJ to pick up the evidence. Maybe we'll get something if the evidence you turned in doesn't pan out."

"Okay, thanks. I've got wall-monitoring duty until Roxie shows up. See you later."

Nicole glanced at Blake, still concentrating on the monitor. She hadn't even discussed with him if he wanted to have an actual wedding ceremony, and she realized they hadn't talked about the kind of house they wanted or about taking a honeymoon. There were so many decisions to be made.

A wedding wasn't a priority for her. Building a house and having a place of their own was more important.

Though she'd never talked to her mother about having a wedding when she found a mate, she suspected her mother would want her to. "Wedding or no wedding? Just a justice of the peace?" she whispered to Blake.

"Wedding. They often have them at the pack leaders' estate. They have a great hall there for feasts, ceremonies, parties, you name it. It would be great fun and a super way to celebrate our union in a human way."

She was surprised he'd really want one. "Okay, sounds good. Your sisters can be my bridesmaids."

"And your brother can be one of my groomsmen, along with my brother." Blake considered the laptop again. "What kind of a house do you want?"

"Two-story? All the bedrooms upstairs? Or us in a separate suite, game room/family room upstairs where the kids will have their rooms? Or a sprawling one-story so we don't have to heat and cool two floors, and we could have one wing of the house as ours and the kids can be on the other side of the house?"

"Two-story so everyone can get their exercise. We'll have a master bedroom and bathroom suite downstairs, and the kids will have the upstairs bedrooms, bathroom, and game room."

She knew couples often got into squabbles when trying to agree on building a house together. She hoped they wouldn't. She would rather she had all her conflict with her cases, not her mate.

———————————————

That afternoon, Nicole went with Kayla and Roxie to the Silver Town Inn to pick up the restored tea set and enjoy Silva's birthday party. Her jaw dropped when she saw the beauty of the tea set, and she pulled her phone out to compare it with the picture of the one Peter had sent her. The tea set was clean and bright and looked like it was brand new.

"That is beautiful." Nicole showed the Wolff sisters the before photo of the tea set, and they were just as impressed with the restoration.

"Silva's going to love this, and it will make up for the distress she's had over her missing tea set." Nicole was ready to return Silva's tea set to her and wish her a happy birthday. She was glad to be included in the wolf pack fun. And so were her mate's sisters. She'd really felt she needed to be watching her own suspects, but Nate would take charge, and Blake and Landon were helping him with it. They all insisted the ladies go to the party. Nicole was still feeling guilty about it when they arrived at Silva's tea shop.

The tea shop was filled with she-wolves from the pack, everyone pretending it was just another day of dropping in to have lunch. Kayla opened the door to the tea shop so Nicole could enter carrying the tea set on a silver platter.

Lelandi was distracting Silva in the back of the tea shop, and then she turned to see Nicole with her tea set and cried out with joy. "You found it!"

The MacTire sisters came in after that, and everyone got up from their seats and called out happy birthday. Silva wiped away tears and hugged everyone.

Nicole said, "I found your tea set. You would never believe where it's been."

Silva smiled.

"The MacTire sisters were having it refurbished, but I couldn't tell you because it was for your birthday."

"You are the best PI ever. Thanks for joining our ranks. And welcome," Silva said to Roxie, whom she hadn't met yet. "And thanks so much to the MacTire sisters for your beautiful gift. You don't know how much this means to me."

But Nicole was sure everyone did.

Silva loved the Bavarian hot chocolate pot set that Kayla, Roxie, and Nicole had bought for her. Nicole realized just how nice it was to have two sisters like this. She could imagine visits to the tea shop with them in the future and shopping trips too.

Then Lelandi brought out a cake for the occasion. After eating soups and sandwiches, then slices of cake, they visited with the rest of the ladies, and Nicole was truly glad that she'd mated Blake and was staying here with the Silver pack.

After everyone ate, they watched Silva open the rest of her presents, and then Blake met Nicole at the tea shop to take her to the grocery store and then back to the lodge. "While I was watching the cousins before I came to get you, I thought there might be something up."

"Oh?" she asked.

"Yeah. Eli seemed to be mad at his brother. I couldn't hear what they were saying, and he stormed off for the slopes. Rhys and his cousin stared after him, and they didn't look happy."

"Sounds like they're getting on each other's nerves." Which wasn't good.

"I think so too."

After Blake told her about the issues between Rhys and his brother, Nicole didn't want to delay getting back to the lodge any longer than she had to. They picked up a few things to eat and would drop them off at the house first, then head over to the lodge.

She was afraid the cousins might end up checking out. Maybe only Eli would, but it concerned her that Rhys might be planning to leave. She still couldn't get used to the idea that Silver Town was now her home and she really belonged with a pack. She couldn't wait to meet everyone who belonged to the pack.

"Hey, no more goofing off for me. Once we drop off the groceries, I've got to stay on these guys the rest of the time they're here, just to ensure they don't try to skip out on us."

"I figured you'd say that. I'm with you on it."

"Where was Clay when the guys were mad at each other?"

"In the men's room. I saw him come out about the time Rhys and William took off to ski. Why would the insurance rep who hired him think he could do a good job? He can't even ski to get close to these guys."

"When he was first assigned the case, the guys were in Florida, not snow skiing."

"Okay. Gotcha. We'll keep on them. No more goofing off."

"You don't really mean that."

He chuckled. "At night, as long as they're sleeping, we're being mated wolves."

CHAPTER 19

As soon as they dropped off the groceries at the house, Blake wrapped his arm around Nicole and headed for the lodge. "I was looking at house plans. I sent you some blueprints if you want to look them over."

"Thanks, I will."

He called Roxie and let her know they were on their way into the lodge. "Where is everyone?"

"Rhys and William are out skiing. Landon and Nate went out to ski too. They're worried something's up with these guys. Eli is in his room."

"That's what I was afraid of." Blake said to Nicole, "What do you want to do?"

"If the guys are skiing, let's head on out."

"We'll be in the office grabbing our ski gear in a moment, Roxie. Let us know if anything comes up."

"I will. See you later."

They reached the office and found Kayla watching the security monitors.

Kayla glanced at the security monitor. "The cousins are coming in."

Blake looked at the monitor. "Okay, it looks like they're getting an early dinner."

"I guess we are too," Nicole said, looping her arm through his. "See you, Kayla. We'll have to skip dinner and a wolf run with you all tonight. Roxie can leave as soon these guys return to their room."

"Okay."

Nicole and Blake went to the restaurant and found a seat near the guys so they could listen in on the men's conversation.

"I can't believe I took three spills coming down the mountain this afternoon," Rhys said.

"Hell, I can't believe I was standing at the base of the mountain and suddenly fell on my ass."

Rhys laughed at his cousin. Then he ran his hands through his long hair. "Okay, listen. We'll stay through tomorrow, and the following day we're leaving. I don't care what Eli wants. We've been here long enough. We need to move on."

The server came and took Blake and Nicole's order for ribs, mashed potatoes, and asparagus.

"Good, Rhys. I was feeling the same way. We've had fun, but it's time to go. I already made our reservations for Acapulco, and we can be there in three days' time," William said.

"It sounds good to me. I'm ready for some heat. Snorkeling and scuba diving. Yeah, man. Until we leave, I want to get in as much skiing as we can. We probably won't be able to ski for a long while."

"Your brother says he doesn't want to come with us right away. He wants to ski longer, then join us."

"He doesn't have a choice. I don't trust him to clean up after himself."

"You can't always look after him," William said.

"Hell, I know that. Okay? He's an adult now." Rhys shook his head. "I just worry he'll leave something incriminating behind." Rhys took a sip of water from his bottle. "We're going to need more money in the near future."

"You're not really going to do the same thing again, are you?" William asked.

"Yeah, unless you want to do it to yourself this time."

"No, you're good at it, if you're going to do it again. Besides, no one will miss you this time. Me? We'd have to deal with upsetting my parents."

Rhys chuckled. "To them, Eli and I are already gone." He got a call on his phone. "Yeah, brother? I'll bring some food up. Yeah, and a couple of beers. We're staying for a couple more days. Don't worry about it."

Blake and Nicole cast each other looks, and then their food was served and they began eating.

The cousins' food was served right after that, but they'd ordered more food and drinks and were waiting on them now.

At least Blake and Nicole knew where the men were headed next if they got away from them before they could get the DNA analysis results. But they still hadn't said anything concrete that would prove Rhys planned to pretend-off himself for more insurance money.

"Hey, when we get Eli's food, I'll run his up to the room. You can wait by the fireplace, and I'll return and eat my dinner with you," Rhys said to his cousin.

"He can join us if he wants."

"Nah, he's watching football."

They got Eli's meal and split up, William taking their meals to the fireplace seating and Rhys going to the elevator with Eli's meal.

Roxie notified Blake in a text that Rhys was in the room telling his brother they were going to Mexico.

Blake: Thanks, we overheard them talking about it.

Roxie: I hope the DNA evidence comes back before they leave.

Blake: We all do.

Roxie: Rhys is leaving again.

Blake: He's eating his dinner by the fire with his cousin. We'll probably move next to the fire, have a couple of cups of hot chocolate, and pet Rosco.

Roxie: Good. He's missed you two.

Blake smiled and finished up his dinner. "Did you want to grab some cocoa and see Rosco?" he asked Nicole.

"I sure do since he's so close to where the men are."

They got their cocoas to go, and then Blake paid the tip for their meals and they left the restaurant.

When they reached the dog, Nicole crouched down and gave him a hug. "Hey, Rosco, did you miss me?" He was wagging his tail like crazy.

She'd made a real impression on their dog. Not to mention she seemed to make a great impression on everyone she'd met. Except maybe the men she helped to arrest and the other PI. He wondered what had happened to him.

Blake glanced around the lobby and saw the guy working on a laptop at a table on the other side. Blake wondered if he was working on another case or trying to get more information on these guys like Nicole had done. Did he know they were leaving for Mexico soon?

He thought Nicole would follow them, but it probably wouldn't work out. Even though having a honeymoon there with her would be fun, these guys might have noticed Blake and Nicole at the ski lodge, and then seeing them in Acapulco could tip the men off.

He suspected this was the last opportunity Nicole had to prove who Rhys was. After that, the insurance rep would have to hire someone else to investigate Rhys. At least she could forward the information to Taggart, and he could take it from there.

"We didn't get to ski this afternoon," Nicole said to Blake, making small talk that wouldn't seem suspicious.

"No, but we can ski tomorrow. We need to figure out when we're going to have the wedding ceremony and where we're going for a honeymoon." Again, Blake figured if the men overheard them, they would sound like a couple who were engaged to be married and not doing any surveillance on these guys.

"Costa Rica? I think that would be a wolf's paradise."

"Costa Rica it is."

That night, they retired to the room, made love, and listened for anything else that might help with the case. But the cousins just watched TV until two in the morning and didn't reveal anything further.

———————————

The next morning, Blake and Nicole heard blasting up on the mountaintop. Before the lifts opened, the ski resort staff had set charges to clear the unstable snow that could cause avalanches once the skiers were on the slopes. When Blake and Nicole headed downstairs, they saw Landon had brought Rosco to the lodge.

"Does he need his morning walk?" Blake asked his brother.

"I took care of it. Once you two move into the house, we can get back to our regular routine," Landon said.

"Okay, thanks. We're headed in to breakfast."

"Enjoy."

Blake and Nicole took their seats in the restaurant and ordered sausage and eggs.

"There's more snow on the way too," Blake said.

"That's not good. These guys might decide to head out of here before the snowstorm hits if they worry about getting out in time to make their plane trip."

"Possibly, but they seem to like the adventure of skiing in the snowstorms too. It hasn't stopped them before."

Once they finished breakfast, they saw the other insurance investigator typing away on his laptop at another table. "Do you want to see if we can slip by him and take a peek at what he's up to?" Blake asked.

"I sure do." They made sure to stay downwind.

When they walked behind him and on past him, Blake saw he was making flight reservations and hotel reservations for Acapulco for that afternoon.

So he planned to skip out on them and arrive in Mexico before the cousins did. Was Clay going to tell Nicole he was leaving?

Blake glanced at Nicole as they slipped out the door. She smiled back at him. "The million-dollar question is will he tell you he's leaving, or will he just sneak out?"

"Maybe he's changed. Maybe he'll be man enough to tell me he's leaving to try to catch up to them in Mexico. I haven't told him I know that's where they're going, but I would have once they were on their way out of here. He must believe he'll have the advantage of learning what he needs to when they arrive in Acapulco. He certainly doesn't have it here."

"Are you upset that he could catch them in Mexico?" Blake didn't think she appeared to be.

"Nah. I mean, I really wanted to solve the case here. But if I haven't before they leave for Mexico, maybe Clay can do it if he can get Rhys extradited," she said as they headed to the office to exchange snow boots for ski boots. "We still have a small window of opportunity. Maybe the DNA evidence will have some hits before they leave."

"If that happens, we arrest them and Clay's sitting in Acapulco waiting for these guys to arrive, only they don't ever show up."

She chuckled. "Yeah. Now for me, that would be the best scenario ever. Especially if he doesn't tell us where he's going and why."

Kayla walked into the office, all smiles. "Your favorite PI 'partner' is checking out."

"Did he say anything about why?"

"No. He just checked out, and he's headed outside with his laptop. Did you want to catch up to him and let him know you know?" Kayla asked.

"I could, but what's the use? Unless he emails me or calls or something, he's doing his usual vanishing act." Nicole fastened the buckles on her boots.

Kayla sat down at her work monitor. "The guy's a jerk of a wolf."

"I'll say." Nicole pulled on her ski jacket and zipped it up.

Blake was glad Nicole didn't intend to chase after Clay to force him to tell her the truth.

Nicole's phone dinged, and she pulled it out of her

pocket. "A text from Roxie. She said the cousins are leaving the room earlier than usual. Maybe because this is their last day for skiing." She texted her back. "I bet she'll be glad when she doesn't have to stay in the room or hide who she is all the time once these guys leave."

"No way," Kayla said. "She's having a blast being deep undercover. That's what she told me."

Nicole laughed. Then she frowned. "Should we have told the pack leaders we were mating and asked if I could join the pack first?"

Blake shook his head and pulled her into his arms. "No way. You know that's why they were all checking you out while eating at our restaurant? Besides, if one of the youngest Silvers had anything to say about it, she would say you had to stay with the pack after finding her Mittens for her."

Nicole smiled and hugged Blake back.

"See you later, Kayla," Nicole said, and she and Blake went outside to ski.

CHAPTER 20

THE SNOW HAD BEEN FALLING AS NICOLE AND BLAKE skied and sometimes caught sight of the cousins skiing, but then Nicole saw her brother and Landon coming out of the lodge to ski. They wore determined PI kinds of expressions as though they were out here to catch the bad guys, not just skiing for the fun of it. She loved them both for helping her with this.

"Hey, they're heading up to the chairlift now," she said to Nate and Landon, the snow swirling around them.

"Did you want a break? You both have been at it for a couple of hours," Nate said.

So they thought they would come out to relieve her and Blake. She so appreciated them for it.

"Since they're leaving tomorrow, I figure this is my last day to keep up surveillance on them," Nicole said.

"I understand. You don't think there will be too many of us keeping an eye on them?" Nate asked.

"No, I think you'll just appear to be two other skiers out here, enjoying the snowfall before they shut down the resort because of the worsening weather."

"Okay, good. Because we want to help you nail these guys," Landon said, looking like a wolf on a hunt, ready to take down some prey.

"Let's go then." Nicole would have liked to stop and warm up with a hot cup of cocoa, but when a mission was winding down like this, she really wanted to spend every minute on surveillance in case something was said that could give her the ammunition she needed to take the guys in.

Landon got a call, and everyone waited to see what it was about.

"Okay, Kayla, I'll take care of it." Landon pocketed his phone. "Sorry, duty calls. I'll be back out here as soon as I take care of a little guest issue."

"See you soon," Nicole said, wanting to get back on the slopes.

"I'll meet up with you when you're able to join us," Nate said, as if Landon was his ski partner.

"Okay, good show." Landon slapped him on the back and then skied back to the lodge.

She was glad Blake's family seemed to really like Nate too.

Nate followed Nicole and Blake to the chairlift, and they spied William, Rhys, and Eli in the line, maybe two chairlifts ahead of them once they loaded up. They watched first William and Rhys load up, and then Eli on the next chair. Two more riders per chair followed them before Nicole and Blake climbed onto theirs. As they were swept up into the air, Nate made the next chair.

The higher they rose, the higher the winds and the more the cold was cutting through her clothes. She definitely needed to get warmed up soon.

When they reached the top, Blake and Nicole off-loaded and moved out of the way. Nate joined them, and the three of them skied to where they thought the men had gone down. It worked better to have two skiers keeping the guys in their sights rather than trying to wait on a third or fourth person coming up on a chair.

They didn't see any sign of the cousins, but then they

smelled that the men had skied beyond where the trail ended and ski boundary signs were posted, warning of the danger beyond that.

"They went past the ski boundary signs." Nicole was irritated to the max. "We're not following them." She saw the expectant looks on her mate's and brother's faces, ready to track the men into danger.

"Right," Blake said, but she knew him better.

If she hadn't been up here with the two of them, she knew they would have followed the cousins' trails.

They began looking through the trees, searching for any sign of them on the forbidden slopes. Nate pointed to deeper snow on a ledge, which was off-limits to skiers for good reason. It was extremely steep, some trees covering the slope, and perfect for creating an avalanche.

She yanked off her backpack and pulled out her binoculars. "Ohmigod, yeah, it's them. All three of them. Foolhardy daredevils who don't give a damn about anybody else," Nicole said, irritated with the men. "If they cause an avalanche, several people on the slopes could be buried." She saw Rhys shouting at Eli. "They're fighting. Rhys is motioning to Eli to return to the marked ski slope."

Nate already had his binoculars out and was observing them too. "You're right. Eli's shaking his head, pointing down the mountain. He wants to go down that way too."

She handed her binoculars to Blake.

"Hell," Blake said. "Those men are nothing but trouble." He handed the binoculars back to Nicole and then called a number. "Hey, this is Blake Wolff up near Dead Man's Leap. We've got three men in the danger zone on a narrow ledge of piled-up snow on North Ridge who could very well cause an avalanche. Can we get the area cleared that might be affected? Thanks."

Nicole was glad Blake could do that.

They all looked down the mountain to see what kind of traffic they still had. At least the ski lifts had stopped because of the weather, but skiers were still making their way down the slopes.

Nicole hoped Blake hadn't called in a false alarm, but anyone with any good sense would know the danger these men could potentially create. "Rhys shoved Eli, and his brother fell on the ledge." After that, ripples of snow spilled down the steep slope, and her heart went into overdrive. "My God, they've started an avalanche."

A cracking sound filled the air, and then snow—growing in volume like a massive wave of frozen water—was picking up speed, rumbling like thunder. The ledge the two brothers and cousin had been standing on collapsed, and the snow carried them tumbling down the steep slope. Nicole and the others looked on in horror, glancing down at the skiers hurrying to ski out of the path of the deadly mass of advancing snow that could travel up to a hundred miles per hour. No one could outski it.

Blake made the call to emergency services with an update. "An avalanche is thundering down the mountain. Okay, good." He turned to Nicole and Nate. "I need to get down there and help with rescue."

"Us too," Nate said, Nicole agreeing.

"Landon will be bringing Rosco to the search for victims," Blake said.

"I'm glad for that. He did great when you were in training with him."

The snow came to a dead stop at the base of the mountain, and Nicole knew what that was like, first to be carried on the fluidly moving snow, then to being buried in it like she'd been entombed in cement. Little ripples of snow continued to fall, and Nicole, Blake, and her brother needed to traverse the hill and ski down the intermediate slope where the avalanche hadn't reached the run.

"I don't see any sign of our suspects," Nicole said.

"Buried," Blake said.

Adrenaline pumped through Nicole's blood as they skied down to reach the others who were already forming lines, using long poles to probe for figures under the snow.

Nate told Nicole, "You don't have to do this."

Blake glanced at her, probably wondering why she wouldn't want to help.

"Nicole was buried in an avalanche and knows all about it."

Nicole said, "I'll be fine."

"You didn't tell me that," Blake said, looking worried. "You don't have to help us if it bothers you."

"No, it's like paying it forward after the men, women, and rescue dog found me. I don't want to ever have to experience that again, and I certainly don't want anyone else to have to either. Or end up in a coma or die."

She didn't know what was the worst: the crushing snow, claustrophobia, carbon dioxide replacing the oxygen in the air, breathing more rapidly, being disoriented, the unending cold, or knowing the clock was ticking and every minute counted if they were going to find her alive and not brain-dead. She'd panicked, screamed, and shouted, to no avail. She'd been lucky and had landed on her face in the snow, allowing for a pocket of air to surround her so that she could breathe for longer. A pocket of air the size of a grapefruit could allow someone to breathe for up to two hours. People who landed on their back in an avalanche usually didn't fare as well. The packed snow could weigh more than a ton.

If they didn't get the victims out within the first twenty minutes, the chance they wouldn't find them alive grew. Half of avalanche victims died within the first twenty-five minutes. Ninety-five percent would die within the next two hours.

She'd been unconscious for some of the time, which had helped save her breath and her life. And when she'd heard the dog's muffled barking from way up above her snowy prison and people talking, she'd had hope.

Already, she witnessed dogs and people digging out four different victims. Not their suspects, but skiers who got hit by the avalanche farther away. Thank God Blake had called in the emergency before it had occurred, giving them time to clear the slopes as much as possible and to have equipment and volunteers arriving soon after. Those who were being pulled out now were unsteady but standing on their feet, a couple of them wanting to help with the search. She hated the cousins for pulling this crap, just to get some thrill, when it would scar others for life, ruining an otherwise fun ski outing for them.

Two German shepherds, a yellow Labrador retriever, and Rosco were bounding through the snow, searching for buried skiers or snowboarders. Dogs and the *lupus garous* could smell humans buried under as much as fourteen feet of snow, which was how a big, old friendly German shepherd had found her. She'd loved him to death for being her savior. The cold, isolation, and not being able to move an inch for three hours had made her pray others were searching for her.

After two hours, little hope remained for victims, so she'd been one of the really lucky ones. She'd suffered from dehydration and hypothermia but no other injuries.

Roxie and Kayla joined them with poles to use to search for victims, but Nicole, Nate, and Blake and his sisters headed for the area where they thought the cousins might be located, closer to where the avalanche started. The search would continue until everyone was accounted for. She knew someone would be gathering information about who was still out here skiing. That was why it was so important that people didn't venture on these trips alone. If they knew they had ten victims, they'd continue to search until all ten victims were recovered, dead or alive.

Landon stayed with Rosco, serving as his handler, sticking with him wherever he was going. That was the thing about the dogs. They didn't discriminate about who they would search for next. Whoever they found was a good thing.

Victims were being taken by sled to the first-aid hut, ambulances arriving in the parking lot already.

The wind was whipping the snow around, the visibility only a few feet as the snow continued to fall in masses of flakes.

Dogs were barking while Nicole was probing the snow, telling herself these men needed to be tried for their crimes. They didn't deserve to die, unless they had murdered Rhys's parents. She had to find them. If they had a real near-death experience, would they finally come clean?

She finally had a hit. "Here!" she shouted.

Some of the rescuers came to help her dig out the person with shovels. He was buried deep, about eight feet, whoever it was. Then she recognized the ski jacket way down below. Eli.

It had been an hour since they had started searching for the victims, and Eli was unconscious, his hat and gloves lost. When paramedics began to work on him, she waited until they'd restarted his heart and then reluctantly left him, continuing to help the others probe for other victims. He might have been brain-damaged. Or he might still die.

Not too far from where Eli had been buried, Nate got a hit. "Here!"

Rescuers joined him to unbury the victim. Nicole continued to probe for other victims while watching to see who Nate and the others pulled from their snow cocoon. William. He was unconscious, too, but after the two men were worked on, they were strapped to sleds and taken to the first-aid hut.

Nate gave her a thumbs-up. The cousin was going to be okay. She noticed the rescuers were all moving in their direction with the dogs. It appeared they'd rescued everyone except for Rhys.

"Who are we looking for?" Jake Silver asked.

"Rhys," Nicole said. "His cousin and brother were there and there." She pointed to the locations. "Rhys is probably somewhere nearby. The last I saw of them was Rhys shoving Eli and knocking him on his butt on that ledge of snow. Then it all came down."

She noticed all the rescuers were listening raptly, needing to know where the last victim might be. Time had already run out for the victim statistically, but miracles did happen. She remembered hearing about a teen who had survived twenty hours under the snow when he and his buddy had gone out of bounds and snowboarded down a ridge between rocks and trees. It took rescuers forever to find him. Their probes kept hitting rocks and tree branches buried under the snow. Fifteen years old with the rest of his life ahead of him, all shot to hell with one adrenaline junkie move. His best friend wasn't so lucky. They discovered his body first, lying face up, and he had suffocated. The other boy had been found facedown, with a pocket of air and unconscious. No injuries other than dehydration and hypothermia, which could have killed him too. At least for him? He vowed no more snowboarding off-trail.

Snow continued to fall all around them, the winds making it so much worse as they continued to probe the area, searching for the last man. She was glad everyone else had been found.

"Did everyone else survive?" she asked Jake.

"Yeah, one broken arm, bruises, lots of scared folks. We rescued six. But everyone else has been accounted for."

"Good." Then Nicole got a call, and she poked her probe in the snow and pulled out her phone. The call was from Peter. She'd assumed he was out here.

"Hey, I'm arresting William and Eli. We got the DNA results back from the evidence you had submitted. We have two hits on the 9mm gun," Peter said. "They're Rhys's fingerprints. Or I should say Oscar Kovac's. That's the good thing about him having been in the military. They had to fingerprint him and do background checks before he could join the service and become an MP. The cigarette butt came through for Eli. He'd been arrested for petty theft so we found his fingerprints in the system. The men are at the Silver Town Clinic being looked after. No sign of Rhys yet?"

"We're still looking for his body, three hours and counting."

"Okay, well, the other two men are waiting for you when you feel you can leave the site."

"Thanks so much, Peter. I could hug you."

"You're welcome. I heard about the other PI. We had to make sure you got the kudos for the job."

"Thanks." Nicole ended the call and told everyone the good news. They all paused for a group hug.

She would be so irritated if they didn't find Rhys alive. Sure, they wouldn't have to waste taxpayers' dollars on trying him, but it didn't seem like justice.

After three more hours, rescuers were returning to the lodge for late lunch breaks and warming up and then switching out with others. The snow conditions were the worst. Even Landon had to take Rosco in for a break to eat and let him rest for a few hours. Most of the other dogs had already returned to the lodge to eat with their handlers and take a long rest.

"We need to take a break," Kayla said.

Nicole heard it in her voice. She wanted to help Nicole finish the mission, but the hopes of finding Rhys alive were dimming by the minute.

"Yeah. The rested crew is coming back out. Why don't we head back in to warm up together? As a family." Nicole smiled at Roxie. "You no longer have to be undercover."

"I'm thrilled for that!" Roxie gave her another hug, and

then the Wolff family and Nate headed for the lodge, eager to get warmed up.

They were worried about more avalanches occurring during the snowstorm. While the family was inside ordering their steaks, intending to spend more hours out working in the cold after they rested for a while, Jake joined them.

"Hey, they're calling off the search for a few hours, letting the dogs get some rest. We're keeping everyone off the slopes so a few wolves can do a search. Because of the low visibility, no one can see them out there, and it is the off-limit area. Peter asked me to see if you want to go into town to speak with Eli and his cousin. Roads are really bad, but I can get you there, Nicole," Jake said.

She glanced at Blake.

"Whatever you want to do is fine with me. If you want me to come with you, I will. Or I can take a run on the wild side and try to find Rhys."

She was torn. She wanted to search for Rhys too, but she did want to learn what she could from Eli and William and then let Taggart know where she was at on the case.

"All right." She knew Blake didn't want to sit around while she interrogated someone. She thought Nate might want to go with her, but she knew him well enough to know he'd prefer running as a wolf on a rescue mission.

"I'll go with Blake," Nate said.

Landon didn't jump right in, but then said, "Okay, I was thinking of holding off on any more searches because I'll need to take Rosco out again in a few hours, but if we can find the bastard as wolves, I'm all for it."

Kayla and Roxie smiled. "I'll help with the lodge," Kayla said.

"I'm going to enjoy my newfound freedom," Roxie agreed.

Nicole smiled at Landon. She suspected he wanted in on the excitement as much as anything. They didn't need to try to break their necks skiing down out-of-boundary ski areas but could get just as much of an adrenaline rush from searching for a victim and finding him.

"Okay, as soon as I eat, I'll go with you to town, Jake," Nicole agreed.

"I'll just grab a bite to eat then too."

"Join us. We'll make room," Blake said to Jake, even though they were already a little crowded at their table.

CHAPTER 21

Jake grabbed an empty chair, and the Wolff family and Nate squeezed in more at the table to give him room to join them. Nicole could tell from the way he was smiling that he was glad to be invited to join the Wolff clan.

Nicole noted that the restaurant was filled to capacity with guests and rescue workers, and even more famished folks were eating their meals in the lobby. Of course, guests could always go to their rooms if they needed a place to sit down to eat. But most everyone was talking about the avalanche and rescues and enjoying the camaraderie, eager to get back out and ski once the weather let up.

Until they found Rhys, the area where he and his kin had started the avalanche would be off-limits while searches continued to try to locate him.

"You know, this makes me think Rhys is really fine, that he escaped the avalanche, and it's just a ploy to obtain another life insurance policy payout," Nicole said as their steak platters were served.

Jake had ordered a steak, too, and it came a few minutes later.

"Does he have another life insurance policy?" Blake asked, cutting into his steak.

Nicole did a search, not having thought of that, though she should have. "Yeah, he does. It's a different insurance company."

"And the payee?" Blake asked.

"Kent Albright."

"Who's that?" Blake asked.

"Maybe Eli's alias?"

"So William wasn't in on this little scam," Roxie said.

"It appears not, which I thought was kind of interesting. Maybe Rhys felt Eli was old enough now to be responsible and pay him half of the money when he came back from the dead. If Eli is Kent Albright. But this time, Rhys could be dead for real," Nicole said.

"It would be suspicious if William kept getting payouts from dead people." Nate took another bite of his steak.

"True." Nicole smiled at Roxie. "I bet you're relieved not to have to stay at the lodge in hiding all the time."

"I am, but if you need my help with any of your new cases, don't hesitate to ask," Roxie said, sounding adamant.

"Me too," Kayla said.

Landon and Blake agreed.

Nate laughed. "Seems you have a whole investigative team."

"That goes for you too," Roxie told Nate. "We're family now."

"All I've got to say is when you arrived to do your mission here in our territory, we all benefited," Jake said, smiling.

"Well, I know where to go when I want some photos for our new house. Do you take wolf portraits?" Nicole asked Jake.

"Sure do. Family sittings, wolf and otherwise, and wolves at play. Some of those can be the most fun," Jake said.

"Okay, then we'll have to get both kinds taken."

After they finished their meals, Nate, Blake, and Landon planned to head out as wolves with the twin ski instructors who would serve as their handlers in their human form in case anyone who shouldn't be out there wanted to help look for the last victim. That way, Nate, Blake, and Landon could strip and shift in the office, then go out through the staff entrance into the swirling snow and off to the avalanche site.

Nicole gave Blake a hug and kiss. "Be careful." She didn't want him buried out there should another avalanche occur.

"I will be. If we hear an avalanche coming, we'll leave."

"By then it could be too late." He knew it and she knew it.

"We'll be careful."

Then everyone hugged Landon and Nate and Blake, and they left to strip in the office.

"Okay, I'm ready to go," Nicole told Jake. She just hoped they didn't run afoul of the weather on the way to town.

After a harrowingly slow drive because of the blizzard conditions, she and Jake finally reached the town and parked at the clinic. A few cars were parked there, buried in snow.

"Our deputies, Trevor and CJ, are on duty, watching over your suspects. Dr. Weber said they're fine, but because of both having been unconscious, he had MRI scans done and they looked good. William's got a broken leg though. Still, they've been told they have to stay here under observation. Eli's been asking about his brother. William's been real quiet."

"All right."

"Did you want me to come into the room with you while you're interviewing each of them? They're in separate rooms." Jake walked up to the glass door, and it slid open for them.

"Just wait. Sometimes when they only have a lone female to talk to, they're more open."

"I'll wait in the staff lounge. If you need me, let me know. I've already read both men their rights, so we're good there."

"Thanks."

"First door on the right is where William is. On the left, two doors down is Eli's room."

Nicole decided to see Eli first. She figured if anyone ended up spilling the beans, he would be more likely to. She walked into the room and smiled at the young man. "Hi, I'm Nicole Grayson. My probe found you buried in the snow. I've been where you were, buried alive. It's not something you ever get over. May I?" She motioned to a chair for visitors.

"Yeah, sure. You're probably not a thrill seeker." Eli smirked.

"You mean the element of danger adds to the thrill? Steep hill, virgin snow, off-limits area, signs posted to keep people out so they don't cause avalanches like the one that buried you, your cousin, your brother, and six other people?"

Eli stared at her wide-eyed. Why? Because she'd made him and his brother and cousin? Or, God forbid, they might have killed other people? She assumed he and his brother and cousin were totally self-centered and could only see the fun in it for themselves, not what they could have done to others. Even rescuers were at risk because of their foolhardiness.

"My... Rhys, is he here?"

She shook her head.

Eli's cocky attitude plummeted, his eyes filling with tears. She glanced at the clock. "Five hours and counting, and they haven't located him yet."

He narrowed his eyes. "Is anyone still looking?"

"Yeah, at great risk to themselves if another avalanche

occurs. The area has whiteout conditions. The snow is falling so heavily it could easily cause another slide."

Eli looked at his hands clutched on his chest. "He's dead, isn't he." It wasn't a question.

"He might be alive. Or brain-damaged. There's no way to be sure. That's a long time under the snow."

"I could have skied down with my brother and cousin if my brother hadn't pushed me. We woulda made it." Tears spilled down his cheeks. "He should have just let me go."

"As soon as any of you started down the mountain, you would have triggered the avalanche. The snow was unstable there," Nicole said. "Others could very well have died because the three of you went beyond the ski boundary."

"Where's William?"

"He's safe. He has a broken leg." She wanted to tell Eli that he would be in police custody soon. Eli too. "You've been read your rights, correct? You know anything I ask you could be used in a court of law?"

"That's what the cop said."

"Okay, then we know you're Eli Kovac, Oscar's younger brother. Kent Albright?"

Eli wiped his eyes. "How'd you know?"

"I know just about everything there is to about you, your brother, and your cousin. I'm a private investigator for the insurance company that paid out the money for Oscar's death. You dumped a cigarette butt in the snow, and you left a coffee cup lying around. We got DNA off both, and since you'd been in jail, they had your DNA on file. It was a match. Not to mention your brother called you by name when we were close by and listening to your conversations. Where did you come up with the names?"

Eli's eyes were as blue as his brother's and cousin's, and they widened noticeably.

"I know Rhys is Oscar and not dead."

"My real dad's name is Percy Albright. I just took his name, and he made me use Kent, my grandfather's name, for my first name. I hated it."

"Okay. When your mother and stepdad died, how did that happen?"

Eli blew out his breath. "I didn't have nothing to do with that."

"With his supposed death? No, I imagine not. That was all on William and your brother."

"They didn't tell me they were doing that. I mean, killing off Oscar in a scam," Eli said. "They never believed I could keep my mouth shut."

"You knew he was supposed to be dead?"

"No. We hadn't seen each other in years. Then he contacted me out of the blue and said he wanted to see me. That he and William were going to the ski resort, and he wanted to know if I wanted to come along. I was shocked to hear he was alive."

"Were you living with your birth father?"

"Yeah." Eli shrugged. "He was okay."

"Not abusive like your stepfather?"

"Arthur was never my father. Once he knew it, he took it out on me," Eli admitted.

"I'm sorry. No one should ever have had to go through what you had."

"But...I never told anyone."

"Your visits to the hospital spelled it out."

"I couldn't tell anyone. Arthur said if I did, he'd take it out on my mother, too, and he'd make me disappear."

"Did your brother ever protect you?"

"He tried. But he couldn't stop Arthur."

"Your mother received the payout for your death."

"She paid my biological father to take me in. Dad knew about me, but he was happy for Mom to take care of me until Arthur learned I wasn't his son. Once the abuse started, Mom felt the only way to help me was to get rid of me. She was still seeing my dad, you know."

Now that was a surprise to Nicole. "You could have just lived with your father. You didn't have to fake your death."

"He wanted the insurance money to support me. He said it was the only way he would go along with it."

Bastard. It also meant Eli's biological dad could be brought up on charges of defrauding the insurance company. He should have been a more responsible dad and taken care of Eli. "What about your mom and stepdad dying in the fire?"

"My stepdad, Arthur, set the fire."

"What?" Another shocker.

"He learned I hadn't died and that Mom and Dad were still having an affair. Arthur said he figured something was up with her, and he followed her to my dad's house. After their big fight at my dad's house, Arthur left, and she went home to try to smooth things over with him. Then the fire happened."

So a case of murder-suicide. "You think Arthur took their lives so she couldn't be with you and your father?"

"Yeah. Arthur couldn't bear losing her."

"I'm sorry about that. Did you receive any of the estate?"

"I shouldn't have. I was dead, but yeah, Oscar came through for me. He gave me half of everything, even though he said I was just a little pipsqueak. But then William had this harebrained idea that my brother should die in a kayaking accident. I would've told him not to do it. Being dead wasn't fun. It was a pain. Though I guess the alternative was that I could have been dead at Arthur's hands. The abuse wasn't fun either."

"So, Rhys/Oscar and William just wanted the money."

"Easy money, new life. And Rhys—I call him that now because he had a meltdown every time I called him Oscar—was obligated to do Army Reserve time, and he wasn't going to do it."

Nicole shook her head. "When you supposedly drowned, how did you manage that?"

Eli ran his hands through his hair. "Mom and I figured it out. Dad came and picked me up. When Rhys learned I hadn't really died, he wanted to kill me. But Mom was afraid he would give away the secret when the police questioned my brother and his friends. I had to sneak off. They were so busy ignoring me, it was easy to do."

"She and Arthur acted angry with Rhys about losing sight of you at the lake because she was trying to keep up the charade?"

"Not Arthur. He was glad I was gone. But yeah, she told me she gave Rhys shit for it, then later, she finally told him the truth, once she was safe, having collected the life insurance. Will…will I go to jail?"

"That's up to the courts to decide. But at least you won't be on the run any longer, hiding your identity."

"No trip to Acapulco, I guess."

She smiled, thinking of Clay being there, sipping a tequila poolside or beachside, waiting for the brothers and cousin to show up. She needed to call Taggart to let him be the bearer of bad news to Clay.

"What about William?"

"He took part in the scheme where your brother 'died' and received the life insurance payout with the intent to defraud the insurance company."

"So if my brother is dead, he won't have to go to trial," Eli said, but he still looked upset about the prospect. Maybe he was just coming to terms with the eventuality.

"Right." She was going to tell Eli that he'd most likely receive an insurance payment for his brother's death, but she decided not to mention it. He probably already knew about it. "The police will investigate your story further about your parents' death. Your own dad could be up on charges if it's shown he knew he received a fraudulent life insurance payout for your death."

Eli looked at his hands again, clutched together. She wondered if he cared. Maybe he figured it served his father right for not just taking care of his son like he should have all those years once he learned about the abuse.

"I know you care about your brother. I hope they find him alive and well." Though if they did, he might want to kill Eli for talking so much. "Is there anything else you want to say?"

"I'm sorry about the people who got caught in the avalanche. And the guys still out there looking for Rhys who could be in danger. But they get paid to do dangerous work."

"They're volunteering their hours and their lives to the cause. They don't get paid." Nicole didn't care if she sounded angry with Eli. Yeah, he wasn't very old, but jeez, wise up!

"Oh. I hope no one else gets hurt. When we fell, I figured that could be the end of me. I thought maybe it was karma for faking my death before. And for Rhys too. I knew the three of us were going to be buried, though it was a hell of a fun ride when I was on top. I never thought it would reach anyone else."

"I'll let you know as soon as we recover him," Nicole said. "I'm going to talk to your cousin and then go back out and help the others look for him."

Eli lifted his gaze to hers. "Thank you."

"You're welcome. We won't stop searching until we find him." Though they might again if they deemed the weather was too risky and Rhys hadn't made it.

Then she left the room and entered William's. She knocked on the door, and William turned his attention from the TV to her. She assumed he'd be hostile, since he would be up on charges of fraud. She spelled out who she was but didn't take a seat. She didn't think she'd be here long.

"How's Eli doing?"

She was surprised he'd ask about the younger brother. She suspected William didn't like Eli butting into his friendship with Rhys.

"He's doing well. Better than you as far as no major injuries. And it doesn't appear the scare of being buried alive has bothered him either."

William snorted.

"How are you doing?"

"In pain. I have a headache the size of Alaska."

"I'll check with the nurse to have her bring you some more pain medication. So you know why I'm here."

"Yeah, to send me to jail. The sheriff already talked to me about it. I want my lawyer."

She shrugged. "No problem."

He looked away from the TV again to stare at her. "Where's Rhys?"

"Buried still. Someone will let me know as soon as they find him. I'm going back out to help with the search."

"You? So you can get your man?"

"I found Eli so he can live another day. My brother, another private investigator who has been helping with your case, found you. Was it a mistake?"

William pursed his lips and looked back at the TV.

"Six other people were buried in the avalanche you and your cousins caused."

That got William's attention, his eyes widening. "I...I didn't cause it."

"You were standing with your cousins on the shelf of snow that was about to go. You are just as culpable."

He rubbed his forehead.

"Thank God they all survived. If you want to pull a stupid stunt like that again, let it be on your heads, no one else's. But the thing of it is, you put the rescuers' lives at risk too. Anyway, you talk to your lawyer. I'm turning the case over to the insurance company. Pay your dues to society, get on with your life, and stay out of trouble is my advice to you." But once someone went down that road where they felt they could make a living off criminal acts, working a regular job was hard to do.

"Good luck on finding Rhys. And thanks for helping."

"You're welcome. I've been buried alive in snow before for three hours. It's a nightmare I'll never get over so I hope we find him and he's fine."

William looked a little surprised to hear it, his brows raised. "Thank you."

She left then, asked the nurse to give William more pain medicine if it was okay, and told Jake she was ready to return to the search. When they walked out into the blizzard to his Humvee, she called Taggart. "Okay, good news and not so good news."

"It sounds like you're standing in the howling wind."

She got inside the Humvee. "Yeah, we're in the middle of a blizzard. I'm sending you all the information you need for your case. Rhys is Oscar, and the DNA evidence proves it. The three men started an avalanche at the resort, and William and Eli are at the medical clinic in custody. William just has a broken leg and can stand trial. Eli's fine. Rhys is still buried. I'm going back out to help with the search."

"Hell."

"Yeah. These guys know how to go out with a bang. Anyway, it's been six and a half hours already since Rhys was buried."

"Okay, so we're looking at only getting our money out of William at this point."

"Very likely. Oh, and you might want to tell your other private investigator Clay that they're not going to Acapulco. So he might want to look for another job."

Taggart chuckled. "Clay thought he was going there ahead of the suspects since you had everything covered at the Silver Town Ski Resort."

"I did. It's all done."

"You know what, the job's yours if you like. I can tell him, but I think it would have more impact coming from you."

She smiled. "Sure, I'll tell him." Then they ended the call. She was watching the road, the wipers going as fast as they could, sweeping away the snow, the flakes coming down even faster. She hoped they were going to make it through.

"I was going to suggest you just stay the night at my place," Jake said, "but I know what it's like to be newly mated."

She wondered about that. She couldn't believe she could go home with Blake and stay in the guest suite and enjoy all the camaraderie with his brother and sisters.

But she also wanted to help Blake find Rhys.

"Yeah, I mean, I could have just run as a wolf back to the lodge. It would probably be easier than driving in this stuff."

"No way. I'm the pack's subleader, and I wouldn't even consider it. Hell, if you got lost, Darien would have my head. Alicia and Carly would never speak to me again."

Nicole laughed. The drive didn't take long from the medical clinic to the ski resort, except in a blizzard. Jake was driving at a snail's pace. He had to. She couldn't see the lanes in the road any more than he could. Twice, he hit gravel on the shoulder, and they knew they were too far over.

"But you can stay at one of the rooms for the night so you don't have to drive back in this," she said.

"That would be very much appreciated. Alicia and my kids would thank you for it."

Nicole called Kayla. "Hey, it's me. Jake's bringing me back, but it's taking forever because we can barely see the road. Can you find a room for Jake to stay in?"

"Yeah, sure. Are you moving out to the house with Blake?"

"Let's see how the search for Rhys goes. We might stay at

the room, get a little sleep, and head back out there tonight if we still can't find him. No word, I suspect."

"No. They're still searching. They've got tons of lights out there, propped up with sandbags, but everything is cloaked in a screen of snow, and the wind is blowing so hard that they're afraid the lights are going to be blown down."

"Okay, Kayla. I'd say we're halfway there, but it might take another half hour or longer."

"Okay, drive safe. Tell Jake he's got a room."

"I will." Nicole ended the call and tried to lean back against the seat to reduce some of the tension she was feeling. It didn't help. "They've got a room for you, Jake."

"Good. I'll let Alicia know I'm staying the night."

Then Nicole got on the phone to call Clay. She was smiling when she got ahold of him. "If you're waiting poolside for the brothers and cousin to show up in Acapulco, don't bother."

"Brothers?"

"Yeah, the case is solved. You can find another one that's even more lucrative."

"Wait, you arrested them?"

"Yeah, they're all confined." The one buried in snow counted as confined, Nicole figured.

"Does Taggart know about this?"

"He does. He told me to pass the word along to you."

The phone clicked dead in her ear. She smiled. "I don't think he liked the news."

"That's the other private investigator?" Jake asked.

"Yeah."

"I didn't like him from the get-go."

"The feeling is mutual." She thought again about locating Rhys and just prayed they could find him before anyone else was injured by avalanches.

CHAPTER 22

BLAKE WAS FEELING AS THOUGH LOCATING RHYS tonight was hopeless. They were looking for a dead man. Yet he didn't want to give up the search either in the event the man was still alive. As wolves, their wool coats kept them warm, and the snow collected on their outer guard hairs, the inner coat keeping them warm and dry. Even so, the blowing snow was getting into their eyes, and the howling wind made it almost impossible to hear what else was going on.

Twice, they'd made out the sound of avalanches, one near one of the ski lifts where no one should be, and another near the searchers that had all the wolves and men running for their lives. The wolves could run a lot faster, and he was praying none of the ones in their human skin were caught up in the avalanche. When the snow had settled, it had buried all their lights.

But everyone had made it out of the avalanche's path.

They checked each other over, making sure everyone was all right. Tom Silver, one of the subleaders, pulled out his cell phone. "Hey, Darien, another avalanche just buried our lights. We haven't found Rhys yet. Yeah, everyone's safe. Okay, will do." He shoved his phone in his pocket. "Darien wants me to put it to a vote. Do we stay a while longer, or give it a rest until daybreak?"

No one said anything, and Blake assumed they were wolf-tired, but they didn't want to give up the search either. Everyone could imagine what it would be like to be buried alive and hoping beyond hope someone would come to their rescue.

Then they saw three she-wolves coming to help with the search—Nicole and his sisters. Hell, if they were coming out to aid them, no way could the guys give up, even if the she-wolves were fresh.

Jake was with them, too, in his human form. "I'm taking over from you, Tom. Go, get some rest, warm up. Some more fresher wolves are joining our ranks. Those of you that need to get warm and rest up a bit, go on inside. The Wolff clan has hot cocoa ready for you, and you can order dinners on the Silvers if you haven't eaten yet." When no one made a move to leave, Jake said, "That's an order." Then he smiled, but Blake knew he still meant it as an order.

The other volunteers made their way toward the light of the lodge that was a warm, welcoming beacon on a blizzardy, cold night.

Blake, Landon, and Nate didn't budge. No way were they going in while their sisters and his mate were out here facing danger without them.

Six more hefty male wolves joined them, and they began hurriedly looking for Rhys's body.

Then more *lupus garous* in their human skins came out to join them too. Some of the wolves found the buried lights and woofed and dug at them. The men hurried over to shovel the snow off them, then set them up next to nearby trees, wrapping rope around the lights and trees to keep an avalanche from burying them again.

Nicole nuzzled Blake, and he hoped they didn't have to do this much longer. He wanted to return to bed with his beautiful mate. But he knew if they didn't find this bastard, they wouldn't be thinking of anything else tonight but recovering his body.

As soon as she was with him, he felt oddly invigorated, like he was a young wolf pup, eager to please her. She rubbed against him, just as happy to join him. Then they helped the others search again for the victim.

Two hours later, Roxie woofed and began digging vigorously at the snow. The wolves and men had been spread out, but they all joined her to help her dig for a body. She woofed again when she reached the victim's hand.

Others were trying to shovel snow away from his head. Blake recognized Rhys's scent and clothes right away, but he wasn't stirring. His face was down, though, and the more they dug the snow away, the more Blake could see Rhys's body was lying on top of a mesh of branches that the snow had torn away from trees on the way down the slope. The good news was that the branches had given him a large area of air that he managed to use to breathe. He was unconscious and cold, but Blake heard his faint heartbeat and woofed, letting the others know he was alive.

Everyone worked even harder, Jake calling for a sled and his brother Tom coming with a medical team. As wolves, they all had some medical first-aid training to take care of their own when they needed to. But Rhys was human, and his situation was critical.

After the men pulled him out of the hole, the medical team stabilized him as much as they could, then wrapped him up on the sled, the snowmobile taking off for the first-aid hut.

Blake nuzzled Nicole's head and licked her cheek. They'd had a long night and needed to get warmed up. He suspected she'd want to speak with Rhys when she could. Tomorrow though. Rhys needed to recover.

Everyone wearing their human skin began to pack up their gear and head back to the lodge.

The wolves headed around to the staff door so they could slip into a room where they'd left their clothes and shift. The Wolff family—which included Nicole, even though they didn't have a marriage certificate to say so yet, and Nate—all ended up in the office, shifting, dressing, and congratulating each other.

"Let's get some dinner," Blake said.

"Here or at home?" Kayla asked. "I think it would be nice to relax at home. I'll cook."

"We'll help, and yes, I think that would be nice," Nicole said.

Rosco hurried to greet them, his tail sweeping out frantically. He was ready to go home.

Over a dinner of spaghetti, garlic toast, spinach salad, and red wine, Nicole couldn't have been more relieved that Roxie had found Rhys and this mission was over. Though the avalanche had been a close call for him.

Nicole squeezed Blake's hand and smiled. "Did you want to stay at the lodge tonight or move over here? You could have the room cleaned in the morning, and it would be available to guests."

"We're done with the mission so we can pack up your bags and mine and return. That works for me."

"Tomorrow morning, I need to speak with Rhys. Not

that I need any more information from him, but I'd love to gloat," Nicole said.

Everyone chuckled.

"Can I go with you?" Roxie asked. "I'd like to gloat too."

Nicole smiled at her. "You sure can. Hopefully, he'll be well enough to speak to."

"And Clay?" Blake asked.

"I told Taggart the news, and he told me to tell Clay the case is wrapped up. He was not happy, to say the least. Not only did he not finish the mission, but he won't be reimbursed for his trip to Acapulco."

"Good," Landon said. "He was one egotistical wolf."

After dinner, Nate, Blake, and Nicole headed back to the lodge. "See you tomorrow," Nate said but gave Nicole a hug and Blake a handshake.

"See you tomorrow," Blake said, and he escorted Nicole up to the room.

She had mixed feelings about moving in with Blake's family. She realized she liked her privacy. She hoped the guest suite at the house would offer that. Still, it was kind of nice getting away from the whole family while staying at the lodge. They couldn't tie up a lodge room until their house was built though. And she knew she'd have fun with Blake's siblings at night. It was just that she'd feel like she was overextending her welcome if she raided the fridge at night or wanted to watch a movie late at night with Blake. Or even if they wanted to slip off to have some private time away from the rest of the family.

"You're all right with packing up and moving to the house, aren't you?" Blake asked as he packed up his bags.

"Yeah, yeah, we can't stay here."

"The suite is like a separate entity, part of the home, sure, but it's set off from the rest of the house, and we'll have our own entertainment center there. Truly, it will be a lot more private than being here."

"It has a TV?" she asked.

He smiled and pulled her into his arms, giving her a sound hug. That was one thing she loved about him. He was nice and physical, loving to share hugs and kisses any time. "Yeah, it has a TV. And everyone's going to understand if we slip away to be by ourselves. There's a desk in there, too, so you can work from there or at the office at the lodge until we can set you up with your PI office with your brother."

"You want to put me to work right away?" she asked.

He laughed. "No. I want to spend all my time with you."

"Okay, good. I was worried for a second." She smiled up at him and kissed him. "I haven't even thought that far in the future. I mean, about working."

"We'll figure it all out. You might want to have an office in town. Though, for selfish reasons, I'd rather you were right here at the resort."

"So we could have lunches together and have time to walk Rosco in the morning."

He smiled. "So we can have time to slip away to do whatever comes to mind."

She chuckled. "Okay." She kissed him again and went back to packing.

She knew it would be an adjustment for everyone, not just her, when she moved in with the family. She hoped it all turned out just fine.

But she didn't know what she was thinking, because as soon as she and Blake returned to the house, everyone was waiting for them to go with them on their wolf run. Even Nate, to Nicole's surprise. They had called him to invite him to run, too, and he had returned pronto, wanting to run free with the rest of the family as wolves.

She loved her new family, and before long, they had dropped off their bags in the lovely suite that was perfect for a honeymooner's getaway, stripped in the room, and kissed each other. But before they got too carried away, she shifted and Blake followed suit. They raced out of the suite, and everyone else laughed. Then they began to strip and shift. Nicole noticed Kayla had removed herself from the living room and soon joined them as a wolf from her bedroom upstairs. It appeared she'd been shy about stripping in front of Nate.

With howls and yips and playing and running, Nicole knew she hadn't just gained a mate but a loving couple of sisters and another brother. After playing for over an hour, they returned to the house. Nate got dressed while Landon and Roxie threw on their underwear. Kayla remained as a wolf, and Nicole and Blake returned to the suite, pulled on robes, and went back to the living room. They all wished Nate good night, as he had declined to stay in Blake's old room. Kayla barked at him and he smiled, then he returned to the lodge. Then everyone said good night and headed up to their rooms while Blake and Nicole slipped off to their suite.

She hoped it was truly private down here when they went to making love and they didn't disturb Blake's siblings.

Like Blake had said, it had a nice big wall television, a desk and computer even, a king-size bed covered in a moose comforter, and big windows that looked out on the mountain and trees. He turned on a gas fireplace, and she smiled.

"Now that is really nice," she said.

She pulled the covers down on the bed while Blake closed the curtains to keep the heat in the room. Otherwise they could leave them open. No worry about Peeping Toms out here, just the wildlife if any came near the house. She suspected with the smell of wolves hanging around the house, deer and other animals probably stayed away.

She checked out the bathroom and loved the setup: a double sink, whirlpool jets in the separate tub, a separate enclosed toilet, and a walk-in shower. "Wow, this is really lovely." Now she knew she could stay here with all the nice touches until their house was finally built. It felt like a lodge room but ten times nicer. Not to mention they were a long way from the other rooms, unlike having a room at the lodge. "In fact, I wouldn't mind having something like this in our home."

She was even thinking Nate could stay with them once their house was built. They'd have plenty of room, and he probably would feel more comfortable living with them until he had a place of his own than living with Blake's siblings.

"Whatever you want, honey."

She smiled and wrapped her arms around his neck. "That's all I wanted to hear."

He chuckled. "Yeah, for you, anything."

She loved how considerate he was of her feelings. She knew if she had said she wanted to stay at the lodge, he would have said that was fine. And his siblings would have gone along with it too. Anything to make her feel like an important part of the family.

"We need to make a trip to Denver so I can pack up my place. I need to give notice too." She ran her hands over his robe, pressing the soft fabric against his chest.

"Yeah, whenever you want to go, we'll do it." Then he untied the tie around her waist and opened her robe to expose her breasts. He leaned down to kiss each one.

When he raised his head to kiss her mouth, she saw his erection poking out of his robe, and she chuckled. "Looks like you have something for me."

"Always."

She loved how he made her feel so desirable. She untied his robe, pulled it off his shoulders, and dropped it to the floor. He slipped his hands under her robe and caressed her shoulders, his large hands warm and soothing. Running her hands over his bare shoulders and chest, she sighed. Whenever he began touching her, besides working up her pheromones, he always made her feel like melting into the floor, spreading her legs, and pleading with him to finish her off.

She loved feeling his rugged muscles under her fingertips, too, making her smile when he flexed them for her, showing off.

He slid her robe off her shoulders and moved her to the bed, kissing her softly at first, then hotly. She kissed him back just as greedily, needing this and needing him. They rubbed their bodies together like wolves would, sharing their pheromones, their scents, claiming each other for their own.

She expected to be lying on her back, but he adjusted her so she was lying on her right side. He knelt, straddling her right leg, and lifting her left leg over his left hip. The

sexual position was a frontal doggy style with deeper pene-
tration, but they still had intimate eye contact. His hand was
free to stroke her clit while he was nudging her folds with
the tip of his rigid erection.

Ohmigod, this felt amazing as he stroked her harder and
then pushed his cock into her and began to thrust slowly,
shallower at first, working her up as he rubbed her clit
faster, and she knew he wanted her to come before he did,
or maybe at the same time. His already dark brown eyes
were nearly black with desire, his kissable mouth parted in
a small smile, his sex hot and full and long. His wickedly
enticing strokes and the way he ground into her, twisting,
angling, made her body scream for release.

Caught up in the heat of the moment, she didn't even
realize she cried out when the climax struck.

He thrust harder, and she clenched her inner muscles
around him. Mine. He was all hers.

He thrust faster, and then he ground out a deep, wolfish
groan.

"Soundproof walls," Blake assured her as he remained
seated in her for a few more minutes, leaning down to kiss
her shoulder and arm. Then he pulled out and wrapped her
in his arms and kissed her cheeks, her eyelids, her lips.

She snorted. "Not with our wolf hearing."

He chuckled. "They will know we're having a good time
if they hear us at all."

From the sex and climax, endorphins and oxytocin
were released into their blood, and she knew the hormones
activated the pleasure centers of the brain, which made her
feel good and relaxed. Though she couldn't help thinking
about what Kayla had shared with the rest of her siblings

about getting a workout while having sex. Nicole was all for having an intimately satisfying workout with her mate as often as they could.

"Have you got any more moves like that?"

He laughed. "Yeah, but I need to refill the pump."

"Hmm, good, because we need to have more of a workout and prolong our youth." Even though they lived longer than humans, thirty years for every year that a human lived, any excuse to have more sex with her mate worked for her.

The next morning during a hearty breakfast with the family, Blake knew Nicole hoped no one had heard them making love again last night. She'd been afraid his siblings would want them to return to the lodge or hurry up building the house, but everyone seemed well rested and cheerful. Maybe a little more cheerful than usual.

After breakfast, Blake drove Nicole and Roxie to the clinic to see Rhys. All three men were doing well, but Nicole and Roxie only intended to speak to Rhys. CJ was the deputy sheriff posted to secure the room. "Morning," he said to them.

"Has everything been quiet?" Nicole asked.

"Yeah. We're all glad the search for Rhys is over."

"I'll say." Nicole was thrilled she could start working on their house and wedding plans and take off from work for a while.

When they entered Rhys's room, Nicole smiled at him. Rhys was sitting up and watching TV.

"I guess you've been read your rights." Nicole told him

who she was, then motioned to Roxie. "You tried to force her to give up her coin collection when you were both stationed at Fort Meade. Well, you went to her apartment off-post and tried."

"I don't know what you're talking about." Rhys looked so smug.

"You're lucky I saved your paltry life after you were buried in the avalanche," Roxie said. "But yeah, I recognized you as the MP who pulled me over earlier in the day for an expired sticker while we were on active duty."

Rhys's jaw dropped, but he didn't comment.

"I identified it was you," Nicole said, not about to say how she and Roxie could identify him.

"But you didn't charge me," Rhys said, so cocky.

"Nope. I've got you this time though." Nicole smiled. "Nice run on being dead…for a while. Good luck with your life."

She glanced at Roxie to see if she wanted to add anything.

"Asshole." Then Roxie left the room.

That about summed him up.

"You're just lucky you didn't pull that crap with my sister when I was there, or you would have been a dead man," Blake said.

This time, Rhys looked a little pale. Blake took Nicole's hand, and they left the clinic with Roxie.

"Do you feel better?" Blake asked his sister.

"I do. I finally had my say to the bastard."

"Yeah, I felt the same way," Nicole said.

"I'm glad you ladies had your say."

Nicole squeezed his hand. "I think you also were glad too."

He kissed her before they got into his Jeep. "Yeah, I needed to do that."

Then they saw the federal marshals arrive and Nicole smiled. "Round 'em up, boys, and head 'em out."

Nicole couldn't be any gladder for the way the story ended with the bad guys being sent to lockup to be tried for their crimes and Roxie finding resolution in Rhys's arrest, even if it wasn't for the time he'd attempted to rob her. Nicole hadn't expected Blake would need it too, so she was glad he had some resolution. She imagined Landon and Kayla might have felt the same way, but they probably were just as glad that Rhys was going to stand trial.

More than anything, chasing after Rhys had brought Nicole to the Wolffs' doorstep and a whole new way of life. She couldn't be any happier than that.

If anyone had told Blake that his sister's armed robber suspect would be caught by the same CID investigator who had tried to find him guilty before and that he'd fall in love with her, he would never have believed it. He loved that Roxie, Kayla, and Nicole had become best of friends. He was also glad Landon hadn't taken too much of an interest in the she-wolf. His brother had probably figured it was a lost cause once he'd seen the two of them kissing in the lobby as if they were already mated wolves. And Nate was just like a brother to them.

Blake had enjoyed all the sleuthing he'd had to do with Nicole in the meantime, though most of that was because he just wanted an excuse to be with her—enjoying the time with her while she did her surveillance. The PI Clay might have been an annoying pest, but his arrival sure had worked in Blake's favor to move the courtship with Nicole along.

Now, as Nicole and Roxie talked about wedding plans while he drove them back to the lodge, he knew all the stars had aligned when he and his siblings had set up the lodge at the Silver Town Ski Resort and Nicole's prey had booked the ski vacation that would be their downfall. And afforded Blake the opportunity to meet Nicole. He also wanted to thank their maintenance man who'd been too sick to blow the snow off the sidewalks that morning. Rosco got brownie points too for leading him on a wild rabbit chase and helping to entertain Nicole. Of course, he had to thank her PI partner, Larry, for getting high-altitude sickness. Most of all, he thanked his lucky stars it had all worked out and he was mated to Nicole. He smiled at her. "I love you."

She laughed. "Good thing too. You're not getting rid of me. I love you too."

He reached over and squeezed her hand, knowing what they were doing when they got back to the resort—slipping away to the suite at the house for some wolfish moves while everyone was at the lodge working and couldn't hear their love play.

Yeah, he was one lucky wolf.

EPILOGUE

"Ohmigod," Nicole said as she looked out at the balcony view of the beach in Costa Rica, the sun setting and the warm oranges and yellows and cooler pinks and purples turning the water into sunset colors too. "This is beautiful." She was wearing her sparkly aqua one-piece bathing suit as Blake joined her on the balcony with margaritas in hand.

"Beautiful," he murmured, nuzzling his mouth against her neck.

"Hmm, so are you," she said, knowing he meant she was beautiful, not just the gorgeous scene before them.

She'd been so wrapped up in the wedding, visiting with her mom and dad before they returned to Denver to sell the business and their home, not to mention building her and Blake's own house and buying her new car, that she hadn't realized Blake had scheduled the Costa Rican trip for them right after the wedding. She thought they were going to wait until the house was finally built. But he only wanted to wait until the wedding was done. This was unbelievably wonderful. They still had snow in Colorado. But here? All sunshine and warmth.

With eleven acres of rain forest surrounding them and white-sugar sand beaches, private use only for the inn guests, she was thrilled. Not only that, but the inn only had thirty-eight rooms, so it wasn't some high-rise tower filled with five hundred guests where everyone was vying for a spot of beach or running into each other in the rain forest.

Nicole and Blake would make the most of the rain forest at night when the guests stayed in their rooms or enjoyed their balconies. She and Blake would run wild.

Tomorrow, they would go zip-lining, and they had a boating excursion. Snorkeling. Swimming. And tonight, well, margaritas first, then…

Blake kissed her again, then set the drinks on the table.

Well, she'd thought they were going to run as wolves as soon as the sun set, but it looked like Blake had other ideas in mind. That was the fun of being in paradise. No real schedules they couldn't break. It was just all sexy fun.

Loving her wolf, she wrapped her arms around his neck and began to kiss him. "Our chilled margaritas are going to get warm."

She thought the world of him for wanting to make the experience special by creating the fun mixed drinks and even more so that she distracted him from drinking them when he saw her in her bathing suit. He was the only wolf for her.

"Always on a mission," Blake said. "I fixed the drinks, then saw you and the sunset, and a hot case of lust came over me." He rubbed against her body, his crotch already aching for release.

She laughed, sweet and sexy. "Bottoms up." She got their drinks, and they drank several swigs, and then he carried her back into the bedroom.

This was one of the great things about the tropics. They had a lot fewer clothes to remove. She had hold of his board shorts, pulling them down his legs before he could say a word. And then he was slipping the straps of her bathing suit off her shoulders and pulling the swimsuit top down to reveal her creamy breasts. This might be paradise, but with her, even more so. He pulled her swimsuit off her the rest of the way.

They collapsed on the bed, kissing and loving each other as mated wolves, not believing they were in a rain forest in another part of the world getting ready for what came next. More wolf loving.

After such a disastrous morning at the lodge that day, Blake couldn't believe the she-wolf of his dreams had fallen for *him*. He couldn't be more thrilled the way things worked out. He wouldn't have done the day over any other way, not when it culminated in this—a beautiful sunset on the beach, his mate half-naked wearing her bathing suit, and him eager to show her just how much he loved her.

He was one lucky wolf.

If you love Terry Spear's wolf shifters, you won't want to miss Kait Ballenger's Seven Range Shifters.

Deep in the mountains, there's danger at every turn. The Grey Wolf clan will do whatever it takes to protect their ranch, and their mates.

Keep reading for an excerpt from this thrilling new series!

Wicked Cowboy Wolf

Available now from
Sourcebooks Casablanca

CHAPTER 1

THE RANCH WAS CRAWLING WITH GREY WOLVES.

The Rogue lingered on the outskirts of the forest, watching the activity in the distance as he leaned against the trunk of a mountain pine. He surveyed the vast ranchlands before him as he tipped his Stetson lower, adding an extra layer of shadow to his face. The old cowboy hat was only a precaution. He knew none of the pack wolves would recognize him. Aside from his scars, it was one of the key advantages to having the identity of a ghost, and a good thing too…

…since he didn't trust anyone else to deliver the target.

He shot a glance over his shoulder toward Bee. The brown mustang gave an angry flick of his tail, the black hair smacking against the pine where he was tied. Bee wasn't mighty pleased with this arrangement.

That made two of them.

"Behave," Rogue warned the horse. "It won't be long."

He strode onto the ranch, ignoring Bee's frustrated huffs. It was easy enough to blend in among the Grey Wolf cowboys. With the Seven Range Shifter clans all meeting at Wolf Pack Run today, there was a plethora of unfamiliar shifters on the ranch. None of the guards so much as raised their heads at him. Not that a rogue werewolf would be their top safety priority. Their focus would be protecting the Pact from vampires—a heightened level of security that would be forgotten once the Pact members left the ranch this evening.

That would be their mistake.

It only took him a handful of minutes to locate his target. An entrance to the kitchens connected to the private conference room where the Pact members were meeting. Rogue was patient, slowly making his way inside, slipping among the shadows. Once near the room, he watched a server enter, allowing him a quick glance inside.

Immediately, he spotted her. He couldn't have missed her if he'd tried. Not with the way his heart was pounding.

Standing in the conference room next to her beast of a brother, talking with animated movements as she pointed toward a massive chart behind her, she was breathtaking. Everything he remembered and more.

He shook his head. The pain in his chest was all the reminder he needed. She wasn't his, and she never would be. She'd stopped being a possibility for him long ago.

He watched her, patiently lingering in the shadows of the kitchen as he formulated a plan. She wouldn't recognize him, though his heart knew her better than the back of his own hand. He would have known those gorgeous green eyes anywhere. The ache in his chest grew.

It's better this way, he told himself.

He'd repeat those words until he was convinced they were true.

He didn't care what it took, or how it hurt him. Her life and the lives of so many others depended on his sacrifice. It didn't matter that she didn't recognize him or that he died a little more inside whenever he looked at her. He would keep his promise to her, to his family. No matter the personal consequences.

And come hell or high water, Rogue would survive losing Maeve Grey again…

"Mae, Alexander is headed this way *again*." Maverick's voice held more than a hint of disapproval. He'd hated her "little backup plan" from the start. Her brother loved her, and as such, he'd always been fiercely protective of her, but packmaster or not, this was *her* choice to make, and she'd do whatever it took to save her pack.

Maeve finished scribbling on her napkin as she ignored her brother's protests. The quick sketch had been a necessary release of tension. The image of a running horse was more cartoonish than her normal work, but it'd been enough to ease her anxiety for now. It was better than ripping her hair out. She'd been trapped at the Seven Range Pact's annual reception listening to Maverick negotiate for nearly two hours now, yet *still* none of the other packmasters had made a firm commitment, and with every passing second, the vampires drew closer to destroying everything she cared for.

And all while she was forced to wear a pair of heels. Her cowgirl boots would have been infinitely more comfortable, but beauty knew no pain when it came to saving her pack, so she'd make do. She'd feared the other packmasters would be wary despite Maverick's best laid proposals, and she wasn't about to waste a perfectly good cocktail dress.

Every summer, the seven shifter clans that ruled over Big Sky Country and formed the Seven Range Pact met at an annual reception held at Wolf Pack Run, a formal soiree complete with suits, ties, and dress Stetsons. This year's occasion was the largest and most extravagant yet. Though typically the annual reception was only held during peacetime and was only attended by the varying shifters of the Seven Range Pact, this year, despite the heightened security concerns, Maverick had made an exception and sent invitations welcoming their usual guests along with several additional Canadian shifter clans. Extenuating circumstances, as he called them.

Mae shook her head. She'd worried this plan wouldn't pan out, but Maverick had been insistent, and while she might have formulated her own backup plans, she trusted implicitly that he'd do whatever it took to steer the pack on the correct course. He always had.

In a normal year, the official purpose of the reception was to build camaraderie among the various packs despite their differences in species. As one of the last living members of the Grey family, one of three founding families of the Grey Wolf Pack, Mae had a personal obligation to represent the pack with grace and poise—and no one was more aware of that obligation than she was. But it was the unspoken reason for this year's soiree that had made her concoct her backup plan.

Mae couldn't allow her lifeblood to be the downfall of her pack.

"Mae," Maverick grumbled again. This time, with even more urgency. "Don't offer yourself up like a lamb for slaughter."

"It's *my* choice." She shot her older brother an annoyed glare. "It's *my* blood they used."

She was tired of Maverick's protesting. On more than one occasion, he'd urged her to marry a pure-blooded alpha wolf, for tradition and all that, but to hear her brother tell it, he only wanted the best for her, and there was no way in hell he'd offer her up like this. She rolled her eyes. She failed to see how her plan was much different. At least seducing Alexander to save her pack was *her* decision.

Mae set down her pen, forcing a smile as her eyes traveled across the table and landed on the alpha wolf headed toward them. Alexander Caron was a massive, muscled wall of a Canadian packmaster from a few hours north of Wolf Pack Run, and the man who could save them all, according to her brother.

A month earlier, the Grey Wolves had discovered the vampires' plans to develop an injectable serum that would allow them to feed from shifters, and the purer the blood, the better. Feeding from humans was mere sustenance, but feeding from shifters would increase a vampire's power tenfold. The development would soon change the outcome of the war between the shifters and the vampires unless Mae's kind found a way to combat it. All their enemy had needed to complete their plan was a blood sample from a pure-blooded Grey Wolf…and they'd taken that sample from Mae.

It was only a matter of time before the serum was in wide use, and then her kind would no longer stand a chance against the bloodsuckers.

Alexander had an army full of alpha warriors that would give the Grey Wolves a fighting chance against the vampires, with or without the serum.

If only she could convince *him* of that…

Alexander joined them at their table and extended a hand toward her. "Care to dance again?" he prompted, casting her a smile. His teeth were beautifully white and his beard perfectly trimmed. He was the ideal image of a handsome cowboy.

Most she-wolves would find the powerful alpha wolf handsome, assuming a woman was into the whole clean-cut male thing, but Mae couldn't have been less attracted to this wolf if she tried. She supposed if she had to put her finger on it, it was because she preferred her men a little more on the rough and rugged side, much like the Grey Wolf cowboys—not that any of them ever gave her so much as a second glance, considering her brother was their packmaster. But even that reasoning failed to fully explain *her* lack of interest.

Still, she'd intended to charm Alexander for the sake of the pack, because they needed this alliance, and thus far, all her brother's efforts had been in vain. Not to mention, her role could pay off twofold. Pack expectation dictated she marry an alpha wolf of pure bloodline if she ever planned to settle down, and considering she didn't want any of the alphas at Wolf Pack Run, Alexander was one of her few remaining options. The pack elders hadn't started to nag her yet, but it wouldn't be long, and the way she saw it, maybe if she faked an attraction to Alexander, eventually she would come to care for him.

Maverick had suggested that if she planned to seduce a packmaster in the name of making alliances, he might as well pull out the hot iron, burn a brand on her ass, and send her off to market like all the other cattle on the ranch.

Mae hadn't been amused with that comparison, but as she'd reminded him, *she* wasn't amused by the prospect of an arranged marriage or the notion of trading herself for some alliance either. For the sake of her pack and their collective safety, she'd do anything. But that didn't mean this whole little charade didn't offend every feminist bone in her body.

Desperate times called for desperate measures.

"Mae." Maverick cleared his throat again.

Ignoring Maverick, she smiled at Alexander. "Of course," she said. "I'd be happy to dance with you."

This would be the fourth time since the start of the reception. He still hadn't offered the support of his pack to them, but apparently, dancing more than once an hour was necessary.

Maverick cast her a frustrated look from the corner of his eye as he signaled for one of the waitstaff to bring another glass of whiskey. Maverick might disapprove, but she could practically hear their father's voice in her head, so similar to Maverick's now that it was eerie.

It's a small sacrifice, Mae.

She'd been raised a Grey, which meant sacrificing herself for the greater good of the pack was expected, even if she'd begun resenting the obligation years ago. Maverick knew that struggle as well as she did. She loved her packmates and would do anything for them, but that didn't mean she always had to be pleased about what that required of her.

Mae set down her pen and accepted Alexander's hand. He guided her out onto the dance floor just as a slow country ballad began to pump through the speakers. The lights strung over the tented outdoor dance floor lit up the summer night with a soft romantic feel as a warm breeze wrapped around them. Gently, the alpha wolf pulled Mae into his arms, slowly swaying her around the floor. She forced herself to smile up at him.

"You have a lovely smile," Alexander said as she finished laughing at one of his jokes.

Mae tried not to let that smile fade. "Thank you," she

replied. The compliment was genuine and sweet, but it didn't stir so much as an iota of her interest.

She fought back a heavy sigh. What was wrong with her? She wanted love, marriage, a family, and there was nothing wrong with Alexander—or any of the other alpha wolves the pack elders had suggested over the years. They just weren't...

They just weren't for her...

Because they're not him, her inner self whispered.

The thought made her chest ache. She could think of only one person who'd ever captured her heart, and she hadn't seen him in over twenty years.

"What's on your mind, darlin'?" Alexander asked. He must have sensed her thoughts were elsewhere rather than on the dance floor with him where they *should* have been, had she not been pining for a dead man.

Now was as good a time as ever. Each passing minute gave the vampires more time to put the serum into wide use. She needed to get this show on the road—fast.

"Alexander, dancing with you all evening has been lovely, but why don't we head back to my—"

The alpha wolf shook his head, the brim of his Stetson lowering slightly as he stopped Mae short. "Save your breath, darlin'. I'm not interested."

Mae nearly tripped over one of his cowboy boots. *Stupid high heels.* "E-excuse me?" she sputtered. She couldn't have heard him correctly.

Alexander chuckled. "I've known the game, darlin'."

Mae's brow wrinkled in confusion. "And yet you've gone along with it anyway?"

Alexander nodded. "I have." He spun her outward

before pulling her back and catching her in his arms again. The move was so smooth and belied a gentility that would have made a more receptive woman swoon.

"Because even though you're attracted to me, you think I'm better than that?" she asked.

Man, did he have to go and be so sweet and make her feel like even more of a tool?

"You *are* better than that, but you're wrong on one part." Alexander let out another bemused chuckle. "No offense, darlin', but I'm not attracted to you."

It was all Mae could do not to stop dancing right then and there. "You're not?"

He shook his head as he lowered his voice. A playful grin crossed his lips. "I'm more of a *Brokeback Mountain* kind of cowboy, if you catch my drift."

Mae's eyes widened. "Oh. I wouldn't have thought..." She struggled to find the words.

"Not every gay man has a feminine side," Alexander said. "It's no secret, but I don't make a habit of advertising my sex life to my fellow packmasters."

"Of course." Mae nodded. Maybe that explained the lack of attraction on her end. Perhaps she'd sensed she would have been barking up the wrong tree? Though if she was honest with herself, she knew deep down the problem wasn't Alexander—it was her. She glanced up at the massive alpha wolf. "So why keep asking me to dance? Why bring your pack here?"

Alexander shrugged. "I like to dance, and you're as good a partner as any. Not to mention, I have a profound respect for your brother. He's one of the fiercest and fairest pack-masters I've ever known, and I like to examine my options.

This serum thing leaves me with some questions for my own pack and some questions for you."

"Alexander, we're desperate, and if you don't get on board in time, your pack will be too. Last month when the vampires took me captive, their intent was clear. The serum they've created allows—"

"I know. My question isn't about what the serum can do or cause."

Mae raised a brow. "What exactly *is* your question then?"

"I've been listening to your story all night, and I'm still unclear about one part," Alexander said.

Mae swayed along with him, allowing him to lead. "I'd be happy to clarify," she said.

That she could do. Even if her backup plan had failed miserably.

Alexander stared down at her, his dark-brown eyes searing into hers as if he were trying to see through her. "How *exactly* did you escape the vampires' cells?"

Mae nearly choked on her own inhalation of breath. It was the one question she *didn't* want the Canadian packmaster to ask, because if the truth was ever revealed to her brother, to Alexander, to anyone here at this reception, their chances of ever claiming more allies would be shot. The consequences for her pack would be deadly.

"That's a good question," she said.

While she struggled to formulate an explanation for Alexander—one that hid the dark truth—the alpha wolf twirled her around again. But as she faced away from him, she let go of his hand, stopping midspin, because at that moment, any hope she had of an explanation was lost.

Mae froze. Slowly, she blinked, standing there like

a deer in the headlights. She couldn't possibly be seeing straight.

It was *him*. The answer to Alexander's question and one of her darkest secrets was standing right there on the other side of the dance floor. As if it were normal, as if *he* were normal.

Nothing about this moment—nothing about *him*—was normal.

Her heart began to pound.

The Rogue. The Dark Devil. The King of the Misfit Wolves. She'd heard the nicknames more than once. And yet he lingered there in the shadows, toasting her with a champagne flute as he cast her an amused smirk. Then he drew a long sip from the glass. Mae blinked, hoping, *praying* the wolf before her was only a memory, a figment of her imagination, caused by the stress of Alexander's questioning and that would suddenly disappear.

But he didn't.

She gaped. The Rogue was one of their most wanted enemies, a criminal wolf who was foe to all and friend to none. He was considered a leader among the packless rogues of their kind, a violent vigilante. His true identity was known to none, and even now, few had seen his face and lived to tell about it. Mae wasn't certain how the leaders of the Seven Range Pact didn't notice him.

From the heels of his leather cowboy boots all the way to the smirk across his face, this devil with a too-charming grin was a man not to be crossed.

And yet she'd struck a bargain with him when she'd been trapped in the vampires' cells, still bleeding from where they'd drawn her blood for the serum. Her freedom and safe release from the cell in exchange for the tool he'd used to make their escape—along with her silence about him and his identity.

In her mind, she was back there again. Inside the vampires' cell as he peered at her from the shadows of the next cell over. She could still hear the deep rumble of his voice as it wrapped around her.

Even from the corner of the dance floor, he commanded the room, towering over the Pact members in both height and hard-earned muscle. Only a handful of the Grey Wolf's elite warriors compared, and yet he was watching *her*. His ice-blue eyes met hers, and a devious grin curled his lips. He was taunting her, daring her to out his identity.

But she couldn't.

Not unless she wanted to negate the deal they'd made, and not unless she wanted to ruin the Grey Wolves' chances with Alexander. If anyone knew she'd partnered with an infamous criminal to escape the vampires, they'd never believe a word she said about the serum. Any chance of them gaining more allies would fly out the window. It would be a death sentence for her pack.

Whatever the Rogue was here for, she needed him to leave.

Now.

The feeling of Alexander's hand squeezing her shoulder in concern wrenched her back into the moment. "Maeve?"

Mae blinked several times, glancing to where Maverick sat at the head table, then over her shoulder to Alexander and then back to where the Rogue had stood. Already, he was gone, the racing thrum of her pulse the only trace he'd been there in the first place.

"Maeve, are you all right?" Alexander asked.

"Y-yes," she stuttered as she tried to recover. "I'm not sure what came over me."

The pink summer sunset had long since faded to nightfall by the time Mae returned to her cottage on the other side of the Grey Wolf compound. As she approached home, she cringed at the thought of the poor excuse she'd given Alexander. There was no way he'd bought her lie. Sure, she and Maverick had scheduled Alexander for a meeting with the Pact, which was a small step forward, but if they didn't get him on board and fast, their prospects were limited.

But Mae was determined. She would find a way to save her pack. She had to.

Feeling more than a little defeated, she shuffled up to her door, scanning the other nearby pack cabins. Hers was one of many adjacent to the dining hall and the main compound building, which housed the elite warriors and the main pack offices. She grabbed her keys from her purse. As she did so, she glanced over her shoulder, as if she might find the Rogue lingering there in the darkness. But she didn't. He'd disappeared without a trace.

She released a long sigh. From what she knew of his dangerous reputation, it was just like the arrogant bastard to trod right into a pack of alphas that would just as soon see him torn apart. He really was a rogue with a devil-may-care attitude to match his title. She gripped her keys tighter in her hand.

After unlocking her front door, she slipped inside.

Immediately, the sound of tiny hooves clopping against tile sounded from the darkness. She flicked on the dim entryway light. Tucker, her teacup pig, stared up at her from the white tiled floor, his beady black eyes sparkling with pleasure at her arrival. He let out a pleased oink. Mae grinned.

Bending down, she scooped him into her arms, coddling him like a baby as she cooed at him. Still a piglet, Tucker was no bigger than a small dog, and according to the breeder, he'd been the runt of the teacup litter and would likely stay small.

With Tucker cradled against her, Mae made quick work of feeding him a bottle of milk replacer before snuggling him into his fluffy, pink dog bed in her living room. Once the piglet was rocked to sleep, she showered before she changed into her nightgown and settled into the comfort of her bedsheets. The day had left her worn out, but her mind refused to calm.

Had she really seen the Rogue, or had it all been in her head?

That question still plagued her. She wasn't sure how he would have gotten onto the ranch without detection, especially considering the heightened security for the reception.

She shook her head. It must have been her imagination, a memory triggered by the stress of Alexander's questions. The Rogue couldn't possibly have shown up at Wolf Pack Run only to disappear again.

Though it had felt so real…

She sighed, sinking deeper into her mattress. It wouldn't be the first time she'd thought of him since their encounter in the vampire coven.

Heat rose in her cheeks. She'd dreamed of him almost

every night since—and not in the way she *should* have. The memory of the night when her life had been threatened by bloodsuckers was a dark one, but when she dreamed of that night, of him, her dream often took a completely different course from reality. Instead of dreaming of the danger she'd faced, she'd woken more than once to the thought of his uncharacteristic heroism as he whisked her from the vampires' cells, only to find her own hand exploring between her legs.

It was sick. She knew it. She shouldn't be attracted to a dangerous criminal like him. Despite that, he stirred something primitive inside her. She knew what sort of dark circles he traveled in, yet she couldn't seem to help it. A wolf like the Rogue was everything forbidden to her: a non–Grey Wolf, a vigilante.

Not to mention one of her brother's enemies, and the antithesis of every criterion she should consider for a mate.

Somehow, that only made him more appealing.

By her birthright, she was destined for a Grey Wolf alpha warrior. She shuddered at the thought. The Grey Wolf warriors were all fine men, handsome cowboys, but they were practically her *brothers*.

Mae tossed and turned in her bed as she tried to put the Rogue from her mind, but still his face taunted her. Eventually, her hand trailed beneath her nightgown. Maybe if she eased this ache, the desire would go away. Maybe then, sleep would claim her. Slowly, her fingers probed the folds between her legs, locating her own clit. She knew her body, what she liked.

Gently, she massaged and probed as she remembered how it felt when the warmth of his breath had brushed against her ear, the deep timbre of his voice thrumming through her.

You won't regret this, he'd whispered.

She imagined his lips trailing downward.

What would it be like to be with a criminal like him? Something told her every touch, every caress would be more powerful, more sinful...just *more*. Soon, she was moaning in climax, the walls of her core tightening in a delicious wave that sent a rush of moisture straight to her center. She cried out, arching her back against the pillows.

As the last throes of her orgasm shook her, she relaxed into her sheets, sated, though it was little more than a fantasy. At that thought, a pang of sorrow thrummed through her. That was all her dreams would ever be—fantasy. Not just him, but *all* her heart's desires. She wanted more than she could have. She always had. She loved her pack, but the duties that bound her to them had never been her choice. She may have been a Grey by birth, but if she were braver, she'd live her own life. She'd make her own choices.

If she were free...

Mae lay there, the weight of the things she'd never have pressing down on her, constraining her chest so much that she struggled to breathe.

If only...

At least she could dream. Her dreams and desires were hers alone. She released a long sigh, switching on the light of her bedside table as she reached for a book to read. Until the sound of a familiar voice came from the darkness.

"Evenin', Princess."

CHAPTER 2

THE DIM LIGHT OF A TABLE LAMP CUT THROUGH THE shadows. Rogue leaned against the bedroom doorway, his Stetson hiding the scarred half of his face as he raked his gaze over her. As soon as Maeve Grey had flicked the light on, she'd scrambled to her feet. She stood at her bedside, wearing little more than a thin, pink nightgown and clutching a large hardcover book from her nightstand like a weapon.

He shook his head.

Despite her pure Grey Wolf bloodline, by both wolf and human standards she was petite, which meant physically armed with knowledge or not, she wouldn't hold her own in a fight against an alpha like him.

But if looks could kill…

She snarled at him. "What the hell are you doing here?"

As if he hadn't made a habit of sneaking into her room hundreds of times before. He shook his head. He'd known when they'd met in the vampires' cells that she didn't recognize him. Twenty years and a half-deformed face changed a man, but still, that didn't make her lack of recognition sting any less.

He crossed his arms, leaning harder against the doorframe as he took in the sight of her.

She gaped at him as if she'd seen a ghost. She *had*, though *she* was none the wiser.

"You're in *my* bedroom," she snapped.

He shrugged a single shoulder. "I gave you fair warning."

She blinked. "I didn't expect you to show up in my *bedroom*."

"And where else do you suggest I find you alone? I couldn't have announced my plans in the middle of that fancy soiree of yours. It would have scandalized the Pact, and then where would that have left you?"

Her lips tightened into an enraged pucker, and she glared at him.

He grinned. Even when they were kids, he'd always had an appreciation for her hot temper. Some things didn't change.

He shoved off the doorframe, straightening to his full height. "You were never taught to check the shadows of your apartment? Seems like something that beast you call your brother wouldn't overlook."

"I must have missed that lesson," she said.

"Pity."

Maverick had been remiss in his brotherly duties then. Hence, the reason she was here, unprotected and alone with *him*, one of the most dangerous wolves in North America. His eyes narrowed as he watched her. Clearly, she didn't recognize the danger he posed.

That was a mistake.

He didn't intend to harm her, but *she* didn't know that.

She'd made his plans easy for him, far too easy for his liking. The spare key to her apartment had been hidden directly under the sunflower doormat. Not that he couldn't have picked the lock, but that trusting inclination of hers would make his job more difficult, get her into trouble. At the very least, if the fire blazing in her green eyes was any indication, he could lead a she-wolf to water, but he couldn't make her drink.

Good girl, Mae-day.

"What are you doing here?" she asked.

"At the moment?" He grinned. "Observing."

Her eyes widened in realization. From the way her shoulders tensed, she was painfully aware of exactly what he'd just observed.

That made two of them.

"How long have you been there?" She sounded breathless, throaty. All too similar to the noises she'd made.

"Long enough." A smirk crossed his lips as he raked his gaze over her. "Don't worry, Princess. I only arrived during the grand finale."

She blushed, and his cock gave an eager jerk. *No.* Maeve Grey was no longer meant for the likes of him, but after that little display, he was still as hard as a damn diamond. Old habits died hard, he supposed. At fifteen, he'd been so crazy in love with her that he could scarcely see straight. But that had been when he was young, naive, before he'd learned the hard way that love was for fools who enjoyed tragedy and that she'd never be his. They lived in different worlds now, universes apart, and it'd been so long since he'd cared for anyone that Rogue wasn't even sure his black heart remembered how.

Even if he wanted to love her, he'd never be worthy of her. But fuck, if he didn't still want her.

He gave her another once-over. Despite her large green eyes and spritely features, many a Montana cowboy would overlook her. With her thin frame and dark-brown hair so short, a lesser man would have said she wasn't feminine enough—boyish even. But only a blind man could miss the plumpness of her pink mouth, the delicate curve of her hips, and the perky breasts hidden beneath her nightgown. They were no more than a handful, but enough to taste, to lick, to tease, and that was all before the scent of her sex had filled his nose. Now that he knew the delicious sounds she made when she came...

That was even more dangerous.

He stepped toward her, and she growled, raising the book higher.

He nearly chuckled. "If I wanted to hurt you, I could have done so while you were..."

"I thought I was alone." Beneath his gaze, the crimson on her cheeks grew deeper by the second until there wasn't an inch of pink in sight. "S-sometimes I need help sleeping," she stammered.

He quirked a brow in amusement. As if she needed an excuse to want pleasure...

Slowly, he prowled toward her, closing the distance between them. She shouldn't feel ashamed. She was fucking beautiful. He plucked the book from her hands, disarming her. "And what keeps you up at night, Maeve Grey?" He leaned in close, his breath a whisper against her ear. "Whose face do you think of as you pleasure yourself? Some valiant Grey Wolf Prince Charming?"

Perhaps the clean-cut packmaster she'd danced with all evening.

Her eyes flashed to the golden color of her wolf, and she snarled at him.

Confirmation enough, as far as he was concerned. The predictability in that annoyed him.

Immediately, she changed the subject. "If it's my brother you're here for, your timing couldn't be worse," she said.

Of course she'd think he was here for her beast of a brother. Her whole life would have centered around living in his shadow.

Maverick Grey was a massive warrior-sized thorn in Rogue's side. Bloodshed between the rogue wolves and the packmasters who treated them as second-class citizens wasn't Rogue's goal, particularly when it came to Maverick Grey. The Grey Wolf packmaster was one of Rogue's fiercer and more formidable opponents, rivaled on the battlefield by only a select few, himself included. In that regard, he had a healthy respect for the self-righteous bastard. He and Maverick had squared off indirectly more than once, battling like a heated game of chess. Rogue was more a thief than a murderer, procuring resources and securing backroom deals for his kind, but if he could screw the Grey Wolves over in the process, all the better.

Not that there wasn't a fair share of blood on his hands.

"It's not your brother I'm interested in, Princess."

Had she been in wolf form, Rogue had no doubt her fur would have bristled. "I'm no princess," she growled.

Clearly, he'd struck a nerve.

"You aren't going to hurt me," he said.

"You say that as if you know me."

"I do know you, Mae." Those words were truer than she'd realize. "I knew you the moment you made a deal with me in the vampires' cells. The only thing I didn't know was how soon we'd meet again." He retreated on that enigmatic statement and sank into a nearby recliner, draping his legs across the arm, his old, black leather cowboy boots crossed at the ankles. "Are you not Maeve, daughter of Thomas and Sharla Grey? Younger sister to Maverick, the current packmaster of the Grey Wolves?"

She didn't respond. They both knew the answer to that.

"Have you not lived a life full of privilege and leisure, sitting atop your pedestal in the Versailles that is Wolf Pack Run? Protected, cared for, safe…"

He'd given everything, nearly lost his own life to ensure she had those comforts and yet…

"All while you turned down your nose at the rest of us."

At all rogues, the packless wolves among their kind.

Wolves like him.

The benefits of pack life were plentiful: a built-in support network, a safe home base, a guaranteed income, bountiful monetary and educational resources, and most importantly, protection from outsiders. Whether they were threatened by other shifter clans, vampires, the hunters of the Execution Underground, or even human law enforcement, pack wolves held a distinct advantage in survival.

It was a sheer numbers game. Rogue knew that firsthand. Rogue wolves were loners by either birth or circumstance, and the numbers weren't on their side. They were outcasts, misfits, the vagabonds of their world. Pack wolves like Mae would never understand. She would never know what it was like to go hungry, to not have a home, to be a pariah among both wolves and humanity.

"I've never done *anything* to the rogues," she said.

"Exactly." He sneered. "Let them eat cake."

Just like the rest of them. He'd do well to remember that. She'd done nothing, said nothing, while those without a pack lived a life harder than she'd ever know. He'd come to expect it by now. They all did, yet she disappointed him more than most.

Because he'd once thought her better than that.

He scowled. They were the ignorant dreams of a silly boy. *She's not for you, and she never will be...*

Mae's hands balled into fists. "My cage may be different from yours, but it's still a cage."

He tilted his head. That's what she thought of the privileged life he'd given her?

He shouldn't have been surprised. They both had something the other wanted. She had the protection of the Seven Range Pact for her family. He had true freedom, what she'd wanted ever since they were children all those years ago. Freedom she'd never known, and from the desire in her eyes, freedom she still wanted—badly.

What he wouldn't give to see her enjoy just a taste of it.

"And what about you? What saint are you to point out my flaws?" she asked. "How are my sins any worse than yours?" She counted off his crimes on her fingers. "Thievery, bribery, extortion, breaking and entering... I'm sure I'm missing some."

"You forgot grand larceny, but I'll excuse it this time." He grinned. Her list only touched the tip of the iceberg, but the challenge in her eyes stirred something low in his belly. He rose to his feet. "But there's one key difference between you and me, Princess."

She bristled at the nickname again.

Slowly, he stepped toward her, lowering his voice into a conspiratorial whisper. "I don't pretend to be the good guy."

Her eyes flashed to her wolf. She was a spitfire, and he liked that more than he cared to admit.

"If you didn't come for my brother, then who? What shifter of the Seven Range Pact are you here to extort, or do you just enjoy taunting me?" Her words were spit like venom, but he'd been bitten by worse vipers.

"I have no interest in the Seven Range Pact."

Her eyes narrowed as if she didn't believe him. "But why the risk then? I could have exposed you."

"We both knew you wouldn't. I walked straight into that reception and practically served myself up on a platter for your brother and the Pact, yet you didn't so much as utter a word."

"Of course I didn't," she snapped. "We had a deal."

"You're a woman of your word, Maeve Grey. I knew that from the start. But even for an honest woman like you, a promise to an enemy is fool's gold in the face of protecting your pack. It's not the deal we struck that made me trust in your silence. It's more than that."

"I kept my word. That's all."

"Don't lie, Mae. Not to me."

"You need to leave." Her mouth drew into that angry, delicious pucker that made him envision what would happen if he pressed his lips against hers. He'd make her melt against him, part those tightened lips with ease.

"Tell me the true reason you didn't expose me, and I'm gone."

And there it was, the challenge sparked in her eyes, and before she could think better of it, she was squaring off with him. "I didn't tell them because I didn't want to." She said the words as if she hated it, as if the truth angered her. "I wanted to keep it my secret. Make my own choice for once."

So Maeve Grey wanted to emerge from beneath the pressure of her brother's thumb, and he was her means to do it.

"That, I believe," he purred. This was the Maeve he knew. She might not have recognized who he truly was, but she was still intrigued…by him, by the darkness, by everything that was forbidden to her. She always had been. He'd known that from the start.

"Now go," she said, pointing toward the door again. "I won't let you ruin our chances with Alexander. My packmates depend on it." From the fire in her eyes, she'd do anything to protect those she cared for.

Their goals were more alike than she knew.

"Don't worry, Princess. I already have what I need."

She frowned. "And what is that exactly?"

A devious grin crossed his lips. "You."

"Me?" Slowly, she backed away. "You said you would leave."

He grinned. "Fool's gold, remember?"

A look of panic came over her. She hadn't been afraid before, but she was now. Good. Let her see the real him. Nothing deserving her intrigue. He was the monster in the darkness, the wolf hidden in the shadows. Everything she should stay away from.

Without warning, she darted past him, but he didn't try to stop her. She wouldn't go far. She ran to the kitchen and grabbed a massive butcher knife from the knife block, wielding it like a weapon. At least it was better than a book.

He sauntered in after her. "Does brandishing cutlery make you feel better?"

Her gaze darted between him and the blade. "Yes."

"Then by all means." He leaned against her granite countertop, ignoring the knife. He knew she wouldn't dare use it. Not this time. "Don't worry, Princess. I'm not going to hurt you."

That wasn't a part of the plan. Even he didn't prey on the

vulnerable. He'd caused trouble for the Grey Wolves more than once, but he had every intention of protecting Mae, even with his life if necessary. It was a shame she had no idea what she was worth or the power she held. Any of the leaders at that reception earlier would have fought any battle, shed any amount of blood, if they knew her true value like he did. But they didn't. Not yet.

A life as a criminal had its perks.

He slid his hand over the granite countertop as he moved toward her. The onyx rings on his fingers flashed in the dim glow. "You wanted to make your own choices, and I'm offering you your first one."

He watched with a grin as she lowered the knife ever so slightly. He saw right through her. She'd made her choice the moment she'd chosen not to expose him to the Pact.

If she knew what was good for her, she'd never make a deal with a wolf like him, but Mae had never been afraid, even when they'd been children and he'd been a scared, mean little boy without a friend in the world.

He was no longer that scared little boy who could save her from the darkness, because he *was* the darkness. And if Maeve Grey wanted the freedom of life lived in the shadows…well, then he'd give it to her.

ACKNOWLEDGMENTS

Thanks so much to Donna Fournier and Darla Taylor for beta reading this book! All their comments were so helpful and much appreciated starting out the new year! And thanks to Deb Werksman for all her helpful suggestions, and to the cover artists, and—yes!—the models who make the book covers drool-worthy.

ABOUT THE AUTHOR

Bestselling and award-winning author Terry Spear has writ-ten over sixty paranormal romance novels and four medieval Highland historical romances. Her first werewolf romance, *Heart of the Wolf*, was named a 2008 *Publishers Weekly*'s Best Book of the Year, and her subsequent titles have garnered high praise and hit the *USA Today* bestseller list. A retired officer of the U.S. Army Reserves, Terry lives in Spring, Texas, where she is working on her next wolf, jaguar, cougar, and bear shifter romances, continuing with her Highland medieval romances, and having fun with her young adult novels. When she's not writing, she's photographing every-thing that catches her eye, making teddy bears, and play-ing with her Havanese puppies and grandbaby. For more information, please visit terryspear.com, or follow her on Twitter, @TerrySpear. She is also on Facebook at face-book.com/terry.spear. And on Wordpress at Terry Spear's Shifters terryspear.wordpress.com.

THE LEGEND OF
ALL WOLVES

For three days out of thirty, when the moon is full and her law is iron, the Great North Pack must be wild...

The Last Wolf

Silver Nilsdottir is at the bottom of her Pack's social order, with little chance for a decent mate and a better life. Until the day she meets a stranger and decides to risk everything...

A Wolf Apart

Only Thea Villalobos can see that Elijah Sorensson is Alpha of his generation of the Great North Pack, and that the wolf inside him will no longer be restrained...

Forever Wolf

With old and new enemies threatening the Great North, Varya knows that she must keep Eyulf hidden away from the superstitious wolves who would doom them both...

"Wonderfully unique and imaginative. I was enthralled!"
—Jeaniene Frost, *New York Times* bestseller

For more info about Sourcebooks's books and authors, visit:

sourcebooks.com

STAT: SPECIAL THREAT ASSESSMENT TEAM

Paige Tyler's all-new, pulse-pounding
SWAT spinoff series

COMING SPRING 2020

STAT—Special Threat Assessment Team—agent Jestina Ridley is in London with her teammates investigating a kidnapping when they cross paths with a creature that savagely kills everyone but her.

When Jes calls HQ for backup, they send her former Navy SEAL and alpha werewolf Jake Huang and his new pack. Convinced that the creature who butchered her teammates was a werewolf, Jes isn't too happy about it. But she'll need Jake's help if they're going to discover the truth and make it back home alive. And with everything on the line, Jes will have to accept Jake for who he is, or lose the partner she never expected to find...

"Paige Tyler has a fan in me!"

—LARISSA IONE, *New York Times* Bestseller

For more info about Sourcebooks's
books and authors, visit:
sourcebooks.com

Also by Terry Spear